THE ROGUE PRINCE

ROYALS OF CARDENAS BOOK 1

ELISE MARION

COPYRIGHT

The Rogue Prince
Elise Marion
Copyright 2019 by Elise Marion
Edited by Elizabeth Williams, ALAREON MEDIA LLC.
Cover Art by Dar Albert, Wicked Smart Designs

All rights reserved, including the right to reproduce this book or portions thereof in any form whatsoever

This is a work of fiction. Names, characters, places, and incidents are a product of the author's imagination or are used fictitiously. Any resemblance to actual events, laces, or people, living or dead, is coincidental.

PROLOGUE

My mother is dead.

The thought reverberated through him in sharp pangs, like ripples on the surface of still waters. Only, there was nothing still about him. The turmoil of such a loss boiled just beneath his skin. He felt as if it would rip him apart from the inside, obliterate him into a pile of bones and organs as his soul flew free of the prison of his body.

What was left of his soul, anyway. With her had died the last shred of good within him. As he stood over the loosely-packed earth covering her freshly-dug grave, he mourned that part of himself as well as her.

The sky was sickening in its beauty, the sun casting bright rays upon the cold stone of her monument. A soft breeze rustled the grass, whispering through the bright green leaves on the trees, and tugging at the hair brushing the collar of his tailored coat. The air carried the sweet fragrance of spring flowers, and somewhere in the distance, the babbling of a nearby stream called to him. He could not have dreamed a more serene resting place himself. He knew—even in the midst of his own hurt—that she was better off now than she'd ever been.

She had battled disease for years, a sickness that seemed to eat away at her from the inside, until she could no longer hang on to the tender threads of her miserable existence. Her condition had been exacerbated by the pangs of a broken heart. It seemed she had always been in possession of a heart rent in two. He'd never known what had caused it until now.

He'd hardly been able to believe his ears when she had entrusted him with her closely guarded secret during what would be their very last conversation, the night before her death. With what would prove to be her last words, she had tipped his very world off its axis and redefined the course of his life forever.

Yet, he remained entrenched in turmoil. Even as he reminded himself that she finally rested peacefully, he remained aware that there would never be anything peaceful about *his* existence again. Staring up at the carved stone figure of an angel looking down on him —her monument—he had only to close his eyes against the bright afternoon sun to remember.

She'd torn his life apart, proving his very existence to be a lie. His father had always hated him, much to his bemusement. His mother's words had shed light upon the truth of his sire's dislike, the reason their marriage had been cold, why she'd spent so much of her life wasting away.

While he returned his father's disdain ten times over, he realized now that the man could not be blamed for his mother's condition. No, someone else was responsible for the secrets and pain that had eaten away at her it had caused her slow and painful death. It had filled her like poison, and with an indifferent husband and an oblivious son there had been no one to confide in. No one to help her carry such a burden.

"It's all right, Mama," he whispered to the wind, to the decaying corpse in the ground. "The burden is mine to bear now."

She'd made it his cross to carry with her dying confession, placing the heavy mantle of anger and pain upon his shoulders.

But, he was stronger than her, his body, mind, and black heart made for this—for what must be done now.

"I understand why you told me," he continued, even knowing she would not answer him. She'd never speak to him again. "There was nothing you could do, young and alone in the world. The royal family forced you into this life, not caring about your thoughts or feelings, robbing you of everything that was rightfully yours."

He paused and closed his eyes, taking a deep, cleansing breath. The crisp morning air cleared his head, leaving him with single-minded focus.

"Now that you are gone, it falls to me to avenge you," he told her. "And I will, Mama ... I *will*. You'll see. Everything that should have been ours ... I'll take it back. I'll make them all pay."

He lingered for a while longer, listening to the whisper of the leaves and imagining that they carried his mother's voice with them She might have disapproved of the depths he'd have to sink to in order to avenge her, but in the end she would have come to understand. She had been the only person to show him love, to treat him as anything other than an afterthought. For all she'd ever given him, there was nothing he would not do, no Hell too hot or too deep for him to descend into. In the end, he would ensure the royal family was made to pay for what they'd done. In wealth, in land, in blood.

He would take it all.

Turning away from the grave, he leaned on his walking stick—the ornate piece serving more for style than practical use. Its custom design had been born of his own mind, a reminder that he need not bow to the dictates of the corrupt who sought to keep him in his place. It featured an eagle straining to take flight, but a two-headed viper had ensnared the majestic bird, poised on either side to strike.

It proved a perfect symbol, a sign of things to come. He would reach out and claim what was rightfully his, and the eagle would do well to beware the viper!

CHAPTER 1

CARDENAS, 1855

*P*rince Damien Alexander Rothchester rolled from on top of the woman who had just been panting and writhing beneath him. His chest heaved with heavy breath as he came down from the heights of his recent climax, sighing at the feel of silken sheets against his sweat-slick skin. Reaching for the decanter he'd stored on the bedside table, he sloshed what was left of the red-brown liquid into his glass. Before he could bring it to his lips, his bedmate eased the tumbler out of his hand.

"That is the last of the brandy," he lamented, turning onto his side to face her.

His mistress, Lady Davina Keane, gave him a cat-like smile and then took a sip of his drink. She showed no shame in her nude form, bursting with curves from her ample breasts and flared hips, her shapely legs seemingly endless despite her petite stature. Before becoming his paramour, she'd been one of the most sought-after courtesans of the royal court—a prize to be flaunted on the arm of a man of wealth and status.

Davina proved one of those women who are very much aware of their own beauty. Auburn hair and brown, feline eyes complimented her alabaster skin to perfection. Her berry-red lips were often parted sensuously or curved into a mocking smile, and her lush figure was enough to drive most men to distraction.

He took hold of her waist when she moved to straddle him, still clutching his brandy in one hand.

"Hmm," she purred, a mischievous glint creeping into her eyes. "I can think quite a better use for it."

She tipped the glass with a little smirk, sending a trickle of the liquor over his chest. He gasped, arching his back as the brandy sluiced down his belly.

They moaned in unison as she dipped her head and dragged her tongue up the center of his chest, lapping him clean. His previously sated prick began to stir again, but he fought against it, divesting her of the tumbler with one hand, while using the other to tip her off of him.

"If you keep doing that, you'll end up on your back again," he muttered, throwing his feet over the side of the bed.

She crawled up behind him, bracing both hands upon his shoulders. "I rather thought *you* could be on your back this time."

Nipping at his ear, she sent a little shiver down his spine, but Damien tilted his head to avoid another bite.

"Davina, I'm late enough as it is."

He would be expected at his club by now, his usual circle of friends likely starting at cards without him. Not to mention he'd been holed up with her for the past two days, the evidence of their debauchery showing in the empty decanters and glasses strewn over various surfaces, the stubs of his cigars in the crystal ashtray, various articles of his clothing and her lingerie strewn about, stacks of plates piled on a tray near the door. He'd gorged himself on brandy, rich foods, and feminine flesh, and supposed it was about time he emerged.

"Must you leave now?" she asked, a whining edge creeping into her voice. "I thought perhaps you would stay for dinner. We could have Anne serve us in here. You needn't even bother getting dressed."

Damien drained the rest of the brandy and set the glass aside, then reached for his trousers. "I have plans for the evening, darling. Perhaps another time."

Rising from the bed, she stormed across the room, taking up a dressing gown as she went.

"Won't you at least come back and spend the night with me? It would be nice to wake up with you here in the morning for a change."

"I have told you before that I sleep more comfortably in my own bed," he mumbled, busying himself with tucking in his shirt and pulling his braces on.

He met her annoyed gaze in the vanity mirror, watching as she pulled a brush roughly through her hair, pursing her lips in annoyance.

"I promise to make it up to you. Perhaps the next time I visit, it will be with a little present for you. How does that sound?"

Her face lit up like a chandelier, her earlier irritation with him seemingly forgotten. It took no more than a new trinket to cool her ire and they both knew it. Fortunately for them both, Damien could afford to keep her happy.

"Well, I suppose it will have to do," she relented.

Damien sat on the edge of the bed to pull on his shoes. Then, he fumbled about, tossing aside her underthings in search of his cravat. He found the wrinkled bit of silk and smoothed it out as best he could before tying it in a haphazard knot.

Glimpsing himself in the full-length mirror across the room, he combed his fingers through golden blond curls mussed almost beyond repair. He shrugged and allowed it to fall how it may. It wasn't as if he'd be in polite company tonight, and he rather liked the haphazard tumble of curls around his head. At least his green eyes shone bright and clear, not bloodshot or watery from drink.

He pulled on his coat while crossing the room to Davina. Leaning over her, he kissed her cheek.

"I'll see you again soon, darling."

He breathed a bit easier once free of her chambers, and even more so once he stood on the front steps, waiting for her butler to have his carriage brought from the mews. She had seemed pacified by his mention of a gift, but Damien never knew when his mistress might choose to express her displeasure by pitching a fit. Beautiful and well-bred she might be, but she had claws and was not shy about using them.

Why did he put up with her fitful moods and childish tantrums?

Glancing over his shoulder at the elegant townhome he had purchased for her on one of the most exclusive streets in the city, he observed its brick facade. She lived here on his generosity, gifted with a substantial allowance each month. In return, she saw to his physical needs and hung on his arm whenever he saw fit to show his face in polite company. Theirs was a typical arrangement between men of means and women of beauty and low funds.

As his carriage appeared, he trotted down the steps with a smile. He supposed he had nothing to complain about when it came to Davina—not when those claws of hers were used against his back when he was on top of her more often than not.

Instructing his driver to carry him to his gentleman's club, he stepped up into the conveyance, making himself comfortable and staring out at into night as they rolled off down the lane.

The past few days of mindless debauchery had left him quite exhausted, but he'd never miss his weekly card game if he could help it. He certainly had the capacity for a bit more reveling in him, and a few hours indulging in brandy and cigars over cards sounded like just the thing.

With few social engagements happening in town this time of the week, the streets remained unclogged by traffic, allowing him to reach the club in record time.

He jumped down from the carriage, taking with him the walking stick he'd left behind while visiting with Davina. Giving it a twirl, he entered the establishment, barely acknowledging the footmen bowing to him as he went. Living as part of the royal family for as long as he had could make one almost entirely unaware of the constant humility of those around him.

Spotting his usual group of associates at a table in the center of the smoke-filled gaming room, he made a beeline toward them with a few of the staff trailing in his wake.

"Gentlemen," he murmured, as one raced forward to pull out his chair.

An attendant appeared at his elbow to take his hat and walking stick, while another placed a fresh decanter of brandy and tumbler before him.

The three men who seemed to have played a few hands without him were all lords of the royal court—landowners born of nobility sitting a bit lower on the social hierarchy than him. Even so, he appreciated that they'd grown comfortable speaking to him as an equal while at the card table. Unlike everyone else, they seemed to have no trouble drinking him under the table, taking his money when he lost a game, or ribbing him as he knew they would due to his tardiness.

He might not consider himself particularly close to any of them, but while at this table once a week he could forget, for a time, his family name and the weight it carried. He could be a man, and not a prince.

"We were beginning to think you wouldn't show," said the brown-haired gentleman across from him.

"My apologies, Lord Huffington," Damien replied, retrieving a slim cigarillo case from the breast pocket of his coat. "I was otherwise engaged and could not seem to tear myself away."

With the expert flick of a match, he lit the cigar and took a deep inhale of the cheroot.

"Otherwise engaged, ha!" Huffington scoffed, placing his cards on the table to reveal the winning hand. "As if we do not know what that means."

Lords Blackwater and Wingate both grudgingly handed over the man's winnings. Damien swiped up the entire deck of cards to take his turn as dealer.

"Ah, the lovely Davina," murmured Blackwater, toying with his mustachio with thumb and forefinger. "Would that I was so otherwise engaged."

"I say, Damien," remarked Wingate, a scrawny eighteen year-old newly come into his fortune. "Never known you to dangle after a female so long."

Damien frowned as he studied his cards. The little whelp had a point. He'd been keeping Davina for well over a year now, and had yet to even consider other options. He had never kept a mistress for more than a few months, and every lady who entered into such an arrangement knew this from the beginning.

It wasn't that he didn't like women ... he loved women. He enjoyed the pleasant lilt of a lady's voice, their sweet smelling fragrances, and the other obvious pleasures to be found with them. He particularly appreciated long legs, an ample bosom, and a firm behind. He loved all these things, as he did good cigars and fine horseflesh.

Yet he had never *loved* anyone.

Davina certainly pleased him, but all that existed between them was lust and a mutual understanding born of honesty.

At least, he thought they understood each other. His friends' remarks made him want to examine their association closer. Her clinging this evening, her complaining over him not wanting to spend the night—something he'd *never* expressed interest in—had him second-guessing everything.

Had she come to expect more from him due to the length of their arrangement? He almost shuddered at the thought. God, he hoped she hadn't gotten the wrong idea.

Even so, he was reluctant to end their association. Throughout their time together, she had been the consummate mistress. Beautiful and well-practiced in the ways of pleasing a man in the bedroom, she knew just what to do to set his blood racing. She was also demanding and spoiled, but Damien didn't mind as long as his own needs were met. She'd certainly cost him a great deal of money, as he constantly found himself purchasing some new trinket or gown to soothe her ire for even the smallest of trespasses.

Perhaps he ought to end it. He'd allowed too much time to pass and he could sense her growing restlessness. If others had begun to remark on the length of their affair, then Davina had certainly caught wind of it. The last thing he needed was for her to think she could demand more from him because of how long he'd been bedding her.

He'd never had a liaison with a woman end badly, and this one would be no different. He would simply settle an obscene amount of money on her, allow her to keep the townhouse, carriage, and servants he had provided, and all would be well. Women like Davina always landed on their feet.

Then what?

The very thought of selecting another mistress made him weary. The process had become tedious, almost boring. Hell, maybe it *was* time to settle down. He shook the thought away before it could take root too firmly in his mind. What a ridiculous notion, marriage! The institution had never made anyone he knew very happy. His parents were a prime example of why it should be avoided all together.

He was grateful that unlike his eldest brother, Lionus, he would be allowed to marry whenever and whomever he chose. As the third in line for the throne, very little was expected of him, and Damien liked things this way. His eldest brother would wed and sire his heirs, while the secondborn would do the same, placing several people between himself and the crown. A man couldn't ask for better—the royal title and all the wealth that came with it, but with none of the responsibility plaguing the elder two Rothchester brothers.

When his attention finally returned to the card game, he realized that several hands passed. His woolgathering had caused him to lose quite heavily. He'd also gone through quite a bit of brandy. Noting how much money he'd just bled over a few hands of cards, he decided it was far past time for him to leave.

Laying the amount he owed in the center of the table for them to divvy up, he rose to his feet.

"Gentlemen, if you will excuse me."

"A bit tired this evening?" Blackwater quipped, taking up his share of the winnings.

His coat and walking stick materialized before he could even turn from the table. After donning them, he was followed into the night by chuckles and bawdy jokes about just what it was that had him too tired to remain for the night. Damien waved them off, though couldn't conjure his earlier amusement. The more he thought of Davina, the more he felt certain the time had come to bring the entire affair to an end.

He would see to the arrangements as soon as possible. Only then would he be able to look forward to what might be next for him.

DAMIEN HAD JUST STRODE through the front doors of Rothchester Hall —the ancestral palace of the royal family—when he was hailed by the butler, Jarvis.

"Your Grace, your brother wishes to see you in the green parlor, immediately."

He paused, tossing his coat and walking stick to the nearest footman, before turning to face the stodgy old servant. Tall and slender, with his dark hair turned mostly silver, he wore immaculate trousers, waistcoat, and tailcoat, setting him apart from the liveried footmen in his command. Like the brass sconces and crystal chandeliers, the man was a fixture here—a much beloved one.

"Which brother?" Damien asked, already knowing the answer.

"Prince Lionus, Your Grace."

He scowled, his hackles rising at just the thought of his eldest sibling. Whatever could Lionus want with him at this hour? He grew certain he was due for his weekly lecture, but was in no mood for a tongue lashing.

"Jarvis, please inform His Grace that I am unavailable at this ungodly hour, and whatever reprimand he has in mind is best saved till tomorrow afternoon."

"That won't be necessary," boomed an imperious voice from the doorway to the green parlor.

Damien stifled a groan when Lionus appeared seemingly from out of nowhere. There would be no escaping him now.

"Come, Damien," his brother demanded before disappearing back through the double doors.

Damien raised his eyebrows at Jarvis—who gave him a smirk and a shrug—before following his brother into the parlor.

"Where the devil have you been?" Lionus thundered as soon as the door closed behind them.

Damien studied the heir to the throne, who was as different from him as the sun when compared to the moon. Where he was broad with chiseled features, Lionus was slender with a more angular visage. Damien was the very image of their father, whereas Lionus had gotten his looks from their mother. He possessed Queen Alexandra's dark brown hair, which he wore long, secured at his nape with an ornate silver clasp. He stood a good two inches taller than Damien, his long limbs enhancing the slimness of his frame. Dark brows arched over deep blue eyes, lending his face a sharp appearance, almost like that of a hawk. And just now, Damien felt very much like his prey.

Crossing his arms over his chest, Lionus stared pointedly at him, waiting for an answer.

"How frightening your voice is when you are wroth, brother," Damien said drolly, helping himself to a splash of brandy from the decanter on the sideboard. "What a fine king you shall make, causing the masses to quiver at the sound of that echoing bellow."

"You have not answered my question," Lionus snapped.

"I haven't answered your question because it seems irrelevant to me, when I know that no matter where I tell you I have been, you will find a reason to disapprove."

"You are damned right I disapprove. If you have not been rutting on top of that woman you insist upon dallying with, then you've been gambling or drinking yourself into a stupor. I would not be surprised if it were all three."

"So shrewd, Lionus ... you've got me all figured out."

He didn't bother to temper the scorn in his voice. What did it matter, when his brother had never bothered to stifle his? The difference between them went beyond simple looks—Damien had been taught to understand that he could never stand head and shoulders with Lionus. The heir had been ingrained with this knowledge as well, putting a wide and endless ocean between them.

"Have you no sense of decency or discretion?" Lionus muttered.

Damien heaved a sigh but remained silent. Arguing would be pointless and he wanted this to end so he could make his way to his chambers.

"You are a disgrace," his brother continued, pacing before the roaring hearth like a caged lion. "You are an embarrassment to this family, to the crown!"

Damien gritted his teeth, his intention of remaining silent forgotten.

"What you mean, dear brother, is that I am an embarrassment to you," he ground out.

"You're goddamn right you are. Is it too much to ask that you conduct yourself in a manner fitting your status?"

Damien set his tumbler aside, stomach turning as the taste for brandy escaped him. He'd be damned if he would stand here and be maligned.

"If that is all, I believe I shall take my leave of you. I know how you so love to chastise me, but I find that I haven't the stomach for it at three o'clock in the morning."

"That's not why I called you in here," Lionus said to his retreating back. "There is something else … it is urgent."

He halted near the door to the parlor, spine tensing. Of course there was something else.

Turning to face Lionus, he balled his hands up, trying to keep a hold on his temper. Whatever it was couldn't be so important that his brother had forgotten to mention it in favor of berating him.

"What is it?"

"Tonight, while you were out doing God-knows-what … another attempt was made on Father's life."

The frayed thread of Damien's control snapped, and he dashed across the room, grasping Lionus by his lapel, fist tightening until his fingernails dug into his palm.

"Why didn't you say that in the first place, damn you! Don't you think that news was more important than you—once again—finding a way to let me know how beneath your sanctimonious self I am?"

Lionus shoved him away, adjusting his coat. He panted, his breath quickening like a raging bull as he made as if to attack him. Damien raised his fists, more than ready for a bout of fisticuffs if that was what his brother wanted.

"Cease this, both of you!" roared a third voice from doorway.

Damien drew up short, turning to find the secondborn prince, and his fraternal twin, striding in to join them.

As the middle brother, Serge often proved the balance between Lionus' sober brooding and Damien's devil-may-care insolence. He was calm and good-natured, could almost always be found smiling, and there wasn't a person in the palace—or the entire kingdom, really—who didn't love him for it.

Serge stood in the middle in regards to his appearance as well. His broad stature was similar to Damien's, as were his chiseled features and pouting lips. His hair stood somewhere between brown and blond, a less intense shade than Damien's shock of golden locks. He kept his hair cropped short like his twin, as well. His eyes, however, were identical to Lionus', as were the slashing dark brows above them.

"If we are going to get the bottom of this, we do not have time for the two of you to come to blows again."

Easing his fists open, Damien voiced his coiled muscles to relax. Finding out what had happened to the king was more important than extracting a few teeth from his prick of a brother.

This would be the third attempt upon their father's life in recent months. What had once seemed like a random act by an angry citizen now seemed to be something else—a plot they could not determine the scope or motive of.

He went back to the sideboard and took up the decanter of again, but only because he knew it would annoy Lionus.

"Brandy?" he offered.

He filled both glasses generously, ignoring Lionus' disapproving glare. Serge accepted the glass and took a sip.

"Would one of you care to tell me what exactly happened?"

"A man entered Father's chambers and nearly stabbed him in his sleep," replied Serge. "We would never have known he was here, if

Maurice had not entered his dressing room to put away some freshly laundered cravats."

"Thank God for a fastidious valet," Lionus mumbled.

"Was the assassin apprehended?" he asked.

"Maurice took him down—would have killed him if Father hadn't stayed his hand," said Serge. "Good thinking, too. Perhaps this one will talk."

"He's being held in the gaol along with the other two," Lionus added. "Thus far, he has remained tight-lipped, just like the other two."

Damien ran a hand over his face, suddenly weary and stone-cold sober. "I do not understand any of this."

"Neither do I," said Serge. "Why attempt to kill a man who is already dying? It is no secret that father has been suffering his illness for years now. We all know it is only a matter of time …"

"The doctors say he has been much improved," Damien protested.

He did not like being reminded of his father's mortality. The loss of King Adare would mean the death of an essential part of himself—and Damien was not ready to face that possibility.

"The physicians tell us what they think we wish to hear," Lionus countered, practical as always. "He has his good and bad days, but the reality of his disease is set in stone."

"Perhaps Father is only the first step in this plot," Serge mused, pacing before the fireplace. "We should consider the possibility that this could be a vendetta against our entire family."

"Then we are all in danger," Lionus declared, raking his fingers through the loose tendrils of hair that had fallen stubbornly into his face.

"We should question the prisoners again," Damien offered. "Obviously someone else is pulling the strings here, and these men are merely pawns. We need one of them to fold and put us on the path to finding the villain."

Serge nodded in agreement. "We should bring the three of them together, perhaps the pressure of seeing that all of their attempts have failed will do the trick.

Lionus crossed to the far wall and selected the tasseled bell-pull to summon Jarvis.

"In the meantime, the level of security at Rothchester Hall should be increased. We will not underestimate this criminal until we know exactly what he is capable of."

After a short wait, Jarvis appeared.

"Your Graces?"

"Attend my instructions carefully," Lionus declared. "The safety of the royal family depends upon it. Firstly, no one is to enter Father's chambers with the exception of the three of us, Mother, Jarvis, Maurice, the physicians when they come to examine him, and the priest. I want palace guards posted at every entrance, in every wing, as well as outside each of our doors at all times. Jarvis, you are to choose a select group of servants. Make certain you consider those who have served here the longest and who are least likely to be a part of some foul plot. I trust your judgment. We will need about ten or so. These chosen few will be allowed to attend us all personally. All others are forbidden from the family wings of the palace and will attend to their duties in the common areas."

"As you wish, Your Grace," said Jarvis with a bow.

"Wait," Serge interjected before the butler could quit the room. "Perhaps we aren't doing enough. This is the third attempt without any indication they will stop any time soon. It might be wise to vacate Rothchester Hall altogether."

"Have you forgotten the wedding?" Damien reminded him. "Lionus' nuptials and the preceding fanfare begin soon. Mother will have an apoplexy if we tell her she must cancel everything."

"I think our lives are bit more important than that—no offense, Lionus, but you can get married any time."

Lionus waved a dismissive hand. "No, Damien is right. Everything should continue as it has been ... from the outside, all must appear to go on as normal. Whoever the mastermind is, he is watching our every move. We cannot show fear, or panic the citizens and royal court, nor can we tuck tail and run. We will present a united front while we work to covertly put an end to this ... whatever it is."

Serge looked as if he wanted to argue further, but, like Damien, had no choice but to bow to Lionus' will. With their father incapacitated by illness, the Crown Prince's word was law.

"Very well," Serge relented. "I will have a word with Maurice and ensure he is armed and ready to protect Father at all costs."

"Good," Lionus agreed, before gesturing for Jarvis to see his orders carried out. "It seems we have accomplished all we can for one night. If there's nothing else, I suggest we all find our beds."

The three exited the parlor, and started up the winding staircase leading to the second floor of the palace. As they went, the sound of footsteps pounding down darkened corridors announced the growing presence of palace sentinels.

Jarvis had been swift and efficient in carrying out Lionus' edict.

Damien parted ways with his brothers on the second floor, gas sconces lighting the way down his personal wing of the palace. As he went, a handful of guards appeared from the shadows, falling in behind him at a respectful but close distance.

A fire roared in his darkened sitting room, courtesy of his valet, Hopkins. The man knew not to wait up for him, but still saw to whatever comforts he could before turning in. Crossing to the bookcase built into a wall flanked by a pair of windows, he took down the cedar chest holding his pair of twin revolvers.

He selected one and ensured it was loaded—just in case. In the event that some faceless assassin managed to slip past the guards, Damien would be ready to defend himself.

Moving back to the sitting area, he sank onto a sofa with a heavy sigh. Fatigue gripped him, but his nerves had been frayed by talk of death and assassins. Finding a recently filled decanter of brandy on the side table, he unstopped it and swigged straight from the glass container.

Before long, the warmth of the fire and the spirits in his belly lulled him into a sound sleep.

CHAPTER 2

Damien was awakened the next morning by a swift kick on the bottom of his booted foot. He opened his eyes, cringing at the early afternoon sun streaming through the opened drapes. The light stung, causing him to squint as his eyes adjusted.

No one dared awaken him so rudely, save one of his brothers. A cursory glance about the room revealed which brother.

"Damn it, Serge. Good morning to you, too."

"More like good afternoon," Serge muttered, kicking his boot once more. "Couldn't even make it to the bed this time, could you?"

He sat up on the sofa he'd spent the night on, running his fingers through his disheveled hair. "I happen to like this couch."

Serge opened his mouth to reply, but Damien silenced him with a wave of his hand.

"Not before I've had my coffee. Ring for a maid, will you?"

Serge pulled on the cord before sinking into a black brocade armchair across from him. Damien blinked his bloodshot eyes several times, then glanced around, finding the revolver he'd dropped onto the floor when he'd dozed off. He'd been drunker than he'd thought last night, and if someone had thought to murder him, they would have likely succeeded.

ELISE MARION

A brief knock sounded at the door a moment later, before a chambermaid entered. Her eyes widened as she took in Damien's state of disheveled half-dress, coat and waistcoat removed, his shirt left hanging open, hair unruly.

As she curtsied to them, her gaze never left the expanse of his bare chest.

"Your Graces ... good morning."

Damien studied her with interest. The frilly mobcap she wore covered her blond hair, save for the few strands that had escaped to frame her round face. Dark blond lashes lowered demurely over limpid blue eyes. Most interesting of all was the voluptuous form pressing against the constraints of her black and white uniform. He felt certain he'd encountered her several times before. What the devil was the girl's name?

Damien smiled at the simpering maid. "Forgive me, my dear, I seem to have forgotten your name."

Surprise registered in her wide eyes. "You are forgiven, Your Grace. My name is Lillian."

"Lillian ... I shall not forget again," he said with a wink.

Serge rolled his eyes and issued a sarcastic snort, which Damien pointedly ignored. Some men gambled when they were bored, others practiced swordplay or pugilism. Damien preferred the sport of bedding willing maids.

"Have a breakfast tray sent up," he ordered. "And send Hopkins to me as well."

The girl curtsied again and backed from the room, her gaze still locked with his. Easy pickings for later, she would be.

"You are insufferable," Serge muttered once they were alone again.

"Jealous?"

"Hardly. One of these days, some maid will turn up with one of your by-blows ... or give you a case of the pox ... who will be laughing then, I wonder?"

Damien shuddered at the thought of both bastards and boils, but chose not to let Serge bait him. He was a rake, just as the rumors of high society had painted him. He knew it, and so did everyone else, so there was not use denying or arguing about it. Being the thirdborn had its advantages.

A short while later, Jarvis appeared carrying a steaming coffee pot and two china cups, followed by a footman hauling Damien's heavy breakfast tray.

"Will you be requiring anything else, Your Grace?"

"No, that'll be all."

The valet entered just as Jarvis and the footman were leaving.

"Hopkins, I'll be riding this afternoon," Damien declared.

"I will prepare the necessary attire. Will you require a shave as well, Your Grace?"

Damien nodded, dismissing his man as he poured coffee into the two provided cups. He stirred sugar and a liberal dash of cream into his, then took a sip and nodded his satisfaction before focusing his attention back on Serge.

"Now then," he began. "To what do I owe your visit? No doubt Lionus is behind this meeting, which means I have done something in the past ten hours or so to anger him despite having been sound asleep."

Setting his cup down the tray, Damien began attacking his breakfast with relish.

"I am only here to remind you how important the next few weeks are going to be. With so much going on, Lionus will be wound up even tighter than usual."

"So you've come to secure my promise to behave, is that it?" he muttered between bites of egg.

Serge snagged a slice of ham from his plate. "It's only for three weeks. Do try not to anger Lionus, or Mother for that matter, as she is the one orchestrating this entire thing and you know how she gets."

Damien needed no reminder. He had been dreading the time when the palace would be overrun with visitors for the festivities leading up to Lionus' wedding.

Their brother was to be married at the end of the month to Princess Isabelle from the neighboring kingdom of Barony. The union had long been anticipated, the betrothal agreement signed mere days after Isabelle's birth. The political state of Barony had been volatile for the past twenty years, and would continue to be until the two realms could be joined through the marriage of the prince and princess.

Rebels seeking to overthrow the crown in Barony had created a dangerous situation for the newborn princess. Isabelle had been a tool, used by her father to form an alliance between Cardenas and Barony.

Not long after the betrothal agreement had been signed, the king and queen, along with several other members of the Guthrie royal family, had been violently and publicly beheaded by the rebels. Barony's grand vizier, a close adviser and friend to the king, had smuggled the young princess out of the country, along with a small group of loyal subjects.

Princess Isabelle had remained hidden in Cardenas, provided for and protected until she came of age to wed. Only then could she could return to her country as queen and take possession of the throne. Cardenas' superior military would serve Lionus in regaining control of Barony. Their vast wealth would refill the diminished resources of the struggling realm.

Within the next few days, Cardenas' court, as well as the loyalists of Barony, would descend upon Rothchester Hall. Three weeks of parties, dinners, luncheons, picnics, a tournament, and a ball to celebrate the greatly anticipated marriage would then ensue.

"How could I forget?" he muttered, rolling his eyes. "The royal wedding of the century between our great prince and his ever-devoted bride."

Serge grinned, snatching a muffin from his tray. Ignoring Damien's icy glare, he bit heartily into the sweet confection.

"I would kill for such devotion, wouldn't you?"

"The woman has been taught from the cradle to love, adore, serve, and obey our brother. The poor girl doesn't know any better. Though, I have to admit she's not bad to look at."

"That has got to be the understatement of a lifetime," Serge scoffed.

Damien shrugged, indifferent.

"The princess is a great beauty, and poised and graceful besides," Serge continued. "But I know what type of woman you prefer, brother: independent, unattached, and worldly. I can see how you would find a woman like Isabelle not to your liking."

Damien arched an eyebrow and smirked. "Back off, Serge. I will admit, the girl is not without charm. One would think she was *your* betrothed the way you carry on so."

Serge pursed his lips and broke Damien's gaze, falling silent. He finished his coffee, then stood and returned his empty cup to the tray.

"I will leave you alone now," he said. "Just try to avoid crossing Lionus until we've gotten past the wedding, if you can. Once he is married, his attention will shift to his coronation and the problems he will soon face in Barony. He won't have time to notice your usual antics."

Damien saluted playfully and returned to his breakfast tray. "I shall endeavor to be a good little prince. If not for Lionus, then for Father's sake."

The sound of Serge's hearty laughter echoed down the corridor as he retreated, causing a slight smile to curve Damien's mouth. For all their differences, the two had always been close—two castoffs standing in the shadow of Lionus' massive royal presence. If sharing a womb hadn't bonded them enough, that had certainly brought them closer over the years.

Adare Oswyn Esmond Rothchester IV, King of Cardenas, had once been a handsome and virile man. He was adored for his pleasant looks and physical strength, and had become known for his charisma and wisdom. His forty years as Cardenas' ruler had shown him to be powerful, decisive, and fair.

Anyone who had not known the great king before illness had ravaged his body would not believe these qualities of the now frail man. Damien's heart plummeted as it always did when he observed his father, who had withered away to a shrunken shell of a man.

He approached the massive bed in the king's chamber on silent feet, not wanting to wake him if he slept. The guards who had allowed him entrance stood on either side of the door. Two more kept vigil in the corridor.

As Damien neared the bed, he saw that his father was not only awake, but shaved and wearing a black and gold brocade dressing gown, with a snowy white shirt and expertly tied cravat at his throat. An emerald stickpin gleamed in the depths of the starched neck cloth, matching the color of his still vibrant gaze.

Adare's smiling eyes, the same shade of green as his, were the only part of him that hadn't yet lost their luster. Damien stared into the face that was so like his own, his smile mirroring that of his father's. His once golden hair was now mostly white and thinning, but still curled riotously about his head and shoulders. Today it was brushed and tamed into a neat queue.

Skin that had once been golden from the sun and stretched over bulging, sinewy muscle, was now papery and held a yellowish cast. It hung from his fragile frame, diminished from its original integrity. Damien reached out and took his father's outstretched hand, relieved to find it warm.

"Father," he said reverently, kissing the large signet ring dwarfing an emaciated finger. "You're looking well today."

"My son," Adare replied, his voice warm with affection. "It is always a joy to look upon your face."

Damien knew, and it was no secret, that he was Adare's favorite. Perhaps it was Fate's way of evening the score—making him first in his father's heart even though he stood last in every other aspect of his life.

"I am sorry I was unable to come to visit you yesterday. I was detained and lost track of time."

His father's chuckle echoed through the large chamber. "Were I keeping such a fine woman as Davina, I would lose track of time quite frequently."

Damien's laughter mingled with his father's for a moment before he grew serious once more. "Lionus does not share your sentiments. He thinks me a disgrace, an embarrassment to the crown. He said as much to me last night.

Adare frowned, his gaze roaming to the great portrait of the royal family taking up much of the wall across from him. Lionus' cold blue eyes, hard as steel, seemed to stare back at them from the painting.

"Much to my regret, your brother has grown into an uncompromising man. Too somber, at times. Your mother and I meant well, but perhaps his education was too rigid, too structured."

"He shall make a great king," Damien offered.

Adare nodded in agreement. "He will rule more than adequately after I'm gone."

"I don't want to talk about that," he protested, gripping his father's hand tighter as if he could gift him with his own young life force if he tried hard enough.

The king's smile wavered and tears filled his eyes. "My son, if I did not love you I would not tell you the truth. The physicians know that I will not live much longer. With the attempts against my life recently, I have come to realize that my time is near. At the young age of twenty-nine your brother will take the throne. I have decided that once he has married Princess Isabelle, he is to be immediately crowned king of Cardenas and Barony. I am no longer fit to rule."

Sorrow clenched Damien's heart, causing his throat to swell and his eyes to sting with tears he only dared to shed in front of this man who loved and understood him so well.

"You have always been fit to rule. Allow Lionus to continue serving as commander of our military; hold the crown as long as you can. You have a few years left in you yet."

Adare's trembling hands cupped Damien's face. "The doctors say I will live longer without the added pressures of governing a kingdom. It is time for Lionus to take his place as king. It is time for Serge to take his place in leading our armed forces."

He nodded, understanding the wisdom of the physicians. Still, he did not want to believe his father could be unfit for anything. Adare was a great king, a warrior. Damien had always thought the man near invincible.

"You and your brother must learn to bear each other," Adare

continued. "He is hard and unyielding, and even a bit arrogant, but he is also under a tremendous strain. The situation awaiting him in Barony is turbulent, to say the least. He will take up the crown sooner than expected, and though he is capable and ready, he will need good men at his back. He will need you."

Lionus would never see him as anything more than a libertine, and a lazy, spoiled prince. But, for his father, Damien would endeavor to do what he could. It was the least he could offer the man who was responsible for the few parts of him that were good and pure. He would preserve those parts at all costs, even if it meant finding a way to tolerate Lionus.

"I will try my best, Father."

Adare nodded and offered him a weak smile. "That is all I ask. Now, leave me. I must be rested to attend your birthday celebration tomorrow evening."

Damien's eyes widened; he had nearly forgotten the event planned for him and Serge's twenty-fifth birthday. The soiree would be the start of the entertainments marking the royal wedding. Funny, how so much drink and debauchery could cause a man to forget his own birthday.

He rose and kissed his father's sunken cheek.

"I will come and sit with you later if you're up to it," he said, pulling the heavy blankets up over his father's chest.

He turned in the doorway to stare at Adare's peaceful face one more time before leaving. He took his time tracing every wrinkled feature, never certain which precious moment shared with his father would be his last.

DAMIEN PREFERRED to saddle his own horse. The grooms and stable boys knew this, so when he entered the stable they did not offer him assistance. Some might think it beneath him, but he enjoyed the moments of anticipation before a ride, the feel of leather in his hands as he attached saddle, bridle, and reins.

His black mare, Persephone, snorted and tossed her inky mane when he approached, reaching out to stroke her glossy coat. She'd grown up with him, a gift from his father on the occasion of his tenth birthday. Serge had been given a red-brown gelding on that same birthday and the beast occupied a place farther down the row of stalls.

"I've been too long in coming to you, my love," he murmured as he took hold of her reins and led her from the stable. "How about a nice long run?"

Persephone nickered as if in response to his murmured words as he swung himself up into the saddle. Soon he was galloping across the manicured lawns and rolling hills surrounding Rothchester Hall. The palace grew smaller and smaller behind him as he streaked across the countryside, toward his favorite spot.

They made quite an impressive sight to anyone who happened to spot them, horse and rider both shrouded in black, Persephone's hooves kicking up clumps of grass and dirt, her massive legs carrying them swiftly across the countryside. It occurred to him that he ought to have brought his revolver, but decided he ought to be safe enough on palace grounds in broad daylight.

He pulled up on the mare's reins as they neared a small, secluded pond hidden by a copse of trees. He dismounted, trusting Persephone not to wander too far.

The little grove had seemed so much bigger when he'd been a boy. He, Lionus, and Serge had run through these trees with their carved wooden swords, battling invisible enemies to save the princess and earn themselves a fortune in gold from the grateful king.

He walked up to the massive oak they had dubbed "king" of Rothchester Forest. The twisted, gnarled wood almost appeared to have the face of an old, dignified man.

"Your Highness," he greeted the large tree as he always did when he visited this private place.

No one came here but him anymore. Grateful for the solitude, he stripped down to nothing and plunged into the cold, crystal clear water. He lay on his back and floated languorously toward the center. He missed the days of his childhood, before he and his brothers had come to understand the differences that would separate them in the coming years.

They had once been equals. At least, Damien had *thought* they were equals. Then, Lionus had turned thirteen and everything changed. Apart from the lessons learned as part of his regular schooling, the Crown Prince began attending separate sessions that would last for long hours after Damien and Serge had been dismissed.

He remembered clearly the day he had finally realized the biggest difference between himself and his eldest brother. He'd been ten years old, Lionus fourteen. He'd come upon their mother outside the schoolroom, observing his brother at work, pride glowing in her cerulean eyes. Damien had tugged on her skirts and turned his eyes up hopefully, daring to wish for the same expression when she looked upon him. Instead, he received a flicker of annoyance directed at him, before she searched the empty corridor behind him for his missing nanny.

"Mama, how long must Lionus stay inside and study? He has promised to take Serge and me out to the pond to sail our toy boats."

Queen Alexandra had removed his hands from her fashionable skirts and gently pushed him away.

"Your brother is much too busy for such foolishness," she'd said, with an imperious tilt of her head. "He is preparing for the day when he will be king, and must concentrate on all he needs to learn. I would not expect you to understand … you are only the third son after all."

Damien had suddenly understood his mother's indifference toward her younger twin sons. Her affections were enough only for the son she favored, the son who would one day be crowned king.

Leaving the water, he found a sunny spot in the grass to lay and dry himself. He clasped his hands beneath his head and turned his face up toward the cloudy sky.

He was glad to be the youngest. Glad he didn't have the weight of the kingdom's responsibility weighing upon his shoulders. He could do anything he wanted with his life, though his usual drinking and carousing were beginning to bore him. But that was the thing about his position … it offered him the freedom to change if he so wished.

The restlessness that had him questioning his relationship with Davina as well as his usual habits must mean something special lay on the horizon.

As he lay in the sun and closed his eyes, Damien was thankful for the opportunity to be able to discover just what that might be.

CHAPTER 3

The back corridor leading to the elegant ballroom at Rothchester Hall was hot and stuffy. Esmeralda Amador fanned herself ineffectually in the stifling warmth. She lifted masses of black, wavy hair from the back of her neck, trying to seek relief. The small crowd gathered in the narrow corridor only added to her discomfort. She peered through the slightly parted double doors, watching the harpist seated in the middle of the ballroom.

She and her group of Gypsy dancers had been waiting for their turn to perform for hours, as the king adored them and always preferred them to appear last. There were nine in all, including six dancers and three musicians. Her younger brother, Desmond, strummed quietly on his guitar nearby, bringing a smile to her face. This would be his first performance at the royal palace.

"Oh, Esmeralda," squealed her cousin Tatiana, from behind her. "Your mother is a wonder! I cannot believe what she's done to this costume. No one would even guess that it was one of her old ones."

She eyed the crimson confection that had been altered for her cousin and nodded her approval. Her mother had made an old dancing costume of her own into an entirely new creation for Tatiana.

"It's stunning. You all look wonderful."

Morgana—another of her cousins—came and stood between the two, linking her arms through each of theirs.

"It is a good thing you're dancing last Esmeralda," she commented, peering out into the ballroom. "I wouldn't want to have to follow your performance. You might even be a better dancer than Aunt Raina."

"*No one* is a better dancer than my mother," she objected.

Raina Amador had been widely known, a favorite of King Adare. However, her mother had not danced since the death of her husband, Esmeralda's father. She insisted that she was happy to help teach younger girls to dance, or make and alter their costumes. With the loss of Matias Amador had come the death of her passion for dance. She might never perform for an audience again.

Esmeralda shook herself from the saddening path of her thoughts. They had a show to put on, and she was unusually nervous. Odd, as she'd been dancing long enough that she almost never grew anxious beforehand.

Taking a deep breath, she released it in on a slow exhale in an attempt at calming her nerves. Palace performances always paid well, and tonight's occasion proved even more lucrative. The king had wanted a festive display for the birthday celebration of the twin princes, and had spared no expense.

Applause resounded, marking the end of the harpist's performance. The woman stood, hands clasped demurely before her, the wide skirt of her evening gown billowing around her as she curtsied and received her praise.

A big, firm hand came against the small of her back.

"You are looking most beautiful tonight, Esmeralda," a deep voice murmured in her air.

She recognized the lightly accented tones of her dance partner, Tristan. His touch and words were meant to stoke her passions, but when she turned, she saw only the face of her childhood friend. They had grown up together like siblings, yet as time had turned her into a woman and him into a man, he had begun to display his feelings to her—and they were not those of friendship.

In any other woman's eyes, he would be seen as a dream—tall, with

ELISE MARION

swarthy olive skin, midnight black hair and equally dark eyes. He had the lithe body of a dancer, with broad shoulders, narrow waist and long, powerful legs.

However, it was difficult for Esmeralda to see herself enfolded in his arms, or imagine being kissed by him.

Among their own people, it seemed understood that they would someday marry, and it was even rumored that Tristan had begun saving the bride price decided upon by her father before his death. Esmeralda seemed to be the only person who did not see marriage to Tristan as inevitable.

"Thank you," she replied, forcing a smile and moving away from his touch.

She turned before being forced to witness his disappointment, the fact that she couldn't seem to return his feelings sending guilt resounding through her. Tristan was a good man, and a loyal friend. But, she had been witness to the love of her parents, a passion that had lasted through the years. That was what she wanted for herself, and settling for a mundane life with Tristan could cause her to miss out on that. And so, she held him at arm's length while wondering if she would ever find her heart's desire.

Peering back into the ballroom, she noticed that the singer who had followed the harpist had nearly finished.

"Tell everyone to get ready, it is our turn."

DAMIEN RESTED his chin on his gloved hand, staring around the crowded ballroom from his place at the high table. His mother had planned quite an affair, complete with several entertainments throughout the evening. There had been acrobats, singers, musicians, and even a troupe of actors.

He'd grown bored with the lavish party, knowing that the majority of the guests had come only to see and be seen, all under the guise of celebrating his birthday. He spotted Davina, seated with her usual group of acquaintances. She smiled at him, leaning forward to give him a better view of her cleavage. Damien's gaze lingered on the breasts barely contained by deep purple silk. His interest didn't rise as fast or as hotly as usual, reaffirming his decision to set her aside. He might not be ready to run off and find himself a bride, but he did know that he was ready to be free of Davina.

Finally, the last act of the evening was announced, drawing his attention back to the center of the room. The Gypsy dance performance would be the highlight of the evening for him, and he knew it to be true for Serge and his father as well. Queen Alexandra found them vulgar, and naturally Lionus shared the sentiment.

Three musicians entered first, standing just left of center. A guitarist, flautist, and drummer struck a lively tune as the first pair of dancers took the floor. The rhythm pulsed through him and his body seemed to vibrate in response to the rhythm, the blood in his veins rushing, his leg bouncing beneath the table.

The pair of dancers who took to the floor were dressed in sumptuous costumes in matching shades of royal blue. Their dance told the story of two cursed lovers, clinging to each other as the man turned the woman swiftly across the floor, her split skirts twirling around her bare legs. Their feet pounded the marble floors, the soles of their shoes clicking in rhythmic harmony with the drums, the billowing sleeves of their costumes flaring with each sweep of their arms.

Damien found himself drawn into the tale they weaved as they danced, their pace quickening maddeningly until they fell to the floor, and in a puff of fragrant white smoke they were gone.

Another duo stood in their place when the fog cleared. Applause echoed from the high ceilings of the ballroom as the second dancers, clothed in deep crimson, glided through the thinning smoke.

Their dance was more sensual than the first, telling the story of a man and woman who seemed to love as well as hate one another. Over and over they circled each other, eyes locked, coming together and separating once more. The man's hands gripped the woman's body in places that would make any man squirm. He held her close, dipping her back and swinging her about, their bodies moving both in tandem and in opposition as the woman seemed to try to maintain independence while the man exerted his dominance.

Another puff of smoke took those dancers from the floor, and in their place rose a solitary man. Dressed entirely in black, a flat, wide-brimmed hat lowered mysteriously over his eyes, he seemed to float through the smoke to the center of the floor.

The music ceased and the dancer created his own pounding rhythm by clapping his hands and stomping his feet. He turned in slow circles, drumming out his own cadence as the guitarist joined him. A series of small turns was followed by another puff of smoke, from which a siren dressed in white surfaced.

Damien was enthralled from the moment the woman appeared. He drank her in with his gaze as she turned in wide loops about her partner.

Her skin was like deep bronze gleaming in the candlelight, and lustrous, wavy black hair fell like a curtain down her back. Her lithe dancer's body was controlled, stretches of taut muscle moving beneath supple skin. A white ruffled blouse revealed her stomach, and her white skirt was slit up both sides to reveal long, graceful legs. His eye was drawn to the glittering gold jewelry that winked around her wrists and ankles. His rapt stare followed the delicate gold chain about her waist as she undulated sensually before them.

Her face was veiled from the bridge of her nose down, but as she turned, he was surprised and pleased by almond-shaped eyes the color of warm honey.

Her partner pursued her around the floor, seeming to yearn for her with the movements of his body, yet she remained always out of his reach. She teased and taunted him with her dance until he could take no more and lunged for her, holding her at her waist and lifting one shapely leg at the knee.

Damien's stomach clenched as he pictured his own hand grasping that supple thigh. The male dancer dipped her backward, and leaned in as if to kiss her. But then, a final puff of smoke billowed up from the floor and they disappeared from sight.

The applause was thunderous, and awestruck murmurs moved through the crowded room in waves. His brother and father clapped enthusiastically, joining several others on their feet in applauding the Gypsies.

Damien searched each of the exits, hoping to catch a glimpse of the woman in white before she could leave. His gut clenched with some unnamed, previously foreign hunger, his blood pulsing as hard as the drums. He didn't recognize this sensation, this desperation driving him to want to keep his gaze upon her, to follow her and … and he was not sure what he'd do, but damn it, this urge just wouldn't let up.

He spied the door the musicians had disappeared behind and stood to move in that direction. The hired orchestra began to play, struggling to be heard through the buzz of conversation that filled the room. His mother would think him rude for abandoning their guests before the affair had ended, but he did not care. He skirted the perimeter of the room, making a beeline for the door.

He found the corridor empty. Muttering a curse, he followed the winding passage toward the servants' back stairs. He knew he had seen the musicians leave through this door. If he hurried, he could catch them before they left.

Footsteps echoed behind him in the darkened hall. He turned to find Davina hot on his heels, skirts held aloft as she hurried to catch up to him. He fought not to groan or let his annoyance show. It was not her fault his desire for her had begun to wane, nor did she realize he had begun making arrangements to cut her loose.

"Thank goodness I found you alone," she breathed hotly in his ear, pressing against him. "I can be in your chambers in ten minutes."

He grunted when she palmed him through the fall of his breeches, a bold and brazen act that had usually worked to get his blood hot in the past. Now, he remained cold, his mind still chasing after the dancer in white.

Davina kissed him, skimming her tongue into his mouth and letting him taste the wine she'd had with dinner, before giving him another squeeze through his breeches and backing away.

"Ten minutes," she purred, before disappearing back down the darkened hallway.

Damien waited until she was out of sight before he continued down the hall at a near run. He exploded down the servants' staircase leading to the kitchen. The cook and her maids seemed paralyzed with shock before they remembered themselves and curtsied as he rushed past. He burst through the back entrance just in time to see the Gypsies' covered wagon speeding off into the night.

"Damn it!" he spat, pounding his fist against the stone wall of the palace, causing a startled maid to squeal and leap away from his unprovoked fury.

"My apologies," he said more calmly when the trembling maid curtsied before him.

"Your Grace," she mumbled before turning to go back inside.

"Wait!" he called, watching the Gypsy wagon grow smaller and smaller against the night sky as it rolled away.

"Yes, Your Grace?"

"Would you happen to know where the Gypsies live?"

"Live, Your Grace?" she said with a slight chuckle. "The Gypsies do not *live* anywhere. They are a wandering people, never staying in one place overlong. They usually make camp on the outskirts of town when they are here."

"My thanks," Damien said with a sigh.

How on Earth could he find the girl before the Gypsy troupe left the city for good?

"Oh wait!" the young maid exclaimed. "I just remembered. A group of them settled here some years ago. They all live in the same part of the city. One of them even owns a tavern."

Damien nodded, weighing his options. What were his chances that the dancer lived right here in Cardenas?

"Thank you," he said, before turning to go back through the servants' entrance.

He took his time, walking at a leisurely pace, his mind filled with images of a woman with skin like bronze, hair like precious ebony, and eyes spitting fire over a gauzy veil. He found the idea of returning to the party distasteful, though he knew it would last long into the late hour of the night, until the wine and food had been depleted.

He decided to take himself off to his chambers instead of going back to the ballroom. Hopefully, by morning, he would have driven away all thoughts of flashing amber eyes burning themselves indefinitely into his memory.

ONE WEEK PASSED HIM BY, and Damien had been unable to forget her. No amount of drink or time spent at the card tables could chase thoughts of the beautiful dancer from his mind. He had searched for days before finding the Gypsy troupe camped out on the outskirts of town. After a few minutes of wandering through the painted wagons and tents, he discovered that no one in this particular group had ever performed at Rothchester Hall. His search for her would become that much easier now that he knew she lived within the city, which came as a relief.

But, how was he to find her; walk about the street amongst the commoners, inquiring about a dancing Gypsy girl?

Then, he remembered what the maid had told him about a tavern. He had heard of the place before, having frequented several establishments in the less reputable part of town. The Golden Dancer boasted beautiful dancers, and Damien thought it best to begin his search there.

As he saw it, the only way to purge his system of this woman was to find her and lead her to his bed as soon as possible. Then, perhaps he could get on with his life with some semblance of normality. This little obsession of his could not be healthy, and certainly wouldn't allow him to move forward until he'd been washed clean of it.

Now he stood near the entrance of The Golden Dancer, searching the smoke-filled room for his prey. Several round tables and chairs, surprisingly clean, were placed in an open circle around a small stage jutting out from the back wall. Men smoking cheroots and holding mugs of ale sat in groups, watching a young woman wrapped in a diaphanous green costume and matching veil move about on the narrow stage.

One of the male dancers he remembered from the palace sat on a low stool toward the back of the stage, strumming a guitar. Serving girls in simple blouses and ruffled skirts moved through the crowd, delivering drinks and avoiding the grabbing hands of some of the bolder men.

Damien found an empty stool at the counter and settled himself there, signaling the barkeep. The massive man standing behind the rough, scratched bar eyed him warily, but filled a clean mug with golden ale for him without question.

Mug in hand, he watched the dancer on stage with interest. She was skilled, her curvaceous body moving in perfect timing to the melody created by the guitar player. But, she was not the one he'd come looking for, her figure a bit more rounded and her eyes a dark brown.

Applause signaled the end of her dance and she disappeared behind the stage amid whistles and stamping feet. Damien waited until the noise had died down to a gentle hum of conversation before turning to the barkeep. Maybe he could help point Damien in the right direction.

"Pardon me," Damien called.

The barkeep approached, narrowing his eyes and studying him more closely. He was very clearly a Gypsy, like most of the other patrons here, his dark olive skin and dark hair helping him to blend in. Damien, however, was very much aware that he did not fit in—and it wasn't only because of his bright shock of blond hair.

He had dressed in the plainest clothing he could manage, but the perfect tailoring and fine quality of the fabrics set him apart. He had hoped to avoid attention and wanted to pass as a traveling merchant or some such. It was why he'd gone without his signet ring, and had come in an unmarked carriage. But, it was obvious his efforts had not amounted to much.

"I am looking for someone ... a dancer. She performed at the king's palace last week."

He realized his mistake in an instant. The other man raised himself to his full height, towering over Damien, gripping the counter and leaning forward to look him in the eye. He could have sworn he heard the wood groan in protest in the barkeep's beefy hands.

"See here, mister," the man said, his voice like hard-edged steel. "The girls what dance here is under my protection and they ain't got time to be bothered with the likes o' you. This ain't that kinda place, and if that's what you be looking for, there's a brothel not far from here."

Damien's reply was smothered by a commotion near the stage. The music had started up again, and a lissome figure in black had entered. The men seemed excited about this particular performance, and he forgot his questioning of the bartender.

It was her. He knew the moment she started to dance, arms lifted high above her head, hips moving in rapid, hypnotizing circles. The other girl had been good, but this one's movements were so natural, so much a part of her. She made the intricate steps seem effortless as she swayed and dipped, working the crowd into a frenzy. Golden eyes flashed, their brilliance further enhanced by kohl. Even the guitar player watched her, his dark eyes following her every move from beneath the hat pulled low over his brow.

Damien remained spellbound until the final chords of the guitar faded away in the dimly lit room. The dancer gave a gracious bow, and even blew a kiss to the cheering crowd before disappearing behind the curtain.

He watched the stage for a few moments, searching for any sign of movement from behind it. The guitar player disappeared behind the curtain as well, but no one else came or went. He supposed her performance would the last of the evening, because most of the patrons finished off their drinks and began preparing to leave. A few stayed behind for more ale and flirting with the serving girls, but the small tavern had mostly gone quiet. Hoping she hadn't left by some back exit, Damien turned once more to the barkeep.

"Perhaps I gave you the wrong impression," he began, hoping the burly man wouldn't break him to pieces before he could finish.

The barkeep let out a sound akin to a growl and dropped the towel he'd been using to clean the counter. He reached across the bar and grabbed Damien up by his lapel, nearly dragging him across the counter.

"I'm done warning you. I think it's time you left. And you'd best do it quietly or else you'll have to be carried out!"

"Leave the poor man alone, Dominic," purred a velvety voice from over Damien's shoulder. "I'm sure he is harmless."

Dominic gave him a mind-numbing shake before setting him back in his stool.

"Only because you asked me to," he grumbled as he went back to his work. "But if he so much as coughs in your direction, I'll snap him in two."

Damien cleared his throat, praying a speck of dust wouldn't be the death of him.

His coveted dancer settled onto the stool at his side, fixing him with her piercing stare. His mouth went dry and he found himself unable to look away.

Unveiled, he found her to be just as lovely as he'd imagined. High cheekbones stood out beneath almond-shaped eyes and a lush mouth curved into a slight smirk as she stared back at him. She had changed into a simple skirt and blouse that draped slightly to reveal one bare shoulder. Her hair hung unbound down her back in lustrous black waves, making Damien's fingers itch to reach out and stroke it. The impact of her presence seemed magnified ten-fold at this proximity, and for a long moment he could only sit there and drink her in.

"I'm sorry," he managed once he'd finally found his voice. "I did not mean to insult him."

She smiled at him, and it drew him in. He found himself leaning forward, his body reacting to her as if he were a bit of metal drawn to a magnet.

"Dominic is very protective of the girls who work here ... particularly the dancers. A lot of men get the wrong impression. They think the girls who work here are available for other things. Things that have nothing to do with dancing. We are not."

Her smile melted away, and her voice sharpened at the end, stabbing through him with all the sharpness of a dagger. The acuity of her gaze told Damien she saw right through him, the very notion making him squirm like a fish on a hook.

"That is not my intention," he lied, his shame at being so easily seen through still not enough to make him cease his pursuit.

He decided on another tactic, one that could be risky, but could prove fruitful if his instincts led him the right way.

"I was told that Gypsies lived in this part of this city. I inquired, and was told you could lead me to a fortune-teller."

The woman nodded and he fought back a smug smile. He had found his opening.

"Yes," she said. "My grandmother is the best. I can take you to her now, if you have time."

"Of course."

"Dominic, I'm taking this man to see Grandmother. You should go home once you've finished cleaning. I'll leave the ledgers until tomorrow."

"Maybe you ought to wait for Tristan," Dominic said, still watching Damien as if he were a snake he expected to strike at any moment. "He'll be upset to learn you've left without him."

He wondered if the mysterious guitar player was this Tristan, and fervently hoped that he was not this girl's husband or lover. And what was this talk of ledgers? Surely, *she* was not involved in the running of this establishment.

She accepted the fringed shawl Dominic gave her from the coat rack behind the bar and draped it over her shoulders. "This gentleman will be with me, and I'm sure I'll be perfectly safe for a few blocks."

Damien nodded. "Of course. Perfectly safe, I assure you."

Dominic's concerned expression aside, he seemed to accept her decision. Damien held the door open for her and then followed her out into the night.

"It is a short walk. Your horse will be safe here for a while," she said, indicating Persephone, who stood hitched to a nearby post.

He fell in step beside her, unsure for the first time in his life how to act around a female. Less than five minutes in her company, and he was already thrown completely off balance. He had come here hoping to slake his lust for her, never considering he could not finesse her in the way he would a woman of the royal court.

Her long strides were nearly equal to his as they navigated down a narrow lane spotted with small cottages. As they walked, he could not seem to stop stealing glances at her out of the corner of his eye, noticing the way the moonlight glinted off her dark hair and bathed her in a white glow.

"What's your name?" he asked.

"Esmeralda," she replied, her voice a velvety caress in the night, filling his mind with images of naked flesh and all manner of other erotic thoughts.

"A beautiful name," he replied, without an ounce of artifice.

Easy to tell the truth when he found everything about her to be more beautiful than anything he'd ever seen or experienced. Funny how seeing her in the dark of night in this modest part of town and dressed so plainly only made that more apparent.

"It is a Romani name," she told him, a little smile curing her shapely lips. "It means 'emerald'."

"That's lovely. I am Damien."

"Yes," she said, turning to study him intently. "I know exactly who you are ... *Prince* Damien."

CHAPTER 4

*E*smeralda fought the urge to laugh. After all, wouldn't such a thing anger the royal prince? But his expression when she had revealed her knowledge of his identity had been priceless.

"I recognize you from the palace. Did you think that I wouldn't?"

How could she have forgotten him? He had watched her at The Golden Dancer the same way he had at his birthday celebration, with the same fiery intensity with which he inspected her now. His eyes were jade flames, causing her skin to tingle slightly when they moved over her.

He had dressed plainly, but his clothes were expertly tailored and of high quality. His bottle green frock coat clung lovingly to broad shoulders and accentuated the tapering of his waist. His buff breeches showcased powerful thighs that moved with dexterous grace as he walked, and high brown riding boots gleamed with polish.

"I would think you were too busy to pay attention to anyone," he replied. "But I did notice you. You are quite a dancer."

She tried not to acknowledge the little thrill that went through her at the compliment. She was relieved when they finally reached the small cottage at the end of the lane, her home.

"Here we are."

Esmeralda tried to see the house through his eyes, which darted about the small sitting room, studying his surroundings. Many of their furnishings were a collection of things that her father had accumulated during his time at sea. There was a hodgepodge of Spanish and Oriental, and the room had been decorated in various bright patterns and colors. The furniture was worn from use but well-made, upholstered in red and gold damask. Various unmatched tables with clawed feet were positioned around the room, holding vases of flowers or various trinkets and figurines. Patterned rugs covered the floor and a low fire burned in the stone fireplace. Beyond the sitting room lay the kitchen. Beaded curtains shielded the doorways to two bedrooms.

"This way," she urged.

She led him quickly up the narrow staircase, past her own bedroom, to the chamber at the end of the corridor where her grandmother resided. She knocked, three raps as the signal that she was bringing a customer.

"Come!" her grandmother called imperiously from the other side of the door.

"She is ready for you," Esmeralda whispered. "Before you go in, you must know that my grandmother is not a simple palm reader, or a con artist. What she sees and shows you is real. Most people are not ready to face the things she has to show them. Before you do this, make certain you are ready for whatever you may hear or see."

Before he could respond, she flung open the door and gestured for him to go inside.

DAMIEN STEPPED into the dark room lit only by candles and a crackling fire in the small hearth. Fragrant incense smoked on a low table in the middle of the chamber. The surface also held a peculiar looking pipe, and a bowl full of colorful glass beads. Reclining on a pile of cushions, he found a slim figure wearing flowing black robes. Her light brown face showed the deep lines of age, and her slender hands were wrinkled and gnarled. A tall turban sat on her head, a large jeweled pin affixed to the front. Several ropes of colorful glass beads hung around her neck and large rings adorned most of her fingers. He found her eyes identical to Esmeralda's, glowing yellow-gold in the firelight.

"Prince Damien Alexander Rothchester," she said, extending one of her hands to him. "Come, I have been waiting for you."

He stepped unsteadily forward. She'd been *waiting* for him? Was that something she said to anyone who came to have their fortune told? He wanted to believe that, but the way she looked at him—as if she could see through skin and muscle, straight to his marrow—led him to believe she'd actually been anticipating his arrival. Which was preposterous...wasn't it?

He crossed the room and lowered himself to his knees on the other side of the table. Now that he'd come here, he had to see this through. The woman would probably tell him some ambiguous hogwash, and he'd pretend to be amazed at her ability to 'see into his future' before going back to seducing the little dancer downstairs. That he had let himself be drawn into this farce only proved how enamored he must be with Esmeralda.

"I am Akira," the old woman said, reaching across the table to take his chin in her gnarled hand.

The strength of her grip surprised him, and yet again he found himself drawn into her enthralling eyes. She inspected him in silence, then smiled and nodded as if satisfied.

"No wonder she is so affected by you."

"Who is affected by me?"

She shook her head, releasing his face. "All in good time, Your Grace, all in good time. You will see only what I see, and what you don't see hasn't yet been set by Fate."

Lifting the pipe from the middle of the table, she held it up between them. A thin line of smoke curled up from it, casting a sticky-sweet odor around the room. Akira inhaled, blowing the aromatic smoke slowly through her nostrils. Then, she offered the pipe to him.

"You must partake in order to see," she urged when he didn't accept it. "Come, come, you may even like it."

Damien choked on the first try, the cloying smoke causing his eyes to water. He coughed, dropping the pipe. Akira chuckled, picking it up and offering it to him a second time.

"Try again," she urged. "This time will be easier."

He wanted to argue that it wasn't possible, as whatever she'd put in that pipe had made him feel as if he'd tried to inhale fire. However, he found himself too curious now to turn back. He'd been expecting cards, or a crystal ball, perhaps a reading of his palm … this was unlike anything he'd come to expect from a fortune-teller and he was overwhelmed by the need to discover how this encounter would end.

This time, he inhaled without choking, exhaling slowly as Akira had done. A thick haze formed around his field of vision, and the Gypsy woman's image before him seemed to waver and then disappear altogether. He could still hear her voice, clear as lightning through the gale of a storm.

"Now you will see," she intoned, her voice seeming to float around his head as he fought to regain his equilibrium. His head spun, and he felt as though he floated over his own body, suspended above reality.

Suddenly, his vision cleared, and he could see.

He recognized an image of himself, his face a contorted mask of unmistakable pain, blood smeared on his hands. This vision wavered and another of himself in Lionus' chambers swam before him. He held his brother's hand as Lionus lay beneath the bedclothes, his face as pale as death. He tried to hold on to the image but it, too, wavered and dissipated. Once more, his eyes focused on the image of himself, this time with Esmeralda clutched in his arms. Tears streamed down her cheeks, she clung to him fiercely. Damien's vision wavered just before their lips met in a tender kiss, the fog melting away altogether.

He jolted, as if he'd reattached to his body, coming back into the room with Akira. Damien gripped the edge of the table, his head spinning as he tried to regain hold of his equilibrium. Whatever he'd smoked from that pipe had clearly altered his state of consciousness. Odd, though, how he'd become clear-headed in an instant, without the lingering fog of drowsiness or lethargy.

"I have seen what you have seen," she said, her voice a near whisper now. "Much remains a mystery, but that is because decisions have yet to be made to set you on this path of your destiny. Esmeralda's fate is in a way entwined with your own."

Damien frowned, recalling the imagery of them locked in a lover's embrace. Certainly something he'd hoped for, but not beyond an encounter or two. However, Akira's words and what he'd seen led him to believe there was supposed to be more.

"But I have only just met her. How can that be?"

Akira shook her head. "That is not for me to say. I know only what we have witnessed, though I believe I understand it better than you."

"Will you explain it to me? Why was there blood on my hands? What is going to happen to my brother?"

"Within the house of the king, there lies a viper," Akira began, her eyes focused somewhere beyond Damien. "If you are not careful, this viper will strike a deadly blow, one that will bring the royal family to its knees."

Thinking of the assassination attempts against his father, Damien fought hard against a lump in his throat. Someone close to his father was trying to murder him. The fact that he had seen Lionus in his vision meant that this plot did not involve only Adare. As they had suspected, the entire family was now in danger. He wanted to discount her words as senseless ramblings, an attempt from a con-woman to frighten him. However, he felt deep in his bones that she spoke truthfully. He could not ignore what had been happening around him when taking in the things she said.

"What must I do?"

He'd known there was a threat, but if this woman could not tell him the identity of the person behind these attempts, he would still find himself at an impasse.

Akira shook her head, her eyes growing heavy-lidded and unfocused. "It is not for me to tell you what to do, but to warn you that the road to your destiny is paved with tragedy. It can be stopped, but only if the people involved make the right decisions. Careful of your own decisions, Your Grace ... one wrong step can set off a chain of events that cannot be undone."

Damien ran a hand through his hair with a heavy sigh. Some fortune-teller. What could he possibly do to stop a killer no one could name? How could he stop things from happening if he had no idea what caused them in the first place. A pit of worry opened in his gut, and he felt as if he'd be sick as he once again recalled the sight of his own hands coated in blood.

Whose blood? Father's ... Lionus' ... Mine?

"And what about Esmeralda?" he asked, choosing to focus on what might be the good news in all this. "How does she fit into my future?"

Akira's smile was both teasing and knowing, only making him more frustrated.

"Ah, surely you know I won't make it that easy for you," she said, her voice laced with laughter. "The two of you must discover this for yourselves. Know that by coming here tonight, you have set your feet upon a path that intertwines with hers ... and not only for a short, meaningless time, Your Grace. My granddaughter ... she is the change you seek, the future you have wanted but could never see. Do not make the error of seeing her as a temporary diversion, for what she can offer you is not so fleeting."

His belly quivered again, anxiety tying him up in knots. These particular words were not so cryptic, and he could clearly read what they meant. It was no coincidence that he would see her for the first time after having just decided to be finished with Davina ... or that he'd been unable to stop thinking about her since the night of his birthday celebration.

But, he hadn't come here looking for a wife, or for love. Realizing that, shame flushed the back of his neck and made his face go hot. Here he was, sniffing about the skirts of this woman's granddaughter, while she had been given some sort of vision about his future—one that would include tragedy and death if her words could be believed. It was a new low, even for him.

He stood, dropping a few gold coins on the table in front of her—far more than he knew the going rate to be, but guilt drove him to include a generous bonus.

"Thank you for your time," he said. "You have given me much to think about."

"You will come to see me again, yes?"

"Might you have more to tell me? Perhaps more about what you've already shown me?"

"Yes," she replied. "As time passes and you, as well as the people around you, make decisions that will affect your future, my vision will become clearer and I will be able to show you more."

"Then, yes ... I will return."

She dismissed him with a wave, reclining back against her cushions. "Then leave me now in peace. I am tired."

PRINCE DAMIEN'S face was drawn when he descended the staircase to where Esmeralda awaited him in the sitting room, leading her to wonder just what Akira had shown him. She had been right to warn him. Most people expected innuendo and trickery when first meeting with her grandmother, assuming her to be some sort of swindler. Others would visit on a lark, simply to say they'd had their palm or cards read and report back to their friends what had been said.

Those same people would leave the encounter shaken to their core by the things Akira would say or show them. No trickster, the old Gypsy woman had the true gift of 'sight', something Esmeralda knew very little about but had learned to trust over the years.

The prince looked quite dazed, so she supposed he'd either been given bad news, or was simply awestruck by being faced with the truth of Akira's power.

"Did it not go well, Your Grace?" she ventured, placing a hand gently on his arm.

He flinched as if she'd seared him with a hot iron and a little tremor ran through her at the feel of his well-muscled biceps beneath her hand. Her breath caught in her throat, a fluttering in her midsection catching her off guard.

What was that all about? He was certainly attractive, but Esmeralda hadn't had such a strong reaction to a man since ... well, never.

"It was interesting," he hedged. "She has given me much to think about."

"Would you care for tea, Your Grace?" she asked. "My mother makes her own special blend. It is known to be very calming."

It would be foolish to entertain him alone—her mother and brother gone visiting a cousin overnight, and Akira likely sleeping soundly upstairs. However, her curiosity about him only became harder to ignore the longer he stood before her. Akira always said that destiny was driven in part by Fate and in part by the actions of the people involved. So, which of those things had brought him here? And now that he was here, what did it mean that she wanted him to stay?

She'd already begun heating the water upon arriving home, and it would be rude to turn him out without offering refreshment. Her mother would never let her hear the end of it if she sent him out into the night without showing hospitality.

The prince looked beyond her, into the cozy little kitchen. "I would love to share tea with you, but only if you call me Damien."

"Of course, Damien," she murmured, his name falling from her lips with an effortlessness that caught her off guard.

His gaze roamed around the small but efficient kitchen as he followed her there. He took a seat at a large table with a marble surface. The space was what one would expect to find in a commoner's home: a simple wood-burning oven, pots hanging from the ceiling, bowls of root vegetables and onions in a large basket on one counter, another filled with fresh fruits on the other.

Yet the tea service she brought to the table was polished silver and the delicate cups she served it in were fine, hand-painted china. He eyed her family's belongings with interest, seeming to try to reconcile the modest cottage with some of the more ornate fixtures and items.

Esmeralda poured the tea and took a seat across from him.

"I know what you might be thinking," she said, indicating the silver tea service. "You're wondering how a family of Gypsies is able to afford such fine things. You are probably wondering if they are stolen."

"N-no," Damien stammered. "I wasn't—"

"It's all right," she interjected, offering him a small bowl of sugar cubes. "My people have a reputation for that sort of thing. But we are not all dishonest thieves, and those who are often become that way as a means for survival. My father was a wanderer who took to the sea. When he met my mother in Spain, he showered her with gifts he acquired from all over the world. Over his life, he managed to obtain quite a collection, so when they settled here, it was all used to adorn our home."

He inclined his head, curiosity alighting his features. "How did he come to settle in Cardenas?"

"Having children made him long for stability. My parents had traveled most of their lives and were ready to settle somewhere. I was seven years old when they happened upon Cardenas and decided they liked it here. Father purchased the tavern, turned it into The Golden Dancer, and retired from his life at sea."

"Your father sounds like an interesting man. I would love to meet him."

The genuine curiosity in his words only made her heart sink.

"I am afraid that's not possible," she murmured, staring into the murky depths of her china cup. "He died a little over a year ago."

His sympathetic wince sent a little twinge of longing through her heart. It never stopped hurting, saying those words aloud.

"I'm sorry to hear that. So, you have inherited The Golden Dancer? Have you no male relatives to assist you?"

"My brother, Desmond, is not yet seventeen. I am teaching him what my father taught me about running the business. I have been dancing there for years, and know more than anyone about managing it."

Her sadness faded, and Esmeralda felt fierce passion gripping her as she spoke of The Golden Dancer. It was merely a small tavern, but it was her father's legacy and she was proud to have taken up his mantle when he'd died. Damien watched her, his chin resting on his hand as he studied her as if she presented a mystery he wanted to solve. The intensity of his scrutiny had her fighting not to squirm in her chair.

"And what about you?" she asked, running her fingertip around the rim of her teacup.

Damien followed that finger with his eyes, and she was very aware of his heated perusal. His fingers flexed against the table and she tried not to think of him reaching across the small space that separated them. If he were to grasp the finger he followed with such interest, would he press the digit to his lips? Would he capture it in his mouth and caress it with his tongue? Esmeralda shivered inwardly and felt heat creeping across her neck.

Damien cleared his throat, flushing as if his thoughts had followed a similar path. "Um…what about me?"

"Well, your reputation precedes you, but I cannot help but wonder if there might be more to you than the stories I have heard."

He laughed, a rumbling sound that caused warmth to spread through her insides. It was thick and heavy, warm like a blanket wrapped around her shoulders.

"And just what stories are those?" he asked. "What exactly have you heard of me?"

"Well, if you must know … you are known as a most disreputable rake, a drunk, a gambler, and seducer of women."

"It seems you have just about summed me up," he said, leaning toward her across the table, his tone growing playful. "Shouldn't it worry you to be left alone with me?"

Esmeralda swallowed. His sudden nearness was wreaking havoc on her sanity. His eyes had grown heavy-lidded and sensual, and he seemed to watch her mouth quite closely, all humor gone from his expression. Inexplicably, she found herself leaning in, hands gripping the table tight as she met him over the scattered cups, saucers, and bowls between them.

"And why should I be nervous?" she replied, forcing a confidence she did not feel. "I know that you are a gentleman, and would never make any sort of advance upon me."

"And yet it is all I can think about," he whispered, his breath warm against her cheek as he brushed his lips against it.

She stiffened, realizing his intent, yet finding herself unable to put a stop to it, to move away from the inevitable. Leaning farther across the table, he brought his fingers under her chin, ever so gently tilting her head. The breath she held came out on a little whimper, the sound emitting against her will. Her insides seemed to liquefy, her limbs losing all strength as he tilted his head, angling to kiss her, inching forward in a way that she could avoid it if she wished.

But she never quite figured out whether she wished to avoid it or not, because then he was kissing her, and she was lost.

He pressed his mouth firmly against hers, gently urging her lips apart. He went slow, as if knowing he couldn't press too hard or too fast with her, yet still wanting to take from her, kiss her, taste her. She was melting into him, dazed by the slow seduction of his lips on hers, intoxicated by the strong, masculine scent of his sandalwood shaving soap. His hand rested lightly on the back of her neck, sending tingles racing down her spine at the delicate touch. All thought of resistance fled as she drowned in sensation, and in him.

His mocking, arrogant mouth worked its magic over her, weaving a spell of seduction so strong that Esmeralda completely forgot herself. It wasn't until she felt the hot stroke of his tongue against hers that she was jolted out of her languid trance.

She pushed swiftly away from him, covering her mouth with a trembling hand. Her breath came in short, unsteady gasps, and as she watched him, she noticed he'd been just as affected by the kiss as her. His chest heaved, his lips reddened and his eyes glittering like emeralds. At first, bewilderment crossed his features before remorse overtook his expression.

"My apologies," he managed between ragged breaths. "I should not have done that."

"No," she said forcefully, fighting to regain her shattered composure.

"You shouldn't have. It is late, Your Grace. Perhaps you should leave now."

She was shaken, her trembling hands balled up into fists at her sides. Anger—at him as well as at herself—rose to the surface. How could she have lost her head so quickly?

He stood, searching her gaze as if he were as confused as she and hoping to find the answers. She wanted to tell him he was looking in the wrong place, because she had been caught completely off guard by what had just happened. He didn't seem to understand it any more than she did, almost as if their mouths had found one another's by accident ... or by some force outside their own wills.

Ridiculous.

"Please," he said, his voice low and at odds with the seductive boldness he'd just wielded a moment ago. "I would like very much to see you again."

"I am certain you would, Your Grace, though you probably will not," she snapped, lashing out in defense of her confused and battered mind. "You will have to practice your seduction on some other unsuspecting female."

Storming to the front door, she swung it open, refusing to meet his gaze. She knew she was overreacting, but somehow found herself unable to stop. There could be no recovering from this, or thinking clearly, while he was still in her presence. His eyes, his lips, those coils of golden hair ... all of it proved an assault on her senses, one she had no defense against.

"Please leave, now."

He was silent for a moment, watching her as if expecting her to change her mind. She avoided his gaze, knowing that one glimpse into those beguiling eyes and she would become lost again.

After a while, he sighed and nodded in acceptance.

"Pleasant dreams, Esmeralda," he murmured before disappearing into the night.

She stood in the doorway a moment, watching his retreating form grow smaller and smaller until he was gone. She closed the door and bolted it, then raced up the stairs to her bedroom. Even with him gone, she needed as much space, and as many walls and doors, between then as possible.

Lighting a lamp, she carried it over to the washstand and began to undress, taking time to carefully remove her dagger from its sheath against her thigh. She never left home without it, and now proved no exception. It would await her on the washstand in the morning when she dressed again.

A good night's sleep ought to clear her head. She felt certain when she woke up in the morning, she'd feel more herself, and might even laugh over how silly she'd been in her reaction to the prince.

She shivered. The fire in her room had burned out hours ago and the chill of the fall night air seemed to sink as deep as her bones.

After washing quickly, she donned a long-sleeved, wool nightgown. Then, she stoked her fire again to chase away the chill in the air. After binding her hair into one long braid, she blew out the lamp and climbed into bed. Once beneath the bedclothes, she stared at the shadows cast on her ceiling by the moon, much too disturbed to find sleep.

Damien's kiss had stirred her, more than she cared to admit. Ever since the day of her father's murder, after the terrible things his killers had done to her, she had felt indifference toward men in general. The very notion of intimacy with a male in any form had always struck terror in her very core.

This supercilious, over-privileged prince, who had women fawning over him, had wanted her. For one moment, she'd allowed herself to revel in it, to be unafraid of the blossoming desire he had stirred within her. That could never happen again.

Remember, she told herself, *always remember the pain and the blood. Most of all, remember the humiliation.*

For hadn't that been the intent of those men who had killed her father? Wouldn't that be all she was left with once the prince had had his way with her? She was certain that he would, for if she continued to find herself alone in his company, she would be unable to resist.

CHAPTER 5

*E*smeralda watched her cousin, Tatiana, approach from where she knelt in the small vegetable patch along the side of the house. Usually, she waited for her mother to tend the small garden together, but after her sleepless night and turbulent thoughts she'd needed the diversion. Raina left early each morning with her grandmother to go into the marketplace, where she sold her handmade jewelry, soaps, and perfumes. Akira told fortunes and sold various potions and charms.

Left alone with nothing to do, she had donned an old skirt, blouse, hat, and worn gloves, then set herself to work.

The late morning weather was quite pleasant and she could see that Tatiana held a basket full of herbs freshly picked from her own yard. She would trade them with Esmeralda for some of her fresh vegetables.

Esmeralda lifted her full basket and met Tatiana near the back door leading into the kitchen.

Her cousin was certainly the beauty of the family. Tatiana's blue-black hair fell straight down her back like a shimmering curtain and her heavily lashed, dusky brown eyes almost always glittered with mischief. Her childlike enthusiasm and adventurous nature were as alluring as her looks, and though she would play coy, Tatiana had most men wrapped around her finger the instant she'd met them.

Esmeralda removed her hat and ran her hands over her riotous waves, pushing the heavy mass over her shoulder, then snatched off her gloves.

"Well, now you've gone and done it," Tatiana said, leaving her basket on the counter and taking a seat at the table. "The gossips were at it early this morning, talking about your mysterious visitor at The Golden Dancer last night."

Esmeralda sighed. She had known she wouldn't be the only one to recognize the prince and that it wouldn't be too long before tongues started wagging. Still, she decided not to divulge too much until she knew how much her cousin had heard.

"What about him?" she asked, busying herself with pouring lemonade. "He came to the tavern and asked if someone could lead him to a fortune-teller. I brought him here to see Grandmother."

Tatiana took a long gulp of her lemonade, wiped the back of her hand across her lush mouth, and grinned.

"Oh? And did he happen to mention that he was royalty?"

She studied Esmeralda intently, narrowing her eyes when no answer was forthcoming.

"You don't seem surprised. You knew!"

"Tatiana, it is nothing to fuss over. He obviously didn't want anyone to know who he was."

"You allowed him to walk you home last night. I hear your Tristan was quite angry when he found out."

"He is not *my* Tristan!"

"He could be yours if you allowed it. Don't pretend you don't know he loves you, Es. Everyone knows. Even though he could have any woman he wants, he wants the only one in our village who does not want him back."

Tatiana was right, as usual—an annoying habit, that. Tristan had pursued her endlessly, since the time they were both old enough to understand the differences between man and woman. No female of her acquaintance had gone unaffected by his looks or his charm. His talent as a dancer and a musician only added to his appeal. He was what most girls dreamed of, yet Esmeralda could feel nothing beyond sisterly regard for him.

She had always been able to keep her feelings on a platonic level with all the men of her acquaintance, yet one man had been able to shatter her carefully laid detachment in the breath of a moment.

"Is he as beautiful as they say?" Tatiana asked, as if reading her mind. "More striking than Tristan?"

"I suppose he's handsome enough," she lied, hoping that if she spoke the words aloud she would believe them.

"According to Tristan, who followed you home last night, you seemed to find him more than handsome enough."

Esmeralda gasped, heat rising in her face. Embarrassment and anger rose up, nearly choking her, and she fought for composure.

"He followed me?"

Tatiana nodded, the gleam in her eyes turned from mischievous to downright devilish. "Oh yes, did I forget to mention? He arrived just in time to see you and the prince in quite a cozy position in the doorway. He believes the prince intended to take advantage of you."

After Esmeralda had been silent for a moment, Tatiana gasped.

"Oh no! He did not, did he?"

"No," Esmeralda said wearily, finally deciding to tell her cousin all. "You must promise not to tell anyone, not even Morgana."

Then, she proceeded to relate the entire story, leaving nothing out. If she could trust anyone with the details, it would be her cousin. She might seem flighty, but there wasn't a more loyal friend. If she knew Esmeralda wanted something kept secret, then it would be. She even told Tatiana of her conflicted feelings following the kiss, her fear as well as her confusion.

"I was awful, Tatiana. I accused him of trying to take advantage of me, though I'm not sure that's what he was doing."

"And just what did you think he *was* doing, kissing a Gypsy girl he'd only known for an hour?" Tatiana demanded as her brow wrinkled. "Esmeralda, you are a beautiful woman and a fine catch, but a man like that will not see that in a girl like you. He probably saw you dancing at the palace and thinks to satisfy his lust with you."

She buried her face in her hands and sighed with a huff. Tatiana could be right, but she just wasn't certain. Her cousin had not been there, hadn't seen the way he'd looked after the kiss—as if he'd been just as conflicted as her.

"You don't understand. I cannot explain it, but there was something there. Besides, when I told him to leave, he did, and he was very polite. If he wanted to ravage me, don't you think he would have done so?"

"Of course not," Tatiana argued. "He is a notorious seducer. His ego would demand that you come to him willingly."

"You have to understand," Esmeralda pleaded, grasping her cousin's hand across the table. "You are like my sister and we have always confided in each other."

Tatiana's face grew serious and she nodded in understanding. "I'm sorry ... you're right."

Few people knew the whole story of what occurred the night her father was killed. If anyone understood how difficult it was for Esmeralda open up and admit attraction to any man, it was Tatiana.

"So, was he charming?" she asked impishly, back to her old self. "Were you overcome and weak in the knees?"

Esmeralda laughed, grateful for her cousin's ability to brighten any room with her smile. "I am ashamed to admit that I was. He was very dashing. Though I'm sure I've ruined it. You don't think he would forgive me for throwing him out, do you?"

"I doubt it, though you could simply apologize next time he comes to call."

"I didn't exactly invite him back, Tatiana. In fact, I told him in not so many words to stay away."

Her cousin shrugged. "Then forget about him. Start planning your wedding with Tristan."

When Esmeralda glared at her, she laughed.

"You know you're eventually going to relent and marry him."

She gave Tatiana's arm a playful pinch. "That's enough about Tristan. I hope you do not make such jokes around him ... he might take it the wrong way."

The last thing she wanted was to hurt his feelings, but she also did not want to give him hope where there was none.

"Fine," Tatiana relented. "We will talk of the prince instead ... far more interesting than Tristan at any rate."

Esmeralda's heart sank at the mention of the prince. "I do wish I could see Damien once more, at least to apologize for my behavior."

Tatiana gave her a wicked grin, her eyes bright with some mischievous plan or another. "I know a way you could make that happen."

"I can't believe I let you talk me into this!" she hissed.

"You want to see your prince, don't you?" Tatiana retorted. "This is the only way."

Esmeralda turned her back to Tatiana so that her cousin could help her tie her apron strings. They stood near the servants' entrance, prepared to infiltrate the palace in search of Prince Damien.

She groaned when she turned and observed the wicked glint in her cousin's eye. When they were children, Tatiana had often involved Esmeralda and Morgana in her escapades, placing them all in a great deal of trouble.

Time had changed nothing, Esmeralda realized as she stuffed as much of her thick hair under the white mobcap as possible. A few strands hung loose around her face and neck, but it would have to do. Tatiana's silken locks fit beneath the maid's cap perfectly, further emphasizing the childlike glee apparent in her face.

"I wonder what the penalty will be if we are caught," she whispered as they edged their way toward the servant's entrance. Probably transportation ... surely death was too extreme for simply sneaking into the palace. Still, being sent away from her home and family did not sound very appealing.

"We won't be," Tatiana insisted. "Do you honestly think any of them know the faces of each and every servant working in this place? There are hundreds of maids here, even some Gypsy ones. We'll blend right in. Besides, the palace is so overrun with guests for the royal wedding no one will have the time to pay us any attention."

"Where on earth did you get these uniforms? Heavens, I don't think I want to know."

"I know a girl who used to be a maid here. She still had these gowns. You're welcome, by the way."

Tatiana's plan seemed foolproof, yet she was uneasy. She'd seen several guards patrolling the perimeter, and though they'd managed to reach the servants' entrance easily enough, she still feared one of the armed guards would come around the corner at any moment and spot them. Of course, they would hardly seem out of place in their disguises, so Esmeralda took a deep breath and willed herself to relax. This could work. They would get inside, she'd find Damien and apologize, then they would leave. Simple enough.

The servants' entrance led right into the large kitchen, which bustled with activity. The smells of freshly baking bread and roasting meat assailed their senses, as did the noisy banging of pots being scrubbed, and the cook shouting instructions to busy maids. Herbs hung from the ceiling, a fire roared in the large fireplace over which a cauldron hung containing boiling water. A row of buckets filled with steaming water sat near the fireplace.

"Hurry up with that water," a footman called from the door to the kitchen. "You know Prince Damien likes his bath water piping hot."

Tatiana shot her a smug look and fell in behind the maids lifting the heavy water buckets. Getting to Damien would be easier than they'd thought. A stack of drying linens was shoved into her arms and she fell in step behind her cousin and the long line of maids headed for the prince's chambers. Her heart hammered in her chest as they filed down the winding corridors, past other bustling servants moving in and out of guest rooms.

Esmeralda lost count of how many turns they took, and hoped they would be able to find their way out. Finally, they reached the door leading to Damien's bedchamber, where footmen had already dragged the largest tub she'd ever seen. Two armed sentries stood guard on either side of the door. She quickly surveyed the room, finding no sign of Damien and at a loss as to what to do next. Surely, she could not be present while the man bathed.

She placed her armful of towels on the small table beside tub where various bottles and vials had been neatly arranged. She felt Tatiana's hand tighten around her arm, and before she could blink, she'd been yanked through the connecting door to the prince's sitting room. Tatiana put a finger over her lips, listening for the footsteps that signaled the other servants leaving the bedroom. Once they heard the door shut, Esmeralda breathed a sigh of relief.

"You'd better get out there before he comes in and starts undressing. Unless that was your intention all along, in which case I say enjoy yourself."

Casting her wayward cousin a glare, Esmeralda pushed the connecting door open a crack and peered inside. There was no sound or movement.

"Are you going to wait in here?" she whispered.

Tatiana shook her head. "Oh no, I don't want to intrude. I will meet you back in the kitchen. I'll continue posing as a maid, and when you are done, we will sneak back out the servant's entrance."

Esmeralda nodded, moving through the door and quickly shutting it behind her. She had been so nervous about getting caught, she hadn't even taken the time to notice her surroundings. Damien's bedchamber was as large as the entire ground floor of her home, boasting a great oak bed with four massive posters stretching toward the ceiling. Chairs in brown, ivory, and gold brocade matched the bedding, while drapes flanked picturesque floor to ceiling windows.

The intimacy of her position remained at the forefront of her mind. The tub sat near the crackling fireplace, hot and inviting; the bed curtains pulled back and held to the posters by tasseled ropes, the bedclothes turned down.

She noticed for the first time that there were a set of glass doors open to a circular balcony. It was there she found Damien, a dashing figure in all black, his hair glowing like a moonlit halo. She was drawn toward him, her voice caught in her throat, hands clenched before her. He half stood, half sat, on the stone rail of the balcony, holding a strange black instrument to his eye, head tilted up to the midnight-blue sky.

She cleared her throat, still too overwhelmed by the sight of him to speak. He lowered the instrument and turned, smiling when he saw her. She saw no recognition in his eyes and realized it must be too dark for him to see anything other than her silhouette.

"Is my bath ready?" he asked, walking toward her.

"Yes, Your Grace," she said, waiting like the coward she was for him to discover the identity of the maid cowering in the shadows.

Damien inhaled as he approached the maid awaiting him on the balcony. Jasmine. The fragrance was unmistakable, and also slightly familiar. In fact, he could remember one recent time in which he'd experienced the scent, and that memory niggled at him with guilt.

Esmeralda had smelled of jasmine when he had kissed her, the scent still clinging to his coat after she'd cast him out into the night.

As well she should have after the way he'd acted. He had sought her for nefarious reasons, only to be shown through Akira's vision that there could be more to their acquaintance if he made the right decisions, if he would open himself up to it.

And what had he done? He'd gone and tried to kiss her like an idiot, likely proving himself to be as much a rake as she'd accused him of being. All the things she'd heard about him were true, and he'd never been ashamed of them ... not until she'd jerked away from his kiss as if afraid of him. He should never have done it, not after she'd been so hospitable toward him, even while suspecting he'd come to The Golden Dancer to get under her skirts.

When the maid's face was revealed by moonlight, he felt as if he'd taken a fist to the gut. Shock washed over him as his gaze traced over the pleasing slopes and planes of her face.

"Esmeralda."

He'd thought he had made such a mess of things with her the night before that she wouldn't want to see him again. Yet, here she stood. The sight of her gave him hope they could start over.

"I came to apologize," she said, hands clasped in front of her. "For my behavior last night."

Damien couldn't control the upward movement of his eyebrows, or mask his disbelief. *She,* apologize to him?

"I am the one who should ask for forgiveness," he insisted. "I acted like a cad, and you had every right to be offended."

"But I wasn't offended," she said, her voice a near whisper, eyelids lowered.

He had assumed when seeing her dance that she was an experienced woman. No one he had ever known moved with such an inborn sensuality. Yet, it was obvious after her response to his kiss and her reticence here tonight that she was innocent and untouched. Realizing that didn't make him feel any better about his behavior.

"You weren't?" he prodded.

She shook her head, causing the ruffled maid's cap to slip back a little on her head. Her masses of hair were fighting for freedom, several tendrils having come loose just in the short time they had been speaking.

Damien clamped down on his desire to snatch the cap away and send her ebony waves cascading down her back. He clasped his hands loosely behind his back instead. Touching her would be a bad idea.

"You took me by surprise," she said, taking a tentative step toward him. "But I shouldn't have thrown you out of my home so rudely."

Damien gestured toward a chaise lounge in the middle of the balcony, and waited for her to sit before sinking down beside her. "I was the one who was rude. You told me about yourself. You let down your guard to me, which is something I sense you do not do for very many people. You gave me a chance to do the same, to share a little of myself with you, and I acted like a moron."

"Well, maybe you can make it up to me," she replied. "Tell me about that thing you were looking into earlier."

He stood and grabbed the long black instrument from the balcony rail. "This? You've never seen a telescope before?"

He smiled when she shook her head.

"My father told me about them," she said wistfully. "I've never seen one in person, though."

"Allow me to demonstrate how it works," he said, handing her the portable telescope and pointing out various constellations.

They went about it for about a quarter of an hour, Damien pointing out star formations and showing her how to get a good look at them. Standing this close to her, he caught a whiff of jasmine each time the breeze blew. It made him want to wrap his arms around her and hold her close, burying his face in all that lush, beautiful hair.

What was happening to him? These urges were nothing like the lust he'd felt upon first seeing her. They felt different, purer somehow, and completely unlike him.

Esmeralda lowered the telescope and smiled at him, the motion making him want to smile back.

"I would not have guessed that you were interested in something as intellectual as astronomy." Then, she gasped and clapped her hand over her mouth, her eyes wide. "I am so sorry. I did not mean to insult you."

Damien merely shrugged and returned the telescope to its velvet-lined case.

"It is not common knowledge," he said, rejoining her on the chaise. "My less reputable hobbies are more known than my intellectual ones. I have several telescopes, of varying sizes and for different purposes, kept in the observatory in the east wing of the palace. My personal library contains several volumes on astronomy, poetry, botany, and biology. I've always been quite fascinated by the sciences ... particularly botany."

Her gaze became pensive, her smile softening as she stared at him.

"The rumors I've heard make you seem so superficial. It is hard to believe that a man who speaks so eloquently of poetry and science could be the same drinking, gambling rakehell I've heard so many stories of. How is it that no one seems to know of your many other interests?"

"That is mostly my fault," he admitted, toying with his signet ring. "I have kept these pursuits to myself, though my family and servants know about them. Publicly, though, I have only allowed people to see one side of me."

Esmeralda nodded. "I know what you mean. Being a Gypsy who dances in a tavern gives people certain ideas about me all the time."

Damien knew he was guilty having misguided thoughts of his own about her.

"Yes, but you are innocent, whereas I am not. People have the right idea about me."

"Then why don't you change it?"

Damien shrugged, trying to seem nonchalant, but her words sparked something deep within him. She made it sound so easy—simply changing. Or, was it that he was making it complicated?

He settled on giving her an honest answer, the truest words he could think to say.

"Because, for all the gossip that exists about me, people are more concerned with my brothers. Lionus will be king, Serge will be general of Cardenas' military, and I will be the third son as I've always been. No one expects much from me."

"But surely you want more than that? To be known as more than just the last son?"

Of course he wanted more than to spend his life standing in Lionus' shadow. He'd felt that way his entire life, and could hardly believe that at the age of twenty-five he'd only just been asked for the first time what he wanted out of life.

"Yes, I want more. It is just that no one has ever expected anything of me, and so I've never expected anything from myself."

"But there must be something," she prodded. "Something you've always wanted for yourself."

His words came spilling out before he could stop them, the truth of his heart spilling forth in an instant.

"I have often thought of founding a university, perhaps even naming it for my father. A place dedicated to the pursuit of knowledge—mathematics, science, philosophy ... a place where anyone can come and receive instruction."

Esmeralda smiled and her entire face nearly glowed. Damien felt that grin tugging at his insides, twisting at his heart. He would have spilled more of his secrets, told her every thought he'd ever had if it would make her smile like that again.

"That's a wonderful idea!" she said, her excitement contagious, sparking something in him now that he had given voice to his idea. "I see no reason why you shouldn't do just what you've said."

Damien studied her face, illuminated by the pale moonlight.

"You are a marvel," he murmured, cupping her cheek with one hand.

He had resisted long enough, the urge to touch her had finally overcome his will.

"Such freshness and passion," he murmured, reaching up to slide the mobcap from her head.

Her hair tumbled around her shoulders. The scent of jasmine grew even stronger. She stiffened when he leaned toward her, but calmed when he pressed his face into her thick locks and inhaled. His instincts led him now, his body acting on all the impulses he'd tempered when first catching sight of her. Still, he kept his movements slow, watching and listening for any sign that she might want him to stop. She gave him none.

"That fragrance is intoxicating."

"My mother makes perfumes and soaps," she whispered.

Damien brushed his lips lightly up her neck, moving over her chin and then finding her lush mouth. She tipped her head back in acquiescence, and he couldn't have resisted the need to kiss her if he'd tried.

He swept her into his arms and crushed her against him, molding her body to his from chest to hip. Though his hold on her was tight, his lips moved with gentle insistence over hers. He took her mouth slowly, careful not to overwhelm her with his growing ardor. He clenched a handful of her hair and tugged gently, slanting her head back to gain better access to her mouth.

He deepened the kiss, his tongue sliding over hers, arousing familiar feelings of lust, combined with something new and exciting that he could not name. Heat suffused through him, spreading from his middle until he was hot all over.

He brought his hands to her waist, sliding them slowly up, his fingertips lightly brushing her breasts. The contact made his hands tingle, his mouth watering as he thought of opening the back of her gown and exposing more of her skin to his touch.

She sighed into his mouth and arched her back invitingly. He lowered his head, showering her neck and shoulders with kisses through the layers of her clothes, working his way steadily downward.

His hand cupping one breast seemed to jolt her senses, as well as his own. Her gasp had him pulling away, clenching his hands to keep from touching her again. She was far more tempting than he'd first realized, not just because of her beauty, but because of her earnestness, her willingness to try to see him as something other than a scoundrel. He couldn't remember the last time someone had given him the benefit of the doubt, but she had, even though he did not deserve it.

"I'm sorry," she panted out between sharp breaths. "You have to understand—"

"But I do understand. You are innocent, and you do not normally allow yourself to be so close to a man. Am I right?"

Biting her lip, she gave him a jerky nod in the affirmative. "Yes, but ... I liked kissing you. I even liked it last night, I just didn't know how to feel about that. I'm afraid my confusion caused me to lash out."

"You do not have to explain anything to me," he insisted. "The truth is ... well, I am not certain how to say this without sounding completely insane."

She gave him that smile again, the one that made him feel as if he could scale mountains and fly. Had she any idea how potent just that little motion of her lips could be?

"Just say it," she urged.

"Something your grandmother said when I was with her led me to believe that something about our meeting is ... special, somehow. And when I saw you again tonight, I got this feeling she might be right."

She lowered her gaze, seeming to wrestle with that as much as he had. Hell, he still wasn't entirely certain how to feel about it, but he did know how Esmeralda affected him. A part of him was desperate to see where it could lead.

"Grandmother has a way of making a person question everything," she replied. "It can be both frightening and exciting."

"I find myself leaning more toward the latter when it comes to you," he murmured, taking her hands in his. Even that small amount of contact electrified him. "Tell me I can see you again ... please. I ... I want to know you."

He felt his face going warm as he realized how he sounded—like some lovesick pup who'd never seduced a woman. Hell, he had the ability to coerce anyone of the opposite sex right out of their drawers ... but that wasn't what he wanted with Esmeralda. It was what he'd thought he wanted, but drawing closer had only caused him to see the truth. Something in her called to something in him, and it was the part of him that craved stability, honesty, something deeper than meaningless sex and drunken revelry.

Relief stole over him when she nodded.

"I would like that very much."

He led her by the hand through the doors of the balcony and into his bedroom. "How on Earth did you manage to get in here? There are guards at every entrance to the palace."

"Not at the servants' entrance," she replied, shoving the mobcap back over her head and tucking her hair into it. "My cousin and I managed to sneak into the kitchen and follow your bath water up here."

"How convenient," Damien said with a laugh. "Let me walk you back."

Even as he found her plan amusing, he decided to have a word with Lionus about ensuring the servants' entrance was secured. She should never have been able to get to him, though he was grateful that she had.

Esmeralda pulled her hand from his with a shake of her head. "It would seem odd, you accompanying a maid to the kitchen. I remember the way out. I'll be all right."

He would worry for her, but she was right. The guards would see her leaving and think a maid had stayed behind for a tryst with the prince. It wouldn't be the first time that had happened. He gave her a swift kiss on the lips and another on the cheek, then opened the door for her. He watched until she had disappeared around the corner before closing the door and leaning against it with a deep sigh.

The water had grown tepid during their conversation, and he had to order it warmed with more hot water. He hated to trouble the servants, but needed to sooth his body and calm his racing mind. Once the tub was filled with fresh, steaming water, Damien lowered himself in. His usual decanter of brandy and glass sat on the table near his drying towels. He grasped the tumbler that had been poured for him and sipped as he thought over the short time that had passed since he'd met Esmeralda.

A WEEK HAD GONE by since she'd come to the palace to dance and set his very soul on fire. Christ, he had told her things he had never admitted to anyone, about his own insecurities as the youngest son and his dream of founding a university. What could possibly have possessed him? He had striven to keep his relationships with the opposite sex fairly shallow. Until now.

He'd wanted Esmeralda to know things about him, to respect him as he did her. It was a bit disconcerting, but more than that, it proved exciting. The 'something more' he had seen looming in his future seemed more an event to look forward to than one to dread. Instead of pressing for the sort of conclusion he always sought with a woman, he would set out to find something more meaningful. He would see if Akira's prediction came true, if there might be some sort of future for him with Esmeralda in it.

He drained the glass and reached for the decanter to refill it, but found he had no desire to intoxicate himself as he did nearly every night.

He'd planned to skip the small musicale planned for the first wave of wedding guests to have arrived, and indulge in a night of cards at his club instead. The idea no longer appealed to him. Besides, he had no desire to incur his brother's wrath so soon after the festivities had begun. He had already ordered his evening clothes readied, so he made the decision to alter his plans.

Davina would most likely be present, though the idea of her company held as little appeal as did cards and drink. He would do his best to avoid her snares this evening and choose a less public place to finally cut ties with her. He'd already had a contract drawn up making her the owner of the townhouse, and would find a nice, expensive parting gift to mollify her.

Satisfied with these decisions, Damien washed, then left the tub and dried. He was determined to make it through the evening, boring as it promised to be. The sooner he got through it, the sooner he could move forward.

He joined the guests downstairs and donned a mask of slight interest for the benefit of his family. His only relief from boredom came when thoughts of a dark-hair vixen came dancing through his wandering mind.

CHAPTER 6

*L*ady Davina Keane rested upon a chaise lounge done in a floral pattern of pink and gold in the middle of her massive dressing room. It was second only to her bedchamber as the largest in the house, and by far her favorite—a place where she could be surrounded by all the fine things gifted to her by her keepers over the years. The best of all, naturally, being those things given to her by the prince.

She lifted her steaming cup of chocolate from a nearby table and sipped it slowly, relishing the rich drink, a large amount of which Damien had procured at her request. Truly, there wasn't a thing she could ask for that he could not acquire.

One of the many perks of my position, she thought, ringing for Anne.

She had spent the previous evening at Rothchester Hall, attending the queen's musicale. The event had bored her to tears, but as part of the royal court, she'd been obligated to attend. She had been surprised to see Damien there and even more astonished by the distraction that seemed to plague him. She hadn't even been able to entice him to her bed. He had claimed fatigue and promised to visit her soon.

His mood was surprising, and his detachment alarming. No matter; he'd probably been just as bored by the night's entertainments as her. She would invite him to dinner one night this week, wear one of her most daring gowns, and he would be hot to have her as he always was.

Anne appeared at her side and curtsied. "Good morning, my lady."

"I believe I'll wear my pale blue muslin dress and white hat with the blue ribbon and plumes this afternoon for luncheon at Rothchester Hall. Have my rose silk evening gown free of wrinkles by this evening for the dinner party. And I shall need you to dress my hair, of course."

"Yes, my lady," Anne replied with another curtsy.

Davina finished her chocolate and refilled her cup using the porcelain pot on the nearby table. She slid her feet into the pink mules matching her dressing gown and moved to study her reflection in the full-length mirror at the corner of the dressing room. Her figure could afford a second cup of chocolate, she told herself with a smug little grin, running her hand down the side of her waist and hip.

What a compliment her peaches and cream complexion was to her luscious auburn locks and velvety eyes. Beauty, grace, and charm were abundant in her personality, as members of her acquaintance had told her several times. All of these things combined to make her the perfect candidate for a princess of Cardenas. She cared not that Damien was merely the youngest son. He was still wealthy beyond all imagining and the handsomest of the three princes. Besides, she had no desire to be wed to the first or second born princes. She would have a husband who had the time to attend to her, not set her aside when he was crowned king or made general.

He would ask her to marry him soon; she could feel it. He was coming to an age where he needed to begin thinking of settling down and she was ready to fill the position. Aside from that, he'd been keeping her for well over a year—far longer than he'd ever dallied with any woman. If that did not prove his intentions, she didn't know what did.

"My lady!" squealed Anne as she rushed back into the dressing room, Davina's blue muslin dress draped over one arm. "The package from Madame Didier has arrived!"

Davina clapped her hands in delight and laughed. "Well, hurry, you silly girl, and have it brought in at once!"

Anne motioned for a tall, broad-shouldered footman to enter with the large box. She had waited weeks for the custom-made ball gown she'd ordered for the masquerade ball to be held for Prince Lionus and Princess Isabelle on the night before their wedding. Davina ripped the ribbon and parchment away and allowed Anne to help her lift the gown, which was quite heavy, from the box.

The maid gasped. "Oh, my lady, how beautiful!"

Madame Didier had charged an exorbitant amount for the extravagant gown and Davina had known then, as she knew now, that the cost was well worth it. Navy blue satin had been sewn to mold to her form before exploding into full skirts swirling with silvery tulle. Silver beading arranged in a swirling pattern covered the bodice and trailed down the front of the skirt to the hem, causing the gown's excessive weight. It would be a damned nuisance to wear, but such discomfort was a small price to achieve the perfect appearance. Matching slippers, reticule, and a painted mask were found at the bottom of the package, along with a bill from Madame Didier.

"I think the sapphires would go best with this, don't you think Anne?" she asked absently, imagining the large gems hanging from her neck and ears. The sapphire set included a tiara that she'd never worn, saving it for a special occasion.

Davina grinned, imagining the sapphire circlet on top of her head. No one would know except her, but for the masquerade ball she would be disguised as Damien's princess.

DAMIEN'S FAMILY had been surprised to see him at the musicale, immaculately dressed and sober. They were even more stunned to find him at the table for breakfast the next morning, promptly at eight o'clock. Even the footmen could barely contain their surprise when he strode in, dressed in riding attire and boots, whistling cheerfully. His brothers were already present.

Adare tried to join them some mornings for breakfast, but

attending the musicale had sapped much of his strength and Damien assumed he was sleeping in. Their guests would all take breakfast in their rooms, and most probably would not be seen until the luncheon that afternoon. Damien wouldn't be attending that, his thoughts already moving him in the direction of a certain Gypsy woman's cottage.

He headed to the sideboard and filled his plate, then took his place beside Serge and across from Lionus. His eldest brother had stopped eating and now eyed him incredulously. Damien winked at Jarvis, who appeared at his side with the coffee pot.

"Armageddon must be upon us," Serge guffawed, his good humor a match for Damien's. "I have never seen you out of bed before noon."

He elbowed Serge in the ribs and dashed his coffee cup with a liberal amount of cream. "Yes, well, I have things to do today. Important things ... So, I won't be attending the luncheon, though I'm sure I will be back in time for the dinner party."

Lionus nodded, turning his attention back to his plate. "I had assumed the musicale would be the first and last of your appearances until the tournament. I appreciate your efforts to attend the planned entertainments."

He took the compliment at face value. It was the best Lionus could do, and Damien couldn't expect more than that.

Queen Alexandra swept into the room, regal as always. Her dark hair was streaked with silver and pulled back in an elegant chignon. Her frigid, hard beauty was only slightly marred by lines and wrinkles around her mouth and cerulean eyes, and the iciness found within their depths.

She took her seat at one end of the table, and a cup of tea appeared at her side before her bottom had settled fully in the chair. She nodded at Jarvis, who materialized at her elbow with her prepared breakfast plate.

Very few servants in the palace were privileged to prepare Alexandra's plate, for most never got it right. She preferred particular foods on certain days, and insisted that none of the items on her plate touch each other. Jarvis had become the master at remembering the queen's preferences.

"Good morning," she said to Lionus only.

Damien and Serge had long grown used to being mostly ignored by their mother. He doubted she even noticed his unusual presence. They ate in silence, even Serge's sunny mood eclipsed by Alexandra's icy manner. He was grateful when Jarvis interrupted them.

"There is a visitor," he announced.

"No need to announce me, dear Jarvis," called a familiar voice from the hall.

"Nicolai!" Serge exclaimed rising to greet their cousin as he stepped into the room. "We weren't expecting you until the end of the week."

Their cousin, Nicolai, older than Lionus by one year, was the son of their father's younger brother. He had been raised alongside the three princes, and it was said that he might as well be their fourth brother. Even Lionus perked up at this unexpected arrival.

"It is good to see you," he said, standing to offer Nicolai his hand. "Jarvis, see to it that Nicolai's usual chambers are prepared for him."

Damien was next to greet his cousin, clapping him on the back and joining him at the sideboard for a second helping. Nicolai carried the looks characteristic of the Rothchester side of the family. Tall with an athletic build, he had the same light blond hair as Damien, as well as the green eyes passed down to many Rothchester men.

"Sorry I did not send word that I was coming early, but there was no time," Nicolai said as he joined them at the table. "Father has been in his cups, and he's been deuced difficult to live with as of late, so I decided to come up early."

"Well, we are glad to have you, as always," Serge said.

"Good morning, Auntie Alexandra!" Nicolai bellowed, deliberately using the form of address detested by the queen.

"Nicolai," she said in a clipped, abrupt manner, with a slight incline of her head.

Her blue eyes narrowed on the nephew she so disliked for reasons none of her sons understood. They knew that Alexandra loathed

Adare's brother, and detested Nicolai's mother, and for that reason did not like Nicolai. However, she didn't seem to like her own sons either, so that wasn't saying much.

"Excuse me, I find I have lost my appetite."

She stormed from the room with a regal swish of her skirts, leaving the men to relax in the absence of her overbearing presence.

"I am also here because I received your message about the attacks on Adare," Nicolai said, once Alexandra had cleared the room. "I thought I might be needed."

Serge nodded. "As you can see, we have severely increased our security."

"And because we have reason to believe that this plot involves the royal family and not just Father, your chambers will be guarded as well," Lionus added, leaning back in his chair and folding his hands over his abdomen. "Only a select group of servants will be allowed to attend you."

"Please tell me that voluptuous maid Lillian is among the chosen few. She is so ... very nice to have about."

"You'll have to practice your seduction well, cousin," Serge said with a laugh. "She has eyes only for Damien these days."

Nicolai chuckled, clapping him on the shoulder. "You devil, you!"

Damien shook his head. "Seduce away, cos. I have not sampled the girl's charms and have no interest in doing so."

"Ah," Nicolai said knowingly, raising a blond eyebrow. "The fair Davina. Shall we be making an honest woman of her one of these days?"

Lionus snorted, rolling his eyes in agitation. "I should certainly hope not."

Rather than defend Davina as he usually would, Damien merely shrugged. "I think not. In fact, I have decided that the time to end our association has come."

"It's about damned time," Lionus muttered.

Ignoring his brother's comment, Damien signaled Jarvis for another cup of coffee.

"Back to the matter at hand," he said sharply, stabbing Lionus with a piercing glare. "The three prisoners still have to be questioned again. We must make time for that."

Serge nodded. "I was thinking we could slip away from the dinner party tonight. All the guests will be occupied and no one should miss us for too long. We could question them then."

Lionus nodded. "A fine idea. I'll speak to the captain of the guard and tell him to have the prisoners brought to us."

"I hope you don't mind if I join you," Nicolai said between bites of coddled eggs. "A fourth perspective could be helpful."

"Of course," said Damien. "This is a family matter and concerns you as well."

"Once you're settled in your rooms, you may wish to rest if you are going to attend the luncheon this afternoon," Lionus said, in command as usual.

"A capital idea. I should like a bath as well, and perhaps Lillian to scrub my back!"

"Well then," said Damien, rising to his feet. "I will see you all at dinner this evening."

He strode quickly from the room, his step lighter than it had been in months as he contemplated an afternoon spent with Esmeralda.

Tristan Molina had loved Esmeralda for as long as he could remember. Their parents had been long-time friends and they had grown up together. One day—he wasn't exactly sure when—he'd turned around and discovered she had become a woman. Her eyes beguiled him, her sumptuous mouth tempted him, and her lithe body set his blood on fire.

He had waited with increasing impatience for her to return his love, knowing that the events surrounding her father's death had made intimacy difficult. Tristan had been there to discover her as she lay, beaten and brutalized on the side of the road beside her father's corpse. He'd taken her in his arms, cradled her to his chest and whispered soothing words in her ear as he'd carried her home. He had been there for her every day since, and still she treated him like she would a brother or a cousin.

Now he sat at the table in her small kitchen, watching her roll out dough for pastries. Her hands were dusted with flour and her feet were bare, but to Tristan she was radiant. Her simple white blouse tucked into a yellow skirt were plain and serviceable, but in his eyes, she might as well have been draped in a silk ball gown.

"Everyone is talking," he said, voicing his concern over her newfound friendship with the prince. "You must know what this will do to your reputation. People will think you intend to become his next mistress."

"You know how little I care about what people think," she murmured absently, her attention remaining on her dough.

"And what of his intentions? Do you think that they are honorable?"

She plopped a basket of green apples on the table in front of him and handed him a sharp kitchen knife. "As long as you're here in my kitchen, you can make yourself useful."

She'd deliberately dodged his questions. Tristan seethed, taking up the knife and slicing into the skin of an apple.

"I only say these things because I care about you," he said. "I am trying to protect you."

Esmeralda stared distractedly through the window, as she'd been doing since Tristan had arrived. Her hands stilled over the dough, and her eyes took on a dreamlike quality as she watched the path winding by the house.

He gritted his teeth in frustration. "Esmeralda, are you even listening?"

She started and moved away from the counter, turning her attention back to him. Sitting beside him at the table, she dusted her hands on the apron tied about her waist.

"I know you are only thinking of my best interest, and I appreciate it. Really, I do. You have always been such a faithful friend, Tristan."

He winced inwardly at the word 'friend'. How he longed to whisk her upstairs to her bedroom and strike the word from her lips forever.

ELISE MARION

"I will always be here for you."

He had waited so long for her, he would weather whatever feelings she thought she had toward the prince. When the other man broke her heart, Tristan would be there to pull the pieces back together.

Esmeralda shot to her feet at the sound of horse's hooves rumbling down the road. She rushed to the window, and from where he sat Tristan made out a figure on a massive black horse trotting toward the cottage.

"It's him!" she cried, with a sunny smile.

He frowned as he watched Esmeralda look down at her clothing in despair, then take off toward the staircase.

"I cannot see him looking like this," she mumbled to herself as she climbed the stairs.

Tristan banged his fist on the table in agitation, then rose and thundered through the front door, unwilling to stay and watch her make a fool of herself over the pompous, spoiled prince. He approached his horse just as Prince Damien drew near, pulling his own mount's reins to slow her.

"Good morning," the prince said while jumping down from the mare's back, tying her reins to the tree that Tristan's stallion had been tethered to a moment before. "You must be Esmeralda's dance partner. Tristan, is it?"

The prince extended his hand to Tristan, but he ignored it, narrowed stare focused on his face. The man was downright pretty, but Tristan wondered if he ran any deeper than what lay on the surface. He very much doubted it. Esmeralda's head had been turned by his status and attention, but she would soon see him for what he truly was—a spoiled boy in a man's skin, spouting pretty lies at her.

"Yes," he replied, his voice dripping with venom. "I am a very good friend of Esmeralda's. She is special to me, and I warn you not to harm her. If I find out that your intentions toward her are anything but honorable, royalty or not, I will spill your blood and prove that is red just like mine!"

Without another word, he mounted his horse and thundered off down the road.

. . .

Damien rapped lightly on the door to the cottage, still puzzled over his encounter with Tristan. It would seem he was in competition for Esmeralda's affections. Nothing else could explain the force of the man's words or the cold glint in his eyes when he'd threatened Damien. The incident was forgotten when the door swung open to reveal a woman who could be none other than Esmeralda's mother.

She was the very image of her daughter, though her face proved distinctly more mature. The same honey-colored eyes that Akira and Esmeralda possessed twinkled with good cheer as she curtsied to him, then stepped back to allow him entrance.

His father had often spoken of his favorite Gypsy dancer, a woman who had graced the palace many times with her presence. Sultry and elegant, Adare had called her, an astonishing combination. Putting his father's description together with Esmeralda's stories about her parents, Damien knew he stood before the 'Golden Dancer' herself.

"Welcome, Your Grace," she said, closing the door behind them. "I am Raina, Esmeralda's mother. I have heard so much about you."

He wasn't sure if it would bode well for him that Raina had heard a lot about him. That would all depend upon the source. However, her smile was kind and genuine as she led him into the sitting room.

"Esmeralda will be down in a moment," she said, sitting in an armchair once he had seated himself in a matching one. "It is an honor to have you visit our home."

"The honor is all mine," he replied. "My father speaks very highly of you."

Raina smiled, a faraway look in her eye. "His Majesty is kind. I have not danced at the palace in ages, and still he remembers. He has always been most kind to me. How is he faring these days?"

"His illness has progressed to the point of no return, according to the physicians. His time with us is short, I'm afraid."

"How tragic," she remarked, reaching across the small space between them to envelope Damien's hand in her warm one. "I will send up a prayer for him."

ELISE MARION

Damien nodded his gratitude.

"Ah, here's Esmeralda," she said, gesturing toward the staircase.

She wore a simple gown of navy blue wool, its long sleeves gathered at the wrists, the bodice clinging to her slender waist and buttoning down the front. The modest neckline flaunted a bit of plain black lace, while the skirt billowed out with the assistance of a petticoat or two. Her hair had been arranged in a soft chignon, though several strands had fallen to hang loose about her face.

It didn't matter how many women he'd seen adorned in silks and satins ... she put them all to shame in simple wool.

Recovering from the initial reaction of laying eyes upon her, he took her hand and kissed it quickly, resisting the impulse to linger on her sweet-smelling skin. That scent of jasmine wafted up his nostrils.

Raina sank back into her chair, taking up a needle and what looked to be the beginnings of a dress, conveying her intention to stay as a chaperone, but maintain a certain distance. Esmeralda led him to the kitchen.

"You cook?" he asked as she donned an apron and began working with a mound of dough resting upon the table.

"I do, but I love baking more. Today I am making apple tarts."

Yet again, he found himself duly impressed. Most women of his acquaintance were at home this very moment, entertaining callers over tea. They were dressed in expensive muslin and lace and discussing mundane subjects over goods baked by a servant. They probably did not know where the kitchen was located in their own home and would never be caught holding a rolling pin or wearing an apron.

"What a coincidence," he said. "I happen to adore apple tarts."

"Well then, you won't mind working for them," she replied, pointing at the abandoned apples and knife on the table beside her. "Tristan was helping me, but he left."

Damien removed his coat and draped it over a chair before rolling up his shirtsleeves and joining her at the counter. He lifted the knife in one hand and a large apple in another.

Esmeralda laughed at the confused expression on his face. "What's this? The prince has never peeled an apple before?"

He shrugged sheepishly. "Madame, I have never had to prepare a meal. Until recently I had never even been in the kitchen at Rothchester Hall."

"Well, there's a first time for everything."

He watched her peel, core, and slice an apple before trying it on his own. It took him longer to accomplish the task than her, but after the first few apples, he found the way of it. She showed him how to roll the dough flat and cut it into squares, and how to mix the apples with sugar and cinnamon and fold them into the little pastry squares.

Nearly an hour later, they and the kitchen floor were covered in a light sprinkling of flour, but the neatly folded tarts were ready to go into the oven.

"So, your friend Tristan seems very protective of you," Damien remarked, trying to sound nonchalant, but he was determined to discover the complete nature of their relationship. If he stood a chance with her, he wanted to know what he might be up against.

She sighed, setting a cup of lemonade in front of him and grasping her own with both hands. "He has been that way since my father died. His parents were friends with mine and we were raised together. He has been my friend for a long time."

Damien sipped the sweet lemonade and continued with caution. "The way he warned me away from you when I approached the house made me wonder if there wasn't more to your friendship."

"Tristan wishes there could be, but I do not feel the same way. Many of our friends and family have expected us to marry."

He did not know whether to be relieved or pity the man. It had to be difficult, finding that your feelings for someone had changed, while theirs toward you had not. However, he did not feel bad enough to cease his pursuit of Esmeralda. It would take far more than a jealous suitor who stood no chance to call him off.

"Tristan means well, though," she continued. "I am sorry if he said anything to you he shouldn't have."

Damien shrugged. "I've experienced worse. Besides, he will have no cause to follow through with his threats. I would never dream of dishonoring you."

He gazed into her eyes, willing her to believe him, to understand that his words were sincere. He would not blame her if his reputation made it difficult to trust him, yet Damien wanted nothing more than for her to give him the benefit of the doubt.

"You do believe me, don't you, Esmeralda?" he prodded.

She nodded, remaining silent as he pressed his lips to hers. He lingered there for as long as he dared, knowing Raina sat a stone's throw away. Cupping her face, he pressed soft, gentle kisses against her mouth, enjoying the small pleasure even as he wished he could kiss her in earnest, taste her, devour her.

Reluctantly, he forced himself to part from her.

"I'm sorry to say I must leave soon," he said, removing his hand from her face and returning his attention to his lemonade. "But, there are affairs I have to attend to at the palace; most of them unimportant, but I am obligated to attend them anyway."

Esmeralda nodded. "I understand. I am glad you came."

"So am I."

He paused for a moment, mulling over the question he'd truly come to ask. Would it be too soon to press for what he wanted? Instinct told him no; however, he was aware that his propensity for leaping headlong into things on impulse might frighten her.

He decided to throw caution to the wind.

"There is a picnic lunch planned for tomorrow afternoon at the palace. I think I would enjoy it so much more if you could come with me."

Esmeralda's eyes widened and her hand went to her throat in a gesture of anxiety. "A picnic? Hasn't the entire royal court assembled for your brother's wedding? Everyone's been talking about it and the city has been flooded with visitors filling the inns and alehouses."

"Yes," he replied. "There are a plethora of entertainments planned for the next fortnight. While I am not obligated to attend them all, I've promised to make an effort to appear when I can. As I said, I think I'd be more likely to *want* to attend if I have you on my arm."

Her eyes darted, and she shook her head slowly as if uncertain. "I don't think I'd know how to behave in such refined company."

Damien took her hand and laughed. "My dear, I am fairly acquainted with nearly every member of the royal court, and I can assure you that you are more well-mannered than most of them. You'll do fine."

"Oh," she murmured gazing up at him when he squeezed her hand. "Wouldn't you be embarrassed … being seen on the arm of a … a common woman, a Gypsy?"

He leaned closer to her, bringing her hand up to his lips for a kiss. He couldn't seem to stop touching her in these small ways that made him feel connected to her. That made him feel alive.

"You are beautiful, charming, and kind. What is there to be embarrassed about? In fact, I daresay I'll be the envy of every man there."

She cracked a smile when he winked at her, but it still seemed tentative. Rising to his feet, he kept hold of her with one hand, using his other to raise her chin.

"I would have you become a part of my life, my world. You would sparkle like the brightest gem there, I'm sure of it. And if it makes you feel better, I will say nothing of your heritage, or where you are from, or any of it. All anyone needs to know is that your name is Miss Esmeralda Amador, and you are attending as my special guest."

She seemed on the verge of giving in, her eyes wide as she soaked in his words.

"May I have some time to think about it?" she asked. "This does not mean I do not wish to spend time in your company … only that a step like this requires a bit more thought."

He tried to fight off disappointment, reminding himself that she hadn't exactly said no. "I'll expect an answer from you by tomorrow morning … deliver a note to me at the palace. Tell the guard at the gate I'm expecting it. If you accept, I will come for you. If you decline, know that it changes nothing. There will be no hard feelings."

He released her hand and allowed her go to the oven to peek at her tarts. Declaring they were ready, she quickly removed them, then offered one to Damien. He bit into the sweet confection, sighing appreciatively and nodded his approval.

"The palace cook could learn a thing or two from you about apple tarts," he said, finishing most of the tart in one bite and reaching for another, heedless to how hot they still were.

Esmeralda giggled. "You'd better get your fill while you can. My brother, Desmond, can smell these from a mile away."

As if he'd heard her, a young man came crashing through the back door, guitar case slung over his shoulder.

"Hello, Es!" he called cheerfully, making a beeline toward the tarts.

Esmeralda raised an eyebrow at Damien and shrugged, prompting a laugh.

The boy had devoured two of the tarts before noticing that his sister had company. He nearly choked, but, coughing and sputtering, quickly gained his composure and offered a bow.

"Your Grace, I'm sorry I did not see you there," he mumbled around a mouthful of syrupy apples and flaky crust.

"You don't see much when there is food in the room," Esmeralda taunted, ruffling her brother's dark curls. They were thick and lustrous, much like his sister's locks.

"Call me Damien, please. You must be Desmond. You are a very talented guitar player. I enjoyed your performance at the palace."

"Thank you, Your Grace… I mean, Damien! Tristan—that's Esmeralda's dancing partner—started teaching me when I was just a boy."

"Yes, I have seen Tristan dance and play," Damien said, recalling the smooth grace with which the man had danced and handled the guitar. "He is quite talented as well."

"He's got all the luck," Desmond said, dropping down into a chair at the table. "Talent, good looks, and charm."

Damien studied the young man. Desmond was nearly as tall as him, and quite thin, though his shoulders were broad and his body beginning to show firmness of muscle. His dark eyes were framed by thick sooty lashes. He could see the beginning signs of manhood on the boy, including half a day's worth of beard on his jaw.

Damien smiled. "You are still young. Give yourself a few more years, and I wager you'll have the girls clamoring after you."

Esmeralda nodded her agreement. "He's right, you know. You're already so handsome ... just like Father."

Desmond rolled his eyes and shook his head, but twin red spots appeared on his cheeks. He shrugged and cleared his throat, turning back to Damien.

"Is that your horse out front?" he asked, crossing the room to procure another tart. "She's a beauty."

"Her name is Persephone. Do you like horses?"

"I love them. Tristan lets me ride his stallion whenever I want. I'm saving up to buy one of my own."

"That's very ambitious," said Damien, a sudden thought occurring to him. "Perhaps I could help you with that. Are you yet employed?"

Desmond's eyes lit up, a wide smile splitting his face. "At the public mews in town. The stablemaster says I'm not ready to go from stable boy to groom, but I know more about horses than any of the others. I think he simply distrusts me because I'm Romani."

Damien would have expected as much. Even with such a large population of honest, hardworking Gypsies in Cardenas, many still held prejudices against them.

"Well, our stables at Rothchester Hall are quite large and we are always in need of grooms to care for the horses. If you would like employment, I could give you work looking after my horses, and in addition to your wages I would give you the mount of your choosing. What do you say?"

Desmond's eyes widened as he looked to his sister, who seemed just as shocked by what had just been said. Then, the boy let out a 'whoop' of excitement, extending a hand to Damien with a bright smile.

"I say you've got yourself a new groom! Thank you, Damien."

He felt Esmeralda's gaze on him as he chatted with Desmond, explaining the details of his duties and instructing him to report to the palace in the morning. Desmond rushed off to find Raina and give her his good news, and Damien turned back to her, wishing that the hours had not gone by so quickly. He was not ready to leave.

"Now I really do need to go," he said, pulling his watch from the fob pocket of his waistcoat and observing the hour. "I've stayed much later than I intended, although I wish I could remain longer."

Esmeralda walked him out into the yard, where Persephone waited patiently for Damien to unfetter her. He turned to face her, reins in hand.

"Thank you for being so kind to my brother," she said, stepping closer to plant a kiss on his cheek. It was becoming easier for her, he noticed, to allow him such closeness.

"It was nothing," he insisted. "And I really am in need of an additional stable groom. I've recently acquired some new beasts, and another pair of hands would be welcome."

"It wasn't nothing," she argued. "You've made Desmond very happy. It has been difficult for him since my father died. Being so young, he feels he must now be the head of the family, yet does not know enough ... cannot do enough yet to fill his shoes. What you've done ... it will work wonders for his pride. Thank you."

"And what must I do to make *you* happy?" he murmured, wrapping one arm around her waist.

"At this moment, a kiss will do," she murmured.

She welcomed his mouth, opening her lips to him and wrapping her arms loosely around his neck. He breathed in her scent and luxuriated of the feel of her lithe arms around him. Once again, he found himself pulling away reluctantly, knowing he must go but wishing he could stay.

"Think about tomorrow," he reminded her before mounting his horse. "I hope you will come."

CHAPTER 7

Damien flicked an imaginary piece of lint from the sleeve of his navy blue coat and stifled the urge to yawn. Davina clung to his arm, indiscreetly pressing her bosom against him as she rambled on about something he'd long lost interest in. In fact, he had long lost interest in *her*. How had he ever found her attractive?

It was as if meeting Esmeralda had opened his eyes. Davina was an appealing woman physically, yet he could not fathom how he'd ever tolerated her company. How had he ever conversed with her without becoming annoyed by her constant jabbering? How had he ever withstood her open flirtation and unabashed seduction of him in public? Where once, such behavior had been permissible, he now found himself embarrassed to be standing next to her. Davina was a woman whose body was for sale, and she flagrantly advertised this in the way she walked, dressed, and acted.

"Damien!"

Her voice splintered his train of thought, forceful and shrill.

"Have you heard a word I've said?"

He sighed. "I'm sorry … I have a lot on my mind this evening."

She stroked his bicep through his sleeve and smiled invitingly. "You should visit tonight. I could ease your heavy mind."

Damien suppressed a shudder. He had been dodging her sexual advances all week, and hadn't taken her to bed since the night of his birthday celebration. Even then, he'd done so mechanically and without much thought. She would not stand his evasiveness much longer. It was time to end things once and for all.

"Perhaps I will come," he hedged, hoping she wouldn't greet him in the nude as she often did. "I have something I want to speak with you about."

Her smile grew even wider and she squealed with delight. "I can hardly wait. Now, be a good boy, and bring me a glass of sherry, would you?"

Choosing to be grateful for an excuse to escape her cloying grasp, instead of annoyed at her command, he wrestled his arm from her clutches.

He had suffered through the seven course meal, Davina's company, and the prying eyes of the royal court, all while waiting for Lionus to inform him that it was time to attend to their other pressing business. Drinks and conversation would continue for at least an hour more in the crowded drawing room, and they ought to be able to slip away soon, unnoticed.

He had just procured a glass of sherry when Nicolai appeared at his side.

"Lionus awaits us in his study," he said in hushed tones. "The prisoners are being brought there as we speak."

Damien nodded. "I'll be right there."

He left the sherry with Davina, then put her out of his mind entirely. He found Serge on the way out of the drawing room, and together they navigated the winding corridors of the palace toward Lionus' wing. He and Nicolai were already waiting in the quiet interior of the darkened study.

His brother paced before the hearth, hands clenched behind his back. He was dressed entirely in black formal wear, his white linen cravat tied in an efficient knot, his hair pulled back into a queue. The firelight cast shadows over his face, but Damien could see the distinct pull of worry around his mouth and eyes.

"Is Father not coming?" he asked, searching the room for Adare.

"I thought to let him enjoy the evening," his brother replied, pausing mid-stride. "He has enough worries without having to deal with this."

Lionus was right, as he often was. Adare had appeared at the dinner party, flawlessly dressed and in his wheelchair. He had been bright-eyed and smiling and Damien would be loath to disturb him as well. The king would trust his sons and nephew to handle this matter and report back to him.

Lionus took a seat behind his massive oak desk, folding his hands in front of him. Serge stood behind him to his left, Damien to his right. Nicolai leaned against the corner of the desk.

The captain of the guard entered, leading six armed sentries forming a cluster around three shackled men. They were bedraggled, their clothes torn and tattered, their odors offensive. One man sported a hideous, festering wound slashing across one cheek.

"Leave us," Lionus said to the guards. "These men are shackled hand and foot and can hardly be expected to cause any trouble. Wait just outside those doors and allow no one to enter."

"Yes, Your Grace," said the captain, leading his men from the study.

Lionus turned his hard gaze on the three prisoners, assessing each one dispassionately before he spoke. "The three of you have been arrested for your part in the assassination attempts made against King Adare. You have been charged with high treason and sentenced to death by hanging. You've each been questioned, but we seek more than the answers you've given us. We wish you to give us any and all details concerning the man who hired you and his reasons behind these attempts."

One man—the largest of the three, sneered at them and then spat upon the rug. "I ain't got a thing to say to the likes o' you. Whether I confess or not, I'll hang all the same."

The impact of the man's words rippled through the room, heightening the already unbearable tension. Lionus' fists tightened, his jaw winding taut. These men had attempted to kill their father ... he would not wish to be merciful.

"You are right," Lionus replied, his voice like the sharp edge of an icicle. "You *will* hang all the same. But whether you tell me what I want to know may make the difference between a short rope that ensures your neck won't snap—resulting in a long, slow strangulation—or a more humane hanging in which you die a swift, painless death."

The man did not seem moved by the threat, simply glaring at them without speaking another word.

"He'll know we told," chimed in the man with the scarred man.

"What difference will it make once you have been executed?" Serge offered with a shrug. "He cannot touch you here."

"But our families!" the man argued.

Damien perked up at that. "He threatened your families?"

The large man scoffed, rolling his eyes. "You see? They know nothin'! A lot of good being born of a royal cunt does when you're as empty-headed as any common moron."

Lionus slammed his fist down upon the desk, his temper flaring to life. "You will remain silent unless you have something of use to contribute to the conversation."

"We can protect your families if you tell us everything you know about the mastermind," Lionus continued, his gaze flitting back to the man with the scarred face. "Otherwise, who is to say he will not simply harm them anyway once you have paid the price for participating in his scheme?"

Damien's gaze fell on the third man, who had observed this all in silence. He clutched rough, wooden rosary beads in his filthy hands, his chin trembling like a flimsy tree branch in the face of a strong wind. This man seemed the weakest of them all; perhaps getting him to crack first would be most effective.

"You do not want to die with this weighing on your conscience," Damien said to the man, purposely lowering and softening his voice. "Wouldn't you prefer to go to your grave with the last of your sins laid bare?"

A tear streaked down the man's grimy face. "There's no priest present … no man of God to absolve us!"

"Confess to us first, and you will have your priest," Damien replied.

"We need to know who this man is and why he wants the king dead. If you make it easier for us to find out, we can make your last days a bit less bleak."

As suspected, the religious man cracked, a rough sob wrenching from him as he lowered his head. "It was the masked man."

Damien exchanged bemused glances with his brothers and cousins.

"What masked man?" Nicolai asked.

"Everyone knows about the masked man," the scarred man said, folding in the face of the religious man's break. "At least all us common folk do. He hires people to do his dirty work, or intimidates us into doing it, is more like it."

The religious man stepped forward, his shackles rattling as he trembled and sniffed, more tears streaking through the dirt caking his face. "You must understand! He threatened my family, said he would hurt my son if I didn't do what he said. Promised me money if I agreed."

"He did the same to me!" said the scarred man. "Seemed to know everything about me and my family."

"So this man walks around the city, masked, and looks for peasants to do his bidding?" asked Nicolai incredulously.

"The masked man don't walk," said the religious man. "And he don't look for nobody. He just knows things. He finds you. And God help you if you refuse him."

A shiver ran down Damien's spine as he soaked all of this in. This villain sounded more like a specter than a man ... one with more power over Cardenas' citizens than they could ever have imagined. How could something like this have occurred right under their noses?

"Why not report this suspicious man to the proper authorities?" asked Lionus. "Why not come to us with this information?"

"Pardon me for saying so, Your Grace," said the scar-faced man. "But we ain't exactly livin' in no palace. Me and my wife got seven children and little money. The amount he offered to see the deed done would have been enough for us to live on for most of our remaining lives."

"So this man is wealthy?" Damien pressed. He'd have to be in order to command so much influence.

The religious man nodded. "He dresses finely and speaks like you do."

Damien and Serge exchanged glances. Could this masked vigilante be a member of the nobility, someone with a close association to the royal family? This tiny bit of information could change everything.

"Why don't you describe everything about this man that you can remember?" Serge said. "Appearance, clothing, anything at all."

"You're all a bunch of fools!" roared the large man. "You think these snotty little pricks give a damn about us or our families? They're gonna hang us all the same!"

"I don't care!" cried the religious man, pointing at Damien. "He's right! We have to do what's right before we die."

"I'll tell you," the scarred man said. "Though as far as looks go there ain't much to tell. He wears this jester's mask, you see … made of pure silver, with nothing but dark slits for the eyes and mouth. You can't see nothing of his hair; he keeps it covered. Even wears gloves so you can't see his hands."

"I remember it that way, too," said the religious man. "Never saw him without the mask … didn't recognize his voice."

Lionus heaved a sigh, resting his head in his hands. They weren't likely to get much more information from these men; it seemed they'd told everything they knew.

"Is there anything else?" Damien asked, hoping for even one more shred of information to add to what little they had.

The two cooperative men seemed to think for a moment before the religious man spoke up once more. "His cane! I almost forgot."

The scar-faced man nodded in agreement. "It was different than anything I'd ever seen. It had a silver handle, shaped like a bird and a two-headed snake."

"Odd," Nicolai remarked. "Perhaps a family crest."

"I'm not sure about that, but, the serpent is wrapped around the bird…maybe it's a hawk…I don't know, but the snake is attacking the bird."

"Must be custom made," remarked Lionus, rubbing his chin. "It certainly does not sound like the crest of any noble family in Cardenas."

"Before you go," Damien said as Lionus went to the door to signal the guards. "Did this man indicate whether or not this plot only involved the king?"

The religious man's eyes widened. "Yes, he did, Your Grace! He said something about how he sought to justify the wrongs done him and his family. He said he was going to make things right, starting with His Majesty."

Lionus whipped around, his face stricken with fear for a moment before his usual calm mask slipped back into place. His gaze met Damien's and an unspoken thought floated on the air between them.

They were all in grave danger.

The palace guards entered to take the men away and Lionus turned to the two prisoners who had cooperated with them.

"I appreciate your assistance. And though I cannot, and will not, repeal your sentences, I can make what precious little time you have left on this earth a bit easier. Tell my captain of the guard where your families are and I will allow them to come here to visit with you before you are hanged. They will then be relocated in order to keep them out of reach of the masked man until he has been ferreted out. You will also be permitted a final confession; a priest will be sent to you."

He turned to his captain of the guard and indicated the larger, defiant prisoner.

"See to it that this man receives forty lashes for his impertinence. I also want his ration of food for the remainder of his time here to be divided between these two gentlemen here."

The man's eyes bulged wide, jaw clenched, his fists clenched. "You arrogant bastard. You can't do that!"

Lionus stepped forward until he and the beefy prisoner stood nearly nose to nose, fist clenching spasmodically at his side as if he wished to strike the man but held back.

"I think you will find that I can. You have committed treason and failed to cooperate in this investigation. And so I will make what is left of your miserably pathetic life a living hell." He turned back to the guards. "Get these men out of my sight!"

Once the room was clear and the men were alone once more, Lionus sank back into the chair behind his desk. The other three took seats across from him and stared at each other for a moment in silence.

Serge was the first to speak.

"So … we are looking for a man no one can name or describe. A man of great wealth, wearing a mask and carrying a distinctive cane."

Nicolai sigh, his face grim. "The odds are definitely against us here. This man slinks around, undetected and unrecognized, coercing the citizens of Cardenas into doing his bidding."

"Have any of you given thought to the fact that this person is probably a member of the royal court?" Damien asked, staring into hearth. "He could be here at Rothchester Hall as we speak."

His belly roiled at the thought of his bastard standing in the same room with his mother and father … close enough to be able to reach out and touch them.

"Then there is only one thing to do," Lionus said, his mouth a harsh line. "I will have mother postpone the wedding, cancel the rest of the festivities, and send everyone away. Once she knows how dire the situation is, I'm sure she will act reasonably and do as I ask. We will continue to fortify the castle with guards and put all our energies into discovering who this masked man is."

"Perhaps that is not the best idea," Nicolai argued. "If he is, in fact, among our guests, it is best we keep it that way. It will be easier to see an attack coming, if he has one planned, by keeping the situation contained here."

"He's right," agreed Damien. "Besides, you were right when you said it would be best to show a united front to this man … show him we are not frightened by his petty attempts. Truly, Father was never hurt by any of them, and all three of the would-be assassins failed miserably. We will simply have to pay close attention to our guests, listen a little more carefully to the gossip. It might help if we could catch wind of whether anyone has a reason to hold a grudge against Father."

"We'll need to ask around about that cane," Serge added. "Perhaps even go about town and ask some questions. I am sure we could find others who have come in contact with this masked man if he is as notorious as our prisoners led us to believe."

"Your ideas have merit," Nicolai relented. "So, we will remain here and investigate while doing our best to keep word of this from getting out. Serge, you go to all the silversmiths in the city—I believe there are only three—and see if you can get information on a custom cane fitting the description we were given. Nicolai and I will circulate among the guests to find out whatever gossip we can. We will also observe the men to see if any of them carry the cane on them. Damien, you will go to the seedier side of town, since you are familiar with it, and find out what you can. Question whomever you must and determine if anyone else has encountered this man."

The four men went their separate ways once they'd left Lionus' study, Damien headed for the observatory. He needed some time alone to clear his thoughts before be confronted Davina.

He wished he could make sense of it, but the web of intrigue surrounding his family threatened to envelop them all. The words Akira had spoken sprang forth in his memory and caused him to shiver with dread. She had told him to beware a viper, that its strike would deal a deadly blow to the royal family. Damien felt certain this masked man was the viper she had spoken of, and that he must be someone close to them. All of this added up too well for him to discount the Gypsy woman's words.

The very thought made him wary, causing him to look over his shoulder to ensure that his guards were present as he walked down the darkened corridor.

WHEN ESMERALDA LEFT the kitchen after cleaning up the remnants of her family's dinner, she found her mother before the hearth, seated cross-legged on the rug. Raina had an array of glass beads laid out on the carpet, and had begun fashioning a necklace with them. Akira sat in a nearby armchair, sipping tea. Esmeralda joined her mother on the floor, watching the beautiful creation take shape as she chose which beads to add to the piece.

"It was nice of Prince Damien to offer Desmond that position at the palace," Raina remarked, a bit of a question in her voice as she paused to glance at Esmeralda. "Desmond's very excited about it."

Esmeralda smiled at the mention of her prince, a warmth sparking deep in her chest. "Yes, Damien is quite generous."

Raina chuckled. "Someone is besotted."

She did not bother to deny it. Anyone with eyes who'd witnessed them together today would have recognized the beginning stages of infatuation. "He's so wonderful. The things people say about him aren't true! At least ... I do not believe they are."

Pulling her knees up to her chest, she wrapped her arms around them, sending her petticoats billowing and allowing a bit of the warmth from the fire to caress her stockinged legs. Damien's face flashed through her mind, and her heart leapt at the memory of him, beautiful and saying all the things she'd dreamt of a man saying to her.

She knew she ought to be more wary of him, perhaps not extend trust so readily given his reputation. Couldn't his words simply be those of a man intent upon debauching her?

"You're not certain?" Raina asked.

Esmeralda stared into the dwindling fire, thinking on her mother's question before answering. "The things he's shared with me ... they are things that aren't common knowledge. Facets he's kept hidden because he's been overshadowed by the Crown Prince for so long. I feel as if he's allowing me to know the real him. Of course, I am aware that none of this erases his past deeds. It is ... confusing. I want to give him the benefit of the doubt.

"He's a good boy," Akira declared, setting her teacup aside. "I saw it in him when I looked into his eyes."

Esmeralda needed no further convincing. Her grandmother had ways of seeing into a person's soul, and apparently saw the same good in Damien that she did.

"Well, then," said Raina. "If he makes you happy, then I approve. You've needed a little happiness this past year."

Akira nodded in agreement. She and Raina had nursed Esmeralda back to health after the vicious attack that had ended in her father's death. They had witnessed the pain caused by the wicked men who had violated her, and the carefully erected defenses Esmeralda had built up around herself as a result.

"So, are you going to the picnic tomorrow?" asked Akira with a grin, her eyes glowing with glee.

Esmeralda's jaw dropped. "How did you know about that?"

Akira laughed, a deep, throaty cackle that resounded through the small sitting room. "I won't reveal my ways, but I will tell you you're a fool if you refuse him."

"What aren't you two telling me?" Raina inquired, setting her jewelry aside and looking first at Akira and then Esmeralda. "What's going on?"

"The royal court is gathered for the wedding of Prince Lionus and Princess Isabelle," Esmeralda replied. "There are entertainments planned, and Damien has invited me to a picnic tomorrow afternoon."

Raina's eyes sparkled and she clasped her hands together against her chest. "How wonderful! Of course you'll go!"

"I do not think it is a good idea," she protested with a shake of her head. "We don't move in such high circles. I wouldn't know how to behave around all those lords and ladies."

"You'll be yourself, and the lords and ladies be damned!" cried Akira, standing from her chair. "You mustn't let those people stand in the way of what is to be."

Esmeralda's pulse raced as the implications of that statement settled over her.

What is to be.

Could that mean she was right to trust Damien, to allow her feelings toward him to grow? It seemed the height of insanity to think that anything could ever come of a liaison between a Gypsy dancer and a prince, yet Akira's words sparked the flame of hope deep within her.

"Mother, would you please find Desmond and have him bring my large trunk down from the attic? He'll know which one. I need a moment with Esmeralda."

Akira glided up the stairs, surprisingly spry for one her age, her robes swishing around her ankles as she went.

Sighing, Raina took her hand and turned to face her. "I have something I want to tell you. I know that you are my daughter, but we are also friends, so for the moment I want you to think of me only as a woman, like you ... not your mother."

Esmeralda nodded, her mother's shuttered expression intriguing her. They had always been close, but much of Raina's past before marriage to her father was a mystery to her. There remained so much she did not know about her own mother.

"I loved your father dearly," Raina began. "When we met in Spain, we knew almost immediately that we loved each other. He gave me two beautiful children, and a wonderful, peaceful life ... I adored him then, and still love him, even after he's been taken away from me. But, before Matias, there was someone else."

That was not difficult to believe. Even now, well into her fifties, Raina was a beautiful woman. She still wore black in mourning for her father, even though an entire year had passed. Esmeralda had no doubt that should she decide to cast off mourning, every eligible man of a certain age in their village would begin tripping over themselves to gain her notice.

"His name was Ramon Bustillo," Raina continued. "*Conde* Ramon Bustillo. He came to the market one day where I sold my perfumes with Mother and our eyes met from opposite sides of the table ... I was stricken by him from the start. Handsome, charming, gracious. He came back every day that week to buy my soap." Raina smiled, her eyes focused on some faraway place and time. "After a while, I realized it wasn't my soap he was interested in."

"You had a romance with a Spanish lord?" Esmeralda asked, eyes wide with shock. She had never allowed herself to think of Raina with any man other than her father, but it made perfect sense for her to have known love in her youth.

"We fell into a secret romance quite easily, even knowing we were only setting ourselves up to hurt one another in the end. He was a member of the nobility, and of course, I was only a Gypsy dancer who sold soap and perfume."

"Oh Mother, you are much more than that! Surely he could see it?"

"Of course he did. That was simply the reality of our situation. He was part of a world in which I did not belong. Oh, he tried so hard to make it so. He lavished me with expensive clothes and gifts. He took me to the theaters, the balls, the dinner parties. We thought we would carry on that way forever…until his father died. He was obligated to take a wife once he became master of his father's holdings."

"So, what happened? Did he not offer for you?"

"He would have if he had been able, but you have to understand the way of their world. His mother already had a bride in mind, and Ramon really had no choice. We went our separate ways, and I never saw him again. I recovered from my heartbreak over time, and eventually I met your father."

"So, you told me this to warn me? You think I should end this thing with Damien before it truly begins?"

The story of her mother and the *conde* had struck dread in her. Heartache was not something she had considered, yet it was almost a certainty. Damien was a prince and someday he would take a wife. That wife could never be a woman of low birth like her, one who had no place in his world of the royal court.

"I told you that story because even though I loved your father more than I could ever have loved Ramon, I would not have changed what happened for the world. I truly believe that none of what I have gained in the end would have been possible without him. People come into our lives for various reasons, Esmeralda. Sometimes that reason is to teach us a valuable lesson, or to show us the way something ought to be. For you, who has been hurt at the hands of men, perhaps that lesson is that pain isn't all there is for you know. And who knows? Perhaps you and the prince will turn out happily … your own story does not have to end in heartache as mine did."

She studied Raina intently, seeing her as she never had before—as a woman, and not just a mother or a widow. Her words held the weight of wisdom born of experience, as well as truth. Never had any man stoked the sorts of emotions in her that Damien did … not to mention she'd never known this sort of desire. In truth, carnal matters struck fear and dread in her ever since the night of her father's death. She hadn't realized until now how weary she'd grown of carrying that weight, of suffocating under that paralyzing dread. Could Damien be the one to help free her from it?

Desmond and Akira appeared at that moment, toting the requested trunk between them. They carried it to the living room, letting it fall onto the rug with a thud.

"What's this?" she asked, as Raina rose to open it.

"You'll need something to wear, won't you?"

Esmeralda peered down into the trunk and gasped. Her mother pulled gown after gown free of its confines, draping them across various pieces of furniture. Beneath the frocks lay slippers in a variety of colors, bonnets, gloves, fans, chemises, reticules, stockings, and even a corset. The items were finer than anything she'd ever owned, seeming like the wardrobe of a fine lady.

Esmeralda lifted a day gown made of pink muslin, its scooping neckline adorned with delicate white lace. It had obviously been made to wear with a corset underneath, its bodice nipping in sharply at the waist before flaring into the full skirt.

"Where did you get these?" she asked, eying the other equally elegant gowns covering the sitting room in bursts of color.

Raina smiled, lifting a pair of short, white lace gloves from the trunk. "These will go nicely with that dress."

"Mother, where did all these things come from?"

"A gift from your father," Akira replied gleefully, lifting a small black box from the trunk. "Meant as a wedding trousseau."

Esmeralda's puzzled expression caused Akira to chuckle as she handed her the box.

"Your father always hoped you would marry someone a little above our means," Raina explained, matching a pair of slippers from the trunk to the pink dress. "He acquired these things for you over the last few years before he died. You have need of them a little early, I think."

Esmeralda studied the small collection of gowns with wide eyes and a slack jaw. Some had fallen a bit out of the height of fashion, but they were beautifully made and far grander than anything she'd ever thought she would own. She'd known her father had hoped she would marry well, but hadn't realized he'd believed that so much that he'd begun preparing for it.

"You'll find that they all fit," said Akira. "Raina gave him your measurements to have them tailored."

"And of course, I can alter wherever needed," her mother added.

Tears filled Esmeralda's eyes as she opened the small black box to reveal a string of iridescent pearls. They were small but luminous, glowing in the light of the fire. She wished he could be here to see her wear them, to accept her gratitude for the priceless gift of his love.

"Well?" said Akira, a smile accentuating the lines around the corners of her mouth. "Any more objections?"

CHAPTER 8

*D*amien pulled the curtain back from the window of his carriage, hoping the windows of Davina's townhouse would be darkened, signaling that she had been too tired to wait up for him.

No such luck.

He could see the faint light of a lamp through her bedroom window. He sighed; no need postponing the inevitable. He wanted to be completely free to explore the burgeoning feelings he had for Esmeralda, and could not do that until he'd cut his mistress loose. It was for the best that she'd waited up for him, even though he dreaded the fallout of the declaration he must make.

A footman allowed him entrance into the house, offering to take his hat. Damien declined, as he did not intend to stay for long. The majority of her servants had retired for the night, so he traipsed the halls undisturbed as he made his way to her bedchamber.

He tapped lightly upon the door before entering.

He found Davina sprawled across the bed on her stomach, wearing a red negligee and poring over a collection of fashion plates. She looked up at him and smiled as he walked in.

"I was starting to think you wouldn't come," she purred, rising from the bed. She approached him, hips swaying beneath the transparent wisp of material she wore. Then, she wrapped her arms around his neck and pressed against him. "You kept me waiting, but I'll let you make it up to me."

Damien struggled to grasp her bare arms and push her gently away. "Davina, I told you we needed to talk."

Seeming to realize he was quite serious, she pulled away with an annoyed huff. She returned to the bed and lay upon her side in a seductive pose, allowing the slit in her gown to fall open and reveal a plump, creamy thigh. He ignored the blatant invitation and pulled up a chair. Once she realized he would not be joining her in the bed, she heaved a sigh of disgust and snatched her dressing gown from the floor. She tied the sash with a jerk and sat on the edge of the bed facing him.

"What is it, Damien?" she snapped, her bottom lip pushed out in a petulant pout.

It annoyed him now far more than it ever did.

"You have been a part of my life for quite some time," he began, trying to find the most delicate words. "I have enjoyed your company, and though I am fond of you…"

Her sharp gasp interrupted him, and her eyes went wide, lips pulling into a wide smile. Clapping her hands, she bounced to her feet, looking very much like a child on Christmas morning.

"Oh, Damien, I knew you would not keep me waiting much longer!"

He shook his head, his heart dropping down into his belly as he realized she had misconstrued him entirely. "Davina…"

"Of course I will marry you!" she cried, throwing herself into his lap an aiming her mouth at his.

He wrestled with her, turning his head to avoid her kiss. Even that mundane an intimacy would feel like betrayal of Esmeralda, whose lips seemed to have imprinted something indelible onto his soul.

"Davina, I was not going to ask you to marry me," he said. "I was actually trying to tell you that I believe the time has come for us to end our arrangement."

ELISE MARION

"*What?*" she screeched, rearing away from him. "You're ending this?"

Damien stood, watching as her joy melted in the face of his declaration. Her lips twisted and her brow furrowed until her face painted the portrait of a woman scorned.

"I think you and I both know that our relationship has run its course," he said, hoping that remaining matter-of-fact would help him avoid any outbursts of rage. "Keeping a mistress is no longer something I am interested in, so you mustn't think of this as being your fault. Of course, you will retain the townhouse. I've already had my solicitor change the deed, so it officially belongs to you. Naturally, any possessions I've given you are yours to keep."

His solicitor had assured him that this was beyond generous, more than any courtesan could command. Damien had hoped it would be enough to placate her.

Davina began pacing, her hands clenched tight at her sides, her face a mottled shade of red.

"You've already arranged a settlement? How long have you been planning this?"

He grasped her hand, hoping to soothe her dismay. "That does not matter. The outcome is the same whether it was a week ago or a day ago. I am sorry if I've hurt you, but this has lasted longer than either of us thought it would, and I have appreciated your companionship, of course. It is simply time for me to move on."

The tears he had been expecting finally came, as did the hysterics. Davina let out a bloodcurdling scream before throwing herself at him. The impact of her body against his knocked the wind from him, momentarily making it impossible to fight her off. She kicked and flailed, just barely missing his face with a swipe of her nails, all while bellowing curses and calling him every foul name that came to mind.

"You bastard! Do you think you can simply set me aside as if I am some common strumpet? I was one of Cardenas' most coveted courtesans before I met you!"

Finally, Damien's patience snapped, and he took hold of her shoulders and gave her a little shake.

"Enough! You're acting like a child."

Kohl ran down her cheeks in inky gray lines, smudged from her tears. Her face was now tinged pink from her exertions. She swiped a hand across her eyes, smudging the kohl even more and glared at him menacingly.

"You think you can just use me and then toss me aside so callously?"

"Now wait just one minute," he retorted. "You and I never made each other any promises. You knew what being my mistress entailed from the beginning. I have lived up to my end for far longer than either of us anticipated. Did you honestly believe this would not end?"

Davina folded her arms over her chest and stared at him a moment longer. She tossed her hair and forced a quavering smile. The swiftness with which she went from enraged to cool and emotionless set him on edge a bit. He had a difficult time believing this would be the end of his troubles with Davina.

"You're right," she relented, her voice shaking with barely controlled anger. "I was being foolish."

He handed her a sealed envelope. "Your settlement ... I've set up an account for you to deposit it into, and there's already to money to cover your servants' wages for a year."

By then, she ought to have found another keeper to take over paying for her lavish lifestyle.

She tore it open and removed the bank draft he had tucked inside. Shock alighted in her eyes when she saw the amount written upon it.

"This is very generous of you."

"You have been my mistress for a long while. I think the amount is fitting considering the amount of time we spent together. You can live off of that for quite some time if you manage it well."

She tucked the bank draft back into the envelope and dropped it onto the bed. She avoided his gaze, her sullen expression doing very little to stoke his sympathy. She'd used this same face to wheedle countless gifts from him, had manipulated and cajoled him to get her way many times during their one-year relationship. He had run out of patience with her, and had come to see that he wanted more than a grasping, spoiled woman clinging to him in exchange for his wealth and favors. He wanted true passion and affection.

He wanted Esmeralda.

"Goodbye Davina," he murmured, taking her hand and giving it a little squeeze—the one concession to affection he was willing to give.

She simply went on standing there, staring off across the room without moving or speaking. He left her behind without looking back.

There was nothing worth clinging to behind him. The time had come to move forward.

ESMERALDA STUDIED her reflection in her mother's full-length mirror, hardly recognizing herself in the pink gown and the accoutrements that had been chosen to go with them. Raina had aired out and hung her new clothing in an armoire, spending hours working to free the day gown of wrinkles. The frock had required only a few simple alterations to fit her like a dream—its long sleeves puffing at her shoulders before tapering in, the bodice clinging lovingly to her torso, the skirts fluffing out with the benefit of several petticoats. Beneath it, she wore her first corset—which would take some getting used to—along with a fine linen chemise edged in delicate lace, white silk stockings, and a pair of pink slippers that proved an almost exact match to the gown.

She wore a simple pair of earrings that Raina had made using delicate pink stones. Akira had tamed her hair, parting it down the middle and braiding it, looping the plaits back over her ears, then arranging the rest into a neat chignon at the nape of her neck. A few strands had been curled artfully at her forehead and temples. A white bonnet with a few muslin pink roses pinned along the brim sat artfully atop her head, its pink ribbon tied at a saucy angle beneath her chin.

Last night, Desmond had carried her message to Rothchester Hall, informing Damien that she would accept his invitation to the picnic. He had penned a response informing her that a carriage would be sent to fetch her at noon, and made sure to tell her how pleased he was that she had decided to join him.

"You look beautiful," Raina said, her voice strained with tears as she handed Esmeralda a pair of white lace gloves and a shawl matching the gown. "If only your father could have seen you like this. He always spoke of a better life for you. He wanted you to have these things so that you would feel worthy of a world greater than ours. I think he was right."

Akira rubbed her hands together with undisguised excitement. "You look like a gem. Just remember to be yourself and those hoity-toity courtiers won't even notice you aren't one of them."

Esmeralda took a deep breath and pressed her hand against her stomach to still the nervous fluttering there. Despite her excitement, she was also nervous. How well could she fit into Damien's world? She wasn't as certain as her grandmother that she wouldn't seem out of place. Yet, wanting to please Damien, to be with him and allow herself to surrender to their burgeoning attraction was too tempting a prospect to resist. It superseded the fear making her want to run back upstairs and hide.

A knock sounded at the door, and Raina opened it to admit Tristan, whose eyes smoldered like hot coals when he took in Esmeralda's appearance.

"You look ravishing," he said. Unmistakable desire threaded through his voice as he eyed Esmeralda's breasts pressed upward at the neckline of her gown by the cinch of her corset. "What's the occasion?"

"I was invited to a picnic at Rothchester Hall."

She didn't miss the dark scowl that crossed his handsome features. "I was looking for Desmond. It's Monday and he usually visits to borrow Storm for a ride. He always comes in the morning, but I haven't seen him today."

"Oh, I suppose he forgot to tell you," said Raina. "Prince Damien offered him a job working as a groom in the palace stables. He started just this morning, and will not be around as much as he was before. He's quite excited about his new position."

If at all possible, Tristan's scowl became even darker. "Well then, I will see you this evening at the tavern, Esmeralda."

He turned abruptly and left, his footsteps drowned out by the sound of approaching carriage wheels. She did not miss the tension in his shoulders, or the curl of his hands into tight fists.

"He is so angry," Akira whispered, hugging herself as she shivered. "I fear it will bring him nothing but misery."

Damien watched Esmeralda as she conversed easily with Serge, laughing over glasses of white wine. He'd known she would adjust well, and seeing her here, dressed like a lady and mingling with the court only confirmed this.

The picnic had begun over an hour ago, and thus far she'd held her own amongst his peers, appearing as if she belonged. No one seemed to recognize her as the Gypsy dancer who had graced the ballroom on the night of his birthday. Whether that was because she had worn a veil over her face, or because her fine clothing tricked them into seeming a different person entirely, Damien would not question it. He was not ashamed to be seen with her, but did not want to invite scrutiny over her background that might cause her to be treated poorly.

He let his gaze linger over her figure encased in the lovely pink gown. He'd expected her to look as beautiful as ever, but the sight of her had taken him aback. In the carriage, she had related the story of her father and his gift to her with tears in her eyes. He had cupped her face and told her how lovely she looked, while swiping those tears away with his own fingers.

Damien looked out over the manicured lawn where at least fifty blankets had been spread, a full hamper beside each one. Members of the court sat eating, or stood about chatting, or strolled the grounds. Liveried footmen walked through the crowd with goblets of white wine and Madeira. In the center, a large awning had been erected over the place where his mother sat with her closest friends, Lionus, and his fiancée, Princess Isabelle.

He procured a glass of white wine and went back to the blanket where Esmeralda sat with Serge and Nicolai beneath the shade of a smaller awning. They nibbled on the fruit lightly dusted with sugar that had been provided for dessert. He sank down beside her and plucked a juicy grape from the bunch she held between slender fingers.

"Damien," said Serge with a grin. "I do not know where you found this woman, but she is far too good for you."

He grinned. "I agree, brother, but I'd intended to let her figure that out for herself."

She laughed, seeming as charmed by Serge as everyone always was. He would make it a point to thank his brother later for being so kind to her.

"Esmeralda," said Nicolai. "Might you do me the honor of taking a turn about the lawn? I have just stuffed myself and now feel the need to walk it off."

Esmeralda stood to join Nicolai. "I would love to."

Damien watched as she walked off on his cousin's proffered arm, captivated by the fluidity in her movements. Even while simply walking, she portrayed the grace of a dancer

"She's beautiful," Serge remarked.

"Yes, she is."

"How angry do you think Mother will be when she finds out that you brought a Gypsy dancer to a palace function?"

Damien sighed. "She told you?"

"No, I recognized her, unlike the rest of our guests. You know how shallow the court can be. They see a woman in fine gown on the arm of a prince and could never let themselves think she is the same woman who danced for them a fortnight ago. Don't worry, you know your secret is safe with me. Besides, I like her a hell of a lot more than the type of woman you usually keep company with."

"Just so you know, I couldn't give a damn what Mother would think. Esmeralda is a rare woman and I am lucky to have her in my company. Her heritage is in no way shameful to me."

"Hear, hear," Serge said, lifting his glass before taking a drink. "I see that Davina is missing today."

"I am relieved. Things did not go very well when I ended our agreement."

Serge laughed. "From what I hear, she never could take rejection well. Don't worry about her; her kind always land on their feet."

"She'll have a lot of help landing on her feet," he grumbled. "The amount I settled on her was obscene."

His gaze found Esmeralda as she strolled about the crowded lawn with his cousin. He observed her smile and felt a gentle tugging on his heartstrings. Simply gazing upon her caused an undeniable twinge deep within his chest. He did not know how to name the emotion, as he'd never felt it before. He only knew that being near her seemed like the most important thing in the world right now, and the thought of her being hurt by anyone—even himself—made him unaccountably angry. It was both heady and terrifying at once.

"I am happy for you," said Serge, as if reading his mind. His twin had always possessed the uncanny ability to guess at his thoughts. "It is obvious that you care for her. I only hope that you will not hurt her."

Damien shook his head. "Not her. She is different … special."

He stood as Nicolai and Esmeralda returned, taking her hand from his cousin's arm.

"If you will excuse us."

He led her away from the awning and the crowded lawn, guiding her toward the palace in the distance. Just now, everyone would be out of doors, which meant they would have the run of the place to themselves.

"Are you enjoying yourself?" he asked once they were out of earshot of any of the guests.

She turned her head to smile at him, the effect of it upon him swift and immediate. "Very much. Your brother and cousin were very kind to me, and it was a pleasure to meet them. Are we leaving now?"

Damien patted her hand, leading her around to the doors leading to the conservatory from the outside. "I want you to myself for a while, and I wanted to share some of my interests with you."

He ushered her inside and past the rows and rows of roses and other blooms grown for use in flower arrangements in the palace. Near the back of the structure, they neared the area he had cleared for his experiments with hybrids. It was an interest he had cultivated some years ago, working with various flowers and cross-breeding them for different effects. He showed her several beautiful plants, including the bright orange roses that had recently bloomed. They flaunted streaks of magenta in the middle, a striation he had been surprised to find when the buds had opened.

"They're beautiful!" she exclaimed, fingering one of the brightly colored buds. "I've never seen anything like it."

"It took a long time to achieve this result," he said, lifting a pair of shears from a nearby worktable and snipping one of the buds to give to her. "Now I am working on the same effect with lilies."

She accepted the rose, lifting it to her nose for a sniff of its fragrant perfume. Once again, her smile struck him like a fist to the middle, knocking the wind from him. And all it had cost him was a flower. He'd have given her a hundred blooms to see her smile like that again.

"Come, there is more."

He guided her through the door of the greenhouse leading into the palace, taking her on a tour of his ancestral home. He led her through the ballroom, then the gallery, which boasted portraits of several generations of the royal family, then the observatory, where his many telescopes were housed.

"I will bring you back here one evening so I can show you how they all really work," he said, taking her hand to lead her on the last stop. "After we've seen the library I promise to take you back to the picnic ... or home, if you'd prefer."

"Oh, I don't mind," she said, following his lead into his wing of the palace. "I have truly enjoyed seeing it all."

He led her through a series of corridors, all guarded, before ushering her into his library. The heavy green drapes had been thrown back to allow in the light of the afternoon sun through floor-to-ceiling windows. A large, well-used desk sat in the corner with several books stacked on top. Chairs and couches were strewn about the room, and along each wall, climbing up three levels high were shelves packed with tomes. She looked up to peer at the skylight, which allowed even more sunlight into the bright room.

"It's a bit dusty," he said, leading her to the center of the room where she turned in a circle slowly, taking it all in. "I don't require the servants to clean it often because it's quite a bit of work."

He showed her the ladders leading up to the various levels, each of which featured narrow railed walkways circling the entire room. Then, watched her walk around the room, reaching out to touch the leather-bound volumes.

"I've never seen anything like this," she said. "How do you know where everything is?"

Damien laughed. "It is a bit overwhelming, but I do have a system. The books are arranged by subject matter—poetry, novels, science, philosophy, and the like. Then, in each section they are grouped by author and in alphabetical order."

He grasped her hand and pulled her into his arms, no longer able to resist the urges that had been eating away at him since he'd first seen her this afternoon.

She came to him with an ease that put a smile on his face, her hands resting upon his biceps. Untying the ribbons of her bonnet, he lifted it from her head and laid it on a nearby sofa. He studied her face, tracing the contours with his gaze. Lifting first one of her hands, then the other, he slowly removed her short lace gloves. The fabric slid over her skin like a slow caress, and Esmeralda's breath quickened when he pressed his lips to her fingers.

He released her hands and wrapped his arms around her waist, pulling her flush against him. His lips came crashing over hers hungrily, savoring the taste of the white wine that still lingered there. He wanted her badly enough to take her down to the floor right there in the library, but he wrestled for control. He was still working on gaining her trust and would not ruin it. That she was an innocent niggled the back of his mind, staying his hand and slowing his actions.

He lifted her in his arms, walking her over to a nearby sofa. He sat her down, then sank beside her, taking her face between his hands and claiming her lips again. She acquiesced to his kiss, tilting her head back and opening her mouth to him. His palms slid down her shoulders and arms before he spanned her waist, his fingertips stroking over the stiff corset underneath. His hands shook when they encountered her breasts, lifted and angled perfectly by the undergarment.

Her back arched, pressing them into his grasp. She moaned, a small sound in the back of her throat, and Damien was nearly undone. He cupped the soft mounds, lifting them slightly, exposing more of her modest cleavage to his view. He kissed the top of each one, delighting in the small tremors that gripped her as he tasted her flesh. He could have remained just like this for hours, feasting on the simple offering of the tops of her breasts. In fact, he found himself believing he might die happy with his head rested on the plush orbs, his ear attuned to the beat of her heart.

She was half sitting, half lying on the sofa as Damien stretched out over her as much as the couch would allow. Passion had overtaken her, quickening her breaths and turning her into pliant clay in his hands. He grasped one of her legs and bent it at the knee, circling her slender ankle. He slowly skimmed his hand up her sinewy calf, over the bent knee and past the edge of her stocking and up to her soft thigh.

His fingers came in contact with something long and sharp. The tip of it pricked his finger, slightly dampening his growing desire. Pulling back abruptly, he whipped her skirt up further and frowned. A leather strap around her thigh held a dagger with a jeweled handle.

She sat up swiftly and shoved her skirts back over her legs. Shock colored her features, as if she'd forgotten the weapon attached to her leg.

"Oh God, I'm so sorry," she mumbled, clearly embarrassed.

Curiosity won out over his desire to take her back in his arms and finish what they'd started. "Darling, why is there a knife strapped to your thigh? Surely you don't think you need to protect yourself from me."

Or, did she? By coming on so strong, had he pushed too hard and too fast? He did not want her to think she needed to defend herself against him, not when a simple word from her lips would be more than enough to stop his advances.

She shook her head, reaching out to touch his arm. "No, it's not that at all! It's just that I always have it on me, and I forgot I was wearing it. You have that effect on me."

Damien's eyebrows shot up. Esmeralda became even more intriguing with each passing day.

"May I see it?"

She nodded, turning modestly away to retrieve the dagger. She held it out to him and he was surprised by the weight of it as it fell into his palm. The heavily jeweled handle made the dagger quite valuable.

"It was my father's," she said, watching him turn the dagger over in his hands. "He acquired it during his time at sea."

"Why do you carry it?" he asked, well aware of the amusement tinging his tone. He simply had the devil of a time imagining her girding herself as if for battle, before putting on this soft pink frock bedecked with lace.

She snatched the dagger from him, placing back in its rightful place against her leg.

"Because the world is full of dangers, that's why," she said, crossing her arms over her chest as if to protect something she kept hidden inside.

Her eyes became clouded with a mixture of fear and something… something else. All at once she appeared haunted and withdrawn, something he'd never seen in her before now.

"I carry this because it makes me feel safe. I won't be caught unprepared."

"Unprepared for what?" Damien asked, brow furrowing as he realized his amusement might have upset her. "I don't want you to think I'm laughing at you. I just want to understand."

She sighed, sinking against the back of the sofa and closing her eyes for a moment, taking a deep breath. "My father was murdered."

Her revelation stunned him. He never asked how Esmeralda's

father had died and was not prepared for the possibility that there had been foul play. He braced an arm on the sofa behind her.

"You do not have to speak of it unless you wish to," he assured her. "I understand how something like that can make you feel fear."

If only he could tell her just how well he understood. That his father had been targeted three times now was never far from his mind.

"No, I think I would like to tell you," she said, her voice low. "It is not something I speak of to anyone, and very few people know the entire truth of what happened that night. But, if you want to understand me ... if we are going to spend time in one another's company, there are things you must know. Things I must tell you."

He nodded, inching closer and bracing a gentle hand on the back of her neck. She sighed when he kneaded the tense muscles, hoping to ease a bit of her anxiety over what she needed to say. He could see it was eating her alive, her hands wringing in her lap, brow furrowed, her gaze darting.

"It's all right," he murmured. "You can tell me anything."

"We had just left The Golden Dancer," she said, staring down at her hands. "It was late. Earlier that night, my father and Dominic had sent some men away for trying to proposition my cousin, Morgana. They were very drunk, but he thought them harmless. It was not the first time men had gotten the wrong idea about the women who dance there. He and Dominic were able to convince the men to leave, and they did not come back. Father and I were walking home together when the men found us in the street. They were angry at him for throwing them out, and thought to seek a bit of revenge. We thought we could escape them by running, trying to get home as fast as we could. My father was unarmed and we were outnumbered ... there were four of them and he was afraid for me."

She broke off for a moment, choking back a sob. Tears glistened in her eyes and her hands shook as she clasped them even tighter, until her knuckles went white.

Damien continued rubbing her neck, wanting to be a comfort in

ELISE MARION

any way he could, but did not speak. He sensed her need to tell the story uninterrupted, to get it out in the open.

"They attacked my father, throwing him to the ground and beating him mercilessly. I tried to help, but I had no weapon to use against them. Two of them held me back as the other two took turns beating him. I fought them...I fought until they began beating me as well. The rest is a blur, but I was in and out of consciousness every few minutes..." she trailed off for a moment, swiping the tears from her cheeks. "When I woke up, Tristan was there. And my father was dead. They had assaulted him until he was hardly recognizable, his face a bloody mess."

Damien waited until he was certain she had finished before he pulled her into his arms. Anger unfurled from deep within him, white hot and furious. He imagined Esmeralda, her face battered and bruised, afraid and trying to save her father. His stomach twisted as he imagined her finding her father's body, seeing the mess that had been made of him. He could not fathom something so horrific.

A sudden thought sprang forth in his mind, causing even more fury to well up in his chest. He didn't want to pry, but the feeling that there was more to the story would not go away. All the signs pointed to his hunch—her skittishness around him, her reluctance regarding intimacy, the knife she carried no matter where she went.

"Esmeralda," he said rasped, wrath straining his voice. "Those men ... they did not just beat you, did they?"

She pulled back, meeting his gaze with her tear-filled one. She shook her head, and his jaw wound tight, his gut clenching with the force of the fury he felt as he realized what would come next.

She lowered her eyes, shoulders shaking with silent sobs. "I kept fading in out of consciousness ... but they were holding me down and one of them was over me ... then a second man took his place. My vision was hazy and I hurt all over from the beating they'd given me, but that pain ... it was unlike anything I've ever known. I begged and pleaded for mercy, but they wouldn't stop ... they laughed at me, delighted in humiliating me after having taken my father from me. I must have fainted, because one moment, it was happening, and the next I awakened and it was over. For a moment I wondered if it had not been a dream, but then ... there was blood ..."

She fell against him again, sobs wracking her slender body. The force of them ripped through him, and an undeniable urge to hunt down the men who had harmed her washed over him. He tightened his arms around her, his need to be here for Esmeralda outweighing all else. She wept upon his shoulder, and he vacillated toward heartbreak on her behalf, and elation that she had chosen him. She had given a part of herself to him that she did not trust with others. The truth of her past might have driven another man away, but it only made him want to cling tighter.

He held her until she calmed, her soft sobs quieting into deep breaths. After a while, he went into his coat pocket for a handkerchief, using it to dry her dampened face. Her eyes had gone slightly puffy, but soon no one would be able to tell she'd been weeping.

"Esmeralda?" he ventured.

"Yes?" she murmured.

"If I were to ever find those men who hurt you, I would ensure that they suffered for the rest of their lives. For you, I would make them pay."

"I've never told anyone the whole story, you know," she replied. "My mother never asked, though she seemed to simply know. But, she never made me talk about it."

"I'm sorry," he said. "I was only curious about the dagger. I had no idea..."

"It's alright," she interjected. "I realize now that I had to speak of it. I've been living in fear since that night. I do not want to be afraid anymore ... especially not of you. I have avoided intimacy since that night, but I do not want to shun it with you."

Damien stood, taking her hand and urging her to follow. "It is time I returned you home, but before we go, I want you to know something. I want you with every fiber of my being."

He leaned his forehead against hers and breathed deeply the fragrance he was coming to love. Stroking her cheek, he placed a tender kiss upon her forehead.

"I would not have you afraid of me, but if you would let me, I'd lay you down and show you so many reasons why you shouldn't fear me. I would banish all memories of pain from your heart, and give you only pleasure. I will wait for you … I will wait until you are ready, and then I will show you how it should be."

She shivered, his words responsible for the effect. Giving no verbal response, she stared up into his eyes without flinching, as if needing him to see that she wanted to be ready. She *would* be; he'd make certain of it. If he never did anything else for her, he would teach her what passion should be, how it should feel when she was in the arms of a man who cared for her.

He replaced her bonnet on her head and re-tied the ribbon beneath her chin. Then, he took her hand and led her from the library to the entrance of the palace, where he ordered his carriage brought around. They rode the distance to Esmeralda's house in silence.

CHAPTER 9

"I vow, Davina, he led her about on his arm, whispering to her as if they'd known one another for years!"

"And there she sat, smiling and flirting with his brother and cousin, right there in front of everyone! It was really quite scandalous."

Davina sipped her chocolate slowly, hardly able to enjoy it with the bitter taste creeping into her mouth. Her two closest friends, Giselle and Ariel, had come to her townhouse to tell her about Damien and the mysterious woman he had escorted to the picnic at the palace. Giselle sat at her left, Ariel to her right, on the sofa in her parlor. They patted her shoulders and cooed to her affectionately, trying to soothe her frazzled nerves. She pressed her fingers to her temple and groaned, a pounding headache starting to blossom.

"That bastard!" she spat, slamming her porcelain cup down into the saucer. "Less than a day after he threw me over, and already he's carrying on with someone new? Does he seek purposely to embarrass me?"

"Perhaps he's been keeping her behind your back for months now, dear," said Giselle. "Maybe he has only waited until now to bring her out in public."

"No," said Davina with a shake of her head. "Damien has had his little flings behind my back, and I have always looked the other way. I myself have not been entirely faithful," she added, lowering her eyes and thinking of the burly footman she had welcomed more than once into her bed.

She had called him in to soothe her the night Damien had left her angry and flustered. With a smile, she remembered that the young footman had done his job well. But now, she was furious all over again at the thought of some other woman moving in on Damien. Flings and affairs were one matter ... cheating her out of the position she had been due as his wife, was quite another.

"It must have been her who came between you," said Ariel. "Didn't you tell me just a few weeks ago that things were going well, and that Damien was visiting you nearly every night of the week?"

She nodded, her mind whirring with chaotic thought. Had Damien tossed her aside for this new woman? If so, who was she, and how long had he been with her behind Davina's back? She didn't mind when he tossed a barmaid or two, but a lady brought in the company of his family and friends was another matter altogether.

How could she have gone to bed one night so certain of her future, then awakened to find it all turned upside down?

"Yes, it must have been. He was on the verge of proposing to me, I just know he was."

Giselle shook her head. "Well, you cannot let something like this come between you. You certainly can't spend your days hiding away like you did yesterday. Why, the entire palace buzzed with gossip when you didn't attend the picnic."

"Yes," Ariel agreed. "You have to get back out there and show him that you are still the perfect lady for him. This woman no one seems to know anything about doesn't stand a chance against you."

Davina stood, squaring her shoulders resolutely. They were right, of course. Before her arrangement with Damien, she had been the most sought-after courtesan among men of influence. There had been bidding wars between men over who she would belong to, who could turn her head with their money and favors.

That woman was still inside her somewhere, and she would not go down without a fight.

"You are the very best friends," she said. "And I shall attend the theater tonight, as I know all of the court is to be in attendance. Now, do come and help me choose the right gown. I mustn't be outdone!"

As Davina led her friends up the stairs and to her chambers, bellowing for Anne as she went, she vowed that Damien would be hers again. She would make him regret leaving her and then force him to crawl back to her on his hands and knees!

Esmeralda looked down at the crowded theater from where she stood in the royal family's private box. The opera would begin in fifteen minutes, but she was glad they had arrived early, giving her the opportunity to revel in her surroundings. She gazed in awe at the high, painted ceilings and massive crystal chandeliers. The luxurious box was situated high above the masses where common folk mixed with nobility—at least, those who could not afford a private box. People milled about talking, laughing, and sipping champagne. She had a feeling that most had come not to watch the opera, but to see and be seen.

Damien stood nearby, conversing with his cousin, Nicolai, though he watched her with admiration in his eyes.

She was particularly proud of her appearance in the ruby silk evening gown her father had purchased for her. She felt luxurious in it, though its restrictive waistline along with the corset were things she had yet to grow accustomed to. Damien had surprised her upon his arrival at her home with an elegant black velvet cape with gold satin lining.

"The fall evenings are getting much cooler, and I wouldn't have you catch a chill," he'd said.

She'd been flattered by his thoughtfulness, and of course the cape had kept her quite warm between the carriage and the theater.

Prince Lionus moved away from where he had stood talking with the queen and his betrothed, Princess Isabelle. He smiled at her as he approached, but the coldness in his eyes hardened his expression so that the smile seemed like something else altogether. He was as different from Damien as any man could be, his hauteur adding an icy edge that lowered the temperature in his vicinity by several degrees.

"Good evening," he said.

She curtsied, the plumes in her hair sweeping low. "Good evening, Your Grace."

"I don't believe we have been properly introduced," he said.

"Miss Esmeralda Amador, Your Grace."

"Amador," he murmured, seeming to think on her name. "I do not believe I am familiar with the name. Does your family in Cardenas as well?"

"My mother, brother, and grandmother are. My father passed away just one year ago."

"My condolences."

The Crown Prince was not very subtle. Esmeralda knew he must be curious about who she was, and sought to gain information. He was trying to intimidate her, but she would not be daunted. She pulled herself up to her full height and looked him square in the eye.

"Where do you come from, Miss Amador?"

"From here in Cardenas, Your Grace."

"How is it that I have never heard of you, Miss Amador?"

"Are you acquainted with everyone in the kingdom, Your Grace?"

A muscle twitched in his face and the corners of his mouth turned down. He was annoyed, but so was she, and she refused to be sorry for her holding her own.

Damien suddenly appeared at her elbow.

"That is quite enough," he said, which told Esmeralda that he'd been listening the entire time.

"I am simply acquainting myself with your lovely companion," Lionus said, his frigid eyes piercing her like a dagger.

"Like hell you are," Damien growled, his voice low as he stepped between them.

Icy blue eyes clashed with fiery green ones and they stood that way for a moment before someone intervened.

"I do believe your mother wishes you to come meet someone," said Princess Isabelle to her betrothed. She pointed to where Queen Alexandra stood near the entrance to the box, speaking with an emissary from Barony.

"Of course," he said, inclining his head at Esmeralda. "Another time, then."

Damien was still seething when his brother walked away, but Isabelle simply grasped his arm and turned her smiling face up at him.

"Damien, be a dear and fetch us some more champagne. Miss Amador's glass has gone empty and so has mine."

He returned her smile, and seemed to calm. "Of course. I will be right back."

Once he had gone, the princess took Esmeralda's arm and led her farther away from Lionus and the queen. "I thought to help extricate you from that situation. I hope I was not too bold."

"No," she replied. "I wasn't certain what to do, and am grateful for your interference."

"Oh, you mustn't worry about Lionus and Damien. I do believe they have been at each other's throats since childhood."

"What a shame. Don't they like each other at all?"

Isabelle smiled again, a flash of perfectly white teeth. "They love each other. They just have different points of view and often cannot see eye-to-eye."

Esmeralda found that she liked the princess already. She had seen her from a distance, but now that she'd met her, she wondered why stories of the princess' kind nature were not as prevalent as those of her flawless beauty.

Isabelle was indeed beautiful. Silvery blond hair had been curled and pinned like a halo about her head, soft tendrils framing her face. Her eyes gleamed a light blue, combining with her pale hair and porcelain skin to lend her an angelic appearance. She was petite, several inches shorter than Esmeralda, but carried an air of confidence that conflicted with her small stature.

"It was very lovely meeting you, Miss Amador," she said as Damien came near with their champagne. "I do hope you will come to the wedding."

"Of course Esmeralda will come with me, if she wishes," said Damien, placing the champagne glass in her hand.

"I would be honored," Esmeralda replied, excitement bubbling inside of her. She had hardly expected to be invited to a royal wedding.

The lamps were dimmed and the orchestra struck up their first notes, a sign that the opera was about to begin. She followed Damien to their seats, allowing him to take her hand as the performance began. She found herself enthralled, pulled into the music and the drama as it unfolded. The man and woman on stage sang with clear, beautiful voices in Italian, which Esmeralda did not understand. Damien whispered the translation in her ear, causing her heart to flutter when his breath tickled her ear and the side of her neck.

By the time intermission came around, tears were streaming down Esmeralda's cheeks. Her parents had taught her appreciation for music of all sorts, and this struck her as some of the most beautiful she'd ever heard.

Damien pressed a white linen handkerchief into her hand. "It's beautiful, is it not?"

Esmeralda nodded, sniffling as she dabbed at her wet cheeks. "How can you be so unaffected by it?"

"I am not. It's only that I have seen this particular opera twice before."

"You must come to the theater quite often."

"Yes, and I will bring you as much as you wish."

She stood from her cushioned chair, stretching her legs. "I believe I'll visit the ladies' retiring room."

"Would you like me to escort you?"

"I remember where it is. I can manage."

She made her way from the box and down the darkened staircase. She found the retiring room and relieved herself, then checked her reflection in the mirror, wetting Damien's handkerchief at the washstand and pressing it to her eyes, which were a tad puffy from crying.

Satisfied, she turned to leave the room when she was cornered by three women.

They looked like any other ladies of the royal court, dressed in opulent satin and silk and draped in jewels. Her gaze was drawn to the one standing in the middle—a petite creature with bountiful curves, gaudy jewelry draping her exposed cleavage, and ostrich plumes stretching up from her rich auburn locks. Quite a beauty, but the glint in her eyes gave her a hard edge.

"Hello there," the redhead purred. "Esmeralda, is it?"

For some inexplicable reason, she felt as if she were being hunted, corned by three jungle cats who would rip her to shreds.

"Yes," she replied, tilting her chin. "And you are?"

"I am Lady Davina Russell, and these are my friends Ladies Giselle and Ariel."

"How do you do?"

"Everyone is talking," Davina continued. "Apparently, you are Damien's latest conquest."

Of course. She ought to have expected to be confronted like this at some point or another. Fortunately, her mother had taught her well, and she knew how to handle people who thought to look down upon her.

"Conquest?" she repeated, raising an eyebrow.

"Oh, never you mind that, dear," said Giselle with a laugh. "When Davina became Damien's mistress, people called her that, too."

Her blood ran cold, and her gaze traveled over Davina once again. The name did ring a bell, and she supposed it was because it had often been whispered in connection with Damien's. This beautiful vixen had once been his lover?

"Ex-mistress, dear," said Davina. "Only recently did we part ways. I suppose I have you to blame for that."

"Oh dear, how rude of him," Ariel simpered. "You see, Davina, he has given her no jewels at all."

Davina touched the gaudy diamond necklace calling attention to her breasts and giggled.

"Davina dear, didn't the prince buy you that stunning necklace?" asked Giselle, in her nasal, high-pitched voice.

Davina grinned, her gaze never leaving Esmeralda. "Darling, he gifted me with everything I'm wearing. Right down to the essentials."

She then leaned closer, her voice dripping with disdain. "You listen to me, you little nobody. Damien has been mine for a long time, and when he is finished with you he will return to me as he always does. You would do well to remember that you can never be anything other than a temporary diversion for a man like him."

That stung, but Esmeralda would not let it show. Whether her words were true or not, she would not stand here and be maligned by this woman and her friends. She lifted her chin and fixed Davina with her haughtiest expression.

"Well, *darling*, I must say that though I appreciate the warning, Damien has assured me he has interest in something *fresh* and not so *worn out*. And if that necklace and that gown are any indication of Damien's personal taste, I believe I shall have to do without his gifts."

With that, she shouldered her way past the three women, leaving a furious Davina fuming in her wake.

DAMIEN WATCHED Esmeralda intently in the dark carriage, wondering at her silence. The sliver of moonlight streaming through the curtains illuminated her face, which was stony and drawn. In the short time he had known her, he found he was more than content to sit in easy, companionable silence with her. However, this was different. Tension filled the space between them and he had no idea why.

He had been charmed by her unguarded response to the opera. She'd returned after intermission, quiet but still interested in the music. Afterward, she had taken his arm and allowed him to escort her to the carriage, though she had done so without a word.

Clearing his throat, he attempted to break through the silence.

"I hope you enjoyed yourself this evening," he said, a questioning tone in his voice.

She nodded, but continued staring out the carriage window and into the night.

"I'm sorry if my brother upset you," he ventured. "Lionus can be an insufferable jackass sometimes."

"Your brother, at least, hid his dislike of me behind a mask of politeness and curiosity. Though I cannot say the same for some of the other people I met tonight."

Ah, so that was it.

"Did someone say something out of turn to you? Tell me who it was and I'll set them straight."

"Your mistress," she said from between clenched teeth. Her eyes stayed fixed on his, focused, measuring his reaction to her revelation.

Damien bit back a string of curses. He had decided against telling her about Davina, but now realized that perhaps he ought to have. It seemed unimportant to him, especially since Esmeralda was one of the few people who didn't judge him based on his past. Davina was definitely behind him.

"You mean ex-mistress," he said carefully. "She is no longer a part of my life."

"How long ago did you dismiss her?"

"It doesn't matter."

"It does to me."

Damien sighed, pinching the bridge of his nose. "A few days ago."

She sucked in a sharp breath at his admission, sitting up straighter in her seat. "After you had found a replacement."

"No!" Damien objected, horrified that such a thought had entered her mind. "No, that wasn't the way of it."

Esmeralda folded her arms across her chest. "Then explain it to me, Damien. You are now without a mistress, and I am a convenient choice to fill the position. Shall you shower me with gowns and gaudy jewelry as well?"

She snatched the velvet cape from her shoulders and hurled it across the coach at him.

"Was this just the first of many of your *gifts*?"

Damien fought to untangle himself from the cloak before tossing it on the seat beside him. He reached across the carriage and grasped her by her upper arms, then pulled her forward until she practically sprawled in his lap. She gasped, but did not struggle when he cupped the back of her head with one hand.

"If I wanted you for my mistress, then it would have happened the night I met you," he declared.

"Oh, you arrogant..." she began, before he cut her off sharply with a kiss. When he had stolen her breath away and left her sagging limp in his arms, he pulled back and smiled. "See? I could have torn down your defenses and whispered pretty lies in your ear had I wanted a mistress. I would have made you mine that very night, in your mother's house, if that was what I wanted from you. It is not arrogance to speak the truth, Esmeralda."

"Then why didn't you?" she asked, the edge of anger starting to slip from her voice. "If it would have been so easy for you, why invite me to the palace, or visit me at home, or give my brother a job?"

Damien smiled, loosening his hold on her. "Because you are worth it. Because I want to know you ... truly know you. I haven't been with Davina since the night I first saw you ... because I didn't want her after that. Everything in me was drawn solely to you."

Esmeralda sighed. "I'm sorry. I suppose I did not think of it that way."

"I'm the one who should be sorry. I should have been honest with you about Davina. You were so determined to see the good in me, and I didn't want to spoil that. I suppose it was selfish of me."

Esmeralda shook her head, brushing her lips over his. "No. It wasn't. So few people see the real you. It's not wrong for you to want that."

Damien claimed her lips, grasping her waist and drawing her close. Relief swept through him as she accepted his kiss, answering his fervor with her own passion. Cupping her face, he stroked his thumbs along her cheeks, their mouths parting and meeting, their tongues touching with heated strokes.

Even as his body came alive in reaction, his blood going hot and the organ in his breeches growing stiff, he held himself in check. He reminded himself that she was worth the wait, worth peeling back her every layer until she lay bare and exposed for him. Keeping his hands in respectable places, he let his lips speak to her of the things to come.

Tristan strummed lazily on his guitar, signaling a barmaid to bring him another mug of ale. He had lost count of how many he'd had, but refused to lose his hold on the euphoria caused by the drink. Tatiana finished her dance on stage, and he ceased his playing, taking the mug from the barmaid who approached the stage. He drained it in a few large gulps and set it aside, waiting for Morgana to appear for her performance. She would be the final act of the evening, since Esmeralda had taken the night off to go to the opera with the prince.

He clenched his jaw, hand tightening around the neck of his guitar. She should be here with him, and among her own people where she belonged.

He had barely seen or spoken to her since that day in her kitchen, when he had pleaded with her to turn away from her liaison with the prince. Tristan knew that in the end, all she would be left with was heartbreak. But, perhaps that would be just the opening he needed.

Morgana signaled him from backstage, and he began to strum. He played mechanically, his mind wandering as he envisioned Esmeralda running to him with tears on her lovely face, her amber eyes wide with sorrow. He would envelop her in his arms and kiss away her tears. Soon, her sighs of sadness would become moans of pleasure when his kisses roamed over her body, as they had in his mind so many times. When her desire had reached fever pitch, he would join their bodies and obliterate all thoughts of the prince from Esmeralda's mind. Then she would be his once and for all.

Tristan smiled. Yes, that is how it would be. He must bide his time and wait for the opportune moment. Meanwhile, he felt as if he would die from the constant state of arousal and need that plagued him. He hadn't taken a lover in months, wanting to remain unattached when Esmeralda finally saw that they belonged together. However, it had begun wreaking havoc on his mind.

He focused his attention back to his playing, noticing Morgana for the first time since she'd taken the stage. Esmeralda's younger cousin was not without charm. Though not as skilled as Esmeralda, her movements held a seductive quality that caused the men to respond wildly to her. Perhaps it was her body, more voluptuous and rounded than the other dancers, with large, swaying breasts and wide hips that drove the men mad for her.

Lust, hot and raw, welled up inside him as he watched, his fingers moving over the guitar in a way they hadn't moved over a woman in some months. His earlier fantasy of a heartbroken Esmeralda had left him aroused, and now he knew that he would ease himself with Morgana.

The song ended, and she left the stage. Tristan followed as the taproom went quiet for the night. One of the dancers' father waited at the back entrance with a wagon to escort the girls home. After the night Esmeralda and her father had been attacked, she had insisted upon an armed escort to see them all safely home. No dancer or serving girl was allowed to walk home alone.

They waited for Morgana, who was changing behind a nearby curtain. The girls smiled invitingly as he approached. They all knew how Tristan felt about Esmeralda, but many still flirted shamelessly, hoping to steal his attention.

"Ladies, I will see Morgana home tonight," he said, putting on his most charming smile.

Morgana appeared from behind the screen, her dark brown eyes wide. She had vied for Tristan's attention for a long time, and while he'd been aware of this, his concern had been Esmeralda. She returned his smile, placing a hand on her hip and tossing her long, wavy hair, so similar to Esmeralda's.

"Go on without me," Morgana said to the other dancers, her gaze never leaving Tristan's.

The girls all filed out through the back door, talking amongst themselves in hushed tones. The gossip would spread, and by tomorrow afternoon everyone would know that they'd left together, but Tristan didn't care. If the silly girl had no care for her reputation, then why should he? Morgana grasped her shawl and wrapped it about her shoulders before allowing him to lead her out into the night.

He silently wrapped an arm around her waist, holding her against him as they walked at a brisk pace, warding off the chilly fall night air. He paused a few times to taste her mouth, leading her in the opposite direction from her home, to his.

Once they reached his front door, he grasped her and pressed her up against it, taking her lips again in a rough kiss. She threaded her fingers through his hair and returned his kiss, pulling eagerly at his clothing.

By the time he reached behind her to open the door, his shirt was unbuttoned, as was her dress. He grasped her hand and led her swiftly through the house where he lived alone. Tristan had never known his father, and his mother was long dead. His only other relative, his sister, preferred the life of a wanderer. He lived alone, so he and Morgana would not be disturbed.

He led her to his bedroom, taking the time to stoke a fire to life in the hearth before ripping his shirt away entirely. Tristan turned to face her in the firelight, pleased by the awe in her eyes as she took in his naked chest and lean abdomen.

"Take your clothes off," he demanded, watching with undisguised hunger as she slipped out of her gown, then kicked off her shoes.

She removed her only undergarment, a simple linen shift, and stood before him in her stockings, breasts thrust forward and back arched in invitation. Tristan crossed the room and pulled her hard against his body. He massaged her ample breasts with his hands, teasing her dusky brown nipples with his fingertips. She moaned and arched her back, thrusting them toward his mouth. Tristan suckled at them like a starving man, kneading and squeezing her round buttocks and pressing her tightly against his erection.

She fumbled at the waistband of his trousers for a moment before unbuttoning them. He pushed her back slightly and finished taking them off himself. She lowered herself to her knees, and he watched as she took the full length of him in her hands. His head fell back and his eyes slid closed when she took him into her mouth, teasing him with her tongue. He groaned hoarsely and grasped the back of her head, seizing a fistful of her thick hair.

He watched her through lowered eyelids, imagining that the shiny black waves he held in his hand belonged to someone else. The body on its knees before him was longer and slimmer, firm and supple. The eyes that looked up at him burned yellow-gold in the light of the fire.

He thrust wildly into her hot, wet mouth, his legs trembling with the force of his lust. Before long, he could take no more and pulled her away. He fought to catch his breath for a moment, then plucked her up from the floor and tossed her on the bed. He spread her legs wide and came between them, pressing to her moist entrance.

"Now, Tristan!" she panted, wrapping her legs around his hips. "Now!"

He obliged her gladly, pushing forward in one sure, firm stroke, tearing into her impossibly tight opening. He was only mildly shocked to find she was a virgin when she certainly had not sucked his prick like one. However, it was not enough to deter him. She winced in pain, but didn't unwind her legs from his waist as he moved inside her swift urgency. He closed his eyes and buried his face in her shoulder, moving faster when her cries of pain turned into sighs of bliss.

He lifted her hips and pounded into her, his rhythm now frenzied, her cries wild and unrestrained. Tristan surged his hips one last time and spilled his seed into her, breathing a sigh of relief.

Then, he rolled to his back, pulling the bedclothes up over them both. She snuggled closer, resting her head upon his chest. He reached out and stroked her hair absently. She fell asleep in an instant, and so did not hear her cousin's name fall from his lips as he, too, slipped into slumber.

CHAPTER 10

The next fortnight passed Damien by in a whirl of endless activity. Esmeralda attended teas, picnics, dinner parties, luncheons, and the theater with him and the court as the day of Lionus' and Isabelle's wedding drew closer. He would have found himself bored with the endless round of mundane entertainments, but having Esmeralda at his side changed everything. She glittered like the brightest of gems amongst the members of the nobility, and had charmed them all, save the queen, Lionus, and Davina. But that was to be expected. Even their impolite behavior toward her could not dampen his spirits.

He had spent quite a bit of time at her home as well, content to watch her work about the kitchen or help her toil in her vegetable patch. His hands had become a bit work-worn as a result and he was oddly proud of the fact.

Being with her wasn't about achieving some nefarious aim. With the women before her, he'd been focused upon the physical payoff of giving his time and attention. But, with her, he was content to simply be near her—drinking in the sight of her, hearing her voice, seeing her smile. If she never allowed him to lay a hand upon her, he'd have still been happy to simply be with her.

The morning of the tournament—the event he had been looking forward to the most—he rose early, as had become his habit recently, and dressed. Then, he joined his brothers in the dining room for a light breakfast. He, Lionus, Serge, and Nicolai would all compete in the tournament that afternoon, along with other men of the court wishing to display their skill at jousting, archery, and swordplay. Princess Isabelle had joined them, then would leave in Damien's carriage to fetch Esmeralda to the tournament. She was beautifully dressed as always, seated beside Lionus and across from him.

"The entire court has been at odds these few weeks, speculating over who she might be," Lionus was saying as Damien took his seat. He lifted his gaze from his plate and fixed it on Damien.

"Who?" he hedged, despite already knowing.

"You know very well who I'm referring to," Lionus retorted, stabbing at a sausage link with his fork. He raised a dark eyebrow at Damien. "Are you going to tell us?"

"You know who she is," Damien muttered, turning his attention back to his cream-laced coffee. "Her name is Miss Esmeralda Amador, and she has become very special to me."

Serge met his stare from across the table, but was otherwise silent. He had held true to his word and kept Esmeralda's background a secret. Damien didn't give a damn if anyone ever found out, but in order to protect her from malicious gossip, he kept his mouth shut as well.

"Well, I think she is perfectly lovely," said Isabelle, sipping her tea. "If you would just talk with her, Lionus, you might come to agree with me."

"I have spoken to her and she is purposely coy when it comes to personal questions," Lionus muttered, pushing his plate aside.

"There is nothing coy about her," Damien retorted. "Perhaps she would be more open to speaking with you if you didn't question her so endlessly, or stare down your nose at her."

Lionus pushed his chair back from the table and stood, his mouth grim, eyes narrowed. "And you know this for a fact, do you? I ask you, brother, what you know about her other than the feel of her open thighs?"

"Lionus!" exclaimed Isabelle, reaching out to place a hand upon his arm. "Do not be crude."

Damien shot to his feet, his chair scraping the floor before toppling over backward. He placed both fists on the table and leaned forward menacingly, the muscles in his biceps and forearms drawn tight. His brother had gone too far. Lionus could say whatever he wanted about him, as most of the insults tended to have the ring of truth to them. Damien had been a rake; he'd been irresponsible, a drunken gambler, and a user of women with no care to anyone's feelings but his own. He'd earned scorn with his past actions and was aware that changing overnight would be impossible.

However, he would not allow any affront to Esmeralda to pass without striking it down.

"Do not insult the lady in my presence," he hissed, his voice quavering with the force of his anger. "If you are ever so foolish again, I will call you out. Do not make the mistake of thinking I'm bluffing, and don't forget who the better man with a sword is."

He stepped over his toppled chair and whirled from the room, leaving his shocked brothers and Princess Isabelle staring after him. He paused outside the door and leaned against it, unable to believe the threat he had just issued against Lionus, surprised to realize that he had meant every word. Esmeralda did not deserve the scorn of his brother, or anyone else. And Damien would make an example of anyone who thought to treat her poorly ... even Lionus.

He heard Isabelle's voice easily through the double doors.

"That was uncalled for."

"Agreed," Serge said. "You don't know the girl, Lionus."

"Do any of us, really?" Lionus asked, his voice calm, yet edged with frustration. "What do any of us really know about her? Has anyone stopped to think that she may be a part of this plot against the royal family? Wouldn't it be clever of the masked man to use Damien's weakness for a pretty face against him?"

A long silence followed, in which no one responded.

"Of course not. None of you are thinking of that, and instead have decided to make me the villain in this little drama. So be it, if that is what it takes to keep this family safe."

Damien curled his hands at his sides and, resisting the urge to go back into the room and smash Lionus' face in, stalked out of the house and off toward the stables.

Esmeralda was grateful for Princess Isabelle's presence beside her, beneath the colorful awning fluttering in the balmy fall breeze. The other woman's warm smiles and idle chatter helped to distract her from the cool stare of Queen Alexandra. Damien's mother had been eavesdropping on their conversation and watching Esmeralda quite rudely—as had become her custom since she'd begun attending these events with the youngest prince. Like Prince Lionus, the queen seemed to despise her, obviously able to see that she did not belong among them. Fortunately, Isabelle, Serge, and Nicolai did a wonderful job taking the sting out of their rejection by making her feel welcome.

Upon arriving to convey her to the tournament, Isabelle had said nothing of her modest home in a quaint little corner of the city. She'd simply greeted Esmeralda and linked arms with her, leading her to the carriage, chattering away as if they'd been friends all their lives.

The princess was clearly excited about the big event. This tournament was a yearly tradition, one the men of the court looked forward to with great anticipation. There would be several contests, Isabelle had explained, including archery, swordsmanship, and jousting. The princes always competed, she'd told Esmeralda, and were almost always the most formidable opponents.

"I vow, Nicolai is the best swordsman I've seen," Isabelle said, her voice lowered. "Damien is a very close second. One of them almost always wins in swordsmanship. Lionus is best with a lance."

"Isn't jousting dangerous?" asked Esmeralda.

She had heard many stories of the ancient sport, though she had never seen it in action. It all sounded bloody and violent to her, though she supposed it could not be so bad if the king would allow his sons to participate.

"The lances are blunted, of course," Isabelle explained. "There are a few injuries every year, though those are caused when one is thrown from his horse, not from the lance itself."

Esmeralda breathed a sigh of relief, no longer worried that she would have to watch Damien become impaled on someone's lance.

"Here they come!" Isabelle squealed, pointing out the parade of tournament participants.

They rode on horseback, each dressed in armor that gleamed brightly beneath the noonday sun. Each man carried a shield boasting the crest of his family. A page followed each horse on foot, carrying his master's lance, bow and quiver, and sword. Lionus led the procession, his hawkish eyes surveying his surroundings, his firm mouth quirked into the beginnings of a rare smile. Damien and Serge rode side by side behind their brother. Esmeralda's heart quickened at the sight of Damien in his armor, regal and proud as he rode on Persephone's back at an easy gait. Desmond walked behind him as his page, and Esmeralda waved excitedly at him as they passed. Desmond, whose arms were full, could only return her smile and nod.

The contestants were presented in order of station, beginning with the Crown Prince. Before the tournament began, each competitor sought out the lady of his choosing for a favor to wear upon his person. Damien brought his horse alongside the canopy where Esmeralda sat with Isabelle and the queen. He smiled at her and dipped his head in a gallant bow.

"My lady," he said, his gaze traveling over her pale green gown and sparkling in approval. "I beg of you, a favor to wear for good luck."

Lionus rode up beside him, holding his hand out for Isabelle's offered hair ribbon. He nodded his thanks and allowed her to help tie it around his left biceps. He placed a chaste kiss on Isabelle's hand and rode away.

Damien sat waiting for her favor, but Esmeralda hadn't thought to wear anything small enough to give him.

ELISE MARION

"Esmeralda, your shawl!" hissed Isabelle, indicating the white and green paisley material draped across her shoulders.

She removed the shawl and stood to loop it around Damien's neck.

"One more thing, my lady," he said, a mischievous gleam in his eyes as he leaned closer. "I require a kiss for luck as well."

Esmeralda hesitated for a moment, wondering if it would be proper. Isabelle looked on with irrepressible anticipation, obviously charmed by Damien's romantic request. The queen frowned, her narrowed gaze fixed on them in blatant disapproval.

All her inhibitions fell away when she looked into Damien's eyes and registered the expectation there. How could she refuse him when she craved the kiss probably as much as he did? Oh, and he did look so gallant in his armor, hair tousled by the soft breeze.

Ignoring the malicious glare of the queen, she raised herself up on tiptoe and pressed her mouth to Damien's. She had meant to kiss him quickly and appease him, while avoiding angering his mother further. But Damien's strong arm swept her off her feet as he lifted her for greater access to her mouth. He kissed her for several seconds, almost causing her to forget where they were. Eventually, he loosened his hold and lowered her back to the ground.

"With such inspiration, no man will be able to beat me," he murmured before moving his horse away to join the others.

"A shameful display," the queen muttered as she rose from her seat. "If you'll excuse me, I believe I see Lady Worthington and would like to have a word with her."

Her final words seemed meant for Isabelle alone, though neither woman replied. She floated away with a swish of her elegant skirts, leaving the two of them alone under the awning.

Isabelle sighed and turned to her with a small smile. "Do not let Her Highness intimidate you. She can be an overbearing woman, but you will learn to abide her."

"I didn't mean to embarrass anyone."

Isabelle laughed. "The only person who should be embarrassed is me. I am the one who is betrothed, and my intended does no more than kiss my hand as he would some distant relative."

For the first time since they'd met, Esmeralda saw despondency in the princess' eyes. The sight was enough to break her heart for the poor girl. She put on a smile and a brave face in public, but Esmeralda could only imagine how difficult this must all be. Her husband had been chosen for her at birth because of the dangers that awaited her in her own homeland. She had lived in exile all these years, her life decided upon by everyone but herself.

"I love him," Isabelle said, sincerity in her every word. "I have loved him all of my life. And I know that he feels something for me, even if it is not love. But I have to admit to envying you just a little. Damien's feelings are so open, and he is generous in his affections. I wish Lionus felt such passion and intensity for me."

Esmeralda was stunned to hear this. Perhaps Isabelle hadn't noticed the way Lionus had looked at her when he'd approached their canopy, or the way his normally cold eyes had warmed considerably as he'd kissed her hand. She had noticed the differences after having spent enough time in the presence of the royal family. The Crown Prince clearly felt affection for his fiancée … perhaps he simply did not know how to show it.

"I think he does, in his own way," Esmeralda said. "He is not like Damien. Open affection simply is not his way. That doesn't mean he does not care."

Isabelle nodded. "I think you're right, but that does not free me from my wishful thinking."

DAMIEN TOUCHED the shawl around his neck as he watched Esmeralda where she sat with Isabelle and his mother. She watched the final event of the tournament, the joust, and did not notice his gaze. Her scent clung to the fabric, making him long to be close to her again, hold her and kiss her. At the moment, he could not, so he forced himself to focus upon the joust.

Serge and Lord Wilmington sped toward each other, their blunted lances in hand, their horses' hooves pounding rhythmically as they drew closer. Wilmington was sent flying, head over heels, landing some feet away from Serge, who had been struck by his opponent's lance but had managed to keep his seat.

A cheer went up from the crowd, celebrating Serge's victory. He would now face Damien, who had defeated all of his opponents as well. Whomever emerged victorious between them would face last year's champion, Lionus, who was preparing for his bout in a nearby tent.

Damien nodded at Desmond, who approached with Hercules, his dappled gray gelding. He patted Hercules' neck before allowing Desmond to help him into the saddle. His heavy armor made it difficult for him to manage it alone. He pulled his helmet on and accepted the lance. He glanced to the awning again and found Esmeralda's gaze. He grinned at her and winked, which earned him a little smile and a tentative wave. His smile almost vanished when he spied his mother, who seemed to watch their every interaction with disgust. He hated that her presence might hamper Esmeralda's enjoyment of the tournament. He was, however, grateful for Isabelle, who put forth a valiant effort to counteract the queen's coldness. She'd been there for them both this past fortnight, sticking close to Esmeralda' side whenever obligation did not have her on Lionus' arm. The two seemed to have struck up a friendship, which he supposed might be good for both women involved. Esmeralda so that she might have a female ally among the court, and Isabelle because her position as a princess in exile did not leave room for very many friends.

Wheeling his horse toward the jousting grounds, he took his place to face off against Serge. His brother was good, and their equal height meant neither had the better reach. However, Hercules was a superior courser—light on his feet yet still powerful. He would be Damien's advantage.

Lowering his face shield, he waited for the flag to drop. Sure enough, three passes saw him besting Serge, meaning he would be the one to face their elder brother.

"It matters not which of us beats Lionus," Serge said with a laugh as he wheeled his horse past Damien, helmet removed, sweat-dampened hair clinging to his forehead. "We cannot allow him the victory two years in a row."

Damien nodded to his brother and returned to his place just as Lionus assumed his. He hated to admit that unseating Lionus would be all the more satisfying after the things that had been said over breakfast. Nothing would make him happier than to literally throw his brother down into the dirt as recompense for maligning Esmeralda.

Thunderous applause met the Crown Prince as he waved to the crowd. Isabelle's ribbon now fluttered on the handle of his lance as he raised it to this betrothed in silent salute. Both men lowered their face shields and waited for the flag to drop.

He narrowed his eyes in concentration. Lionus had the longer reach and thus the advantage, but Damien could still win. The flag fell, and Damien dug his heels into Hercules' sides. The horse raced him toward Lionus, concentrating on the figure in gleaming silver armor charging at him with lowered lance.

Suddenly, the front legs of his brother's horse buckled and the horse began to fall, face forward into the dirt. Horrified, Damien yanked up on Hercules' reins, pulling the beast up short. He lifted his face shield just in time to see Lionus pitch forward from the saddle as the horse toppled. He soared through the air for a few feet before landing in a heap of battered metal.

Isabelle's shrill scream rang out amid a chorus of gasps. Alexandra fainted in the arms of a nearby servant. The royal court came to their feet as one, hands over their mouths as they waited to see if the prince would move. Damien leapt from his horse, racing toward the crumpled heap that was Lionus. Nicolai and Serge appeared from where they had been watching and joined Damien at his side.

Nicolai rolled him onto his back before gingerly removing his helmet. Though it had probably been the only thing protecting him from death, there was still a large gash marring his forehead. Blood trickled down the side of his face and back into his hair, which had mostly come loose from its binding. Lionus did not stir, but Damien detected a strong, rapid pulse at his throat.

"He's alive," Damien announced, as Isabelle and Esmeralda appeared beside them. "He is only unconscious."

Tears streaked Isabelle's cheeks as she knelt beside Lionus, using her pink shawl to staunch the blood trickling from his head. The queen had been left in the care of several ladies of the court, who had awakened her with a vial of smelling salts and now sat in a cluster around her, holding her hand and fanning her flushed cheeks.

Serge commanded a page to send a footman for the physician. Then, he helped Damien and Nicolai lift him and carry him to his chambers. Esmeralda and Isabelle followed, clutching each other's hands tightly.

CHAPTER 11

They carried Lionus to his chambers, where maids already scurried about with hot water, towels, and bandages. A physician had been sent for, and they need only await his arrival. Isabelle sent them all away, electing to tend to his wounds herself, with Esmeralda's help. While the blood was washed from Lionus' face and hair, Damien went to his chambers to have his armor removed. By the time he returned, Nicolai and Serge had removed Lionus' armor and tucked him into bed. The doctor arrived shortly after to clean and stitch his head wound. He judged the injury to be minor, and told them that while the prince had been battered and bruised by the fall, he'd suffer no lasting effects.

Damien's shoulders deflated with relief at the news. While he had wanted to unseat his brother, he certainly hadn't wanted him to be grievously hurt.

"You may want to have a bottle of spirits or laudanum nearby for when he wakes up," the physician suggested. "He is going to need it."

Isabelle ordered both brought to his chambers, electing to remain by his side and send word when he had awakened. Damien, Nicolai, Serge, and Esmeralda left her there with a handful of armed guards.

"Well, I suppose it's safe to say the rest of the day is shot," Nicolai said.

Since the last event had come to an abrupt halt, Queen Alexandra had herded the entire court inside for the planned luncheon. They spied the small crush inside the yellow drawing room, milling about and chatting as they waited for lunch to be served. With the panic abated over Lionus' accident, everything had returned to business as usual. Even his mother would not shun her duties as a hostess following the injury of her son. Only his death or maiming would have taken her away.

"Does anyone else think that accident seemed a bit strange?" asked Serge, stopping a few feet from the drawing room doors, his voice lowered. "Lionus was practically born in the saddle of a horse. He knew how to handle his mount. Besides which, we had the animals inspected for lameness or injuries just yesterday."

Damien frowned. "You think this wasn't an accident?"

"It seemed odd, the way his horse went down," Serge said. "Something isn't right."

Nicolai wrinkled his brow. "Are you sure you aren't just making something out of nothing? Accidents happen all the time—in jousting especially. We ought to be grateful he wasn't hurt worse, or killed."

Damien wanted to agree with Nicolai. Each year, the tournament saw its fair share of minor injuries. However, Serge was not prone to dramatics, and given the recent attempts on the king's life, the notion was worth exploring.

"The least we can do is have the horse inspected, and even the area around the tent where prepared for any suspicious signs."

"I'll have it done right now," Serge declared, heading off toward the door. "Tell Mother I will miss lunch."

"It's not as if she will notice with Lionus laid low," Damien replied, taking hold of Esmeralda's hand. "I will not attend either."

They left Nicolai alone, and he made his way into the crowded drawing room to join the others.

"Are you all right?" she asked, following him in the direction of the kitchen. "That must have been terrible for you, watching your brother fall that way."

"I am fine," he assured her. "Glad that Lionus is all right, of course. I just need some time away from the crush. Besides, I have something planned for you."

He led her to the palace kitchen, where he acquired a large basket from the smiling cook.

"All the things you asked for, Your Grace," she said with a smile and knowing look in Esmeralda's direction. "I hope you and the lady enjoy it."

"If you made it, I know we will, Doris," he said before dragging Esmeralda off toward the stables.

"Where are we going?" she asked, trotting to keep up with his long strides.

"Somewhere special," he said, accepting Persephone's reigns from Desmond, who had come to groom Hercules and put him back in his stall. "Take the rest of the day off," Damien told him, handing him a small sack of coins. "This is your share in my winnings for the day. You made an excellent page."

"Thank you, Damien," Desmond said with a smile, thrusting the small sack into his pocket. "Should I have a mare saddled for Esmeralda before I go?"

"That would be good. I think Cinnamon will do."

Once the chestnut mare had been saddled and Desmond had set off for home, Damien secured the basket to his saddle. Then, he mounted Persephone and led Esmeralda across the open green lawn at a slow canter. She had never before ridden in a sidesaddle, and so she sat astride, revealing much of her long legs and the stockings encasing them. Damien found himself staring and grasped for a distraction.

"How about a race?" he suggested, desperate to calm his racing blood.

Being a gentleman was not difficult when it came to her, but his body often reacted to her in ways he could never hope to control.

The more time he spent in Esmeralda's company, the more he wanted her. A fortnight had turned him into a starving man, craving sustenance in the small kisses and caresses she allowed him.

"A race?" she repeated with a laugh, her face tilted upward to the sun, her skin shimmering in the afternoon sunlight. "How will I race you if I don't even know where we're going?"

"See that little copse of trees over there?"

He pointed toward his private domain, which stood in the familiar circle of trees some distance away.

She nodded. Then her smile turned mischievous. Before Damien could guess her intent, she spurred her horse forward and took off toward the little glen.

He chuckled and followed her. He could have easily overtaken her, but was content to ride behind her. He watched, dazzled, as her hair unwound from its coiffure to stream out behind her like a banner. She looked at him over her shoulder, her smile competing with the sun's brilliance. He'd be content to let her win every time, if the view always proved so pleasing.

Esmeralda slowed as they neared their destination, allowing Damien to pull up alongside her. Together, they approached the glen at a slow cant.

"It's so quiet here," she remarked as he helped her dismount.

Holding the basket in one hand and a saddle blanket in the other, he led her through the trees toward the little pond he so loved.

"This is my favorite place," he told her, spreading the blanket on the ground. "My brothers and I used to play here when we were boys. No one comes here but me these days."

Esmeralda turned in a slow circle, taking in the little glen that had once seemed so big to three little boys. He enjoyed the sight of her here, her green gown making her seem like part of the landscape, all of it a picturesque frame to her beauty.

Sinking onto the blanket, he motioned for her to join him. She obliged him, sinking down at his side, her skirts and petticoats billowing before settling around her like the spread petals of a flower.

"I don't know about you, but I am starving," he said, revealing the small feast prepared by the cook.

Doris had provided meats, bread and cheeses for sandwiches, an assortment of fruit, a bottle of white wine and tiny lemon tartlets for desert. Damien poured the wine into the provided cups and handed one to Esmeralda. They sat mostly in silence, enjoying the privacy and serenity beside the pond, disturbed only by an occasional breeze. He helped Esmeralda piece together their sandwiches and portion out the fruit.

They ate in companionable silence, something Damien found to be comfortable with her in a way he didn't with anyone else. He liked that she didn't seem to feel the need to fill the quiet with meaningless chatter. When Esmeralda did speak, it was always with something worthwhile to say. It made him eager to hang onto her every word.

Once they were full, he repacked the basket and stood. Stretching his sore muscles, made so by the long day of activity, he ambled toward the pond.

"How about a swim?" he said, bending down dip his hands in the cool water. "The water might be a bit cold, but the weather is warm. We'll adjust."

Esmeralda glanced about as if afraid they would be seen. "What if someone comes?"

"Trust me," he said, removing his shirt with one swift motion. He'd left off his other layers after stripping off his armor, leaving him with less to remove.

"Everyone is listening to my father's stories of his tournament days over partridge pie as we speak. Besides, I can assure you that we are quite alone here. The trees provide added privacy in case someone should ride past."

Esmeralda's gaze fell to his bared torso and held, causing the surface of his skin to tingle. It was not as if a woman had not looked admiringly upon his body, honed by years of riding and swordplay. However, her gaze felt different, making him far more aware of her than he had been of anyone else.

Thank God the water will be cold.

He bent to remove his boots and stockings, but left on his breeches for her sake. Not only did he not want her getting the wrong idea, he also didn't want her too uncomfortable to get into the water with him.

"Are you coming?"

She nodded, looking away from his half-naked form and turning her back, starting to unbutton her gown down the back. He wanted to offer his assistance, but didn't think he could resist the urge to kiss every inch of skin as he bared it. Instead, he went to the water, desperate to cool his ardor and squelch his arousal.

He was already swimming around in slow circles by the time she made her way into the pond, hands covering her breasts, separated from his view only by the thin chemise she wore. The layers of her gown, petticoats, stockings, and corset lay in the grass.

She ducked her head under the surface to quickly grow used to the temperature, and then they circled one another in the pond. Damien soon began to realize that a swim might not have been the best idea. The cold water had killed the erection swelling in his breeches, but the sight of her with all those wet tendrils of hair falling around her, knowing she was wearing only a chemise ... it brought him right back to life, heating his blood to an unbearable degree.

"Care to race again?" she challenged when he caught her eye.

He couldn't resist her wide smile, or the mischief flashing in her eyes.

"Of course."

They trudged to one end of the pond, and on Esmeralda's count, plunged back into the water. Damien gave it everything he had this time, needing the exercise to tire him out and keep him from doing something reckless. Being nearly naked with her in a secluded place was wreaking havoc on him.

He won the race, coming up from the water seconds before her. Laughter welled in his chest as she re-emerged, glaring at him as she swiped her hair out of her eyes.

"You only won because I let you, you know," she grumbled, coming toward him through the water.

The laughter died away as she came close enough for him to notice the way the damp chemise clung to her body. His nostrils flared, and that scent of hers wafted up his nostrils, floral and alluring.

The smile faded from her face when her eyes met his, and she seemed as incapable of looking away as he was. He kept his movements slow as he reached out for her, his hands shaking with the force of his anticipation. His hands fell on her shoulders, and he smoothed them up and down in her arms in a slow caress as he allowed himself to drink her in, looking beyond the beckoning call of her eyes and the slopes and planes of her face.

Her hair hung wet and curling down her back, a few strands plastered to her face, neck, and shoulders. One lock rested alluringly over her collarbone. Tiny droplets of water had formed on her bare skin and a few trickled in tiny rivulets down into the valley between her breasts. Damien's tongue crept out to wet his lips and an undeniable urge to lap up the tiny drops overwhelmed him.

His hands still on her shoulders—because he didn't trust himself to put them anywhere else—he pulled her closer and kissed her. Accustomed to his touch now, she parted her lips for him immediately, and met his tongue with hers. He groaned and sank into her, resting against her soft, womanly body. She tangled her hands in his wet curls and drank from his lips.

Tremors rippled down his spine in reaction to her touch, the acquiescence in her parted lips and pliant body too much to resist. He lost his grip on control and reason, and simply allowed himself to feel, to taste, to touch. His hands moved around to her back, his fingers trailing through the thick strands of her soaked hair. They traveled lower, skimming the sinews of her back and the curve of her waist before finding her hips.

She gasped against his mouth when their bodies mashed together, the hard length of his erection pressing against her belly. Instead of trying to avoid it, she wiggled against him, as if desperate to take it inside her body. He groaned into their kiss, shaking with the need to claim her, but knowing he must hold back. He wanted her, but not here, not like this.

However, that did not mean he could not give her a little taste of what they would have together once she was ready.

Lifting her from the water, he urged her legs around his waist. Cupping her bottom, he held her tight against him as he walked back up the bank.

He walked slowly, his lips still connected to hers as he carried her to a sunny spot on the warm grass. He laid her there and came down on top of her, his hips sinking into hers. The fit couldn't be more perfect, the cradle of her body open to let him in.

He propped himself up on his elbows and gazed down at her, awed at the unwitting seduction that radiated from her, beckoning to him. She was the most tempting sight he had ever seen. Her rapid breaths caused her upturned breasts to heave and for the first time, Damien realized he could see the outline of her dark brown nipples through her soaked chemise.

The roaring in his ears increased until he could think of nothing more than taking one of those perfect peaks into his mouth. He lowered his head to capture her lips once more while using one hand to slip the chemise off one shoulder, and then lower. She arched her back, causing her legs to spread wider, pressing her even tighter against him. He could feel the heat of her core through the layers of her chemise and his breeches, the sensation sending another deep pang of longing rippling through him.

Gazing down at her bare breast, he dipped his head and captured it in his opening mouth. She gasped, her arms tightening around him as he teased her nipple with soft tongue strokes and sucking pulls of his mouth. He delighted in her response, the soft moans that fell from her lips as he suckled at one breast while palming the other through her chemise and plying the tip with his thumb and forefinger.

"Damien," she whispered, his name on her lips holding wonder and awe.

It urged him on, making him less reticent as he realized she was enjoying the things he did to her.

With his mouth still working at her breast, he snatched up the hem of her chemise, pulling it to her waist. Then, he reached between them and found her heated, moist center. She moaned, a silky sound from the back of her throat that stroked at Damien like a caress. He bit his lip and closed his eyes, reminding himself to go slowly, to be careful not to frighten her, and keep his own needs in cheek. This would be about her.

He massaged her gently, kissing his way up from her breast to her neck, then her jaw, and at last, her lips. He parted her velvety folds, finding her most sensitive place and teasing it with his first finger. She moaned and thrashed beneath him, grasping his shoulders tight while her hips undulated in time with his movements. He inserted one, and then a second finger into her tight, pulsating sheath, relishing every cry of pleasure he forced from her lips. He moved them within her at a slow but steady rhythm while stroking her little nub with his thumb, watching the pleasure build up in her as she climbed toward ecstasy. At last, her eyes widened and a sound that could only be described as a scream was torn from her lips as she writhed and trembled. Then, she threw her head back and trembled, her insides pulsing and squeezing his fingers tight as climax washed through her.

He stilled his movements inside her and took her mouth with his own, gently `nibbling at her lips as she climbed down from the height of her pleasure. He was still hard and burning for her, but kept himself under control. Now was not the time to make Esmeralda his. He lowered her chemise over her hips and reluctantly pulled away from her.

She sat up and wrapped her arms around her knees, her eyes a bit glassy and dazed when she looked at him. "That was… not what I expected."

Damien laughed. "It was exactly what I expected. I've always wondered what your face would look like when overtaken by passion. I was not disappointed."

"Shouldn't I…do something…for you?" She indicated the bulge at the front of his breeches, seeming embarrassed but earnest in her question.

His belly clenched in reaction to her question, the hardened length of him downright painful locked away in his breeches. He wanted nothing more than to take her up on her offer, but knew to follow his original instincts to wait.

"Not here, and not like this," he said, reaching for his shirt. "This was not my intention in bringing you out here. I only wanted a moment away. When I do finally make love to you, it will not be on the ground like an animal. I will lay you on my bed and take my time. I will learn all there is to know about you and teach you everything there is to know about me."

After tucking in his shirt, he helped her to her feet and set about helping her get dressed once more. His shaking hands stilled after a moment, and focusing upon the task helped distract him from his physical discomfort.

Once she was fully dressed, he grasped her shoulders pulled her against him one last time. He pulled the curtain of her hair aside and graced the side of her neck with a tender kiss.

They cleaned up the remains of their picnic and rode back to the palace in silence. After what had just happened between them, there was not much to be said. He was not certain how to tell her how honored he was that she'd trusted him enough to be nearly naked with him, to let him kiss and touch her in a way he knew no other man had. And so, he said nothing, hoping that in some way he could show her his gratitude.

He stole little glances at her as they rode, pleased with the affect his touch had on her. She'd managed to pin her hair back into place and looked mostly as she had upon leaving the palace. To the casual observer, there had been no change in her since she was last seen at the tournament. But, he noticed the brightness of her eyes and smiled. He had done that to her—made her glow with the look of a woman well-loved.

They dismounted near the stables, and Damien ordered the carriage brought around for Esmeralda.

"I would love to escort you home, but I must see to my brother," he said, before handing her into the spacious carriage.

"I understand," she said, allowing him to kiss her hand. "I will see you soon?"

"Of course."

Nothing could keep me away.

CHAPTER 12

"I knew something wasn't right. I just knew it!"

Lionus frowned, folding his arms over his chest. He studied the horseshoe that Serge held up for all of them to see. The Crown Prince's head had been bandaged, and though he admitted it throbbed and pounded, he'd refused the laudanum and brandy offered to him once he had awakened. He'd wanted to be lucid for this meeting. He sat amongst the bedclothes wearing a black silk dressing gown, his freshly washed hair hanging down to his shoulders. The only visible injury was that of his head, though the fall had battered his body as well.

"Unbelievable," murmured Damien as he studied the twisted, mangled horseshoe. "No wonder your horse went down, Lionus."

"You're saying that this shoe was on his horse during the tournament?" Nicolai asked, his face a mask of disbelief.

"All but one of the nails had been removed," Serge said. "It must have been only slightly bent at the beginning of the tournament. But as the day wore on, it became worse." He turned to Lionus. "When you started charging at Damien during the joust, the shoe cut into your horse's opposite leg, causing him to go down."

Lionus took the horseshoe and studied it with his sharp eyes.

"None of the grooms would be careless enough to allow this. It was done on purpose."

Serge nodded, his mouth a firm, hard line. "Exactly."

"Have anyone who was anywhere near the stables this morning questioned," Lionus said to Serge. "And while we are here, let us discuss what we do know. Nicolai and I have made our inquiries at the various gatherings and have learned nothing new. Several of the nobility have even heard of this masked man, yet none of them seem to know his true identity."

"He's like a phantom," Nicolai added. "He comes and goes, paying or threatening people in order to get them to do his bidding. Apparently, his threats aren't idle. There have been injuries and deaths for those who haven't complied."

Damien frowned. "I had the same problem."

He had taken a few nights away to visit some of the seedier establishments in town. Many people had stories to tell about encounters with the masked man, yet none of them could offer any clue to who he was, other than the description already given.

"No one has seen his face, or know where he's come from. It is as if he doesn't even exist."

"But he does exist!" roared Lionus. Through his anger, Damien could see the pain reflected in his eyes. "The man is not a ghost or a specter! Obviously, he is very real if he is able to make attempts on my life and the lives of my family. I want him found!"

Serge nodded. "I think it is time we put out a description of this man…at least the little that we do know. Perhaps if we offer a reward someone will come forward with more substantial information."

"I did not want to have to do that," said Lionus, rubbing his bleary eyes. "But I suppose it must be done."

"I will see to it," said Serge. "In the meantime, we should increase security. Specifically, around you since you are the latest target of these attacks."

Lionus nodded his agreement, but was otherwise silent.

"Why don't you take a little laudanum?" Nicolai suggested, lifting the bottle from the nightstand beside the bed. "You are in pain."

"And if I do, do you suppose the masked man will send an assassin to murder me as I sleep? No, thank you. The pain is tolerable."

"Nevertheless, we will leave you to your rest," said Damien, following Serge and Nicolai from the room.

Serge still clutched the horseshoe in his hand, his countenance filled with worry. "It seems this man will not rest until he has achieved his ends."

"Or until he is caught," said Damien. "The sooner he is found, the better."

THE FOLLOWING AFTERNOON, Damien watched with pleasure curving his lips as Esmeralda was draped with length after length of satins and silks. He had brought her to Madame Didier's establishment to have her fitted for a gown for the masquerade ball to be held at the end of the week, the night before the royal wedding. Esmeralda had asserted that Raina had promised to make her a suitable costume, but Damien insisted she have the best. The dressmaker was known as the best in Cardenas, and had dressed royalty, as well as many wealthy members of the royal court.

She stood on a small raised platform in a private room of the boutique, while Madame Didier watched two shop girls drape her with various fabrics. When she wasn't covered in yards of material, she stood in her undergarments, including a stiff corset and layers of petticoats.

"Bring the gold silk," Madame Didier commanded, studying Esmeralda with a critical eye. "It will compliment her skin very nicely. Such exotic looks."

She circled Esmeralda as the two shop girls held a bolt of gold silk up against her skin. Madame Didier issued a dramatic gasp, throwing her hands up in the air.

"Magnificent!" she cried. "It is perfect!"

She draped and pinned the silk in various places, looking to Damien for his approval. She'd observed the latest fashion while taking care not to let the gown overpower Esmeralda's natural beauty.

"It's beautiful," he murmured, his mouth watering as he observed the way the silk draped over Esmeralda's frame. He did not think he'd ever seen a color that looked so alluring on her. If he had his way, she'd be swathed in gold every waking hour of every day.

Madame Didier held a scrap of black lace against the gold material. "This will do nicely over the bodice, I think. Many people cannot pull off black, but your coloring will only enhance it."

Esmeralda reverently touched the lace held out to her, teeth worrying her lower lip.

"It's so fine," she said, turning to Damien. "It is sure to be expensive."

"No expense is to be spared," he replied with a smile.

She still looked uncertain, but did not argue, knowing it would be futile. He would have his way in this, just as he had about the cape, as well as the riding boots and hat he'd given her just the week before. He had the means to give these things to her, and took pride in seeing her happily wearing each item. This gown would set her apart the ball, and the tongues would wag—but all about how stunning she would look, not about who she was or where she'd come from.

Madame Didier returned his smile and focused her attention back on Esmeralda. "A neckline that flaunts the shoulders … it's all the rage. Oh, and an elaborate bustle and short train as well."

Esmeralda nodded her agreement. "That sounds lovely."

"Matching slippers, reticule, and of course a mask. It will be an exquisite creation."

Esmeralda stood for nearly an hour while Madame Didier and her assistants pinned and draped until the beginnings of a gown had been formed. She seemed relieved when it was over and the fabric had been removed from her body.

Damien waited until she left to dress in the adjoining room, before pulling Madame Didier aside.

"I would like to order more," he said, his voice low. "You have her measurements, and I'm sure you will choose fabrics and colors that are suitable."

"But of course, Your Grace," she said, smiling at the prince. "What would you like?"

"Day dresses, evening gowns, ball gowns. Four of each should do. And a riding habit."

"Accessories? Undergarments?" Madame Didier began making notes on a small scrap of paper.

"Yes ... all the makings of a proper wardrobe. I will leave the particulars up to you. You know what is fashionable. Send the bill to me at Rothchester Hall and have the clothing delivered there as well."

The seamstress' eyes glittered at the mention of the commission she was sure to gain for such an undertaking. "I shall see it done."

Esmeralda emerged from the dressing room and allowed him to take her arm. She did not notice the conspiratorial glance exchanged between him and Madame Didier. He could hardly wait for the garments to be completed so he could present them to her. Beyond the royal wedding, he wanted her with him everywhere he went. He wanted to share everything with her, and if that meant she must have new clothes in order to fit into his world, then she would have everything she could ever need.

Before long, they were in the swaying carriage, on their way back to Esmeralda's home.

"I really wish you had not spent so much on a gown for me," she said, threading her fingers through his and resting her head upon his shoulder. "My mother could have altered one of my gowns, and it would have been just as suitable."

"Nonsense," he replied, squeezing her hand and kissing her forehead. "You need an appropriate costume, and Madame Didier is the best. She'll make you the envy of every woman present."

She smiled and nestled closer to him in the intimate confines of the carriage. He savored moments like this, when they could be away from probing eyes and whispers.

He pulled her closer and whispered in her ear. "I wish I could have you to myself more often. But, you have become wildly popular at court and ... what the devil?"

She followed his gaze out of the carriage window. A black coach sped alongside them on the narrow lane, swerving dangerously close. The carriage's curtains were closed, and there were no identifiable crests or markings on it anywhere. It was pulled by a team of impeccably matched black bays, being driven by a figure also shrouded in black, his face hidden by the scarf wrapped around the lower half of his face. Damien banged on the wall of the carriage, trying to gain their driver's attention.

"Slow down and let him pass, Rawlins!" he shouted, struggling to be heard over the clatter of wheels. "The reckless bastard."

He pushed the curtains back to try and better identify the carriage and driver. Just as he peered from the window, the vehicle swerved, perilously close to ramming them. Their driver shouted and cursed, trying to bring the startled horses under control. The carriage swayed and rocked, tossing Esmeralda about. Damien grasped her and pulled her close, trying to keep her in the seat.

"Goddamn it all, Rawlins, get the horses under control!" Damien shouted to the driver, pressing Esmeralda up against the cushioned seat. "Hold on to me, love."

The horses seemed to be picking up speed, carrying the coach down the dusty road at a dangerous pace.

The black conveyance swayed toward them several more times before it rammed into the side of them, causing their carriage to tilt to one side before slamming back down to four wheels. This time, a scream escaped Esmeralda's lips, and Damien could do nothing more than hold her tighter against him.

The horses were out of control now, terrified by the attacking carriage and their panicked driver. If Damien were alone, he would simply throw open the door and try to leap to safety. He would not risk such a move with Esmeralda. She could be crushed under the wheels or trampled by the horses, and he would never forgive himself.

"Cut the horses loose, Rawlins!" he shouted, praying the driver could hear him.

Separating themselves from the horses seemed to be the only way, and Damien hoped Rawlins would be successful before the other carriage succeeded in tipping them over. Gunshots rang out overhead, and Esmeralda shook in his arms at the explosive sound. Rawlins' cursing and yelling were the only indications that the man still lived, but the bullets flying overhead obviously slowed his progress.

"Got it!" shouted Rawlins just as he cut the last horse free.

Damien felt the carriage slowing to a halt as the racing horses left it behind. He breathed a sigh of relief and loosened his hold on Esmeralda.

"Thank God," he said with a sigh. "As soon as we have stopped, we'll—"

The carriage lurched, causing him to go flying across the vehicle to the other seat.

"Damien!"

Esmeralda shrieking his name was the last thing he heard before they began to roll.

DAMIEN HELD his hand over his pounding forehead, almost afraid to open his eyes. He knew without looking that his body lay at an odd angle—nearly upside down, his legs bent and over his head, his shoulders supporting all of his weight. The sound of gentle sobs brought him fully into consciousness and he slowly opened his eyes. He was staring at his shoes. He frowned. They were extremely scuffed.

He flexed all of his joints before determining that nothing was broken. His head hurt like the devil, and he was certain to find bruises once he was able to look in a mirror.

"Esmeralda," he said, causing the sobbing to cease in an instant. "Are you all right?"

"Damien! Thank God, you're alive!"

"Of course I'm alive, love. Where are you?"

"Right beside you."

"At this impossible angle, I don't even know where the side of me is located," he said with an ironic laugh. "Would you help me make sense of myself?"

With a few tugs and pulls, she managed to turn him onto his side, where he was better able to assess their situation. First, he satisfied himself that she was all right. Her dress had torn in places and she had a few bruises. Her hair was hopelessly disheveled and tangled in a mass around her head, but she seemed otherwise fine. He made her move all of her joints and limbs just as he had done to assure himself she hadn't been injured. Satisfied that nothing was broken, he began gazing around the overturned carriage. Damien guessed that it had probably turned a few times before stopping. They were now laying on one of the doors, with the other directly overhead.

"We'll have to climb out," he said, studying the bent carriage door above them. "I am just tall enough to push it open, and perhaps I can jump out. Then I'll lean in and pull you up."

Esmeralda grasped his arm. "Perhaps we should call for Rawlins. Maybe he can help."

Damien met her gaze, his mouth tightening. "If the carriage has overturned, Rawlins may not be able to hear us."

"Oh no," she cried, tears springing to her eyes.

"Let's not make any assumptions," he said, remaining calm for her sake. "Perhaps he is just unconscious. In that case we had better hurry … he may need our help."

Esmeralda nodded resolutely and raised herself to her knees. Damien struggled to stand, pausing several times to catch his breath. He felt a knot forming on the side of his head. His eyelids were heavy, and his vision blurred, his movements slow and uncoordinated. The blow to his head had begun to take its toll.

Nonetheless, he reached upward with his long arms, determined to have Esmeralda free before he succumbed to the full extent of his injuries. Every muscle in his body ached, but he ignored the pain and managed to shove the carriage door open. He grasped either side of the doorway and pulled himself upward with a groan and every ounce of his strength.

"Give me a moment, love," he panted once he had surfaced, wiping the perspiration from his forehead. "I have to summon the strength to pull you out."

Esmeralda waited silently, watching as he took several deep breaths and closed his eyes. He finally nodded and opened them, using his last ounce of willpower to force himself to concentrate on the task at hand. His eyes had grown heavy and his head pounded relentlessly, and all he wanted to do was lie down on the ground and fall asleep.

He lowered the upper half of his body into the carriage and held his arms down to Esmeralda. "Take my hands and don't let go."

She clenched his hands tight and tried with all her strength to help him pull her from the carriage. After a few tries, they managed it together.

They collapsed on the ground in a heap, a tangle of arms and legs. The horses were long gone, and the other carriage had abandoned them. He searched for Rawlins' lifeless form, but could see nothing but dusty road, grass, and trees. His strength waning, Damien could only focus on Esmeralda's face. It blurred and faded to nothing as he lost consciousness.

When Damien awakened, he lay in his own bed. He recognized the familiar ivory canopy above him immediately. He waited for his vision to focus before trying to move his head. Drowsiness pulled upon his mind, yet he fought its grasping tentacles as he struggled to recall what had happened since he'd pulled Esmeralda from an overturned carriage on the side of the road.

"Esmeralda!" he exclaimed, shooting upright.

His vision blurred once more, and an overwhelming dizziness claimed him, forcing him back onto the pillows.

A hand found his, and Serge's face appeared within his field of vision.

"Damien, you must lay still," he said, working to prop Damien up with more pillows. "The doctor says you have a concussion and will be dizzy for a little while."

He fought unconsciousness and focused on his brother's face, creased with worry lines. His normally merry blue eyes proved and cloudy and turbulent.

"Esmeralda," he repeated, remembering her battered form

collapsing beside him on the side of the road. "Is she all right? How did I get home?"

"She is here," Serge replied. "I saw to it that she was placed in a room nearby. Rawlins left the carriage when it overturned to get help. He thought you were dead."

"We could have been," he said, accepting the glass of water pressed into his hand. He drained it greedily and placed the cup back on the bedside table. "Some bastard driving a black carriage ran us off the road."

"Rawlins told us everything. He's hurt as well ... a couple of broken ribs and a sprained ankle. If he hadn't left to find help, you might still be out there."

"Someone should send for Esmeralda's family."

"It is already done. Her mother and grandmother arrived not long ago. They are tending to her now."

Damien swiveled his legs over the side of the bed, pausing for a moment to gain his equilibrium.

"I want to see her."

"I know you're concerned," Serge said, grasping his arm, "But you are in no condition to be up and walking around."

"I have to see her," he disputed, grasping his brother's shoulder for balance. "Either help me, or get the hell out of my way."

With a shrug, he allowed Damien to lean on him as he fought against the dizziness that threatened to unman him at any moment. Serge helped him into a dressing gown and led him slowly from his bedchamber. He felt like an invalid and despised the fact that he had to lean on his brother for support. He cursed his weakness, but would do whatever he must to see for himself that Esmeralda was all right.

Serge ushered him into the room she'd been placed in, where they found Isabelle, Akira, and Raina clustered around her.

Esmeralda's mother turned as they entered, eyes filled with worry for her daughter.

"She's been asking about you," she said, her voice at a near whisper. "We have tried to convince her to rest, but she worries for you."

"I am here," he said, releasing Serge's arm and limping over to the bed on his own.

He squared his shoulders and fought the urge to scream out in pain. He approached her bedside and breathed a sigh of relief.

Besides a few visible bruises, Esmeralda appeared to be fine. She lay beneath a thick counterpane, dressed in a prim white nightgown that Damien supposed had been brought for her from home. The white ruffles around the neck and shoulders added a feminine appeal. She had been bathed, her hair washed and brushed until it gleamed, fanned around her head against the pillow. He sat on the edge of the bed and grasped her hand in both of his. A lump had worked its way up into his throat and he felt the unmistakable sting of tears behind his eyes.

When had she become so important to him? He wondered at his own uncharacteristic display of emotion. The room was full of people who would see him if he allowed the tears to fall from his eyes and he couldn't care less. All that mattered to him was her.

"I'm glad you're all right," she said, reaching up to cup his face. Damien leaned against her open hand, grateful for a touch he had thought he'd never feel again. Yet here she was, warm and alive and here before him. His gratitude knew no bounds.

"I see that you have been well taken care of," he said.

"Your maids were very helpful. They had me cleaned up in no time."

Akira stepped forward, offering him a small, stoppered vial. "A few drops of this in your bathwater, and you will feel as right as rain. It will take a few days, but it'll do you much good."

Damien gave the old woman a grateful smile. "Thank you."

Then, he turned to Esmeralda. "You should rest. I will leave you now."

She grasped his sleeve and held tight. "No. Please, don't go."

Damien glanced around the room. Serge, Raina, Akira, and Isabelle waited silently, each seeming unsure about whether to go or stay.

"My dear, it would be highly improper."

It wasn't what he wanted to say at all, though it proved the right thing to vocalize with her mother and grandmother in the room. What he really wanted was to climb into bed with her and never come out again.

"Nonsense!" Akira interjected. "She is hurt and needs comfort. Who better to give it to her?"

Isabelle nodded. "We'll leave strict orders not to let anyone into this room. No one ever has to know."

Akira had already grasped Raina's hand and began pulling her toward the door. The woman did not seem worried about leaving her daughter alone with him, which spoke of her trust in him. Serge placed a hand at the small of Isabelle's back and led her away, as well.

He turned back to Esmeralda, who had moved to the other side of the bed to make room for him. She turned down the covers invitingly and smiled. He groaned as if in pain and lowered himself to the mattress beside her.

"Are you all right?" she asked, stroking his hair as he lowered his head to her breast. "Are you in pain?"

"Damned right, I'm in pain," he said, wrapping his arms around her. "Here I've been dreaming of getting you into bed for weeks and when I finally do, I am too weak to do anything about it!"

They laughed together and burrowed beneath the blankets. The comfort of the bed and the soft warmth of the body beside him created a drugging effect. Before long, he slept peacefully with his head upon her breast and her scent washing over him with a comforting effect.

CHAPTER 13

The crowded ballroom was overrun with people in elaborate costume. Fairies and wood nymphs promenaded by on the arms of Shakespearian heroes and Greek gods. Damien searched the room for Esmeralda, trying to see past the masks of the various ladies walking by. He knew that an air of mystery was essential for a masquerade ball, but at the moment, he found it a damned nuisance.

He had sent a carriage to fetch Esmeralda, since he had been unable to go himself. He'd spent the afternoon trying to soothe Lionus' ire.

Though he and Esmeralda had fully recovered from the incident with the carriage and the rest of the week had passed uneventfully, Lionus remained as uneasy as a caged beast. He had paced about the library, questioning Rawlins for the third time, trying to squeeze every possible clue from his version of the story. And though Damien, Serge, and Nicolai had worked to soothe his temper, the feeling was not lost on them. Damien fully understood his brother's apprehension, especially since they'd come no closer to identifying the masked man than they had a few weeks ago.

Damien sighed, flexing his fingers around the champagne flute he held. This last attempt would not have rattled him so much had it not involved Esmeralda. He'd been wracked with guilt for days, knowing that if not for her association with him, such a thing would never have happened to her. He had been helpless to protect her, able to do nothing as the carriage had hurtled uncontrollably down the road.

Damien knew she was doing well, as was he, thanks to Akira's potion. He had no idea what was in the small vial that the Gypsy woman had given him, but a few drops in his bath water each night had soothed his bruised and sore muscles. Now, he felt like himself, stronger than ever even.

For the event, he'd chosen to adorn himself as a pirate. A red, military-style jacket decorated with gold and black braid and shining gold buttons, clung to his shoulders and arms, hanging down to his knees. Beneath the coat was a starched white shirt, rakishly unbuttoned to reveal his chest. Ruffled lace spilled from his wrists from beneath the cuffs of the jacket. Black breeches clung to his legs, and a pair of black polished boots reached up to his knees. A tri-corn hat sporting several feathers and an eye patch completed the ensemble.

Nicolai appeared at his side, dressed in a green tunic and matching hose. A green hat with a bright red plume sat at a jaunty angle on his head. A green mask covered his eyes and nose. What appeared to be ivy vines had been fashioned to intertwine about his limbs, making him look as if he'd just climbed someone's trellis.

Damien doubled over with laughter. "And what, pray tell, are you supposed to be? A woodland sprite?"

"I will have you know, dear cos, that the ladies find it charming," said Nicolai, humor twinkling in his eyes. He bowed before Damien, sweeping his hat from his head as he did so.

"Just be careful not to rip those hosen of yours!" Damien guffawed, clapping Nicolai on his shoulder.

"I've another pair ready in case that happens," Nicolai whispered with a wink.

Damien procured another glass of champagne from a passing servant. Nicolai did the same.

"Davina's looking well," Nicolai said, gesturing toward a figure in blue with his glass. "It would seem being tossed over by you can do wonders for a woman."

The woman in question stood nearby, surrounded by her lady friends and a few gentlemen admirers fawning over her jeweled hands. Even the elaborate, bejeweled mask she wore could not disguise her. Damien had received the bill for the gown she wore a few days after ending his liaison with her. The creation bore the clear stamp of Madame Didier, though it was so encrusted with beading he was certain Davina might topple over at any moment. The sapphires he had purchased for her glittered at her wrists and throat. The tiara had seemed like a frivolous purchase, but it was fitting to Davina's taste.

The rare black diamonds set in gold that Damien had sent along in the carriage for Esmeralda would eclipse Davina and her blatant flaunting. He fought a smile as he pictured Davina's face when she saw the twinkling jewels around Esmeralda's throat.

"Would you mind terribly if I approached her?" Nicolai asked, seemingly hypnotized by the indecently low bodice of Davina's gown. "I believe we would get along well together."

Damien shrugged. "She is no longer of any concern to me. By all means, have at her."

"Good man," Nicolai said with a grin.

He watched his cousin make his way toward his former mistress with a raised eyebrow. Nicolai knew how grasping and calculating Davina could be. It would seem that was a risk he was willing to take. It was none of his affair, and he wished his cousin luck with her.

All thoughts of Davina fled from his mind when he heard a soft murmur rippling through the crowd. Something had shifted in the atmosphere, making the hairs on the back of his neck stand on end. Nearly every head in the room swiveled toward the entrance, so he followed them, nearly losing his breath at the sight of the woman in gold standing at the top of the curving staircase.

Madame Didier had outdone herself. The black lace over the bodice offered a peek at the gold silk, which billowed out into her full skirts. An elaborate bustle had been fashioned at the back, and a short train trailed behind her as she walked. The gown was sleeveless, cut daringly low, with a high, black ruffled collar that rose up behind her neck. Her hair had been brushed and smoothed to the top of her head in a series of twists and coils, where two golden butterfly combs had been placed. A gold mask in the shape of a butterfly covered the upper half of her face, and the black diamonds winked and sparkled at her ears and neck.

The crowd seemed to part as if by magic to allow her passage. Damien started through the opening, unable to tear his gaze away from her. Hands were held over mouths and whispers swept from one corner of the ballroom to the other as he made his way toward her through path made by the parted crowd.

It was just as he had wanted—Esmeralda appearing here and putting every one of the ladies to shame.

When he reached her, he took her hand bowed over it, his kiss lingering a second longer than was proper before linking her arm through his. All around them, the ball resumed, though those standing closest to them seemed to strain to hear them, craning their necks for a better look at her ensemble.

"You look beautiful," he whispered near her ear, resisting the impulse to press his lips against her fragrant skin.

"And you look positively charming," she replied. "I was very surprised to find these jewels waiting for me in the carriage. Really, Damien ... I would say it's too much, but I know you will argue the point."

"No woman should attend a ball without the proper jewels," he said, pulling her near the buffet table. "And you, my dear, deserve the very best. Of course it isn't too much."

Esmeralda's eyes widened at the assortment of food presented at the buffet table. It was hard to believe any one group of people could devour so much food in so little time.

"I know," Damien said, leading her toward the line that had formed on one side. "It is a bit excessive, isn't it?"

Esmeralda could only nod and follow him down the line. It seemed she could hardly decide between the various meat pies, fruits, tarts, breads and cheeses. And the wine! Champagne, port, brandy, sherry and Madeira all flowed freely.

She chose a glass of Madeira and followed him to a quiet corner where they could sit to eat in peace. The curiosity over them had seemed to wane for now, as everyone anticipated the arrival of Lionus and Isabelle, who would lead the assembled guests in the first dance of the evening.

"How are you feeling?" he asked. "You look well."

"I am well," she murmured between sips of wine. "Good as new."

"I must impress upon your grandmother to learn her secrets. That mixture she gave me worked better than any laudanum or spirits."

Esmeralda smiled. "The Gypsies are wise in the ways of healing. My grandmother is also very taken with you."

"Ah, so I may be able to learn her secrets after all," he quipped, wiggling his eyebrows.

She giggled. "You might have better luck than the rest of us anyway."

They fell silent and began to eat, pausing here and there to remark upon the various costumes as the guests milled about. He saw the masquerade in a new light through her eyes, noticing the way the costumes, decor, and hundreds of candles glowing from the chandeliers overhead seemed to awe her. With her, all the things he'd come to see as mundane became new. She made him aware of how privileged he had been to experience these sorts of things, when there were so many others who may never see the inside of such a lavish ballroom. Like so many other aspects of being with her, this experience proved humbling, driving home just how much he'd taken for granted. At the same time, it made him all-too aware of how spoiled he'd been, how ungrateful. Esmeralda made him grateful to be alive, to have her near him, to be able to call her his own in some way.

As Lionus and Isabelle appeared—the prince in unrelenting black with white linen, the bride in brilliant white—they finished their food and stood to join in for the first dance.

Taking her hand in his to lead her onto the dance floor, Damien experienced a sudden feeling of rightness settling over him. He pulled

Esmeralda into his arms for the waltz, smiling down at her and noting the way candlelight made her gown and the matching mask shimmer with a life all their own. Tonight … tonight he would make her understand the depth of his feelings for her, as well as his intention to make her a permanent part of his life.

It might seem sudden to her, but now that he'd found her—the one person who could make him feel like something more than a wastrel—he did not think he could ever let her go. Time would not change that; it would only cause his feelings for her to grow stronger.

"What are you thinking?" she asked as he spun her into the dance. "You have that look on your face … the one you always wear when you're deep in thought."

He shook his head, tightening the hand on the curve of her waist. "Not now. Later, I have something I want to tell you. For now, I want to enjoy our first waltz."

The first of many, he hoped. As they danced, he couldn't help but notice how different it felt with her. He'd been taught to dance as part of his education, but had never enjoyed it so much. In the past, dancing had been an obligation to fulfill, something his mother urged him to do for the sake of appearances.

But, as he held Esmeralda in his arms, the blur of candlelight whirling by around them, he realized he could have danced with her like this for the rest of his life.

Esmeralda clung to Damien's arm and allowed him to lead her through the palace gardens. She'd never seen a garden so large, so lush and fragrant, in her life. She admired the rows upon rows of azaleas and gardenias and roses, all which would be shriveled and gone soon, until the harsh winter was over.

Already, the night air had grown colder, biting at her bare shoulders and arms, but she didn't care. She'd danced nearly every dance and not just with Damien. Dozens of men had approached to ask her to dance, and she'd hardly been able to rest between songs. She was grateful that her mother had taken the time to teach her the various ballroom dances, as she had put each of her lessons to use.

They had escaped for a reprieve, and now walked through the moonlit garden, where they were blessedly alone She had been nervous about attending such an important event with him, worrying that she would commit some egregious faux pas and embarrass him. But, she'd had a wonderful time, and he seemed to be enjoying himself as well. If someone had told her weeks ago that she might find herself here tonight, she would have laughed in their faces. Now, she found she wouldn't have wanted to be anywhere else.

Damien led her through the hedgerow maze to the fountain hidden inside. Walls of greenery shut them away from the rest of the world, offering them solitude. He sat her on the edge and knelt before her, lifting her feet to rest on top of his thighs. He ran his hands slowly up and down her legs to gift her with his warmth. He rubbed vigorously, his hands gliding over her silk stockings.

"You should have allowed me to fetch your cloak. It is cold tonight."

Esmeralda shook her head and tilted her head back to view the cloudy night sky. "Winter is coming. It is my favorite time of year. The trees die and lose their leaves, but then the snow comes and covers everything with tiny white crystals. It's beautiful."

Damien stopped massaging her legs and circled each of her ankles with his hands.

"Winter is my favorite time of year too," he replied.

She glanced down to meet his gaze, and they stared at each other a moment in silence before he spoke again.

"I do hope you've enjoyed yourself tonight."

Esmeralda laughed, spreading her arms wide and leaning back as if embracing the heavens. "How could I not enjoy myself? The dancing, the music, the food. It was better than I imagined!"

Damien removed his hat and eye patch, placing them on the fountain beside her. "You are the lady of the evening. Everyone's talking, wondering who the mysterious butterfly is. It seems you're all they seem capable of talking about these days."

He leaned in close, searching for her eyes through the golden mask. She removed it and rewarded him with a smirk. He returned her smile.

"Some are even saying that you are a foreign princess, come to be my bride."

Esmeralda's laughter rang out to mingle with his in the silence of the hedgerow maze, where the surrounding foliage sheltered them from the outside world.

She chuckled, her shoulders shaking with glee. "That's ridiculous! A princess?"

He was suddenly serious again, the intensity of his stare setting her on edge. The air around them seemed to shift and change, and she felt as if something monumental hung over their heads. Something big and frightening, yet wonderful.

"You could be." He grasped her hands and held them to his lips, kissing the knuckles of each one. "You have more refinement in these fingers than most women have in their entire bodies. You walk with confidence and speak with grace. You are good and kind. You may not have been born a princess, but I want make you *my* princess."

Her eyes grew wide as she looked down at him, disbelief stealing her breath. Surely he could not be serious. Oh, but he was. His earnest gaze and the tremor in his hand gave truth to his state of mind. He was serious, and possibly a bit nervous.

He drew her near and pressed his face against her middle, beneath her breasts, squeezing her tight. She wrapped her arms around his neck and held him close, sharing in his terror and experiencing the niggle of hope deep within.

"I love you," he whispered on the night air.

His words wrapped around her and warmed her from the inside out. She knew that if he looked into her face, he would see that she fairly glowed. The effect of his words upon her had been immediate, making her feel as if she might take flight right then and there.

She had known he cared for her, that he wanted her. But love? She'd never thought she would hear him say those three magical words.

"I think I've always loved you," he and, running his hands up and down her back.

Tiny tremors ran along her skin, causing her to shiver, although she could no longer feel the cold. She could only feel him.

"From that first night I saw you dancing in the palace, I wanted you. I thought to make you mine in body, but when I finally found you I knew I wanted to make you mine in spirit as well." He lifted his gaze up to her. "I want you to be my wife."

Esmeralda's hand flew up to cover her mouth, stifling the tiny sob that escaped from the back of her throat. He was saying the most delightful things, on the most beautiful night of her life, and all she could think was that she was unfit to be a princess. How could Damien, a prince, wed a Gypsy woman? It was simply unheard of. She shook her head to clear her thoughts, then gently dabbed at her eyes with his offered handkerchief.

"Please, say yes," he whispered, searching her face as if desperate for an inkling of her thoughts. "Please, tell me you will do it."

"Surely you cannot mean it. You can't mean to marry me."

He came to his feet. "And why not? No one will tell me that I can't!"

"Think what you are saying, Damien," she pleaded, standing as well. "You must take a wife who was raised to take on the role of being a princess."

She pointed toward the ballroom, which only a few moments ago had seemed worlds away.

"Any one of those women in there would be more suited to be your wife than I."

"*None* of those women are more fit to be my wife than you." He shoved his hands through his hair, exasperated. "I don't want them, I want you! I *love* you."

Esmeralda smiled, though her eyes were cloudy with sorrow and tears. "And I love you."

His expression flickered with momentary surprise, though he must have had some idea how she'd felt. Otherwise, he might never have asked her to marry him. But, she could not fight off the voice in the back of her mind telling her that saying yes would be selfish. Taking her for a wife would bring him nothing but hardship.

"Can't you see?" she added. "You think you want this now, but I would never fit. I wouldn't blend into your family or your life. I do not know the first thing about royalty, what being a permanent part of your world would entail."

"Damn my family. Damn it all! I would give up being a prince if it meant we could be together."

Esmeralda allowed the tears to fall freely now, beyond moved by his words. She almost wished he would stop, because she knew that if he continued, she would be ensnared and unable to resist his offer. It was bad enough he had declared his love, now he would break down her arguments by telling her that he would sacrifice everything he was for her.

"You could not do that," she murmured, reaching out to cup his face in her hands. "I would not ask you to leave your family, to forsake all that you have known, what is yours by right of birth. You belong here Damien. You have responsibilities."

His laugh was dry, dripping with scorn. "Responsibilities? I am merely the third son. Everyone has a duty except me. No one will care who or when I marry, and I like it that way. I am freer than Lionus and Serge to make my own choices … and I'm choosing you."

"But your dreams of opening a university…"

"I would never have found the courage if it weren't for you. You made me realize that it was more than a foolish dream. You made it a reality for me. Don't you understand? I cannot do it without you."

He grasped her about the waist and pulled her against him, molding their bodies together. Then, he grasped the nape of her neck and tilted her head back until her lips were parted and ready for his. He ravaged her mouth with his own, clinging to her as if she held his last breath. His fingers tightened, holding her captive. She issued a soft whimper and leaned into him, standing on tiptoe to offer him more of her mouth.

How could she give this up? She'd never known such a depth of emotion toward another person, this need to be near them always. It went beyond anything physical or rational. It felt a lot like the Fate her grandmother always spoke of.

"Say yes," he murmured between kisses, his voice a mere sigh on the night air.

He showered kisses over her neck, working his way up to the sensitive place behind her ear.

"Marry me," he whispered before taking her earlobe between his teeth. "Don't deny me."

Her legs buckled as if she had been drugged, and if not for his arms around her, she would have fallen at his feet. He never ceased his assault, whispering love words in her ear as he nibbled at her vulnerable flesh.

"You're not being fair," she managed, clinging to him as his mouth lowered to her shoulder. "I can hardly say no to you while you're kissing me like that."

"Then I shall never stop kissing you," he whispered hoarsely, claiming her mouth once more.

Esmeralda pushed at his shoulders, fighting for breath, fighting for control over her tempestuous feelings. It was inevitable, she realized now. She had known it from the moment he had tried to kiss her the night they'd met that she would never be able to resist him. Everything he was offering both frightened and thrilled her at once. Even so, she couldn't have refused if she'd wanted to. No matter how afraid she might be, she realized she would not have to face it alone. She would have Damien as her love, her husband.

"Yes," she whispered, tearing her lips away from his. "Yes, Damien, I will marry you."

For a moment, his face portrayed a degree of shock before it was replaced with elation. His grin was broad and his eyes grew bright as he lifted her in his arms and twirled her in circles. Esmeralda lifted her face upward to the starry night, exulting in his joy and claiming it as her own. The dizzying sensation washing over her had more to do with her happiness than the spinning.

He set her on her feet and kissed her again, short and swift.

"We must go to my father."

Before she could respond, he had grasped her hand and began dragging her through the maze.

She trotted to keep up with his long strides. "The king? Now?"

Damien nodded, but didn't decrease his pace. "I must tell him of our plans to marry. He will support us, even if no one else will."

"And Serge will as well, I believe."

He smiled. "You're right. Nicolai, as well. See? There are more people on our side than you thought."

"But now is hardly the time. Your father wasn't even present at the ball. Perhaps he is not well enough for visitors."

"He is merely resting up for the wedding tomorrow. Normally, he would not miss a masquerade. Trust me, he is likely awake and would want to be the first to hear this news."

Esmeralda could only relent and allow him to lead her around the side of the palace, away from the crowded ballroom. She had yet to be introduced to the king, and the trepidation of earlier began to steal back over her. Clinging tighter to Damien's hand, she reminded herself yet again that she did not have to go through any of this alone. Tonight, and for the rest of her life, she would have Damien at her side.

She had seen King Adare in the paintings Damien had shown her throughout the palace gallery. She had also seen him in passing at the many functions she'd attended at the palace over the last few weeks. Seeing him up close, Esmeralda could hardly believe the difference that prolonged illness had made. The once strong, virile man was now a former shadow of himself, wasting away before their very eyes.

Esmeralda tried not to let the pity show in her eyes as she approached the gigantic four-poster bed erected on a platform in the midst of the king's chambers. She smiled demurely and executed her best curtsy.

Adare smiled and stretched out his hand toward her. "Come, my dear, and let me have a look at you."

Esmeralda rose from her curtsy, pleasantly surprised at the

strength still to be found in the king's voice. The sound was like music to her ears, echoing off the walls and high ceilings.

"It is a pleasure to finally meet you, Your Highness," she said as she approached his bedside.

Damien walked a few paces behind her. The ever-watchful guards stood a discreet distance away, their eyes focused forward. She allowed Adare to take her hand and place a kiss upon it, pleased by the radiance sparkling in his eyes. They reminded her of Damien's, so bright and green and full of life.

"I have seen you from afar and heard much about you," he said, each word seeming to draw upon an excessive amount of his breath. "It is good to finally meet you. Raina Amador used to grace the palace ballroom with her radiance. I am pleased to see that there is much of her in you."

"You remember my mother?"

"How could I forget? She is a remarkable woman, and a wonderful dancer as well. Seeing you perform at my sons' birthday celebration made me feel as if I was watching her."

Damien approached the bed, placing a kiss on his father's hollowed cheek. "You look well tonight, Father."

"That is good to know. I hope to look my best for your brother's wedding." Adare turned to Esmeralda. "You will be in attendance, young lady, will you not?"

"Yes, Your Highness. In fact, Princess Isabelle has asked me to stand up with her, as her maid of honor."

The request had come as something of a surprise, but she had been elated by it. Apparently, being in hiding and enclosed behind palace walls for her protection hadn't allowed the princess to make many friends. Esmeralda was glad to be able to fill that void for her.

"Speaking of weddings," said Damien with a smile. "I have asked Esmeralda to be my wife, and she has agreed. I wish us to be married as soon as possible."

The joy that leapt in Adare's eyes was unmistakable. He smiled and clapped his hands together, issuing a hearty, gleeful chuckle.

"This is wonderful news. I never thought I'd see the day! You know, this young rascal has been avoiding the noose of matrimony for years," he said to Esmeralda with a wink.

"That's enough of that, old man," Damien chided with a laugh. "We don't want to scare her away."

"No," said Adare, suddenly serious. "Your mother will try enough for us all. And I fear Lionus, as well."

"That is why we came to you first. I knew you would be supportive."

Adare nodded. "You've made a splendid match. A love match. That much is obvious from the look in both your eyes. I could ask for nothing better for my son. I only hope that your brothers will find such happiness."

"With all due respect, Your Highness," Esmeralda interjected. "I believe Lionus already has. Princess Isabelle loves him dearly."

"She is very astute," Adare said to Damien. "She has seen what not many others have been able to see between Lionus and Isabelle."

Damien seemed surprised by this, but then he couldn't have noticed the looks Lionus gave his fiancée when he thought no one was looking. Esmeralda had hope that the pair would find happiness in their new marriage.

"We should leave now, and let you rest," Damien said, taking Esmeralda's arm. "I should return Esmeralda home soon."

Adare kissed Esmeralda's hand one last time before allowing Damien to pull her away. "I know the two of you will be happy together. If it means anything to you, you have my most ardent blessing."

"It means everything, Father. Thank you."

Esmeralda let him lead her from his father's chambers. She saw the unmistakable glistening of tears in his eyes, but chose not to comment on them. He'd had an emotional night, and she had done her share of crying as well. But the time for tears was now over. She held tight to his hand, turning to face him as the door to the king's bedchamber closed behind him. She'd been waiting for the right time to invite him somewhere with her, and found now to be perfect.

"So," she said with a wide grin. "Do you want to go to a real party?"

CHAPTER 14

Damien sat beside Esmeralda, sipping a mug of warm, spiced wine, and sharing a blanket with her to ward off the chill of the evening air. They rested near a campfire, shielded from the wind by a circle of colorful Gypsy wagons. The aromas of roasting meat and aromatic spices filled the air. The strumming of guitar and the whistle of flutes could be heard, mingling with boisterous laughter and conversation. All around them, the swish of women's skirts filled the space with vibrant splashes of color, while a jumble of voices speaking with various accents proved as melodic as the music.

Esmeralda had advised him to change clothes before coming to the Gypsy celebration, and Damien was glad that he had followed her advice. He had never been so comfortable at a party before, seated on the ground in his plain trousers and coat, wrapped in a coarse, wool blanket. He'd also never had more fun.

"What are we celebrating?" he'd asked when they had first arrived.

"Life," she said with a laugh, grasping his hand and leading him to the center of the camp. "In this village, we jump at the chance to gather with music, food, and dancing. Many of my friends' relations are passing through—thus the wagons. It is a good opportunity for us all to be together and simply enjoy ourselves."

A strange notion, that. Damien had never before been to a party that was not for the purpose of flaunting one's wealth, or creating a situation for the nobility to see, be seen, or indulge in scandal and gossip.

Small children ran in groups around the fire, squealing and laughing, watched closely by a group of mothers and grandmothers who sat nearby preparing food. Akira and Raina were among them. Desmond sat beside Tristan, strumming lightly on his guitar and sipping the spiced wine.

Damien tried not to notice the venomous looks the other man leveled at him from the other side of the campfire. The orange flames cast a demonic glow over the handsome Gypsy's face, lending it a sinister appearance.

Her family had been overjoyed at the news of their engagement, but Damien had not missed the shock and anger that had registered on Tristan's face in visceral reaction. Esmeralda had been so busy accepting the boisterous hugs and offered congratulations of her family and friends to notice. Damien brushed it off and vowed to enjoy the evening. Esmeralda's happiness was his only concern. Perhaps, now that she was engaged to marry him, Tristan might turn his attention elsewhere.

She smiled up at him, and he pushed her jealous admirer completely out of his mind.

"It's not exactly a palace ball."

Damien returned her smile and kissed the tip of her nose. "No, it's not. It is much better."

Then, he gave her a light squeeze and rested his chin on top of her head, inhaling the sweet scent of jasmine wafting from her hair. He had been walking about in a dreamlike state ever since she'd accepted his offer of marriage. He could hardly believe that she would be his, for the rest of his life.

It would not be easy for them at first, with Lionus and his mother sure to oppose the marriage. But, they would come to accept her eventually, or forget her presence altogether. Besides, they did not have to spend all of their time at Rothchester Hall. Damien had three properties of his own, all fully staffed and secluded. He would be content to pass his time alone with her in one of those places, perhaps even watching her belly grow with his children.

Whatever life brought them, they would face it together, and it was all that mattered. That he would come to love her so deeply had never occurred to him when he'd first decided to pursue her. However, now that he'd come to terms with his feelings, he could not imagine that he'd ever stop loving her.

Suddenly, Tristan and Desmond, along with a man with a flute and another with a small set of drums, struck up a lively tune. A group of young women rushed into the clearing near the fire, their skirts swishing and their hair whipping about their faces as they began to dance. Their smiles were contagious, their laughter ringing out as if in accompaniment to the music as they swayed and dipped in time to the music. The group swelled by the second, with more women, both young and old, joined in the dance. Men made their way in, finding partners and falling into the dance as seamlessly as their women.

Esmeralda grew restless in his lap, moving in time to the music and humming. She seemed drawn to the unmistakable call of the notes, entranced by the slow hum of the sensual melody flowing through the night air.

"Come on, Esmeralda!" called Tatiana, who appeared from the edge of the sea of dancers, holding a hand out to her cousin.

Her dark eyes sparkled with mirth, her cheeks flushed from her exertions.

"Go," Damien encouraged, giving Esmeralda a nudge.

He had not seen her dance since that night he'd come searching for her in the tavern, and found he longed to watch her now. She left him after he assured her he would be just fine on his own, the shawl she'd worn slipping off and falling into his lap. She and Tatiana joined the fringes of the group, remaining in his line of sight as they fell into the rhythm.

His mouth went dry as he watched her move. She smiled and laughed as she danced beside her cousin, arms raised high above her head, her body swaying and dipping in time to the music. She had changed into a simple black skirt that swirled about her legs as she danced, and a ruffled white blouse that bared her shoulders. She had unpinned her hair and allowed it to fall down her back. Gold bracelets and anklets clanked together with every step. Damien's fingers tightened around his mug as he watched, hypnotized by her.

This dance was nothing like the precise, controlled routine he had seen at the palace—what Esmeralda had referred to as *flamenco*, a style her mother had learned during her years living in Spain. This dance was freer, more spontaneous, and far different than any ballroom dance he'd been taught.

Esmeralda was vibrant, bathed by both moonlight and firelight at once, her expression one of genuine joy.

Suddenly, she turned and locked eyes with him. Their gazes held, even as she danced, never ceasing in her movements in perfect time to the melody. Her movements became decidedly more sensual as he watched her, lips parting as if she'd become breathless. Damien had trouble drawing in air himself, his mouth going dry.

He could not resist when she reached her arms out to him in invitation, urging him to her. He dropped their blanket to the ground alongside his empty mug and allowed Esmeralda to pull him into the midst of the twisting, writhing bodies.

This dance was unlike anything he had ever experienced. There seemed to be no clear pattern of steps; one just simply allowed the music to speak and followed its natural rhythm. He held Esmeralda far closer than would be considered decent in a ballroom. But, he was not in a ballroom. He was beneath the open sky, surrounded by a sea of writhing, undulating bodies, the woman he desired more than anything else in the world in his arms.

Heat suffused his entire body, though it was not caused by the fire. It was her, stoking his desire to fever pitch, her body pressed tight against his, her breath tickling the side of her neck as she leaned into him. His hands shook where they rested on her waist, his belly clenching with raw, unfettered need. The way she moved against him … it filled his mind with imaginings better untouched. However, the longer they danced together, Damien becoming more comfortable with the unpredictable rhythm, the harder that became.

Her gaze flicked up to meet his once more, and he noticed that her pupils had expanded, an unmistakable glimmer sparking deep in the amber irises. He was not alone in his thoughts or his desires, as became more and more apparent in the hitch of her breath and the rise and fall of her breasts. He lowered his head toward hers, but stopped just short of kissing her. He fed off the air she supplied, practically quivering from the need to taste her, touch her, strip her bare and lay her down right here, right now.

The music had died away, and they ceased moving, though neither made a move to release the other. They clung to each other, bodies melded together, gazes holding. Damien read the meaning in her gaze with ease, and relief stole over his tense body. She wanted what he wanted—he could see and feel it. Even so, he waited in silence, needing her to confirm with words what her eyes had already given away.

He waited with baited breath for her to tell him what he needed to hear in order to act.

"I am ready to leave," she said, her voice low and thick with the tension clogging the air around them.

"Are you certain?" he asked, knowing he had to allow her the opportunity to withdraw.

She nodded, her stare never wavering from his. She seemed resolute, and it was all Damien needed to know. He grasped her hand and led her to where Persephone was tethered to a tree on the edge of camp. Wordlessly, he swung up into the saddle and pulled her up before him. Arms tight around her, he clutched the reins and steered the beast away from the gathering, heading back in the direction of the palace.

THEY STOOD before the hearth in silence, face to face. Like him, she did not seem to know what to say, though he felt unsaid words of love and longing hanging on the air between them. He was determined to show her all that was in his mind and heart, leaving her without any doubt.

Damien had removed his coat and stood with his shirtsleeves rolled to the elbow, his buttons undone. Her gaze fell to the exposed skin of his chest, and she pressed her hand into the opening, right against his heart. The touch sent a jolt of awareness to him, causing his blood to race and his pulse to flutter at the base of his throat. Resting is hand over hers, he pressed it tighter against his chest and letting her feel the pounding cadence of the organ within.

"See what you do to me?" he murmured.

No woman had ever caused him to feel so undone. He had always gone about lovemaking strategically, assessing every woman carefully and planning his assault upon her body with deliberate skill. Now, he realized that he had never truly made love to any woman. He did not know where to begin, for he wanted all of her and he wanted it all at once.

He decided to start with her mouth, which was open and ready for him as he lowered his head to claim a kiss. He kept his hand over hers against his heart, while wrapping his other arm around her, to draw her in. He was gentle at first, brushing his lips back and forth over hers. Then he eased her mouth open, his tongue gliding over hers so slowly, so achingly, he thought he would die from the thrill of it. She tasted of sweet desserts and spiced wine, the combination so heady he thought he could have spent the entire night simply tasting of her lips.

He nipped at her lower lip, pulling a swift breath, then a low sigh from her. His fingers came up to thread through her hair, and the ardor of his kiss increased. He slanted her head, taking full advantage of the offering of her lips.

She swayed, leaning against him for support as she returned his kisses, urgency seeming to build in her the same way it did in him. They panted in unison, mouths meeting and parting in a perfect, synchronized dance.

His earlier urges rushed over him again—the compulsion to lay her down and claim her. However, he stayed his hand and slowed his movements, understanding that on this night, more than any other, he must take his time with her. Their first joining should be something she never forgot, washing away the pain of her past.

Tearing his mouth away from hers, he put a bit of space between their bodies. His gaze fell to the clothing shielding her from his view.

"I want to see you … all of you."

He flicked open the top button of her blouse with a shaking hand. His touch against her breasts was feather-light as he undid the rest of the buttons slowly, savoring every inch of skin he revealed. He pulled it off over her head and let it drop, then skimmed his hands up her bare arms toward the straps of her plain linen shift. The material felt coarse in comparison to her soft skin.

"When I make you my wife, the only things that will touch your body other than me will be silk and satin," he murmured, lowering his head to press his mouth against her ear.

She shivered, goose bumps rippling over her bared skin as he skimmed his lips down the side of her neck to her shoulder. He placed soft kisses against the supple slope as he took his time pulling the straps of the shift down, peeling the fabric away from her breasts. He left the garment at her waist, studying the perfect teardrops of her breasts and the dark brown nipples capping them. Her hair fell over her shoulders, one thick lock resting decorously against one of the soft swells.

She took his breath away, and she was only halfway undressed, her chest heaving as he drank her in, from the top of her head to where the revelation of her skin ended at the waistband of her skirt.

He wrapped his arms around her and lifted until her feet dangled off the floor and those tempting orbs hovered just within his line of sight.

Esmeralda moaned at the first touch of his tongue against her breast. She arched her back, grasping his shoulders as he gently suckled at first one, then the other. He traced slow circles around her nipple with his tongue, causing her to shudder and quake against him. She melted in his hold, her body going pliant, her limbs heavy. Her head fell back as she submitted to his kisses, letting him taste her throat, her chest, her nipples.

"I love the way you taste," he murmured against her skin, his mouth moving slowly back and forth from one peak to the other. "Never could I have imagined you would be so sweet."

She seemed shocked by his words, but he couldn't stop—wouldn't stop loving her in every way that came to mind. That meant lavishing her with his words as well as his touch and his kiss. By the time he was finished with her, she'd no longer fear the physical. If she had any doubt in his devotion, he would obliterate it from her mind.

Setting her back on her feet, he let his hands fall to her waist. He worked at the fastenings at the back of her skirt, meeting her gaze and holding it. He felt her stiffen, her breath hitching a bit as he began pulling the garment down. He paused for a moment, but she did not protest. She simply went on staring at him, her chin trembling as fear mingled with the lust and need shining in her eyes.

"You can trust me," he assured her, dropping the skirt at her feet before reaching for the string holding up her single petticoat. "You can trust me with all of you, Esmeralda—your heart, your mind, your body…"

She nodded as the final layers of her chemise and petticoat fell away, leaving her nude except for her stockings.

"Yes," she whispered. "I know. Don't stop, Damien."

He wouldn't. He couldn't. Letting his gaze stray below her face, he took her in—the nip of her waist tapering in from the swells of her breasts, the flare of her hips, her long, sinewy legs. The shadow of dark curls between her thighs.

"Beautiful," he whispered, tracing his fingers over the curve of her waist and hip.

She was just as he had imagined her, just as he had seen her in his mind so many times before. Her shoulders sagged a bit, a slow breath releasing from between her lips as if in relief.

"I want to see you, too," she blurted, the words coming out fast as if she hadn't wanted to lose her nerve.

Damien nodded his acquiescence and began pulling his shirttails free of his trousers.

"Let me," she insisted.

She batted his hands away and took over the task herself, her lower lip clenched between her teeth. Her hands trembled, but she steadied them and got the shirt off over his head. Dropping the garment on top of her discarded clothing, she reached up to rest both palms on his chest.

Damien stood as still as possible, his muscles tensing as she explored him, her fingers ticking over the fine blond hairs sprinkling his chest.

"You are beautiful, too," she said, her voice sounding breathless. "So … perfect."

He could hardly think of an appropriate response when her mouth found him, her open mouth skimming his throat, his collarbone, the swell of his chest. She gazed up at him while tentatively flicked her tongue at one of his nipples, mimicking what he'd done to her earlier. His eyes slid closed and he groaned, which seemed to embolden her, because she did it again, then again, before crossing to the opposite one.

His fingers tangled in her hair, holding her to him as she kissed and tasted him, sending little shivers of delight over his skin. They all ended in lightning strikes in his groin, making the organ in his trousers swell even more, his need for her becoming more urgent by the second.

She trailed a fingertip down the center of his abdomen, through the trail of hair leading down into his trousers. Once she reached the placket, she wasted no time unbuttoning them and letting them fall. Then, she knelt and helped him out of his shoes and stockings, all while avoiding looking at the part of him that was hard and aching for her, rising proudly toward his navel.

Once he was completely undressed, she came back to her feet, now unable avoid looking at him. Her gaze dropped to his thickened shaft, lips parting and breath hitching at the sight of him.

He lifted her chin until she looked him in the eye once more. "I will not do anything until you are ready, understand? We have all night."

She nodded, then glanced back down at the rampant erection he wanted to bury deep inside her.

"I am not afraid ... I just ... I don't know what to do."

Her eyes told him otherwise, but he chose not to point that out. If her fear was rooted in ignorance, then that was something he could overcome.

"Fortunately for us both, I know exactly what to do," he told her, before sweeping her up into his arms.

She clung to his neck as he carried her to his bed. He laid her down, then climbed on after her, kneeling near her feet. Taking hold of her ankle, he lifted it and slid his hand up her leg, caressing over her wool stockings. She whimpered, shivering in reaction to his touch, her eyes gleaming like molten gold as she watched his every move. He leaned over her while loosening her garter, then pressed his lips to the top of her thigh. She mewled, her back arching as he kissed his way down her leg while simultaneously dragging her stocking down. Gooseflesh rippled in his wake, her soft sighs urging him on as he kept going until he had her stocking off. Then, he repeated the ritual with her other leg, taking his time and driving her back toward the level of desperate need that could banish what remained of her fear.

He grasped her knees and pulled them apart, causing her to gasp and stiffen a bit. She melted when he laid between her spread legs, pressing soft kisses against her lower belly. Gazing up, he watched her eyes slide closed as he kissed his way down toward her center, his tongue darting out to tease her now and then.

They moaned in unison when his mouth came against her, him from the taste of her womanly flesh upon his tongue, her from the pleasure of it.

"Oh God ... Damien," she whimpered, hips arcing up off the bed as he went on tasting her, lapping at her, delving his tongue into her opening and then tracing up toward that most sensitive part of her.

He held her legs open and feasted on her, closing his eyes and losing himself in her taste, her scent, the feel of her on his lips, so silken and soft. His own need grew and swelled to nearly painful limits, but he was determined to teach her a woman's pleasure, to show her that he wanted give her something as opposed to taking.

It did not take long, her arousal winding her taut like the string of a crossbow. Her fingers clenched the sheets tight as she cried out, shuddering and writhing beneath him as climax washed over her. Damien chased her to the finish, keeping up the ministrations of his mouth and tongue until she'd gone still.

He rose and came up over her, resting his hips in the cradle of her open thighs, his chest coming against hers as he found her lips in a tender kiss. She trembled beneath him, returning his kiss with a desperation born of her need for more.

Cupping her face, he stroked her cheek. She opened her eyes and looked at him, her gaze radiating wonder and awe.

"I ... I've never felt anything like that before," she confessed.

He grinned. "I've only just begun, love."

She smiled back at him, wrapping her arms around him. She seemed more comfortable now, her body limp and open beneath him. She was ready.

"What you just did to me ... is it something I can do to you?"

Her curiosity and ignorance, as well as her eagerness, had him dropping his head, a rough groan falling from his lips.

"Yes," he rasped. "Yes, it is, but ... if you do it to me right now, I cannot promise I will last long enough to get inside you. And Esmeralda ... I need to be inside you."

She shivered again, tightening her arms around him and raising her hips in invitation. "I need that too. Now ... please."

He kissed her again, wanting to be connected to her in every possible way. Taking hold of her hands, he intertwined their fingers, holding fast as he nudged at her tight, wet opening. The heat of her beckoned to him, her slick entrance gripping tight to his tip. He held his breath as he entered her, fighting to maintain control while he pushed into her inch by slow inch.

His breath came out on a tortured groan as he fell all the way into her, her breathy sigh tickling his cheek. She clenched him tight, her body opening to accept him. The urge to move, to create the friction and heat his body craved, slammed into him. But, first, he sought her gaze, wanting to ensure she was still here with him, that she was ready and willing, not retreating behind her fear.

He found only desire and love when he looked at her, as well as a bit of shock—as if she hadn't realized the joining of their bodies could feel so good.

She tightened her hold on his hands, undulating beneath him and urging him silently to move. He gasped at the way that movement sent ripples of pleasure through him, and from there he lost himself in her. His hips moved in a timeless rhythm as he made love to her with slow thoroughness, reaching as deep into her as physically possible.

Releasing her hands, he grasped her legs, urging them around his waist. She complied, the long limbs clenching around him and holding him close. His mouth traveled from her lips, over her chin, down her neck, then back up again. All the while, he moved inside of her, the slow drag of his swollen length against her insides creating the perfect blend of warmth, friction, wetness, and bliss.

"Esmeralda," he murmured against her ear, nuzzling the shell and nibbling on the lobe. "I love you. God ... I love you."

She cried out, her legs tightening around him as the beginning flutters of a climax rippled through her. He felt it around his shaft, urging him on toward his own finish.

He released her hands and she used them to cup his face, bringing his head up so their foreheads touched. She gazed up at him, her breaths swift and uneven.

"I ... love you, too ... Damien."

His name fell from her lips on a sharp moan, and she released, her sheath clenching around him in swift spasms that took his breath away. He followed close behind her, stroking inside her a few more times before he could no longer hold back. He clamped his mouth over hers, moaning against her lips as his body jerked, and his hips surged, his release tearing through him like a hurricane. Shuddering against her, he let go, his seed flooding her in a warm rush, the tension in his middle finally unwinding until he fell limp on top of her.

They lay that way for a long while, limbs intertwined, Damien still lodged inside of her. After he'd found the strength to move, he rolled from on top of her and faced her. He gathered her against him, waiting for his pounding heart to slow, and his breathing to return to normal. She rested in his hold for a long while without speaking, but when she finally turned her face up to look at him, he found her eyes filled with tears.

Swiping at her damp cheek, he frowned. "What's wrong?"

She shook her head, then smiled, making him realize that her tears were not those of sorrow.

"I never imagined," she whispered. "I never knew it could be that way."

"Neither did I," he replied with honesty.

He had set out to teach her about lovemaking, and instead had learned something new himself. Nothing he'd ever experienced had come close to the bliss of being with her. He felt new, reborn, redeemed.

"Thank you," she said. "Thank you for teaching me how it is supposed to be … how it can be with the person you love."

He smiled at her, using his thumb to wipe away her final tear. "I am the one who should thank you for teaching me the very same thing."

CHAPTER 15

The following morning, Esmeralda stood in Princess Isabelle's dressing room, watching as the bride studied herself in a full-length mirror. She looked like an angel in her wedding ensemble, enveloped in white satin and lace, her white-blond hair arranged into an elaborate coiffure of slender braids and spiral curls. Esmeralda helped the princess' maid fasten a sheer veil over her hair and lower it into place until it swept the floor behind her.

"You look stunning," she said. "Lionus will have a difficult time keeping his composure when he sees you."

"That's the idea," Isabelle replied with a giggle, turning to face her. "Oh, thank you so much for standing up with me. I know we haven't been friends for very long, but I feel as if I've known you my whole life. You truly are the best friend I've ever had."

Esmeralda clasped Isabelle's outstretched hands and held them tight. "I feel the same way. I am honored to stand beside you today."

"Who knows?" said Isabelle with another giggle. "Perhaps someday you and Damien will wed, and we will be sisters-in-law."

When she did not respond, Isabelle turned slowly and studied her face. Esmeralda's lips fought a smile, but she felt as if she might burst from trying to contain it. Isabelle gasped, gloved hands coming up over her mouth.

"He didn't!"

"He did," she confessed, her smile widening. "Last night at the masquerade ball, in the garden. I suppose Damien will tell Lionus and the others soon. We went to the king, and he has already given us his blessing."

"Oh, it must have been so romantic," Isabelle said with a sigh. "This is exciting. We are going to be sisters."

The two embraced, and Esmeralda clung to Isabelle, a bit of the former anxiety rearing its head. It proved easy to forget her reservations when in Damien's presence, but seeing the evidence of what it took to plan a royal wedding once again had her questioning her place here, among these people.

"I will need your help, Isabelle," she said as they pulled apart. "I do not know the first thing about being a princess."

"Sure you do," Isabelle countered. "You are kind and gracious—two things already working in your favor. The rest can be learned. Truly, you have nothing to worry about."

She wasn't so certain, but now was not the time dwell on it.

"Oh, I almost forgot," she murmured, opening her reticule and retrieve the item she had stashed there for the bride. "A gift from my grandmother."

She produced a small vial, holding it out to the princess.

Isabelle opened the tiny bottle and sniffed, smiling at the heady fragrance that drifted up. "Perfume?"

"Grandmother made it herself. It's a special blend. She said it was for your wedding night. It is meant to *attract* the groom."

"In that case I'd better put it on right now!" Isabelle said with a laugh, dabbing the sweet smelling oil on her wrists.

"Not too much!" Esmeralda exclaimed. "It is very potent. We wouldn't want Prince Lionus trying to lay you over a table at the reception."

Isabelle lifted an eyebrow before dabbing even more behind her ears. "Then perhaps this will get me to the marriage bed much faster."

The pair doubled over with laughter, and this was the way Queen Alexandra found them when she entered the room. The warmth in the little chamber seemed to evaporate in her presence, the echo of their laughter fading away into silence.

"What on earth could be so funny?" she muttered, her eyes narrowing when her gaze fell on Isabelle.

She'd objected when Isabelle had announced her intention of making Esmeralda her maid-of-honor. Yet, the princess had been unwilling to change her mind and the queen had no choice but to suffer Esmeralda's presence.

"Nothing, Your Highness," said Isabelle, fighting to hide her smile behind her hand.

Esmeralda turned her back to the queen and choked down laughter. She pretended to fix her hair in the mirror, watching their reflections behind her.

Alexandra held a large, polished wooden chest out to Isabelle. "My dear, I came to give you this. It was given to me by Adare's mother on the day that we wed. It has been worn by the Rothchester women for generations, and now it will be yours."

Isabelle lifted the lid of the box, revealing a thin silver circlet encrusted with diamonds resting on a black cushion. She gasped and traced the edges the delicate tiara with her gloved fingers. Alexandra lifted it from its box, and placed it on top of Isabelle's head over the veil. The circlet rested perfectly within the curls of her coiffure, and would sparkle when the candlelight within the church fell upon it.

"Today, you become a part of our family," she said, clasping Isabelle's hand. "We have waited a long time for this day. Soon you will be queen. I could not be prouder."

Despite her words, not an ounce of warmth of affection made itself apparent in her voice, making Esmeralda wonder if she were even capable of portraying true emotion.

"Thank you, Your Highness," Isabelle replied with a gracious smile.

Alexandra patted her hand before turning to Esmeralda.

"As for you," she said, lowering her voice and stepping closer.

Esmeralda turned to meet the frigid gaze of the queen.

"My husband has told me of your so-called *engagement* to my son."

"Yes, Your Highness," Esmeralda said, squaring her shoulders, determined not to let herself be intimidated. "Damien and I love each other very much, and he has asked me to be his wife. Of course, I've said yes."

"You may think to wile your way into the palace by marrying my son, but I promise I will do everything in my power to stop it. You may look the part—" her eyes swept over Esmeralda's pale blue silk gown and elegantly dressed hair with contempt, "—but you and I both know that you are merely a common whore who has attached herself to my son in order to gain money, privilege, and status."

Esmeralda gasped, her face flaming hot as if she'd been slapped. The insult stabbed through her with savage effect, and she nearly doubled over from the ugliness of it. Before she could attempt to muster up a response, Isabelle had swept forward, coming to stand at her side.

"Your Highness," she said, her usually sweet voice cold and hard. "I hope you are aware that once I am queen, I would hold the power to have you banished from Rothchester Hall."

Alexandra placed a hand over her chest and gasped in horror.

"Isabelle! How dare you speak to me this way?"

"I dare as Lionus' bride and the future queen. You would do well to keep yourself in my good graces, for we both know that a queen has great influence with her king. I could convince him that you are no longer needed here and ought to be banished forthwith."

"You wouldn't!"

Isabelle's voice rose and she drew herself up to her full height, which was nowhere near that of the queen's, though that hardly seemed to matter at the moment. The princess proved formidable in her own right.

"I would! You welcome me into your family, and within the same breath tell this lovely girl that she is barred from it? Well, I won't have it! Should I find you acting ungraciously toward Damien's betrothed at any time, I shall do everything in my power to see you gone."

Alexandra remained silent for a long while, her eyes narrowed as she looked from Isabelle to Esmeralda, and back again. Her icy glare was no match for the chilling fury that radiated from Isabelle. She had clearly been beaten.

"My apologies," she murmured so low, they had to strain to hear her. "I shall go and ensure that the carriage is ready to carry you to the church."

Alexandra turned and made her exit, but not before spearing Esmeralda with another hateful scowl. She merely stared back, knowing there was nothing left to be said. She was not foolish enough to believe her troubles with the queen were over, but was glad for a temporary reprieve.

"You should not have done that for me," she said to Isabelle once they were alone. "But I am grateful that you did."

Isabelle grabbed her bouquet and linked her arm through Esmeralda's. "Nonsense," she said, pausing to allow her maids to lift her train. "We princesses have to stick together. Now … to the church! I have a wedding night to get to."

THE WEDDING HAD GONE off without a hitch, the ceremony carried off with all the pomp and opulence expected for the marriage of a Crown Prince and his bride. Damien now watched the newly wedded couple as they danced their first waltz together as man and wife. Lionus had eyes only for Isabelle as he twirled her gracefully about the ballroom. He was elegant in a dove gray tailcoat and black breeches, a brocade waistcoat, and snowy white linen. She was exquisite in her wedding gown and sparkling tiara, an heirloom passed down by the women of the Rothchester family. His brother's stoic expression had softened around the eyes, and Damien could have sworn he saw the beginnings of a smile pulling at the corner of his mouth.

"They look happy," Serge said, appearing beside him with two glasses of champagne, one of which he handed off to Damien.

He nodded, accepting the glass. "Yes, they do."

"I envy him."

Damien turned to glance at his brother. His eyes were lowered to the contents of his glass, his jaw clenched tight. He had not said much, but those three words revealed much more than Serge had meant them to. He experienced a stirring of pity for his brother. He had not realized that his brother's admiration of Isabelle had gone beyond appreciation of her beauty. As he stood watching her dance with Lionus, he looked as if he might be ill—though not from the food or the champagne. Serge was heartsick.

Damien scrambled for the words to comfort his brother. "Someday you will feel the same for a woman."

"That's just the thing," he murmured. "I already do."

Serge left his side, draining his glass as he went.

Damien watched his brother go, hoping someday he would find a way to rid himself of these feelings. They were dangerous and inappropriate, and would only serve to drive him and Lionus even further apart. That was the last thing they needed, considering the deep rift that already existed between the Rothchester brothers.

His thoughts were quickly turned from Serge when Esmeralda appeared at his side. His gaze came to rest on the daring neckline of her gown, heat surging in him as he recalled having his mouth on the plump flesh revealed by her décolletage.

"My love, you have no idea how much I want to whisk you away to my chambers," he whispered, resting a hand at the small of her back and leaning in.

Esmeralda swatted at him with her painted fan playfully, sipping on a glass of champagne.

"Damien, it is still early," she chided. "Besides, it would be rude to abandon the reception when the food has not been served, and the bride and groom have not yet left."

"Very well, then," he replied with a heavy sigh. "I suppose we will be polite this time. But mark my words ... when you and I are married, we will shock many with our rudeness, for I will carry you away to our bed whenever the urge strikes."

Esmeralda flicked her fan before her face, and he felt a shiver run through her. It made him smile, the evidence of her continuing desire for him, the proof that he was not the only one so affected. Everyone else had been captivated by the bride during the ceremony, but he had spent the entire time staring at her, unable to take his mind away from the night they'd spent together, recalling her passionate response to him. He wanted more, and he wanted it now. He wanted to lose himself in her, showing her that their night together proved only the tip of the iceberg when it came to all that they could share.

Nicolai appeared, jarring him from his wandering thoughts and requesting Esmeralda for a dance. Damien urged her to go, needing a few moments to compose himself so he could make it through the rest of the wedding. He would have his time alone with her later.

As he stood watching her dance with his cousin, Lionus crossed the room toward him, purpose in every stride.

"Damien, a word," he said curtly, gesturing toward the open doors leading out to the garden.

He followed, resolute, knowing that only one order of business could be important enough for Lionus to pull him aside at his own wedding reception. He'd hope it would wait until after his brother and sister-in-law had returned from their wedding trip, but true to form, the Lionus had decided that now was the time to have this discussion.

"I have heard about your engagement," he stated once they were alone.

He stared at Damien with tight lips and raised eyebrows, waiting for an explanation.

"Have you called me out here to offer your congratulations?" he asked, inclining his head and returning Lionus' stare.

"I called you out here to talk some sense into you. What can you be thinking, marrying a Gypsy girl?"

A ripple of shock resounded through him as he wondered how Lionus had come to that conclusion. He might have thought he'd realized it just by looking at her, yet knew that many others in the royal court had laid eyes upon her without being any the wiser. He ought to have known his brother would ferret out the truth and use it to argue against their union.

"Did you think I would not find out?" Lionus went on. "I have not revealed her true identity to keep from embarrassing our family, though the knowledge brings me shame."

"Why should her origins shame you?" he challenged, indignation welling within him. "She cannot help where she comes from any more than you or I can. But she is a *person* ... a wonderful person who understands me, who sees me in a way I never even saw myself."

"None of that matters if word gets out," Lionus countered. "I ought to have known it would be you ... that you would be the one to find a way to bring disgrace upon this family."

He balled his hands up into fists. "This has nothing to do with indignity. I am not seeking to destroy or besmirch anything, you idiot. I love her. I do not understand how that is somehow shameful to you. I am marrying her because I love her, nothing more."

"You do not understand because you are so unbelievably selfish," Lionus snapped. "You go out looking for unsuitable women on purpose, so naturally, you have found a common woman to take to wife. It is almost as if you *enjoy* making yourself look the fool, and by proxy, this entire family is made to appear uncouth."

Damien winced as if he had been struck, anger and sadness tangling in his gut in a mixture he could never think to sort. Anger on behalf of Esmeralda, who did not deserve to be spoken of this way. Sadness because no matter what he did, Lionus would always find a way to hate him for it.

"Nothing I've done has ever met with your approval. You lectured me when I gambled, or drank, or kept women you did not approve of. I have stopped doing all of those things, and you would have Esmeralda to thank for that. What difference does it make who her parents are, when she has changed me for the better?"

Lionus grasped his coat in a tight fist, giving Damien a rough shake. "Listen, damn you, I am not going to stand out here on my wedding day and argue with you about this. You have a responsibility to this family—"

He shrugged out of Lionus' hold, pushing his brother away before he was tempted to strike him. "And what responsibility does this family have to me? Love? Acceptance? I have received none of those things, least of all from you."

Lionus shook his head, jaw flexing and clenching as he ground his teeth. "I will not allow you to marry her."

"Until you are king, you can do nothing to stop me. Esmeralda will be my wife well before your coronation."

Lionus snorted and shook his head. "As usual, you spite me."

Damien wrinkled his brow, both baffled and hurt by Lionus' mentality toward the happiness of his own brother.

"I thought you would understand. You love Isabelle, don't you? The fact that she was chosen for you by Mother and Father ... that you had no say in the matter ... does that have any bearing on how you've come to feel about her?"

His brother's nostrils flared as he seemed to wrestle with himself before answering the question. Matters of the heart had never been Lionus' forte.

"Of course I love her," he ground out. "That she and I were betrothed as children hardly matters."

"Then neither does that fact that Esmeralda is not of noble birth."

"It is hardly the same thing," replied Lionus.

"It is exactly the same thing!" Damien railed, threading his fingers through his hair in frustration. "Am I to be denied my happiness because Esmeralda is not of noble blood and Isabelle is?"

Lionus sighed, running his hand through his own hair in the same unconscious gesture shared by Damien. The two were like mirror images just now, yet their minds and hearts could not be farther from one another's.

"I must return now or I will be missed. If you insist upon doing this foolish thing, then you had better do it before I am king. Otherwise, I will do everything in my power to put a stop to it."

LATER THAT EVENING, Esmeralda stood in the doorway to the balcony off Damien's bedchamber, watching him gaze out into the darkness of the early morning. He had seemed distracted during the wedding celebration and had hardly spoken a word since bringing her upstairs to his chambers. He had made love to her with as much passion as he had the night before, scorching her with hot kisses and fiery caresses. She'd fallen asleep immediately after, but had awakened just now to find him gone. It was here she'd found him, the tension still showing in the tight pull of the muscles of his back.

She slipped into his dressing gown, belted it at her waist, and ventured toward him. He wore only his breeches, but seemed not to register the cold. A soft breeze ruffled the hairs at the back of his neck, but the rest of him was hard and unmoving as he stared silently into the distance. She came up behind him and wrapped her arms around his waist, pressing her cheek against his back.

"You should be sleeping," he said, resting a hand over one of hers where it laid against his middle.

"I was sleeping until I found the bed beside me empty."

He turned to take her into his arms. She studied his face, finding it tight and drawn.

Esmeralda frowned. "Something is bothering you."

"Yes."

"Will you tell me what it is?"

He rested his head on top of hers, burying his face in her hair. "I do not wish to trouble you as well."

"It troubles me already, seeing you this way."

He remained silent for a long while, making her worry that he would not speak of it. At last, he sighed, drawing back to look her in the eye.

"Lionus has warned me that when he becomes king, he would stop me from marrying you."

She gasped, holding him tighter as if Lionus' phantom presence had appeared to drag him away from her.

"Can he do that?"

"My father has the right to choose a bride for me," he replied, stroking her hair. "When my brother becomes king, that right will become his. I would be powerless to stop him."

"But, surely Isabelle—"

"Will not be able to persuade him otherwise. When Lionus has made up his mind, he can be quite unyielding."

"Why would he do such a thing?"

Of course, she had a feeling she already knew why. But, she needed to hear it, to hear him say the words that would strike her like a dagger to the heart.

"He chafes at the idea of me marrying a Gypsy dancer. I do not know how he uncovered that information, but he knows and he does not like it."

The pain of his words radiated through her. She had known her heritage would present a problem, but had been unprepared for how it would feel to hear it said aloud. She had never been ashamed of who she was, or where she'd come from, yet knowing Damien could suffer for loving her made her feel physically ill. Would loving one another be enough, or would forces outside either of their control force them apart?

"I refuse to let anyone or anything come between us. My father has already approved the match. Until Lionus is king there is nothing he can do to stop us. Once he returns from his honeymoon trip with Isabelle, they will be crowned king and queen."

"Then we shall simply have to get married before then," she offered.

Damien breathed a sigh of relief, holding her tighter. "You don't know how happy I am to hear you say that, love. We will have to elope as soon as possible. I can make arrangements to have it done in a few days. It will not be the wedding I could have given you, but we'll be together."

Esmeralda placed a finger over his lips and smiled. "Damien, I don't need a lavish wedding. I just want you."

"And I, you," he murmured, his voice a velvet caress against her ear.

He circled her waist with his hands and lifted her onto the stone railing of the balcony. His hands found the sash of the dressing gown and untied it. He pulled the garment from her shoulders, finding her naked underneath.

He sank to his knees before her, lavishing her body with kisses as he went. He parted her legs and pulled her forward to meet his waiting mouth. Esmeralda's eyes slid closed, and she moaned at the first touch of his lips against her. When his tongue flicked out to taste her, she cried out and laced her fingers through his hair. He held her captive with his hands on her hips, devouring her womanly flesh, sending overwhelming jolts of pleasure straight through her.

She trembled in his hands and begged him to take her, but he continued as he was, hurtling her closer and closer to a rapturous ending. When she threw her head back and shattered the silent morning with her climactic cry, he rose to his feet and entered her, bringing her legs around his waist. She wrapped her arms around his neck and kissed him with all the love and devotion contained within her, her hips moving against his and matching his rhythm inside her.

The sun had begun its slow ascent on the horizon as they reached the height of their desire together, his low groans rising up to mingle with her soft sighs of delight on the chill air of the swiftly arriving dawn.

"Lionus has disappointed me. I would have thought he would be more reasonable about this."

Damien sat at his father's bedside. He'd just finished telling Adare of Lionus' plans to prevent his marriage. Adare's outrage was clear as he sat abed, green eyes bright with fury.

"I will not stand for it," he continued. "I am still king, and if necessary I will postpone Lionus' coronation until the deed is done!"

"There is no need for such drastic action, father. We intend to elope as soon as the arrangements have been made."

Adare smiled, grasping Damien's hand. "That's my boy. If only I'd had the courage to do what you are doing. My life would have been drastically different."

Damien frowned. He knew his parents had not been exactly happy in their marriage, but he'd never heard his father express any regrets aloud.

"I once loved a woman more than life itself," Adare continued. "I find that even now, I love her still. I should have carried her away and made her my wife as you plan to do with your beloved. But, I let my duty to the crown come between us and married your mother instead, as my father commanded."

This revelation stunned him, though he realized it shouldn't have. It stood to reason that his father had had a life before meeting his mother, marrying her, and becoming king. Of course he'd had years before then to have loved and lost.

Who was this mysterious woman? What had become of her after Adare had been forced to turn away from her?

"If you could go back and do it all again, would you change it? Would you be with the woman you loved against your father's wishes?"

He found himself hoping his father would say yes, even knowing that without Alexandra, he would never have been born. He also knew that his father would have lived a much happier life.

Adare smiled. "My son, I would change nothing. From your mother, I have been given three beautiful sons to carry on our name and family legacy. That is more than most men receive from an arranged marriage. I can only use my experience to advise you, Damien. I can tell you that you will regret it until your dying day if you do not follow your heart and make Esmeralda your wife. You may marry another, and you may even find contentment in your life. But you would always wonder what your life could have been."

Adare was right, of course. He knew now more than ever that he was making the right decision. It did not matter what Lionus did or said to try to stop him; he would go through with the planned elopement and live the rest of his life in happiness with the woman he loved.

"Thank you, Father. Your words have given me the resolve I need to carry through with my plans. Knowing that you are on my side makes all the difference in the world."

"It is my pleasure to see the man you have become. I only wish Lionus could be more like you."

Damien's brows shot up in surprise. No one had ever described his brother as lacking in any capacity. In fact, he had been told numerous times that he should endeavor to be more like Lionus.

"Surely you don't mean that, Father."

"I do," said Adare. "Lionus is a strong leader. He is unwavering, proud, and sure. He will make a good king, but he could be a *great* king, as I suspect you would be were you in his place."

Damien shook his head. "Father, you are mistaken. Lionus is more fit to be king than anyone. Were the crown left in my hands, I would let it fall to the next in line. Such a thing is not meant for me."

"Do not sell yourself short, my son. Sure, you've committed your share of youthful follies, but so did I. So do most young men still finding their way. But, you are passionate, fiercely loyal, generous, and kind. You lack the arrogance that so defines Lionus' character. I believe you would rule Cardenas fairly, and with a heart for the people. I am not yet certain that your brother understands how to do that. This is why the two of you must learn to abide each other. Once I am gone, he will need someone to remind him that a king's first duties are always to his people."

Damien watched his father in silent awe. He had never imagined that he felt this way. To think that Adare believed him more fit to be king than his own heir. He found the idea preposterous, but kept his thoughts to himself out of respect for the old man. Perhaps illness had muddled his mind. Whatever the case, he would never be king. Lionus was firstborn, and now that he was wed, he would produce his own heir. He did not yet know what his own future would hold, only that Esmeralda would be part of it in some way. Together, they would build their own life and legacy.

"I should go now, Father. You need to rest, and I have to make arrangements."

"Wait. Have you purchased a ring yet?"

"No. That is my first order of business, actually."

Adare tossed the blankets aside and eased his legs over the side of the bed. Damien rose to help the man to his feet, though would rather have assisted him back into the bed.

"Father, where are you going? You shouldn't strain yourself."

Adare dismissed Damien's concern with a wave of his hand and crossed the room, his white sleeping gown billowing around his emaciated frame.

"Nonsense. I'm not going far."

He disappeared into his dressing room, making quite a bit of noise once he was in there. Damien realized he must be opening the safe where many family heirlooms had been stashed. The clicking sound of the vault being opened drifted out into the bedchamber. Adare reappeared a few moments later with a slender wooden box held under one arm. He shuffled back to the bed, huffing and panting with exhaustion but with a wide smile stretched across his face.

"These belonged to my mother," he said, presenting Damien with the box. "I think you will find that they suit your fiancée to perfection."

Damien opened the box to find a ring, earrings, and a necklace cushioned against soft velvet. The yellow topaz stones sparkled up at him, reminding him of Esmeralda's eyes. He could imagine her wearing the gems, perhaps at a ball or dinner party. Her smile would be vibrant and her eyes would sparkle to match the jewels. He imagined undressing her at the end of the night, taking her to bed wearing only the topaz.

He looked up at his father, his chest tight with emotion. "They are perfect. I cannot thank you enough for this."

Adare smiled, allowing Damien to settle him back into the bed and tuck the bedclothes around him. "Give her the ring now, and the rest as a wedding gift. I wish you a lifetime of happiness together."

Damien pressed a kiss to his father's forehead and hugged him tight. "The next time you see me, I will have my wife on my arm."

"I look forward to it."

Damien walked from his father's chambers, lighter than he had been when he'd entered. His steps were jaunty and he even found himself whistling, the box containing Esmeralda's engagement ring and its matching pieces clenched tight in his hand.

CHAPTER 16

The king's chambers were dark and smelled of medicines and herbs. A lit lamp rested on Adare's bedside table, bathing the dying man in a soft yellow glow. It had not been difficult for the masked man to climb the ivy-covered trellis to the balcony where he stood now, watching King Adare fight for his last breath. He'd timed it perfectly, ensuring that the patrolling guards had turned the corner while he clung to the shadows, staying out of sight.

Little did anyone know that the inevitable had been set in motion. That night, when Adare's evening meal had been brought to him, his fate had been sealed. The guards for the night shift were changing places with the afternoon guards just outside the doors. He could be discovered at any moment, but would only remain for a few moments. The time for Adare's death was at hand.

It had been easy to ensure that a lethal poison found its way into the king's food. It was so brilliant, he could hardly believe he had not thought of it before. His first attempts had been clumsily executed failures. Relying upon paid assassins to see the job done had been a mistake. He'd finally taken matters into his own hands, and now he would have the first taste of his sweet revenge.

The man who'd sold him the poison claimed that its effects would take hold within hours. The fatally ill king would not be strong enough to fight it. He stood at the foot of the king's bed, watching him struggle and fight for breath as the toxin worked its way through his body. The physicians had come and gone earlier, declaring him to be no worse off than before. They expected him to live at least another year now that he had given up the duties of ruling a kingdom. How surprised they would be to find him dead in the morning.

Adare trembled, unable to control the shudders that wracked his body. Sweat dampened the bed sheets and dripped from his brow, plastering his thin gray hair to his forehead. He opened his eyes and found the masked man standing at the foot of his bed. Fear flickered briefly in the emerald green depths, along with confusion.

"Am I dreaming?" he asked, his voice barely discernible in the ominous room. "Or are you the angel of death, come to take my soul from this wretched body?"

"You are not dreaming," said the masked man, stepping more fully into the candlelight surrounding the bed. "And I am no angel, but before I leave this room your soul will leave your body, you can be sure."

"You!" Adare spat before powerful coughs racked through his frail body.

He held a handkerchief over his mouth as he coughed and hacked. When he pulled it away it was stained with blood.

"Why have you pursued my death so endlessly? What have you to gain from my demise?"

"I have more to gain than you could ever imagine, though you shall not live to see me take all that will be mine once your sons are dead as well."

Adare coughed and sputtered into his handkerchief, fighting even harder to draw breath into his lungs. "Would you show me the face of my assassin before I die? Or are you too much a coward to reveal who you really are?"

He smiled behind his mask. "Far be it from me to deny a dying man his last wish."

The silver mask was pulled away and Adare gasped, pressing the back of his hand to his mouth.

"No ... it cannot be," he whispered, shaking his head from side to side, tears running down his sallow cheeks. "Why have you done this?"

The masked man stood over him, his face a twisted expression of anger and despair. He grasped Adare by his nightdress, pulling him upward to stare into his eyes.

"You abandoned me. You pawned Mother and I off on the man who raised me, and then you went about your life pretending I did not exist, as if your time with her never even happened!"

"That's not true," Adare sobbed. "I wanted to keep you, but my father was still king and I was powerless to go against his wishes. I loved your mother dearly, and would have made her my wife if I'd had the choice. Alexandra was forced upon me, and she would not raise a child that was not her own."

The masked man was taken back for a moment, shock rippling through him at Adare's words. Had the king truly wanted him all along? He shook his head to clear his mind of such thoughts. The path to his destiny had been set, and he would not be swayed. If Adare had wanted him, he would not have been pawned him off on the man who had raised him—a man who had hated him because he had been sired by another man. He wouldn't have had to watch his mother drown in despair, dying her slow and painful death.

"You are a liar," he roared, giving Adare a shake before dropping him back against his pillows. "You cared nothing for her, though she pined for you every day for the rest of her life. Because of your abandonment, a little piece of her died with each passing day until she was no more than an empty, hollow shell. Even on her deathbed, she called out your name."

Adare squeezed his eyes shut as if to escape what he was hearing. "I did not toss her aside. I arranged a marriage and a comfortable life for her. I wanted you to have the best of everything, even if I could not have been the one to give it to you. I'm sorry if my decision brought you pain. I only wanted to give you as much as I could."

"Crumbs, swept from your table, the same as you would give a dog. And you would have Lionus inherit the throne, when you and that whore you married have known all the time that he is not truly the firstborn son."

"Contrary to your belief, I always loved you," Adare whispered. "I watched you from afar, proud of you always, knowing that you were the child of my heart, the child I'd created with the woman I loved."

The mask back in place, he turned to face Adare one last time, a smile twisting his features as the king's last breath left his body.

Then, he disappeared into the night, his mind already working on his plan of attack against his half-brothers.

DAMIEN SMILED AT ESMERALDA, holding her close by his side as they waited for his carriage to be readied. He could hardly believe his luck. It had taken him only a few hours to make the arrangements for them to elope. Morning had come, and now they stood a short time away from being husband and wife.

Esmeralda was lovely in a white day gown, several layers of petticoats making her skirts flare out from her slender waist. Bright yellow lace adorned the neckline and bodice. Matching ribbon festooned her upswept hair, and the topaz ring glittered on her left ring finger in the brightness of the sun.

Damien cupped her chin and lifted her face upward for a light kiss. "You make a beautiful bride, Esmeralda."

Esmeralda nuzzled his nose affectionately and smiled. "And you make a very handsome bridegroom."

He watched the sun cast its rays over her face, illuminating the golden depths of her eyes. His euphoria was so great that at first he did not hear the devastating cries that intruded upon their private moment. He tore his gaze away from Esmeralda, eyes widening as he noticed Jarvis walking briskly toward them. He was out of breath, and beads of sweat had broken out along his forehead.

"Your Grace," he called out as he came nearer. "Your Grace, you must come at once!"

Damien's heart plummeted into his stomach. His grip on Esmeralda's arm tightened as dread roiled through him. There could be only one reason the usually stoic butler had come searching for Damien himself, and at a near run at that.

He knew the truth before Jarvis had even spoken, the somber expression and turbulent eyes telling him everything he needed to know.

"It's my father, isn't it?" he asked, his voice hoarse.

Jarvis nodded, reaching out to clutch his shoulder. "I know that you are to be married today, but your family needs you."

Damien needed no convincing. He turned to Esmeralda, heart sinking into his stomach.

"I'm sorry, love. It seems our wedding must wait."

Esmeralda nodded her understanding, her eyes filled with unshed tears at the pain he felt certain radiated from his face. "Would you like me to come with you?"

He nodded and grasped her hand, leading her toward the palace.

"Has Lionus been sent for?" he asked Jarvis as they neared the king's chambers.

"Yes, Your Grace, word was sent immediately."

The door to Adare's chambers hung open when they arrived, so they swept right in. Serge, Nicolai, and Alexandra all stood at the foot of the king's bed, looking down upon his lifeless body. Damien's knees buckled, and he held Esmeralda close for support as he walked slowly forward. The king's body had obviously been cleaned and prepared to be viewed. He lay amongst the bedclothes, richly dressed, his face more peaceful in death than it had been during the last few months of his life.

Damien paused, unable to come any closer. Grief welled up at the back of his throat, threatening to cut off his air supply. He breathed deeply and forced it back down. He would not lose control in front of his family. He would weep for his father in private.

"When?" he managed, his voice a strangled sound.

"Maurice found him dead this morning," said Jarvis. "I suppose he passed sometime during the night."

Alexandra sniffled and dabbed at her red eyes with a handkerchief, quiet and composed, her back ramrod straight. Damien wondered at the little display of emotion. He knew there was no love lost between his parents, but more than thirty years had surely created at least affection and respect between the two.

She lowered her head as the tears began anew, her shoulders shaking as she wept.

"Oh, Adare," she cried, burying her face in her handkerchief.

Her sobs wrenched at Damien's heart until he could bear it no longer and reached out to comfort her. At the touch of his hand on her shoulder, she cringed and pulled away as if he'd burned her, her blue eyes filled with venomous.

"Don't," she spat, rearing away from Damien's touch. She turned to Jarvis. "Notify me the moment Lionus arrives."

As she walked away, Damien felt the familiar twinge of pain he had experienced as a boy, when he'd first realized how much closer Lionus was to their mother's heart than him.

Serge stared after her, his face twisted with the same agony Damien felt.

"The selfish bitch," he muttered as she made her exit. He swiped his hand over his tear-filled eyes. "Does she not realize that we all grieve as she grieves?"

Nicolai wrapped one arm around Serge's shoulders.

"You were fortunate enough to have the love of your father," he said in comfort, his own eyes damp and red-rimmed.

"There is something else," Jarvis said, eying them nervously. "I was waiting for Her Majesty to leave before I mentioned it."

"What is it Jarvis?" Damien prodded.

"I do not think His Majesty died naturally," he said, his voice a near whisper. "I believe that our masked man has finally succeeded."

"What could possibly give you that idea?" asked Nicolai, his expression melting into one of incredulity.

"He was fine yesterday. He asked me to wheel his chair through the gardens in the afternoon so that he could enjoy the fine weather. He was happy and strong ... stronger than he has been in weeks. The physicians had come just a few hours earlier and said that he could live another year at best. He was doing well."

Damien recalled having visited yesterday afternoon, finding his father in good spirits. Jarvis' words held the ring of truth, and yet …

"But there seem to be no signs of foul play," he pointed out. "He has not been shot or stabbed, for there is no blood. There are no marks around his neck, so he was not strangled."

"I was not thinking that he was killed violently, Your Grace."

"Poison," Serge gasped. "But that is impossible. All the servants who handled father's meals have been here for years and are loyal. Jarvis, you chose them yourself. They are all trusted. Who would do such a thing?"

"I do not know," said Jarvis with a sigh. "Perhaps I made a mistake in my choosing. I am to blame for His Majesty's death."

"No!" Damien argued, unable to believe what he was hearing. "You have been a loyal friend and a trusted member of this household longer than I can remember. You acted in Father's best interest—we all did. If what you're saying is true, then no one is to blame. It would seem the masked man found a way to reach him, just like you said."

"What other proof is there that Adare was murdered?" asked Nicolai, studying the seemingly peaceful corpse. "He was sick for so long. Perhaps the doctors were mistaken about the amount of time he had left to live."

Jarvis shook his head. "When I found him, there was a significant amount of blood on one of his handkerchiefs. There was some also on his face and his nightclothes. I studied him for wounds, but found none."

"So, you suspect he coughed up the blood last night?" Esmeralda asked. "Was this something that happened often?"

Damien shook his head. "No. That was not one of the symptoms of his illness."

"Something happened," said Serge. "I know it's possible that father merely succumbed to his illness, but all of the signs here point to murder."

"What do we do now?" asked Nicolai. "Surely we are all still in danger."

"We'll wait for Lionus," said Damien. "After all, he is now king."

Esmeralda met his gaze, and he found the same dread in her eyes he knew must emanate from his. He could not voice his worry aloud, but she must share the same thought.

Though Adare had just died and it was selfish to think of anything else but that, sorrow settled deep in his chest as he was forced to consider another matter.

If Lionus was now king, they would never be able to marry.

Lionus drummed his fingers on the surface of his desk, watching the double doors of his library without blinking. Damien, Serge, and Nicolai sat in chairs on either side of him, not showing their restlessness quite as much as Lionus, but feeling it all the same.

The Crown Prince had returned from one of his country estates the day following Adare's death. He had planned to spend a few days there with Isabelle before continuing on their trip, but the news had reached him first. He had ordered Jarvis to bring all of the servants who'd had access to Adare into the study for questioning. He believed, just as the butler had, that the king had been murdered.

Damien studied his brother's profile, unable to decipher any trace of emotion. He stared straight ahead, eyes cold and hard, his mouth drawn down into a frown. Alexandra had been delighted to see her son, of course, and had cried upon his shoulder for a full hour upon his arrival. They had left her with Isabelle to tend to the pressing business of finding their father's murderer.

"There can be only one explanation," Lionus had said before ordering the servants brought before him. "There were only a select few allowed to attend father. One of them has to be the culprit. We must find out who it is before we all find ourselves poisoned."

Damien agreed. He had been too grieved to eat anything, but even if he'd allowed himself to succumb to the hunger gnawing at his insides, he would be too paranoid to put anything in his mouth.

There was a great commotion in the hall before the doors swung open to admit Jarvis. He held fast to the arm of a chambermaid, pulling her alongside him. Two armed sentries escorted him, hands upon the hilts of their swords. The girl fought Jarvis with all her might, but the old butler was surprisingly strong.

"You may as well stop fighting, girl," he snapped. "There is nowhere for you to run."

"Jarvis, what is the meaning of this?" Lionus barked. "Where are the other servants?"

"Your Highness."

Lionus winced at the new form of address but did not interrupt the butler. He waved a hand for Jarvis to continue after he'd executed a swift bow.

"This woman almost boarded a ship headed for God-knows-where. She was in quite a hurry and was carrying a rather large sum of money upon her person."

"Lillian?" Damien gasped, recognizing the blonde maid he had once flirted with.

He had hardly thought of her again since meeting Esmeralda. She'd served at Rothchester Hall since she'd been a young kitchen scullion, having worked her way up to the status of chambermaid.

"I suspect her as being our culprit, and found it unnecessary to involve the other servants," Jarvis continued. "Doris says she was the one tasked with bringing your father his evening meal."

Lionus' eyes narrowed on the trembling girl. Her dress had been torn at the shoulder and her face was streaked with tears. Her hair hung in a tangled mess around her face. It would seem she'd put up quite a fight to keep from being brought back to the palace.

Jarvis released her arm and she fell to her knees before them, her head lowered and eyes downcast.

"What have you to say in your defense?" Lionus asked, his voice deceptively calm.

Damien heard how it wavered with barely contained fury as they looked upon the woman who had taken money to assassinate their father. For his part, he felt surprisingly numb, more shocked by the revelation than anything else. He supposed anger would set in at some point, but he was still grappling with what had happened and what it all meant.

"Speak, girl!" Jarvis commanded, looking as if he would like to strike her. Adare had not just been his master; he had also been a close and faithful friend. He appeared even angrier than Lionus, and Damien wondered if he were not also feeling a bit guilty as he'd hand-chosen this maid to service the king.

Lillian lifted her wide blue eyes, which brimmed with tears. "Please ... I will tell you everything you want to know if you would promise to spare me long enough for me to give birth to my unborn child!"

For the first time, Damien noticed that the girl had begun growing heavy with child. She clutched the slight swell of her belly protectively as she gazed upon each of them, eyes darting as if she sought an ally.

"If you have done what you stand accused of, then you have no right to ask promises of me," Lionus ground out, his teeth clenched so hard Damien was surprised they didn't shatter.

"I would have your word," she cried, clutching her stomach tighter. "I merely want to give my babe a chance to live. My parents would take her and then you may punish me as you please."

Lionus rose and circled the desk swiftly, grasping a fistful of the girl's hair. He yanked roughly, pulling Lillian to her feet. She screamed, trying to twist out of his hold.

"Do you think your sniveling will save you?" he growled.

"Lionus, the woman is pregnant," Serge interjected.

Lionus silenced him with a wave of his hand. "Do not think to intercede on this murderer's behalf, brother. She does not deserve your sympathy." He turned back to Lillian, pulling her head back to stare her fully in the face. "If I were you, I would think carefully about this. Your choices are limited. You can die quickly, or you can die a slow and agonizing death. Either way, you will face the penalty for treason and murder."

She began sobbing in earnest now, babbling incoherent words as she clutched the front of Lionus' coat. Lionus shook her like a rag doll, the frayed threads of his control snapping completely. His raised voice mingled with hers, unintelligible. From them, Damien gathered that he would throttle the maid if she didn't start talking.

Having had enough—and not trusting Lionus to keep from hurting the woman—Damien leapt to his feet, rushing to get between them.

"That's enough, damn it!"

Taking hold of Lionus' shoulder, he pried the maid from his hold before giving him a rough shove. Lillian fell in a crying heap on the ground, while Lionus stumbled back, his face reddened and his hair mussed as he glared at Damien. Serge had stood, and came to insert himself between them as well, making it to where Lionus would have to get through them both to get to the maid.

"Pull yourself together," he hissed, before turning back to Lillian.

He knelt to help her to her feet, keeping a tight hold on her arm lest she thought to try to fight him. He wouldn't hurt her, but he would have the truth.

"Listen carefully. I am going to ask you a question, and I want an honest answer. If you do not tell me what I want to hear, I will hand you back over to my brother. Do you understand?"

She nodded, but did not speak. Her gaze kept shifting to Lionus, as if she feared he might lose control again and attack her. He seethed in the corner, staring daggers at her. Ignoring him, Damien pinned her with his stare and asked his question.

"Did you kill my father?"

He could see her defenses crumbling, her facade cracking until she collapsed against him, sobbing and shaking.

"Yes! Yes, but I didn't want to ... *He* came to me and told me he would take my child once it was born if I didn't do what he wished. He said if I tried to run away, he would kill me. I had to think of my child ... I had no choice ..."

"He, who?" Serge blurted, crossing the room toward them. "The masked man?"

She nodded, struggling to catch her breath between sobs. "I told him I would never do such a thing. The king had always been gracious and kind to me. Any other master would have let me go once I became pregnant, but not him. I loved him ... I loved him as much as the other staff here. But, everyone knows that the masked man will find you no matter where you go. I had to protect my baby, I had no choice!"

"You could have come to us," Nicolai stated, his voice sharp like the edge of a knife as he glowered at Lillian. "You have served me in my chambers since I arrived. You've had numerous opportunities to come forward with the truth."

"I wanted to ... believe, me I did," she argued. "But I was afraid that he was watching me ... that he would know if I told you. So I took the poison he gave me and poured it in His Majesty's wine goblet. He told me it would be a quick death, and that the king would not suffer."

Lionus pushed Damien aside and stood almost nose to nose with the cowering maid, though he managed to keep his hands off her. "So you chose instead to make my family suffer by killing my father."

"I'm sorry," she wailed, exploding into another bout of forceful sobs. She fell to her knees again, bowing low at Lionus' feet. "I beg of you to allow my child to live. I don't care about my own life anymore, but please don't allow my child to die!"

"Damn the child!" Lionus roared, rage contorting his features. "You will hang by morning, so help me God!"

"No!" interjected Damien. "I won't let you do that."

Lionus quirked a brow at him and laughed, the sound harsh and ugly. He seemed half-mad with grief, anger and sorrow a turbulent combination.

"You think to stop me?"

"I do," Damien replied, standing his ground. "Father would not want this. He would not allow you to murder an innocent child, no matter what the mother has done. Do not forget who the real enemy is, Lionus. Save your fury and your savagery for him!"

"He is right," Serge agreed. "Allow her to live long enough to birth to the child and then give it to her parents. She can spend the next several months reflecting on what she has done before facing the gallows. That's as good a punishment as any, I'd say."

Lionus looked from one brother to the other in disbelief. Then, he turned to Nicolai. "I take it you are in agreement as well."

Nicolai shrugged, seeming less adamant than Damien or Serge, but still reasonable. "It does seem awfully cruel to allow the child to die with the mother. I would not advise it. You may frighten and anger some of your citizens. That is not the way to begin your reign."

Lionus sighed, deflated, but still a far cry from his usual self. He turned to the palace sentries, who had stepped forward with a pair of shackles to take her into custody.

"See her to the gaol and relate my orders. She is to be held until such time as she has given birth to her babe, at which point her parents will be sent for to take custody of the child. Then, her execution is to be scheduled immediately after."

As the sentries began to shackle her, Lionus turned his attention back to Lillian, upper lip curling into a sneer as he stared down at her.

"Should you start to die during childbirth, I will command the midwives to do everything within their power to save your miserable life. You *will* hang for what you've done."

Lillian did not seem as afraid now, simply nodding her head and accepting her fate as the sentries guided her from the room.

Once the door had closed behind them, Lionus paced toward the hearth, hands clasped tight behind his back.

"I am ordering a complete evacuation of Rothchester Hall," he murmured, voice low and raspy. "Until the masked man is found, it is not safe for us to remain. I will do what should have been done from the start—we will retire to one of our country estates until the villain is brought to heel. The location will be disclosed to no one. Once father is buried we will leave under armed escort."

"Lionus, none of this is your fault," Nicolai offered. "The man was determined to see Adare dead."

Lionus did not respond, head bowed as he stared into the fire. Damien exchanged glances with his cousin, who shrugged as if to indicate he had tried. They all knew Lionus well enough to understand that he would hear nothing resembling comfort right now. He would not feel better until his orders were carried out and he felt they were all safe.

Serge backed away toward the door. "I'll inform Mother."

He made his exit, with Nicolai upon his heels.

"And I will send a message to my father, informing him that he should remain at our country home where it is safe," he added. "He had planned to attend the coronation, but … well, all things considered …"

Then, he was gone too, closing the door and leaving Damien alone with his brother.

He approached the hearth, his gaze fastened on Lionus' back. What he needed to say might sound trivial, but he could not rest until he'd made certain that his brother wouldn't try to destroy the one joy he had left. With Adare gone, he needed to know that Esmeralda would still be his.

"Lionus, I will bring Esmeralda with me. We will be married."

His brother turned, piercing him with a glacial stare. "I have told you I will not allow it."

"We were going to get married yesterday," Damien argued. "We never got the chance."

"I am relieved," Lionus snapped, stepping away from the mantle and toward Damien. "That only means that I am now in a position to stop it from happening."

He could hardly believe his ears. Lionus was still determined as ever. Even in the midst of their grief, even knowing it would tear him apart to lose the woman he loved as well as his father, Lionus would still prohibit him from getting married.

Damien nodded decisively, arriving to the decision he had mulled over earlier. It had seemed daunting at first, but now he realized it was something that must be done if he and Esmeralda stood any chance of being together.

"Then I won't be leaving Rothchester Hall with you."

Lionus scowled. "Are you mad? You will not disobey my orders in this! We are all leaving together and that is the end of it. When this has blown over, we will return and I will arrange a suitable marriage for you."

"I did not say I wouldn't be leaving Rothchester Hall," Damien replied. "I merely said I wouldn't be leaving with you."

"What *are* you saying?"

"I am saying that I'll take Esmeralda as far away as I must to escape your reach. I will marry her, with or without your approval. If I must live someplace else in order to do that, then so be it."

"You would abandon your family, your country?" Lionus asked, looking as if he'd been punched in the gut. "You would leave Mother and Serge just after Father has died, with no care to their feelings in the matter?"

Damien scoffed at that. His mother would hardly care what he did, and Serge would understand that he'd done what he thought was right. He would praise Damien for fighting to keep what was his.

"I will abandon things that do not matter—such as titles and bloodlines and your expectations—for the one thing that does," he retorted.

If at all possible, Lionus' countenance hardened even more. He turned his back to Damien once more, dismissing him with a wave of one hand, as if he shooed away a bothersome fly.

"Very well," he said, his voice once again sharp and even. "Do what you wish. I do not care."

"That has always been plainly obvious," Damien said to the back of Lionus' head. "Tell me, brother, have you shed even one tear for our father? Have you asked Serge how he is faring in the face of this loss? Have you given any thought to how badly I need Esmeralda right now—how badly we all need each other? Or is this all about you, your lust for power, and your need to constantly be in control of the people around you?"

He did not wait for a response before quitting the room. He faltered in the corridor, leaning back against the study door and closing his eyes.

He had just pledged to leave his family, abandoning the only home he had ever known, but knew in his heart that he had done the right thing. His father had told him to not let go of love and he would not. He would build a new home and a new life with Esmeralda away from the pressures of court life and the tyrannical rule of his brother.

As he turned to walk away, he heard a strange sound. He glanced up and down the darkened passage, trying to discover its source. When he opened the door to the study to peek inside, he discovered that it was Lionus.

His brother still stood before the fireplace, one hand resting upon the mantle. The other hand was pressed against his face. Gut-wrenching cries racked his body, shaking his shoulders with the force of grief. Damien wavered in his resolve, wondering if he ought to go back inside, and once more try to comfort his brother and reason with him.

But, even as Lionus' sobs tore through him like the sharpest of swords, Damien hardened his resolve. Like his mother, his brother had proved time and time again that he despised weakness in himself as well as those around him. He wouldn't want to be seen weeping, nor would he accept Damien's comfort. And in the end, he would hold true to his decision concerning Esmeralda.

As far as Damien was concerned, there was nothing left to be said between them.

Just before he closed the door, Lionus dropped to his knees, head lowered as he went on weeping. His guttural sobs followed Damien down the dark corridor.

CHAPTER 17

*E*smeralda had been unable to sleep. She had not seen Damien since the day of Adare's death. She longed to see him, to offer him whatever comfort she could, to tell him that she understood what it was to lose a father. Yet, she knew that the business of ferreting out the king's murderer, as well as the resulting fallout, would consume his focus. Which meant the matter of their marriage, and whether or not Lionus would allow it, must wait.

She left her bed and paced the length of her room. What could be done if the Crown Prince—no, she must think of him as the king now—held firm on his decision to prevent them from marrying? Would Damien defy him in order to go through with their plans? Would she let him? The last thing she wanted was to come between two brothers.

She paused to open the window and allow in the crisp breeze, then continued pacing.

As she tread the floorboards, she fiddled with the ring Damien had slipped onto her finger only a few days past. It might as well have been a year ago, so uncertain was her future with him. All she could do was hope he discovered a way. In that, she could trust him.

"Esmeralda!"

She glanced about the room, certain she was alone, but also sure she had heard someone whisper her name.

"Esmeralda!"

It was unmistakable this time; someone was definitely whispering her name. She rushed to the window, craning her neck and listening for the sound again.

"Down here!"

She glanced down to find Damien standing beneath her window, poised to climb the uneven brick. This late in the night he likely hadn't wanted to wake the entire household. By the time she fixed her lips to offer to come down and let him in, he was already halfway up the wall.

"Damien, be careful!"

When he was close enough, she offered her hand and helped ease him up over the windowsill.

He fell into her arms, trembling and sniffling as if he could no longer contain the storm of emotions within. She nearly buckled under his weight, but held fast, determined to lend him her strength in his time of weakness.

"I know I should not have come so late, but I needed to see you," he whispered, his face pressed against her neck, soaking the neckline of her nightgown with his tears. "I had to hold you."

Esmeralda pulled back slightly to study his face. He sported dark circles under his eyes, as well as a day or more worth of stubble on his jaw.

"You look exhausted."

"I haven't slept," he said. "I haven't slept in almost two days."

She stroked his hair, allowing him to rest his head against her breast.

"You will lie in bed with me until you fall asleep. I won't take no for an answer."

"I would ask something of you first," he said, taking her hands in his.

"Anything," she responded, her heart in her throat.

He guided her to sit on the bed, then lowered himself to one knee before her.

Would he now tell her they could not marry? Her stomach clenched and her chest ached at the thought. However, she must accept whatever came now. Any decision he had reached must have been a difficult one... she would not make it harder on him.

"If I asked you to come away with me, to leave Cardenas and start a new life someplace else, would you do it?"

Esmeralda was too stunned to respond immediately. She stared at him in shock for several seconds, unsure of what she had just heard. It certainly was not what she had been expecting.

"You would leave your home?" she asked in disbelief. "You want me to leave my family?"

"My brother will not allow this marriage to happen," he said, tightening his hold on her hands. "If you'll agree, I can arrange passage to anywhere else in the world. We can start over, Esmeralda, begin our own family. Your mother could come—hell, your entire family could if they wanted. It would be perfect."

"Where would we go?"

"I haven't puzzled that out yet... but the possibilities are endless. Europe, perhaps. Someplace we can begin again, where we can be together and happy."

"Would we ever come back?"

Damien shook his head, his expression somber. "I doubt it very much, love. Once we leave, we would have no reason to come back."

"Of course we would. What about Serge and Isabelle and Nicolai? What about Lionus and your mother?"

"To hell with both of them! They would only seek to come between us and I won't have it! I only want you."

Esmeralda considered this carefully. She knew that her mother would never leave Desmond, so unless he wished to come along, the two of them would remain in Cardenas. She would probably never see her grandmother, Tatiana, Morgana, or Tristan ever again. She would be leaving behind her closest friends and part of her family.

She would abandon the only home she'd ever known, and The Golden Dancer, which her father had left in her hands.

"I know I am asking a lot of you," he said. "But my father told me I should do whatever it took to ensure our future together. He told me that if I didn't, I would regret it, and he was right. I will travel to the ends of the earth if it means we could be together."

Esmeralda smiled, stroking his face with an affectionate hand. He was right, of course. She would leave Cardenas behind, and be happy with the man she loved. Her family would not begrudge her that—in fact, they would encourage it. As he'd said, they would make their own family. Her heart warmed as she thought of growing round with Damien's children and watching them grow up. It would be a dream come true, no matter where they chose to live.

"All right," she relented. "I'll go with you."

Damien lifted her in his arms and twirled her about the room, kissing all over her face. She laughed with him, delighted at the thought of a new life, one that had endless possibilities.

"I will not be a prince where we're going," he warned.

"You'll always be a prince to me."

"We will have money," he added. "It will be enough for a comfortable life for us and for any of your family who wish to come along."

"Will you not miss Cardenas? It is your home, after all."

He shook his head, taking her face in his hands. His lips hovered inches from hers.

"How could I be sad to leave a place that is only soil and stone? Where you are is where my home is."

He claimed her lips, the kiss desperate and searching, taking her breath away.

"This is home," he murmured against her mouth, running his hands over her body.

Trembling in his arms, she met his ardor with her own avid desire. He ran his fingers through her hair, caressing the softly curling tendrils as he made love to her mouth with his. She felt the cool night air against her skin as her nightgown slid to the floor. He carried her to the bed, coming over her as soon as he was unclothed. She welcomed him eagerly, opening her body to him as well as her heart. Their loving was joyous, a celebration of their life to come, an uninhibited expression of their love. When it was over, they clung to one another, sated, happy, hopeful.

Damien slept peacefully that night, his curly head resting on Esmeralda's shoulder.

THE MORNING of Adare's funeral brought the first snow of winter. Damien stood between Esmeralda and Serge beside his father's freshly dug grave, warmly bundled against the cold. Usually, the king's body would be prepared and placed in the massive cathedral at the heart of the city for one week, to allow the inhabitants of Cardenas a final look at their sovereign. However, the circumstances surrounding Adare's death had forced them make his funeral a private affair, including only family and close friends.

As the last of the dirt was packed over Adare's grave, they remained while the priest spoke his final words.

Then, one by one, they drifted away toward the warmth of the palace. Lionus and Alexandra first, Serge and Nicolai second, Jarvis and Hopkins third. Finally, Esmeralda turned to walk inside, her arm linked through Isabelle's. Damien waited until he was completely alone and approached his father's headstone. Resting against the cold monument lay a bundle of the freshly cut black orchids from the conservatory. They were another of his hybrids, the insides of the petals stained with a vibrant pink. Speckles of powdery snow clung to their edges.

He shoved his hands into the pockets of his greatcoat and stood in silence for several minutes.

"Father, tomorrow, we are all to leave Rothchester Hall," he murmured. "Mother, Lionus, and Serge will return, but I fear I may never set foot on these grounds again. I am doing what I promised you, and following my heart. I have already made arrangements to take Esmeralda to Europe. I can remember your stories of visiting the place—its art and culture, the food and museums. It sounds like a wonderful place to make a fresh start. We plan to travel a bit before deciding upon a permanent place to live—a honeymoon trip of sorts, I suppose."

He paused for a moment to choke back the tears that threatened to weaken him. Saying good-bye to his father proved the most difficult part of this entire ordeal. He'd wept off and on for days, wallowing in his grief over not just Adare's death but the rift between himself and his brother. It only made this entire thing all the more painful.

"I am sure Lionus will get along just fine without me. It seems there are many things we cannot see eye to eye on, and I think it is best that I'm leaving."

He knelt before the headstone, reaching out with his gloved hand to touch it. The stone was cold and hard, and he wished that some part of his father's spirit would impart upon it, so that he could feel it for himself one last time. The stone was, of course, unresponsive.

Damien sighed, rising to his feet. "Esmeralda and I will depart in a few days, and I just wanted to say goodbye. Thank you for everything you've taught me, for being patient with me when everyone else was determined to see me as a failure. I love you."

He turned and walked back toward the palace, taking a few deep inhales to calm his roiling emotions. The cold, crisp air was cleansing and he took it deep into his lungs, marveling at how renewed it made him feel. He felt a little less anxious about his new start, perhaps more ready than ever now that Adare had been buried.

He found Nicolai standing in the circular courtyard in front of the palace, watching as his luggage was loaded onto a coach.

"Leaving already?" Damien asked, watching the liveried footmen as they carefully lifted Nicolai's heavy trunks.

"I'm going home for a day or two to look in on Father," Nicolai replied. "Someone's got to make sure the old man doesn't drown at the bottom of that liquor bottle he's been wallowing in since … well for as long as I can remember. The masked man won't have to kill him when the brandy is driving him into the grave at an astonishing rate. Anyway, we'll join Lionus and the others by the end of the week."

Damien clapped him on the shoulder and smiled. "Have a pleasant journey."

Nicolai turned to him, his features alight with curiosity. "So, you're really going to the Continent? At first I thought it was a threat … you know to get Lionus to agree to your marriage. But you really are going through with it."

"I am. I won't allow Lionus to dictate the course of my life. I want Esmeralda for my wife, and a life of my own choosing."

Nicolai nodded. "I understand. I just hope you do not come to regret this."

"Never," Damien declared.

"Well then, I suppose now is the time for good-bye." He extended his hand to Damien. They shook hands first, then embraced. "Good luck with your new life. I wish you all the happiness in the world."

"And good luck to you, Nicolai. I hope Lionus does not try to arrange a marriage for you."

The two traded amused glances before bursting out laughing together.

Nicolai sobered quickly, giving Damien a thoughtful look. "I wonder…"

"What?"

"If, by some inexplicable twist of fate, the crown were to fall to you, would you come home to claim it?"

Taken aback by the question, Damien wrinkled his brow and frowned, mulling it over. It was something he didn't like dwelling on, because his ascension to the throne would mean the deaths of both his brothers and any heirs Lionus and Isabelle might produce. Even if he did covet the crown, he didn't think he'd be willing to pay such a price to gain it.

"No," he replied with a shake of his head. "I once told Father that such a thing is not for me. If, God forbid, the crown should ever come to me, I would let it pass down the line. Naturally, your father being next in succession, it would eventually make its way to you."

Nicolai chuckled and turned toward his carriage. "Of course, these things hardly ever happen. With our luck, Lionus will live to be one hundred and fifty! And thank God for it ... I do not believe I'm cut out to rule, and quite like my life of debauchery and drunkenness."

Damien laughed, realizing that his cousin sounded much like he might have before finding Esmeralda had changed him. "I will miss you, Nicolai."

"And I will miss you. But we all have to make our own fortunes, don't we?"

"Truer words were never spoken."

Damien stood in the courtyard and watched as Nicolai's carriage disappeared against the horizon, then he turned to go back inside. He had much to accomplish if he and Esmeralda were to leave by the end of the week.

WHEN TRISTAN CAME EXPLODING through the door of her office at The Golden Dancer, Esmeralda knew why he had come. She'd been expecting him, in fact, and was not the least bit surprised by his anger. He had heard that she was leaving, perhaps for good. She sat at her scratched, worn desk poring over ledgers as he stormed in, slamming the door behind him.

"What is this I hear about you leaving for the Continent?"

Setting her quill aside and stoppering her inkwell, she folded her hands upon the desk and glanced up to meet his gaze. She had hoped to have a civilized conversation with him about this, but it seemed that was highly unlikely. He was furious, his face reddening, his eyes wide and wild. His hand shook as he ran his fingers through his hair.

"I'll be leaving at the end of the week," she replied. "I'm leaving The Golden Dancer to you and Dominic until Desmond is old enough and ready to take it over. With Tatiana and Morgana here, I have no doubt you can keep the place running. If it turns out that Desmond does not want the place, then I hope you and Dominic will continue running it together."

"I don't give a damn about The Golden Dancer," he muttered, coming around her desk to stand before her. He grasped her by her shoulders and forced her to look up at him. "I care about *you*. This is madness, what you're doing, running away to marry this man. What would your father think of this?"

"My father would want me to be happy," Esmeralda snapped, weary of Tristan's interference. Despite the fact that she did not return his amorous feelings, they had always been such good friends. Only recently had this rift grown between them, caused by his jealousy.

"I know that you feel the need to protect me, but I don't need that anymore. Damien will be my husband, and my protector. What I need from you is your assurance that you will keep The Golden Dancer open for Desmond's sake ... at least until he comes of age. It is his birthright and I'd hate to see it go to waste."

Tristan stared at her silently for a moment, a muscle in his jaw working as he clenched and unclenched his teeth. His hands curled into fists at his sides until his knuckles grew white, and he fairly trembled with the force of his anger.

He spoke finally, his voice ominously low. "I had always believed that you would come to love me. I hoped and wished for it like a fool. All this time you've kept me waiting, and now you expect me to just let you leave? You think I will just stand by and let you get on a ship and sail half a world away?"

Esmeralda took a deep breath and fought for patience. She understood that this was difficult for him, and perhaps she ought to have been clearer about her feelings from the beginning. Maybe she had done or said something to make him believe the things he was saying. But, she needed him to accept her decision. If it ruined their friendship, so be it. Damien was her choice.

"Tristan, you have no say in this. This is my decision. You can either support me by taking over The Golden Dancer, or I will find someone else to do it."

"You ask much of me, yet you are willing to give me nothing in return," he said, his voice a low growl as reached out and pulled her roughly against him.

"Tristan, don't," she cried, pushing against his unyielding chest. "What about Morgana? I thought that you cared about her."

Tristan scoffed. "Your cousin is a nice enough woman, and I've enjoyed her company, but I would turn my back on her in a moment if it meant I could have you."

Esmeralda shook her head as Tristan's face inched closer to hers. His lips found hers and crushed them in a bruising kiss. She twisted in his hold as his arms came around her, holding her captive against him. There was no need to fear that he would hurt her—even as he forced his kiss on her, Esmeralda remained aware of this. Still, she would not allow him to get away with it.

When he released her, her arm lashed out and her palm connected with his cheek. The sound of her hand against his face resounded through the small office like a gunshot.

Tristan was first shocked, then immediately repentant.

"Forgive me," he said, pressing his hand against his reddened cheek. "It's just that I have loved you since I was a boy, and have often wondered what that would feel like. I ... I am not taking the news of your leaving well, as you can see. But, I know you. When you have made your mind up about something, you do not change it."

"Then you will you do what I've asked?"

He nodded with a heavy sigh. "You know I would do anything you ask of me."

"Then I would ask for one other thing."

"Anything, Esmeralda."

"Have a care for my cousin's heart. She is young and naive. I would hate to see her hurt."

Tristan nodded, and turned to leave. Esmeralda sat back behind her desk, lowering her head over her ledgers once more.

The entire encounter with Tristan had put a bitter taste in her mouth. She hated hurting anyone, but needed him to relinquish his infatuation with her and move forward with his life.

"Goodbye, my friend," she whispered to the closed door of her office. "I hope you find your happiness someday."

CHAPTER 18

The convoy of vehicles bearing the royal crest loomed only a few yards away. The newly crowned king and his queen rode in one carriage, the Queen Mother and her son in the other. The masked man watched from his position amongst the trees.

His hired men lurked in their strategically chosen places, waiting for his signal. The mercenaries had been easy enough to sway to his side, his own wealth enough to ensure their loyalty. They were a nasty lot, but would get the job done. Bastards, poor men, desperate men ... all of them with no stake in this other than the coin they were being offered to ensure he stood over the broken and bloodied bodies of the royal family.

He tasted victory, but would not allow himself to rejoice just yet. The success of his plan would depend entirely upon timing. The royal caravan would be heavily guarded, but he was confident that he had brought enough men to bring the royal guard under submission. He sat in the saddle of his horse on the side of the road, partially concealed by the cover of the approaching night and shadows of the trees.

When they were merely a few yards away, he lifted his pistol into the air and fired a single shot. This threw the king's horses into a panic. It also communicated to his men that it was time to act. They came from their places of hiding with weapons drawn, surrounding the convoy as the drivers fought to regain control of the frightened horses.

"Stand down!" shouted the captain of the guard, unsheathing his sword. His men followed suit. "By the authority of King Lionus, I order you to remove yourselves from our path or be cut down!"

He smiled behind his mask, pulling his own sword from its sheath, relishing the fight to come. "I do not follow the orders of your king. Tell your men to step aside and let the mighty Lionus fight his own battles. There is no need for your men to die."

Even as Serge and Lionus stepped from their separate carriages, swords at the ready, the armed guards formed a protective circle around them, blocking the king and prince from harm.

"So be it," said the masked man, signaling his men to attack.

THE SOUND of metal against metal shattered the silence of the night, the grunts and groans of fighting men echoed among the trees. Lionus fought his way through the aggressive band of men, who all wore dark, coarse wool over the lower halves of their faces. Their eyes were visible, filled with a malice that he did not understand. Who were they and what loyalty did they have to this masked man that caused them to commit treason and ambush their king and his family?

There was no time to puzzle that out now. His life and those of his brother, mother, and wife were in danger. He focused all his attention and energy into the fight, battling off the men in black who had managed to get past the royal guard. He swung his sword—the Sword of the Kings that had been passed down to him by Adare—cutting down one, then another.

When Lionus lifted his head, turning away from their corpses, he found his enemy awaiting him. His mocking laughter rang out, both eerie and enraging as it echoed through the trees from behind the silver mask he wore. The thing was twisted into the expression of a jester, the gaping holes for the eyes and mouth taunting him.

"Hail, King Lionus!" he bellowed with a chuckle, dipping into a sweeping bow.

Lionus stepped forward, steeling himself to face the man who had murdered his father. Aside from protecting his wife and mother, he would avenge Adare by sinking his sword into the assassin's black heart.

"Tell your men to stand down or I will run you through," he commanded, searching the soulless black eyes of the silver mask.

Lionus charged when the man did not respond, his sword raised in a two-handed grip. The masked man was ready for him, bringing his blade up to parry Lionus' downswing. They backed off and circled each other, and as he watched the masked man, taking in his stance and grace, he realized his opponent was no stranger to the art of swordplay. The man held the weapon as if he'd been born that way, wielding it with deadly precision. Lionus fought calmly, too disciplined to allow his white-hot anger to affect his concentration.

He soon had his opponent backed away from the battle that ensued behind them. Amongst the royal guard, Serge fought to keep the mercenaries away from Alexandra and Isabelle.

Lionus parried his enemy's thrust, and lifted one of his long legs to catch the masked man in the center of his chest with his heavy riding boot. With a grunt, his enemy lost his footing and Lionus was over him in an instant, but not before the masked man regained his hold on the hilt of his sword. He loomed over the masked man, his sword angled down at the other man. However, the tip of a blade was aimed right back at him, a single thrust away from running him through his middle.

They both remained as they were, weapons pointed at one another, locked in each other's eyes. The darkness and cover of the mask made it difficult for Lionus to try to identify the man, and the frustration of that ate away at him.

"Unmask yourself," he growled. "I would look into the eyes of my father's murderer before I run him through."

A gloved hand reached up to slide the mask away. When Lionus looked into the eyes of his father's killer, he felt as if the wind had been knocked from him. The face of his enemy was so familiar, yet the malevolence that he saw in the handsome features had never been present before. He staggered, his sword falling limply at his side as numb shock seemed to grip his limbs.

"No," he rasped, feeling as if he might choke on his shock. "It can't be!"

A man he had once called friend stood to face him. "I'm afraid it's true ... brother."

Lionus' shock was paralyzing. He could only stare at the man, open-mouthed.

"*Brother*? What are you ..."

Of course, this man was his brother. How could he have not recognized the signs?

Lionus had never truly looked him, not as he studied him now. The now-unmasked man had many of his father's features. His mind spun from the implications of this, what it meant for his family, the things that had been hidden from him. Part of him wondered if it might be a lie, but then he realized that it must be true. Or, at least this man believed that it was. Why else would he have gone through so much trouble for revenge?

"Whatever Father did ... whatever pain it caused you ... we could have mended it. I would have tried, I ... Why have you done this?"

"To take back what is rightfully mine," his enemy rasped, before striking out with lightning quick speed.

Before Lionus could react, the steel found his shoulder, sinking in deep. He dropped his sword with a roar of agony and then drew back his fist to connect with his opponent's face. The man staggered backward from Lionus' blow.

Lionus reached up to pull the blade from his flesh, gritting his teeth against the searing pain shooting through his arm. He threw the bloodied sword at the feet of the man he'd never realized was his brother, and lifted his own with his uninjured arm.

"Stand and fight me, you coward."

. . .

SERGE FOUGHT WITH FIERCE DETERMINATION, cutting down the men who had been dispatched by the masked man to kill his family. He could see Lionus through the chaos that surrounded them, and noticed that their father's murderer no longer wore his mask. However, he had his back turned and Serge could not see his face.

Raw fury raced through him, and he battled to make his way to his brother's side. He would not allow Lionus to face the villain alone.

He was drawn up short by the shrill screams of a woman behind him and turned to find three men surrounding the carriage his mother had taken shelter in with Isabelle.

An inhuman battle cry was the only warning the attackers had. Serge hacked his way through them, decapitating the first, severing the sword arm of the second and running his blade clean through the middle of the third. He looked up to find Isabelle watching him from the window of the carriage, her eyes wide with fear. He must look like a man possessed, and could feel the sticky wetness of someone else's blood across his face. Nevertheless, he reached through the window to take her hand, ignoring the tiny shivers of awareness that shot through him at her touch.

God, how he loved her. He had loved her for so long, he could hardly remember a time when his heart didn't ache at just the sight of her. If she died … no, he couldn't let that happen. She might be Lionus' wife, and he'd never laid a hand upon her—hell, the woman didn't even know how he felt about her—but he cared about her like he'd never cared for anyone in his life. If no one else made it out of this debacle alive, then she would … he would see to it. He'd gladly stay behind and die if it meant she would survive.

"Isabelle, are you able to drive this carriage?"

She glanced beyond him to see that one coachman lay dead and the other fought amongst the guards. Every other available man was busy trying to keep them alive. There was no one else.

"I can," she said, her soft voice filled with a strength he had always known she'd possessed.

Others saw her as beautiful and sweet, but Serge knew better. There was so much more to her than what met the eye.

"Good. Take the reins and drive this thing as fast as you can, back to the palace. Damien is not scheduled to leave until tomorrow. You must find him and tell him what has happened. Tell him to send aide."

Isabelle nodded, exiting the carriage to climb onto the driver's perch. Alexandra cried hysterically in the confines of the carriage, the shrill sounds grating against his nerves. There was no time to comfort her, so he turned back to Isabelle, who held the reigns in a tight grasp. He lifted his pistol from beneath the carriage seat and handed it to her.

"Do not hesitate to use it," he said.

She took the pistol and pushed it down into the pocket of her skirt.

"Go!" he bellowed, slapping one of the lead horses on the rear. The beasts whinnied and were off like a shot, carrying the two women to safety.

Relieved, Serge turned back toward Lionus, who still fought the masked man. Blood now trickled down his arm and soaked the front of his coat. He was slowing down, swinging his sword with sluggish, ungainly movements. The injury must be grave. Serge leaped over two men who had fallen to the ground, locked together in a struggle. Most of the men from either side lay dead or dying, but Serge's main concern was his brother.

He had just raised his sword, prepared to strike out, when pain exploded at the back of his head, bringing him up short. His vision blurred as he fell to his knees, ears ringing and his entire body seemed to vibrate from the force of the blow. He fought for consciousness, knowing that if he lost himself to oblivion, he and Lionus would both be dead within moments.

One of the masked man's accomplices grasped him by the arms and held him down. A pistol pressed against his temple.

"Hold still or I will gladly blow a hole through your head," a man's voice rasped in his ear. "Then my employer will be furious with me, since he's determined to kill you himself."

Serge could only watch Lionus fight as his blood rapidly drained from his body through the gaping wound in his shoulder. His heart twisted painfully in his chest when Lionus finally dropped to his knees, too weak to go on.

"No!" Serge cried as he watched their enemy drive his sword through Lionus' middle. His brother jolted from the blow, crumpling in on himself, unable to remain upright.

"Lionus," he rasped, watching his brother's lifeless body fall into a heap on the ground as the masked man pulled his sword free.

He struggled against the arms that held him, enraged, but the blow to his head had sapped much of his strength. Darkness shrouded the face of his enemy as he approached, wiping his sword clean of Lionus' blood. Serge growled like an enraged beast, straining against his captor's hold. Another blow to the head subdued him and he waited for his adversary to show his face, his body slumping as if he no longer had any control over it. He must have been hit harder than he thought.

"No," he whispered, when the man finally came into view. Could it be? This man had been a part of Serge's life for as long as he could remember, yet the evil and hate he found on this man's face hurt worse than his injured head.

"It can't be true."

Serge shook his head and narrowed his eyes, determined to see someone else, but the face and form before him did not change. It made no sense.

"Why?" he whispered, his voice having grown hoarse from his screams. "For the love of God, why?"

"Because our father abandoned me," the man said with a shrug of his shoulder.

Serge scowled, uncertain if he'd heard correctly. Surely he'd been hit far too hard and wasn't thinking clearly. He and this man didn't share a father...

Did they?

Serge fought with renewed strength, anger numbing the throbbing pain in his head as desperation set in. Lionus was likely dead, and there was no one else here to assist him. He now stared death in its face … and that face was one he'd known and loved. It simply defied all reason.

"Tell your men to release me and fight me, damn you! Let me go, goddamn it!"

Serge fought and screamed as the man motioned more of his men toward him. He kicked and flailed as ropes were tied around his ankles and wrists. He cursed his enemy for the coward he was, as his ankles were tethered to the back of the remaining carriage.

The face of a man he'd once held dear loomed over him.

"I will not stand by and watch you inherit everything that is rightfully mine. When you awaken in the afterlife, you can thank Adare for this."

The man lifted his pistol above his head, firing a cracking shot into the dead of night. The horses reared and whinnied before dashing off down the road, dragging the carriage and Serge behind them.

Damien bent over the lens of one of his most prized telescopes, alone in the observatory. The instrument was far too big for him to bring on board the ship that would carry him across the world in the morning. So, here he stood, gazing through it one last time at the clear night sky.

The palace was eerily quiet now that his family had gone, leaving behind only a handful of servants and guards. The majority of the staff had left ahead of them to prepare one of Lionus' country estates.

A tingle of excitement worked its way through him and he smiled, lifting his head to study the heavens through the domed glass ceiling. A new beginning awaited him in Europe, and he could hardly wait. He and Esmeralda would live a comfortable life away from kings and royal courts, scandals, intrigue, and the constant gaze of courtiers upon them.

Damien looked away from the sky just in time to see Jarvis entering the room. The faithful butler had stayed behind to see him off, and planned to join the family once he had escorted Damien to the waiting ship.

The old man's face was white as a sheet as he drew near, his clenched hands trembling.

Damien stepped away from his telescope. "What is it Jarvis? Is something wrong?"

"Your Grace, Her Majesty and the Queen Mother have returned," he began, wringing his hands until his knuckles turned white.

"Alone?" Damien frowned. "Where are Serge and Lionus? What's happened?"

"They were attacked."

"Where are they?" he demanded, already striding through the doors of the observatory with the butler on his heels.

Before Jarvis could respond, the sound of Alexandra's wailing drifted down the hall. He followed the noise until he found Isabelle and his mother seated in the green parlor. Alexandra sobbed hysterically while Isabelle paced before the fire.

"Damien!" she cried when he entered. She flew across the room at him, clutching his shoulders. "You must gather up more men! You must go to help them!"

Her face was streaked with tears, but her voice remained calm and her words clear as she struggled to be heard over Alexandra's noisy crying.

"How did you get back here?" he asked. "Did you come alone? Where are my brothers?"

Isabelle turned to Alexandra. "S*hut up*! I can barely hear myself think!"

Alexandra clamped her lips together and glared at Isabelle, but was otherwise silent.

Isabelle continued. "I drove the carriage back. Serge … he saved us … we were attacked by a band of men along the road led by the masked man. Your brothers stayed with the guards to fight them off."

Damien turned to Jarvis. "Get as many guards together as you can, and have them assembled in the courtyard at once. Send one of them to the barracks for soldiers … we may have need of them, too. Have Persephone saddled, and bring my sword and pistols."

Jarvis hurried from the room to carry out his command as Damien turned back to Isabelle.

"Did you see his face, Isabelle ... the masked man?"

She shook her head, letting out a little helpless sob. "No. When I left, he was locked in a sword fight with Lionus. Oh Damien, I fear they may both be dead! Lionus was severely injured and Serge and the guards were greatly outnumbered!"

Damien held her against him, patting her back and fighting to keep his hands still. As it was, panic had him feeling as if he vibrated from head to toe, the tremors of dread rocking him from the inside out. But, his family needed him to remain calm and composed ... they needed him to be decisive and calm.

"Don't worry, I'll find them. They could very well have routed the attackers and started on their way back to the palace."

Even as he said the words, they rang false.

He left Isabelle with his mother, and found Jarvis in the front hall waiting for him. The butler handed him his greatcoat, gloves, and a belt holding his sword and a pair of pistols. Damien fastened the belt around his hips and pulled on the gloves. Then, he swung the greatcoat around his shoulders and turned to Jarvis once more.

"Send for a surgeon, Jarvis. We don't know what ... condition, we will find them in. Have some maids standing by with supplies and bandages as well."

"Your Grace, do you think..."

The words hung between them unsaid, as the butler seemed to wrestle with them. Damien's heart plummeted as he was forced to think of the reality of this situation. He did not think he could ever adequately prepare himself for what he might find when he arrived at the scene of the attack.

"No, Jarvis. We won't think that way until we have to." He turned back in the doorway and added, "Send a messenger to Esmeralda's cottage in the city. Her grandmother has a knowledge of healing; she may be able to help."

. . .

DAMIEN LED the small group of palace guards down the darkened road, gaze sharp as he scanned their surroundings. He had clung to the hope that he would find his brothers along the way, headed back toward the palace, unharmed. The longer he rode, the less likely that became. He stayed on alert, aware that a trap could be set to ensnare him, as well.

Eventually, they came upon a lone carriage, observing the crest of the royal family upon its side. The horses stood calmly, pawing at the hard earth. He looked inside and found it empty.

"Search the area," he commanded the guards. "They have to be close by."

He stood and turned in a slow circle, searching the line of trees on either side for the slightest movement.

Nothing. The entire area remained silent and as still as death.

"Your Grace!"

The panic in the guard's voice brought Damien running around to the back of the carriage where he was greeted by a sight that caused his stomach to turn.

He barely recognized Serge, who lay lashed to the back of the carriage by his ankles. His clothes were torn to bloody shreds. Blood caked his hair and soaked the snow-white ground beneath his head. One of his arms lay twisted at an unnatural angle, and Damien was quite certain it must be broken in several places. Bitter bile rose up in the back of his throat at the same time tears welled in his eyes.

"Serge," he whispered, reaching out toward the prone form of his twin as he fell to his knees in the snow.

A lone tear fell as Damien pressed his fingers against the base of his throat. He was shocked to find a slight fluttering, the only sign that Serge remained with them. A huff of relief rushed from him, and he choked down the sob that had begun welling up in his chest.

"He's still alive!" he cried, hope expanding in his chest. "Get him into the carriage! One of you drive him back to the palace. The rest of you keep looking."

Damien knew that Lionus must be out there somewhere, injured. Fury swept over him and he prayed that the masked man was still near, alive, so that he could squeeze the life out of the bastard with his bare hands. If Lionus was in as bad a state as Serge, then he would make the villain's death slow and painful.

Two guards cut Serge free of his bonds and lifted him gingerly into the carriage.

"Hold on, Serge," he whispered as he watched the vehicle hurtle off into the night.

He continued his sweep of the area, passing several bodies strewn out along the way. He recognized some of the palace guards laid out amongst the killers hired by the masked man. Damien gazed into the face of each corpse, relieved as he realized his brother was not among them.

He swiveled around and drew his sword at the sound of a low groan. The crumbled form of a man shifted nearby, and he ran toward it, followed by the faithful guards.

"Lionus," he whispered as he drew near and recognized the man. "Thank God, you're alive."

His brother groaned again, both hands pressed over his stomach. Damien sucked in a sharp breath at the sight of so much blood soaking his fingers, his shirt, the front of his breeches. His brother had been completely impaled, the sword that had done the damage withdrawn to make matters worse.

"Goddamn it," he growled, dropping to his knees beside this brother just as he had the other. "That son of a bitch."

He lifted Lionus into his arms as carefully as he could, then stood and trudged toward his horse, straining with the effort it took. Lionus might be slender, but he was tall and at dead weight proved heavy as a bag of boulders.

Lionus mumbled incoherently, his head lolling on his shoulders as he seemed to try to look at him.

"D-Damien," he managed. "I ... I'm ... s-sorry."

"No," Damien interjected, holding his brother tight against his chest. "I am the one who is sorry. I should have been here. Perhaps the outcome would have been different."

"Serge," Lionus rasped. "Th-they dragged him..." His voice cracked and tears sprang freely to his eyes. "I saw ... I saw them d-drag him."

"He is still alive," Damien reassured him as they neared his horse.

The guards helped him lift Lionus into the saddle. Damien climbed on next, allowing his brother to lean back against him, heedless to the blood wetting the sleeves of his coat, its metallic scent stinging his nostrils. He placed his arms on either side of Lionus, and grasped the reigns.

"I need you to stay alive, too. Do you hear me?"

Lionus had already lost consciousness, but he still breathed. The sound was shallow and ragged, not a good sign. Damien dug his heels into Persephone's side and urged the mare on as fast as possible. He thundered down the road toward the palace, his men following close behind.

Esmeralda and Isabelle sat in silence, waiting to hear news of Damien's return. The queen's skin was pallid and cold, and she stared listlessly into the fire without speaking, or even blinking. Esmeralda was at a loss for words to comfort her friend. She could not lie and tell her that everything would be all right, because she was not certain things would ever be the same again.

Raina and Akira sat on the other side of the room, also silent. Akira clutched the small pouch containing her medicines and herbs, watching the open doors of the parlor for any sign of movement. If someone were brought back injured, she would be ready. The physician had not yet arrived, but Jarvis had assured them he would be here soon. Esmeralda dared to believe that Lionus and Serge would be found alive and unharmed, but each passing minute chipped away at that hope.

A commotion in the front hall brought the women to their feet. Esmeralda clearly heard Damien's commanding voice shouting instructions to Jarvis, who fluently passed them on to the waiting servants. She followed Isabelle into the vestibule and reached out to support her friend, who muffled a strangled cry against her hand and crumbled at the sight that greeted them.

Serge was being carried as swiftly up the stairs as possible by two footmen. His clothing hung from his body, tattered and torn, his limbs twisted at impossible angles. Damien held Lionus in his arms, his cheeks tinged pink from the biting winter cold, snow sprinkled over his greatcoat. He handed Lionus over to two more waiting footmen.

There was so much blood. Lionus' shirtfront and coat were stained with it, and Damien's clothes had been smeared with it, as well. Esmeralda was relieved to see it was not his own, even as her stomach roiled at the sight of his brothers' injuries.

All was in chaos when the surgeon arrived. Maids bustled about with hot water, towels, bandages and fresh linens. The doctor was brought up to speed on both patients' conditions and decided to see Serge first, as he was the worst off. Akira chose to tend to Lionus. Damien exchanged his blood-soaked shirt for a clean one offered by the stalwart valet, Hopkins, and swiftly followed the doctor to Serge's chambers, leaving Isabelle in Esmeralda's care.

She wrapped both arms around her friend, holding her tight. Isabelle seemed on the verge of collapse, her legs weak and her entire body trembling as she appeared to fight against losing hold of her emotions.

"Oh, God," Isabelle moaned. "Do you think he'll die? I don't think I would survive if he does."

"I don't know," she whispered.

She had seen the wound through Lionus' middle. His chances did not seem good, and neither did Serge's.

After leading Isabelle back to the parlor, she settled her on an overstuffed sofa beside Raina, who had brought along some of her soothing tea. She'd had Jarvis prepare a pot upon their arrival.

"Drink this," Raina said, pressing a cup into Isabelle's hands. "It will calm you and you must be strong now for your husband. We can do nothing but wait."

. . .

THE ROGUE PRINCE

"They are both still alive for now," Damien told them an hour later. He ran a hand over his tired face and sank into a chair across from Isabelle and Esmeralda. "Akira mixed a potion to help Lionus sleep. Serge never awakened, even when the physician set his broken bones."

"Will they survive?" Esmeralda asked, clinging tight to Isabelle's hand. Her friend had cleaved to her an hour ago and refused to let go.

Damien shook his head with a heavy sigh. "We have no way of knowing right now. They had the devil of a time trying to stop Lionus' bleeding. He sustained two wounds, one in his shoulder and another in his belly, both through and through. But, his injuries are nothing compared to Serge's. Three of his limbs are broken—his left leg taking most of the damage—and the surgeon suspects internal injuries. They do not expect him to last the night."

Isabelle was silent, staring blankly ahead as she had been for the past hour, her hand clenched tight around Esmeralda's. She didn't even react to what was being said around her.

Raina patted her shoulder, giving her a gentle shake. "Did you hear that, Your Highness? Lionus is all right. Maybe you can go up and see him now."

Damien nodded. "That's a good idea. I believe I'll go look in on Serge."

"I'll come with you," Esmeralda said, rising to follow him.

Damien braced a hand at the small of her back, leading her out into the main hall and toward the staircase. Raina took Isabelle's hand, and eased her to her feet, murmuring to her in soothing tones while leading her along in their wake.

They found Akira hovering over Serge's prone form when they arrived, trying to pour a thin broth down his throat. The prince remained unresponsive, the bruises marring his handsome face deep purple and ugly, swelling edging his eyes and jaw. Even with the blood washed away and his broken bones set, he looked nothing like the cheerful, smiling man she'd come to know.

His breathing was nearly imperceptible, almost nonexistent. One had to strain to see the gentle rise and fall of his chest.

"He'll need his nourishment if he's to fight for his life," Akira explained, placing the bowl aside and mopping Serge's chin with a handkerchief.

Akira gathered her various herbs and placed them back into her little pouch.

"He is broken," she said, her voice a low whisper. "But, is he strong. He has the will in him to fight."

"Thank you for your help," said Damien. "I will have a carriage readied to escort you home."

Akira nodded, turning to Esmeralda. "You stay here and watch over him for me," she said, and Damien wondered which of the Rothchester brothers she referred to. As of now, they could use all the help they could get, himself included.

Esmeralda nodded. "Of course, Grandmother."

"I'll return in the morning with a tonic for His Majesty," she said as she turned to leave. "If he survives the night, it'll do him much good."

As Akira exited, the butler entered. His face mirrored the exhaustion and angst that Damien felt within.

"You should retire, Jarvis," he suggested. "You've certainly earned a decent night's rest."

"Of course, Your Grace. There is just one other matter that requires your attention. I thought it should wait until morning, but the man was quite insistent he speak with you tonight."

"Who the devil would be here at this hour, Jarvis? Send him away. I have far too much on my mind to be bothered tonight."

"Mr. Forth was most insistent," said Jarvis. "He said he would not leave until he had spoken with you."

"Forth?" Damien asked, his interest piqued. "As in August Forth, the silversmith?"

"The very same, Your Grace."

Damien turned to Esmeralda. "Will you stay with him until I return? I'll only be a moment."

"Of course," she said, settling into the chair beside Serge's bed.

Jarvis informed Damien that he had shown the man to his library, and had taken the liberty of offering him a drink. Damien thanked him and made his way there.

Serge had gone to all three silversmiths in the city in an effort to learn the identity of the owner of a very remarkable walking stick. Two of the smiths denied ever having heard of such a thing. They'd both advised Serge to seek out the only other silversmith in the city, a man who was most known by members of the aristocracy for his extravagant, one-of-a-kind creations. When Serge had gone to see the man, he had been informed that the smith was away on holiday and would not return for several weeks. That silversmith's name was August Forth.

CHAPTER 19

"Thank you for seeing me, Your Grace," said August Forth, standing to bow as Damien entered the room. The tall, bony man removed his beaver hat and waited for him to be seated first.

He took his place behind his polished mahogany desk and motioned for Mr. Forth to sit.

"Jarvis assured me that your visit was of the utmost importance," he said, helping himself to a liberal splash of brandy.

"My business is actually with your brother, Prince Serge," Mr. Forth said, adjusting his wire-rimmed spectacles. "But your butler informed me that he is ill and cannot receive visitors."

Had Jarvis been in the room, Damien would have kissed him. The butler understood as well as he that discretion was critical. No one needed to know what had occurred on the side of the road tonight. He would give Lionus and Serge time, give the doctors time to make a better guess at their prognoses.

"I give you my word that whatever information you have for my brother will be communicated to him as soon as he is well enough to receive it."

"Very well," Mr. Forth replied, reaching into a slim leather portfolio. He removed several sheets of thin parchment and laid them on Damien's desk. "Your brother left a message at my shop that this was of the highest importance. He inquired about a custom walking stick, featuring this figure in pure silver."

Damien looked down at the drawings of an eagle, wings outstretched as if in flight. The eagle was entangled in the vicious hold a two-headed snake poised on either side with fangs exposed as if to strike.

Akira's cryptic words came back to him in a rush of memory.

Within the house of the king, there lies a viper...

He studied the drawings carefully, knowing he had never seen this symbol before.

Mr. Forth cleared his throat. "Your brother seemed quite insistent I inform him immediately of the identity of the man who commissioned this remarkable cane. I found the request quite odd, to say the least."

Damien's brows snapped together in confusion. "Why should you find it odd?"

"Because, Your Grace, the owner of this cane is a member of your family. I found it strange that Prince Serge seemed oblivious of this fact."

Damien's blood ran cold. A tremor of dread ran through him, and he stood watching the silversmith, still as death.

"Oh, God," he rasped, his hands curling to fists on the desk. "Nicolai."

Mr. Forth's nod confirmed it.

He did not want to believe what he was hearing. Surely someone had stolen the cane from his cousin, or had seen it and had an exact copy made. There could be no other explanation.

Fighting for composure, Damien turned to the man with a forced smile. "I appreciate your coming tonight, Mr. Forth. I cannot tell you why, but I would appreciate your discretion in this matter. Tell no one that you spoke to me tonight."

The silversmith stood, shuffling the drawings back into his portfolio and donning his beaver hat. "Of course, Your Grace. I spend too much time in my shop to gossip. I only know that your brother seemed quite adamant that I inform him of the owner's identity immediately upon my return. I hope the information proves helpful to you."

"Oh yes," Damien murmured. "You've been most helpful."

Once the other man had gone, he began pacing the length of his library, thinking over the events of the past few weeks. Nothing added up. How could Nicolai possibly be the culprit? He searched his mind for any inkling, any speck of truth that could prove or disprove his suspicions.

He thought objectively, and first pondered all the reasons that Nicolai could not be the perpetrator.

He had been just as dedicated to finding Adare's would-be assassin as he and his brothers had been. For another thing, the criminals who had been hanged for their part in the masked man's plot had told them that the man sought justice for wrongs committed against him by the royal family. What possible revenge could Nicolai seek to gain by murdering members of his own family? The final reason was the most obvious. Nicolai was like a brother to him, and to Lionus and Serge. The four of them had been that way their entire lives. He could not imagine that his cousin could nurse even an ounce of hatred.

Though it pained him, he turned his mind over to all the reasons that Nicolai could very well be the villain.

The first reason seemed almost silly, but he could hardly keep the ominous words of Akira from his mind. She had warned him of a viper and advised him that the viper was close to him. Could she have been referring to Nicolai?

He also realized that his cousin had left a few days before the rest of the family, an action that had seemed harmless at the time, but now Damien saw it as a strategic move. It would have placed Nicolai in a position to strike out at them. He had been one of the few who knew their destination, what day they would depart, which roads they would travel upon.

If the crown were available to you, would you come home to claim it?

The question had seemed innocent enough when Nicolai had

asked it, but now Damien wasn't certain. Was his cousin trying to position himself to take the throne? With Adare and his sons out of the way, Nicolai's father would take the crown. Upon his father's death, he would naturally be next in line.

Damien left the library on swift feet, his brow furrowed and his body feeling as if he'd been pummeled by fists from all sides. He found Jarvis in the empty family dining room, where intimate meals were taken each day, enjoying his usual evening glass of sherry. He silently sat at the large oak table beside the butler and accepted an offered glass.

The butler leaned back in his chair, his coat removed, cravat untied and the top button of his shirt undone. Just then, he looked older than his years, as haggard and exhausted as Damien felt.

"I heard," Jarvis admitted, lifting his glass to his lips for a healthy swallow.

Damien laughed dryly and took a large gulp as well. "Jarvis, I am old enough now to realize that you have been eavesdropping at keyholes since well before I was born."

Jarvis straightened his shoulders and inclined his head. "My dear boy, I never eavesdrop. I merely listen in on occasion. It is my duty to see to your welfare. After all that has happened today, I thought to wait nearby with a loaded pistol in case you needed me."

Damien smiled at that. Of all the people who resided within the walls of Rothchester Hall, he knew that Jarvis could be trusted. He could just imagine the somber, gray-haired man toting a pistol in the hall outside of his library. Though the image itself amused him, he knew for a fact that Jarvis could fire a pistol with deadly precision.

"What will you do now?" the butler asked, refilling each glass with the crystal decanter nearby.

"What would Lionus do?"

Jarvis chuckled. "You know, I have watched you boys grow into men, and I know as well as anyone that even though you and Lionus do not get along, you love each other. You, my dear boy, cannot seem to free yourself from a younger sibling's desire to be like the elder. You admire and respect him, even if you do not like him very much.

Now, Lionus ... he frets over you like a mother hen, trying his best to put a sober face upon his disapproval of your actions. The two of you make quite a pair."

Jarvis blinked and shook his head, circling back to the point.

"Your brother would objectively observe the facts."

"I have done that!"

"And?"

"I have decided that Nicolai is a highly likely suspect, though it pains me to think that way. I can see no reason for him to commit such a heinous act. For God's sake, I am thinking of accusing my own cousin of murdering my father! How can I do such a thing? The man is like my brother."

Jarvis cleared his throat and shifted in his chair as if uncomfortable. "There is a reason for that, Your Grace."

"What is that supposed to mean?"

He ran a hand through his thinning hair and sighed. "Your father may have told you of a great love in his past, one he was forced to give up in order to marry Alexandra."

"Yes, he told me the story. He said his father had already arranged a marriage to Mother and he was unable to change that."

"Did he tell you that there was a child?"

Damien felt the beginnings of apprehension curling in his stomach as he realized where this story was going.

"No, he did not tell me that."

Jarvis nodded. "He wouldn't have. It is a little known secret, one that has been closely guarded. Adare knew that Margaret carried his child, and begged his father to allow him to wed her. He did not want his first child to be born a bastard. Your grandfather would not be swayed. He forced your father into a union with your mother. Adare was devastated. But, he wasn't content to just let Margaret go on her way with his child. He did the only thing he could do to ensure a life for her and a future for the child. He sought out his brother, who'd always had feelings for Margaret himself. Adare asked him to marry Margaret and claim the child for his own, and of course your uncle agreed. It was on that day that

Nicolai Rothchester went from being your brother, to being your cousin."

Damien could hardly believe he had never known this. Even now when he thought back, he realized his father had been quite interested in the details of his nephew's life. He'd supposed it had only been because Nicolai's father had seemed so *un*interested, but now Damien understood why. He also realized why Nicolai bore a stronger resemblance to Adare than Lionus, why he looked more like Damien's twin than Serge, and why his relationship with his own father had always been strained. His Aunt Margaret had always been a quiet, sickly woman, appearing perpetually sad... and it was no wonder. She'd had to watch the man she loved rise to become king, marry someone else, and sire three sons upon her.

"It all makes sense now," he said, his fingers tightening around his glass. "The prisoners we executed told us that the masked man meant to right the wrongs committed against him. Nicolai must feel slighted because father gave him away and did not claim him as his legitimate heir."

"Yes," said Jarvis. "And by killing your father, and all of you, he would be gaining the throne that he feels should have been his to begin with. So, to repeat my earlier question, what do you intend to do now?"

Damien stood, his blood chilling until it felt like ice-water in his veins. "It's very simple Jarvis. The man has killed my father and viciously maimed my brothers. I intend to find him. I intend to kill him. As long as he lives, none of us are safe."

Davina slowly opened her eyes and found that one of them stung with the effort. Her muscles ached, and with every movement she had to stifle the urge to cry out in pain.

Nicolai Rothchester had left her chambers while she slept, and she was relieved to finally be free of him—for however long it took for him to return.

She had known for some time that Damien's cousin held an

interest in her. Davina had not been entirely indifferent toward him; after all Nicolai was devastatingly handsome. But who would pass up the chance to become the mistress of Prince Damien? Davina had passed Nicolai over for his cousin, and now it would seem Fate had conspired to make her pay for the transgression.

When Nicolai had approached her at the masquerade ball, she had thought to use him to make Damien jealous. Perhaps seeing her on the arm of another man would cause him to lose interest in Esmeralda and return to her. Of course, the ploy hadn't worked, and now she suffered at the hands of Damien's cruel cousin.

The first time she'd taken him to her bed, she had enjoyed it. She'd known there were men who liked to apply the strap to a woman's behind and found that she herself liked a bit of rough play in the bedroom. However, it soon became apparent that Nicolai was not the sort she'd thought he was. She came to see that Nicolai gained pleasure from inflicting pain, from watching the fear he could cause to well up in her eyes. His sadistic urges were barely controlled, and he often allowed them to take him—and by proxy, her—to dark and painful places. Before long, he began to ramble on for hours after rough intercourse, telling her of his plans to take the throne. He warned her that if she were a good girl, she could one day be the king's mistress.

Davina had given no credence to Nicolai's mad ramblings at first. She thought only of ways to escape him, but he would not allow it. The man came and went from her townhouse as he pleased and seemed to know her every move. He attended every soiree she did and clung to her possessively as they mingled among the guests.

When news of Adare's death had spread through the kingdom, Davina had known Nicolai to be at fault. She also understood that if she told anyone what she knew, she would be killed. Nicolai had issued no such threat aloud, but then, he didn't have to.

Now, hours after another bout of violent intercourse, she stepped gingerly from her bed, pressing her hand against her throbbing temple. She had protested Nicolai's rough treatment and had been rewarded with an open palm on the side of her head, thus her sensitive eye. Peering at her reflection in the mirror, she found a nasty bruise. She sighed and pulled a silk dressing gown around her naked body. If she didn't do something soon, Nicolai would either kill or permanently disfigure her.

She cursed Damien for leaving her to this fate. Damn him for being swayed by another pair of pretty eyes and shapely legs!

Yet, angry as she was at him, the only way out of this predicament was to find a way back under his protection. It would not be enough to go to him with the evidence of his cousin's abuse. Damien, gallant romantic that he was, would probably rush to her defense if he believed her, but that would be the end of it.

No, she needed a more permanent way to bind herself to Damien, to make him take her as his wife as she'd always thought he would.

She studied her reflection with a smile, an idea beginning to take shape in her mind.

LIONUS WAS AWAKE, though in a great deal of pain, when Damien arrived in his chambers the following morning. Isabelle, her face haggard and drawn, still wore the same gown she'd had on the night before, having refused to leave her husband's side.

He and Esmeralda had spent their night in Serge's room together. They had talked most of the night, though they'd also taken turns sleeping. Damien had reassured her that his intentions were unchanged.

"No matter the outcome, I will make you my wife," he'd said resolutely, clutching her hand in his.

Their ship was setting sail without them and their new beginning was temporarily on hold, but Damien was more determined than ever to make it happen.

He had told her of Nicolai's treachery once he'd dispatched soldiers to comb the city for his cousin. Every citizen of Cardenas was to be questioned, and Hensley Hall, where Nicolai lived with his father, would be searched extensively. So far, Damien had received no word from the captain of the guard, but he waited patiently for news.

It would only be a matter of time before he was found or turned up on his own. Nicolai would not leave Cardenas without ensuring his plot had played out to its end.

"Are you certain you will be able to go through with it?" she'd asked when he had informed her of his decision regarding Nicolai. "I know what he has done to you, to your family, but can you honestly say that you can kill him when the time comes?"

Her question had given him pause. His fury was great, yet he realized that taking Nicolai's life would hurt. However, it was a burden he was willing to bear. He knew without a doubt that it was what Lionus would do—choose to deal the fatal blow himself. So, for him, and for Serge as well, Damien would do what must be done.

He'd sent Esmeralda home at dawn, ordering her to rest before returning with Akira and the tonic she was preparing for Lionus.

Damien was relieved to find both brothers still alive in the morning, though they still hovered precariously on the brink. He stood beside Isabelle, placing a hand upon her shoulder.

"Have you had any chance to rest?"

She nodded, pulling her shawl tight around her shoulders. "He slept through most of the night, so I was able to doze off right here in this chair. The maids came a few hours ago to change his bandages. He is still bleeding heavily from the wound through his middle. I fear he has lost too much."

"Stop talking about me as if I am not in the room," Lionus rasped, his cobalt eyes swiveling in their direction. "I may have a hole through my middle, but I haven't gone deaf."

Isabelle was up and at his side in an instant, shoving a bowl of broth into his hands.

"Drink this," she commanded. "You need to regain your strength."

He complied, then allowed his head to fall back against the pillows. His face was ashen and pale, and Damien feared, just as Isabelle, that he had lost too much blood.

"Nicolai," he croaked, his eyes widening when Damien approached his side.

Damien placed his hand on his brother's uninjured shoulder. "I know. I have soldiers combing the city for him. He will not go unpunished, I swear to you."

Lionus raised his eyebrows in surprise. "*You* sent out soldiers?"

He shrugged. "Seemed like a good idea. I only thought to do what you would have done were you in my shoes."

Lionus nodded, a weak smirk tugging at the corners of his mouth. "I find myself strangely proud of you. Serge?"

"He survived the night, but … it does not look good for him. Three of his limbs are broken, and the physician fears that there could be bleeding inside his abdomen. He has yet to awaken."

Lionus squeezed his eyes shut, pressing his hands to his middle, a rough sound of both agony and grief emitting from him. He grew even paler, trembling as if a great earthquake shook him from the inside.

"That bastard!" he cried, thrashing wildly against the pain.

Damien was unsure if it was his wound, or his heart that hurt him more. For all his emotional shortcomings, Lionus loved his family, even if he did not always know how to express it. Nicolai's betrayal must be more painful to him than any wound sustained from a sword.

Lionus' grunts and groans continued and he squirmed, obviously lost in the throes of his torment. This was more than heartbreak … he was in true, physical pain.

"You must hold him," Isabelle cried, rushing around the other side of the bed to pin down his injured arm. "He'll rip the stitches in his shoulder!"

Damien saw the blood seeping through the bandage in his middle and realized that the shoulder was now the least of their worries. He pressed his full weight onto Lionus, who was surprisingly strong for one who had lost so much blood. He stared down into his brother's tear-streaked face while trying his best to keep him still.

"Lionus, I know you are in pain, but you cannot move about so much," he murmured. "Doctor Keane would be upset to find you have ripped his fine stitches."

His words had fallen on deaf ears. Lionus was delirious with the pain by now, and blood flowed even faster from the gaping wound in his middle.

He turned to Isabelle. "Doctor Keane stayed the night in case he was needed. He is in a room just down the corridor. Go and find him. Hurry!"

Isabelle hesitated for a moment, lip clenched tight between her teeth.

"Go," Damien urged. "Doctor Keane can do more for him than either of us."

His words seemed to spur her into action, and she rushed from the room without a look back.

Damien found fresh linens and pressed them to Lionus' wound, praying that the pressure would staunch the flow of blood. Lionus groaned and fought against him, his eyes frantic and glazed.

Moments later, Doctor Keane came tearing into the room with Isabelle on his heels. He quickly peeled back the linens that Damien held to find they had soaked through. The doctor commanded Damien to continue pressure, while he rifled around in his bag.

"Do something!" Isabelle shrieked from the foot of the bed.

"He's hemorrhaging," the doctor replied, his tone grave. "All we can do is apply pressure to the wound and pray that it will stop. I can give him something to ease his pain, but we must get that bleeding under control."

Doctor Keane produced a bottle of laudanum from his bag and forced Lionus' mouth open. He poured a generous amount of the liquid down his throat and then proceeded to help Damien apply pressure.

Isabelle leaned against the wall, sobbing and shaking her head rapidly from side to side.

"Please," she prayed, her voice a whisper. "Please don't let him die."

Within minutes, the laudanum began to take its effect and Lionus stilled, his pain seeming less acute. He focused his glassy eyes on Damien. Doctor Keane lifted the blood-soaked linens away and shook his head.

"There is nothing else we can do," he declared with an anxious glance in Isabelle's direction. "I'm sorry, but he will not last another hour."

"Why won't you do something?" Isabelle cried, throwing herself at the doctor with a guttural wail. "You have to try and save him!"

Doctor Keane looked to Damien with pleading in his gaze, seeming not to know what to do with a hysterical woman. He appeared relieved when Damien plucked her from his arms. The physician bent back over Lionus, leaving the business of consolation to Damien.

"Isabelle," he said, taking firm hold of her shoulders and giving her a gentle shake. "You must cease this. Lionus is going now, and there is nothing we can do to help him. Do you understand? You have done everything you can. So have I, and so has Doctor Keane."

Isabelle released another sob and a hiccup, but nodded her understanding.

"You cannot let him go without saying good-by. You have to tell him how much you love him. You cannot let him go without telling him."

He and Doctor Keane stepped aside, allowing her to sit on the edge of the bed beside him. Blood soaked her gown, but she seemed oblivious to it as she ran her fingers gently through her husband's hair.

"Lionus," she sobbed, pressing her lips to his. "I love you so much. Please, don't leave me. Please, don't die."

Lionus lifted one hand to her pale cheek, his face softening as he studied her angelic face.

"My love, I will never leave you," he said, his voice a raspy whisper. "You will always carry me in your heart. For that is where you have always held me."

Isabelle pressed her lips to his again and clung to him for dear life, heedless to the blood. Lionus wrapped his good arm around her. He locked gazes with Damien over her shoulder.

"Brother," he said. "I cannot leave this earth without telling you what you have meant to me."

Damien was beside him in seconds, reaching down to take his

empty hand. "I have always known, Lionus. Even when I was angry with you, I knew."

Lionus shook his head, grim determination furrowing his brow. "Marry Esmeralda. Marry her and keep her close. Don't let her slip away. I was wrong to try and stop you, I know that now. Don't leave Cardenas ... stay here and ... give her everything ... give her the world."

Damien could no longer hold back the tears. They fell in warm drops onto the back of his hand. "I will, Lionus ... I will."

"There is one other thing. It is important. You must not fail me. Take up my sword."

He searched the room, his gaze falling onto Lionus' sword, propped up in the corner beside the bed. He lifted the weapon and held it where Lionus could see it in his hand.

His brother inhaled, his chest swelling with pride as he nodded his approval. "That is the Sword of the Kings of Cardenas. It has been wielded by Rothchester men for generations. I am giving it to you."

"But surely you would want Serge to have it," Damien argued, too stunned to say much else. "He is next in line."

"Serge may not live, and that would make *you* king," Lionus pointed out, much to his dismay.

"No," he objected, having never fully considered what Serge's death could mean. "I can't be. I won't be!"

"You must be," Lionus insisted, holding Isabelle closer with one arm, clutching Damien's hand tighter with the other. "You are the son of Adare. His blood runs in your veins. You were born for this, the same as me."

Damien shook his head, as if the movement could shut Lionus' words from his ears.

Lionus released his hand, too weak now to hold on any longer. "You will take my sword and avenge our father," he whispered, closing his eyes. "And you will rule Cardenas in my stead if Serge should die."

Damien fell back against the wall with the sword clenched tight in his hand, watching Lionus whisper his final goodbye to Isabelle. His gut twisted as he read the words '*I love you*' from his brother's lips, confirming what Esmeralda had tried to convince him of.

His brother really had loved his princess bride.

A few seconds later, he was dead. Isabelle collapsed over her husband's lifeless form, her shoulders shaking with sobs that seemed to tear through her from as deep as her soul. Damien could only watch with tears in his eyes, clutching Lionus' sword against his chest.

Doctor Keane ushered in a small group of maids who busied themselves with stripping Lionus of his bloodied clothes and linens. Isabelle composed herself enough to help, still sniffling and muffling little sobs.

Damien turned and dashed from the room, unable to abide the stench of death any longer, the scent of Lionus' blood, or the sound of Isabelle's cries. He ran through the twisting, turning corridors, seeking to flood his senses with fresh air. He raced through the main hall and burst through the heavy front doors. Then, he collapsed at the top of the stairs, welcoming the biting cold that reached out to grasp him with its icy fingers.

He inhaled, closing his eyes, willing the cold winter air to cleanse him. When he opened his eyes, he noticed for the first time that his palms were smeared with blood, just as they had been in the vision Akira had shown him. Little had he known that the blood would turn out to be Lionus'... that even more blood will be spilled before it had all ended.

Anger rose within him, hot and swift. He threw his head back and allowed a guttural, pain-filled cry to spill from his lips. Damien sobbed until he could no longer breathe, his lungs contracting powerfully with the force of his cries.

CHAPTER 20

amien sat in the first pew of the church he had recently occupied for Lionus and Isabelle's wedding. Only now, as he sat listening to the droning voice of the priest, he stared at Lionus' casket instead of a happy couple exchanging their vows. With Esmeralda on one side, and his mother on the other, his pew was filled out with Isabelle and Jarvis farther down. Other members of the household staff sat near the front of the church with the family, as Adare had loved and respected the people who had served him. Members of the court and the loyalists of Barony filled the rest of the sanctuary, with not a single pew unfilled.

He barely registered the words being spoken, his mind overrun with chaotic thoughts—most of them focused upon Nicolai.

His cousin had yet to be found, though the soldiers he'd sent out had brought back some interesting news. He'd last been seen at Hensley Hall, where he was presumed to have gone before launching his attack. His father had been found lying face down in the garden fountain, a bottle of port clutched in his icy hand. The man had been in his cups ever since the death of his wife, so an accident was possible, perhaps even inevitable. Nevertheless, Damien suspected foul play. He had come to believe now, more than ever, that Nicolai was killing off members of their family one by one.

He assumed Nicolai thought Serge had died upon the side of the road that fateful night, and wanted to keep it that way. If he thought that the only person who stood between him and the throne was Damien, he would come directly to him. For his part, Damien would not be caught unaware once the time came. Even now, he felt the cold steel of a pistol tucked into the waistband of his trousers, and Jarvis carried one as well. He slept with both his sword and pistol at his bedside. At least, when he managed to drift off. Most nights, he lay awake thinking of his brothers, his father, of the family that had been torn asunder by secrets, lies, and revenge.

His gaze fell to the gilded casket, still open to display Lionus' lifeless body. He could not even summon the tears to cry for his brother, or his father, any longer. He'd spilled the last of them on the front steps of the palace. Since then, all he had been able to feel was a black rage, a sensation that had planted itself within him like a seed and now grew to the farthest reaches of his body. It ate him alive, but at the same time propelled him forward, giving him purpose. He would not rest until Nicolai was dead, and what remained of his family was safe.

He turned to glance down the pew at Isabelle, who remained outwardly composed. She wore traditional mourning attire, layers of shapeless black bombazine that made her fair coloring appear almost sallow. A black veil had shielded her face as she'd entered the church, but she had pushed it back to hang over her hair and reveal her face once inside. Her puffy, red-rimmed eyes betrayed her composure, and he was certain she'd been weeping as recently as this morning.

He returned his attention to the service, as Lionus' coffin was closed and lifted. Soon they would follow the box out into the swirling snow to the royal cemetery on the grounds of Rothchester Hall. He would stand in the bitter cold and watch them lower his brother into a dark hole in the earth. Damien determined with every ounce of his will that this grave would be the last one dug for years to come.

He would will Serge to live and take his rightful place on the throne. Nicolai would pay for what he had done, and Damien would marry Esmeralda. He refused to allow it to happen any other way.

Later that evening, when the palace had grown quiet, Damien encountered his mother coming from the kitchen. He was surprised to find her wandering the corridors at night, holding a pot of tea and a china cup, a long, dark braid streaked with gray hanging over one shoulder. In her prim white nightgown and matching wrapper, she appeared much younger and softer than Damien had ever seen her. In fact, he did not think he'd ever seen her anything other than impeccably groomed and fashionably dressed.

She halted in her tracks when she saw him, seeming to struggle internally for a moment before speaking.

"I have been meaning to talk to you. I had hoped to find you alone, and I suppose now is as good a time as any."

Damien folded his arms across his chest and gave her a slight nod. He would hear what she had to say, in hopes that she would leave him to return to Esmeralda, who he'd left waiting in his chambers.

He'd had very little to say to her after she'd spurned him following Adare's death, and found he still had no words of comfort for a woman who used her pain to lash out at her own sons.

"Lionus is dead," she rushed on. Damien discerned a slight faltering in her voice, but Alexandra pressed on. "Serge is not at all improved. Doctor Keane and the other physicians have said that he is in a coma. They do not believe that he will ever awaken ... or if he does, he will not be himself."

She paused for a moment and watched Damien intently. Her scrutiny made him uncomfortable, and he shifted from foot to foot under her watchful eye.

Alexandra continued when he did not respond. "Because your brother's condition is so uncertain, I believe it is time for us to consider your succession."

"No," he protested with a shake of his head. "We will not have this conversation right now."

"When would be a good time, then? When Serge is already lying cold and dead in the ground?"

Alexandra's words sliced through him with ruthless intent, and Damien closed the distance between them, his fingers itching to reach out and throttle her. He clenched them behind his back instead.

"Serge is not dead," he hissed through clenched teeth. "I wonder, Mother, if you would shed tears for him, as you did your beloved Lionus."

Alexandra lifted her chin and stabbed Damien with her cold blue eyes. "You have always been a romantic like your father. But you cannot go on dreaming forever. Do you honestly think I *want* to have this conversation with you? That I would not rather be content in the knowledge that Lionus and Isabelle will rule Cardenas and Barony well, as they were born to do? Well, I tell you now that I wish none of this had ever happened, but we have to face reality. Serge could die at any moment and you must be prepared to take the throne. It is your birthright, as well as your duty."

A sudden weariness settled over him, weighing upon his shoulders with crushing force. He had never allowed himself to consider the possibility of Serge's death. His injuries were severe, but Serge was as strong as an ox and stubborn as a mule. He must survive this.

But what if he doesn't?

The question nagged him, taunted him with the near certainty of his future. He, Damien Rothchester, third son of Adare, would be crowned King of Cardenas. It was the one thing he'd never wanted.

"I will not take the throne while Serge lives," he replied. "We will wait and see what happens. I won't take something that is not rightfully mine."

"I am not asking you to," Alexandra replied. "According to the law, if the king is unfit to rule, then the High Council must be assembled. It is among them that the decision must be made to pass the crown down to you. Doctor Keane can testify to your brother's condition. I do not doubt the council will rule in your favor. The kingdom will fall into chaos without a king. We can only give Serge so much time to recover before it all comes crumbling down around us. It is what he would want ... what Lionus would have wanted."

Damien had never known such anger before. Perhaps because her words—however ruthless and heartless—were true. Or maybe it had to do with the matter-of-fact way she presented them, as if she discussed the weather. He advanced on her, hands balled into fists as he fought the urge to shake her like a rag doll. She backpedaled as if afraid, her china cup and saucer falling to shatter upon the marble floor. He stopped when she came against the wall, looming over her with his lips twisted into a snarl.

"You are a pitiful excuse for a mother," he growled. "You have rejected me my entire life, showing me nothing but disinterest and contempt. Now you seek to manipulate me, as well. Allow me to make this clear to you. I will not assemble the council and convince them to wrest the crown from my brother while he fights for his life. Until he awakens I will act as steward to the throne. That will ensure the realm continues to function as it ought, without me having to stab Serge in the back to take something that isn't mine."

Alexandra regained her composure, drawing herself up and tilting her chin at him, her cool eyes once again like frigid icicles.

"Very well," she relented. "I can see that you are still very hurt over your father and Lionus' death, and Nicolai's betrayal. Time and perspective will change your view, mark my words. You must eventually come down from the cloud you have been living on and face reality. Serge will more than likely die. The fate of both Cardenas and Barony will rest in your hands. Don't tarnish your father's legacy by being indecisive. Do what must be done."

When he did not respond, she turned to leave, but stopped suddenly and glanced at him over her shoulder. "Oh, and you might think of poor Isabelle as well. She was meant to marry a king, and now her life, as well as those of the people of Barony, are more uncertain than ever."

With that, she was gone, not even bothering to retrieve the broken cup and saucer from the floor.

Damien cursed her under his breath as he made his way back to his bedchamber. He had almost reached the door when he remembered his reason for going to the kitchen in the first place. With a heavy sigh, he turned and walked back.

He hated himself for the pattern of his thoughts, but Alexandra's words had the nasty sting of truth in them. It was as if someone had doused his face with cold water, waking him up from a horrible dream. Only now, his life proved as nightmarish as what he faced whenever he closed his eyes.

Esmeralda shivered and wrapped her thick shawl more snugly around her shoulders. December rapidly approached and the bitter cold became harsher by the day. Akira stood and gently poked at the dying embers of the fire before adding more coal. The flames leapt upward and Esmeralda held her hands out toward the radiating warmth.

"The days grow colder," remarked Akira from where she sat near the hearth, staring into the flames. "This year, winter will be bitter and cruel."

Esmeralda frowned as she studied her grandmother. The old woman had been quite distracted lately, and that could not be a good sign. Whenever Akira sank into one of these moods, it was because she had seen something in one of her visions that disturbed her. Esmeralda wondered if it concerned her or Damien, but dared not ask. If Akira wanted her to know something, she would speak of it on her own. That she revealed nothing meant either the future was uncertain, or she did not think telling her would help matters.

She had not seen Damien in days, and missed him sorely. However, with winter coming her mother and grandmother needed her at home—helping to prepare the house for the change of the season and take part in preserving food and making candles for light. Besides, Damien had a lot on his mind as well as his plate, acting as steward to the throne while Serge was incapacitated. She had not had a chance to tell him yet how proud she was to see him stepping into the role—one that many others likely thought he would have shunned or failed at. It only reaffirmed what she'd always seen in him, the strength no one had thought him capable of.

Suddenly, a pounding at the front door interrupted her train of thought. She leapt to her feet and rushed to the door, but Akira was already there.

"He's late," she murmured before swinging the door open.

Damien strode in, bringing in a great deal of snow on his boots and the shoulders of his greatcoat. His eyes were wild, as was his hair, which she could tell had been mussed by anxious fingers. Worry sagged his shoulders and left dark circles beneath his eyes, but even so the sight of him quickened the beat of her heart.

He took her in his arms, taking a moment to place a lingering kiss upon her lips before turning to Akira.

"I need to know where he is," he stated. "I have to know where to find my cousin, and I need your help. The visions you shared with me before came true … perhaps you can find him for me."

Akira reached out and grasped his hands tight, craning her neck to look up and into his eyes. She studied him for a long moment, as if trying to come to a decision. Then, she nodded decisively and gave him a tug.

"Come," she said, motioning toward the staircase. "Esmeralda, be a good girl and brew some of Raina's special tea. Your beloved will probably need it when we are through."

AKIRA'S BEDCHAMBER was just as Damien remembered it. Though it was mid-afternoon, dark curtains kept the light of the sun away, shrouding the room in darkness. She lit a lamp and led the way to the same low table they had sat at before. Damien took his place, kneeling across from her, and waited for her to offer him her pipe. Anxiety had kept him on edge for days, and it was all he could do not to urge her to hurry things long.

She removed it from one of the pockets in her voluminous robes and stuffed it with tobacco from a small glass jar nearby. The familiar blue smoke curled around her as she lifted it to her lips.

He took his turn eagerly, relieved that the fragrant smoke did not choke him as it had before. Once his vision had cleared, he saw himself standing in the courtyard before Rothchester Hall. Snow fell all around him, yet he wore no protection against the cold. He stood in his shirtsleeves with Lionus' sword clenched at his side, the moon edging its steel with a menacing glow.

A figure in black moved toward him through flurries of falling snow, his weapon drawn as well. As the man came near, Damien recognized the unmistakable glow of Nicolai's blond hair and the flash of eyes identical to his own. Just before the image faded, he saw the two figures rush toward each other, their swords clashing together between them.

Damien fought to hold on to the image, but it was gone and a new one rose in its place. Before him stood a woman, and though he could only see her back he recognized Esmeralda. She wore a gown of pristine white, her hair unbound and flowing to her waist. Her head was covered with a white lace mantilla, and Damien could faintly make out a small bouquet of flowers in her hands. Joy flooded him at the sight of her dressed as a bride. His heart swelled even more as that vision faded and the third one sprang to life before him.

A child ran across the sprawling green lawn of the palace grounds. He recognized the circular band of trees behind her and the little pond in the distance. She giggled, waving at some unseen person. Her eyes were as green as the grass beneath her feet.

Damien was smiling when the haze dissipated and he found himself back in the room with Akira.

"Patience will serve you well," she said, leaning back against her many cushions with a tired sigh. "You will not find your enemy, but do not despair. He will come to you."

Damien nodded. He and Nicolai had confronted each other on the steps of the palace and he could see from his vision that the attack was well anticipated. He had only to wait. He shot to his feet, his smile growing wider.

"Thank you," he murmured, his words coming out on a sigh of relief.

She closed her eyes, not replying to him with words ... but that didn't matter. There was nothing to be said when he'd seen everything for himself.

He left Akira to rest and took the stairs two at a time, rushing to the kitchen where Esmeralda waited for him.

She gasped in surprise, then laughed as he swiftly drew her to him for a kiss, lifting her feet off the ground and holding her tight.

"What has gotten into you?" she asked. "I suppose the news was good."

Damien set her on her feet with a smile. "You have no idea."

"Are you going to tell me what you saw?"

He studied her for a moment before responding. She did not yet show signs of pregnancy. The child in his vision had been at least two or three years old, so she might not have conceived yet, but the possibility had lifted his spirits beyond belief.

"I saw you as my bride."

He did not wish to unnerve her by speaking of the child, and he certainly wasn't going to tell her about the duel with Nicolai. All of these things could be dealt with as they came.

He left Esmeralda's cottage filled with hope. Damien turned to see her watching him from the doorway and his spirits lifted as he thought of the new beginning to come and the life that could now be growing inside the woman he loved.

THE SNOW WAS RELENTLESS, falling in flurries that swirled around the still form of a man on the precipice of one of the mountains bordering Cardenas and Barony. Nicolai stood, his legs wide as if on the deck of a rocking ship. His black greatcoat whipped about his body with the shifting of the biting wind. Its fur lining served to keep him considerably warm. He stood with his gloved hands shoved deep into his pockets, his gaze surveying the land below him.

Soon, everything as far as the sparkling ocean beyond would be his. The end was near, and Nicolai could taste the inevitable victory.

Two brothers down.

He glanced over his shoulder at his loyal band of men, milling about the campgrounds they had established high in the mountains. Each of them was discontented with their lots in life, money hungry, and willing to do anything to better their own circumstances. So far they had proved invaluable, his own private little army.

However, Nicolai knew they'd begun growing restless. They were watching him, huddled around the small campfires between the opulent tents he had provided. The men slept on fur rugs, had all the ale and spiced wine they could ask for, and more than enough food. It would keep them content for now, and he'd assured them that it would not be much longer before they dealt the final blow. Once he was king, he would keep them in his employ, paying them well enough that they could remain at his beck and call. After all, even a monarch could have need of men such as these.

When the king's soldiers had come looking for him, Nicolai had known that one of his brothers had lived long enough to reveal his identity. He had been ready for such an occurrence and immediately led his men into the mountains. They were impatient, and some even questioned why they didn't just have done with it and kill Damien.

Nicolai had decided to give it time, hoping that he would be wise enough to follow through with his plans to whisk his fiancée off across the world. He would allow his cousin to decide his own fate. The moment he received word that Damien had set sail, he would take his rightful place. The second he heard otherwise, Damien would not live long enough to regret it.

CHAPTER 21

Another fortnight passed without any change in Serge's condition. Damien and Esmeralda had spent much of their time at his bedside, watching and waiting for any sign of life. Damien had begun to believe that his mother and the physicians were right. Serge wasn't going to wake up.

The time had come for him to go to the High Council. Alexandra had said no more to him on the subject, but Jarvis had informed him that the she'd already petitioned the council on his behalf. He had only to call on them and they would assemble, ready to rule in his favor.

And so, a few days after making this decision, he stood at the foot of Serge's bed attired in formal court dress—a military-style jacket and sash boasting the navy blue and gray colors of the royal family. The coat fit him well in his broad shoulders and tapered in at the waist, where a black belt holding a jewel-hilted saber was fastened. The garment boasted rows of silver buttons down his chest, with epaulets and silver braid at the shoulders; snowy white linen was tied at his throat, and highly polished black boots gleamed on his feet.

Damien remained silent for a while, watching his brother breathe, seeming to struggle with each inhale. Serge's fluttering pulse at the juncture of his jaw and throat was barely detectable. Damien sighed, wondering how a person could hover so precariously on the line between life and death. He had hoped and prayed so fervently that his brother would wake up, but the heavens seemed to be ignoring his requests.

Perhaps it would have been better for Serge to have died that night. It was no worse a fate than being trapped inside a broken body and a dormant mind, unable to speak, or move. He had never counted upon how empty Rothchester Hall felt without his brother's presence, how hollow it was without Serge's laughter to fill it.

"I am prepared to make my statement to the council," said Doctor Keane as he entered the room to find Damien there. "You have no need to worry, Your Grace, the council will rule in your favor."

"Is that supposed to reassure me?" Damien groused, his voice low and menacing. "You think I want this ... that I want to take from my brother what is rightfully his?"

The physician stammered and stuttered in the face of Damien's anger. When he could come up with no suitable reply, Damien dismissed him with an imperious wave of his hand.

"Leave us," he said, turning back to Serge. "The council should be assembling now. Go there and tell them I'll be along in a moment."

Doctor Keane rushed from the room as fast as his feet would take him, passing Esmeralda and Akira in the corridor, who had come as they did almost every day to look in on Serge.

He turned to face Esmeralda, his shoulders sagging. "It's time. The physicians all agree that if he does not awaken soon he will either die, or remain as he is for many years."

She rushed forward to wrap her arms around him. "He would understand, Damien. He would not hold this against you. It was not his way, and you know it."

Damien nodded, wrapping one arm around her. "I know. But that doesn't make me feel any better about doing this."

A light knock upon the door preceded Alexandra's entrance into the room.

"You must come now. The council awaits."

Damien stepped from the circle of Esmeralda's arms and placed a light kiss upon her forehead.

"Will you be here when I return?"

She nodded. "Whatever you need."

"Good."

He would most certainly need her here, for him to hold and love and look upon—a reminder that all was not lost. He stood in a position he'd never wanted to be in, but he could face it all with her at his side.

He stopped in the doorway one last time and gazed back at Serge over his shoulder. His heart rent anew every time he looked upon his brother's prone form, and he wondered if a day would ever come where he could no longer bear to be in this room.

"Forgive me, brother."

The fifty members of the council were gathered and ready, each seated in their designated place in the Hall of the High Council. Damien's boots clicked against the marble floor as he walked to the center of the chamber, where he was to stand and plead his case to the men gathered. Alexandra and Doctor Keane took available seats against the side wall, waiting silently for their chance to speak. Damien stood beneath the domed, painted ceiling, gazing up at the members of the council, men who had all been chosen specifically by his father to advise him on important matters and vote new or amended laws into existence.

Lord Francis Boswell, the most senior member and Speaker of the High Council, began the proceedings.

"Prince Damien," he said, his voice echoing off the walls and ceilings. "You have summoned us here today to discuss the condition of your brother and current heir to the throne, Prince Serge. If he has been found incompetent by his attending physicians, then you have every right by the dictates of the law to succeed to the throne in his stead. You may now state your case."

Damien clasped his hands behind his back, hoping that no one would notice how badly they were shaking. He knew this must be done, yet could not seem to find any sort of peace about it. He forced himself to square his shoulders and speak.

"My lords, I gather you here today with great sadness in my heart, and a heavy burden upon my conscience. My father and eldest brother are dead and another brother lies upon his deathbed. As the third son of Adare, I never thought to be in a position to take the throne. It is with great remorse and regret that I come here today to do just that. I have brought Doctor Keane, the senior physician attending my brother, to speak on Prince Serge's condition. I will ask him to come forward now."

"Doctor Keane, do you swear before this court that what Prince Damien says is true?" Lord Boswell asked, swiveling his gaze to the physician.

Doctor Keane stepped up beside Damien and cleared his throat. "Gentlemen of the council, I have conferred with my fellow physicians, each of whom has examined Prince Serge personally. He has sustained a catastrophic amount of trauma, and we are doubtful that he will ever recover. Even if he were to live, he might continue to lie in a comatose state, just as he is now. We can do nothing more than care for him until the day of his passing. There is a small possibility that he could awaken. But in my experience, people who rouse from comas are never the same as they were before. Some never speak or move on their own. They simply sit and stare blankly into the distance. Others are unable to speak clearly or even feed themselves. Considering the amount of trauma that the prince has sustained, it seems highly unlikely that he will ever be able to function as a normal man ever again. He certainly would not be fit to rule."

Lord Boswell nodded and dismissed Doctor Keane with a wave of his hand. "If you will give us a moment, Your Majesty, we'll now adjourn to discuss our decision."

Damien silently agreed and watched as the men of the council disappeared one by one through a door at the back of the Hall. He took a seat beside Alexandra and waited.

Half an hour later, the doors opened and the men who had decided his fate filed silently back in. He stood to face them, dread unfurling in his belly.

"We have reached a decision," said Lord Boswell, once every member had been seated. "We have reviewed the signed testimonies of each physician who has examined your brother, as well as the letter from the Queen Mother beseeching us on your behalf. We believe what they say to be true and have decided to name you King Damien Alexander Rothchester, ruler of Cardenas and Barony, as is your right as the next in the royal line. For what it's worth to you, I believe your father would have been proud."

Damien felt the cruel weight of finality crushing down upon him. This was not what he had wanted. Never could he have imagined he would be here, accepting the responsibility that came with ruling two kingdoms. He inclined his head in acknowledgment of the council's verdict, but said nothing.

Lord Boswell stood, and the other members of the council followed. "All hail King Damien!"

"All hail King Damien!" The council members echoed, their voices ringing in Damien's ears as he turned and strode swiftly from the Hall.

ESMERALDA LINKED her arm through Damien's and allowed him to lead her down the winding path through the garden. Nearly all the flowers had died now, and the frost of winter snow had settled on the remaining branches. Snow crunched beneath the soles of her boots and clung to the bottom of her fur-lined cloak. The cape had been another of Damien's numerous gifts, one she was grateful for now as they strolled through the beautiful garden clothed in a soft white blanket of snow.

The tension that had been present before Damien's meeting was now gone, though she knew his mind must be burdened with the many duties awaiting him as king. Esmeralda was relieved, but in a way nervous as well. He still spoke of marrying her as if his becoming king had not just changed everything. As his wife, she would become the queen of two kingdoms. Though Cardenas and Barony were small realms, the thought of ruling as queen of anything caused the butterflies in her stomach to flutter their wings mercilessly.

"You should begin planning the wedding at once," Damien said. "I've informed Jarvis that he is to be available to you at all times to lend his assistance. We will have to be wed as soon as possible, three weeks or less if we can manage it. Once we are married, I'm afraid we'll have to forgo a wedding trip. The state of Barony can be ignored no longer."

Esmeralda nodded slowly, but her mind was reeling. She hadn't the faintest idea how to plan a lavish wedding fit for a king and queen. Normally, she would turn to Isabelle for guidance, but her friend had not quite been herself since Lionus' death. She walked about as if in a dreamlike state, shrouded in her black mourning clothes. However, she was always there to take up the vigil at Serge's bed whenever Damien and Esmeralda were not present. Sometimes she would read or talk to him, convinced that he could still hear what went on around him. Other times, she merely sat in silence and stared out of the window.

"A decision must be made about Isabelle's future as well," Damien said, as if reading Esmeralda's thoughts. "Though, I daresay she is not ready to discuss the matter just yet."

"She is hardly recovered," Esmeralda replied, glad for the change of subject. She would worry over the planning of the wedding later. "Give her a bit more time. Perhaps she could remain here with us."

Damien shook his head. "I know that she would if I asked her to, but Barony is her home. She was meant to return there and continue the royal family line. It hardly seems right the way things have unfolded."

She patted his hand. "I'm sure you will think of something. You cannot blame yourself. You can only take things one step at a time. Eventually, we will find the peace to live a normal life."

Damien stopped and smiled down at her, lifting her chin with his fingertips to capture her mouth in a tender kiss.

"I will be the most fortunate of men to have you for my wife," he said, brushing his lips across her cheek and down to her neck.

The hood of her cloak slipped back from her head and Damien caressed the loose tendrils of hair that had fought their way from the neat chignon at the nape of her neck.

"I'm not so sure," she replied, fighting the waves of exhilaration that rippled through her at his touch.

She could barely think with his hand cupping the back of her head, drawing her in for another kiss, his thumb tracing light circles on the sensitive spot behind her ear.

"If you are king, then that makes me queen."

"Mmm," he rumbled against her throat, nibbling gently and sliding his hands inside her cape to span her waist. "And you shall be the most beautiful queen to ever sit upon the throne."

"What on earth does a queen *do*, anyway?" she asked absently, closing her eyes and giving herself over to the pleasure of the moment.

"Whatever she wants," he replied, pulling back to look at her. "Devote herself to charity work, bear lots of children, spend obscene amounts of money, lounge around all day nibbling on chocolates, plan lavish parties ... take your pick."

Esmeralda laughed. "I think I'll stick to charity work and bearing children. I don't care much for spending money, and chocolates and lavish parties are sure to ruin my figure."

"More than anything else, I simply wish you to be my wife. In the same way you would if I were still a prince, or a simple farmer, or a Gypsy."

He was right, of course. She had a lifetime to learn how to be a queen; she would spend that lifetime as his wife and the mother of his children.

"Anything you say, Your Highness."

Damien laughed, a sound that Esmeralda had come to miss over the past few weeks. It warmed her more than her fur-lined cloak had in the chill of the winter afternoon.

"You know," he said. "I have not been very fond of that title, but I rather like the sound of it coming from your sweet lips."

Esmeralda smiled. "Then I'll have to say it more often, Your Highness."

Keeping his arm around her waist, he turned to guide her back to the palace, declaring that it was too cold for them to remain outdoors for much longer.

Jarvis awaited them when they returned from their walk. He took Esmeralda's cloak and Damien's greatcoat and ordered hot tea for them both.

"Have mine delivered to my library, Jarvis," Damien said. "I've pressing matters to attend ... things that have been neglected long enough."

"Of course, Your Highness. Might I suggest having your things moved to the king's chambers? I thought you would like to start getting used to your new quarters."

Damien nodded. "I'll leave that task up to you. I would prefer to bring the furniture from my library, though, and my books as well. Have them switched out with those in the king's study."

"I shall see it done today."

"Good. Make yourself available to Esmeralda as well. I am trusting you to see that all goes smoothly with the wedding arrangements."

"Of course, Your Highness."

Damien gave Esmeralda a swift kiss on the cheek and was gone up the winding staircase in the span of a few seconds. She waited until he was completely out of sight before she turned to the butler.

"Jarvis, what am I going to do? I haven't the faintest idea how to go about planning this wedding. I would ask Isabelle for help, but she is hardly in the right frame of mind, and I know that Damien's mother will only laugh in my face if I ask her."

Jarvis smiled and grasped her hand, leading her to the sitting room where her tea awaited. He lowered her into an armchair and handed her a steaming cup.

"You must calm yourself, my dear," he said. "I think you will find my assistance invaluable in this. If you will allow me, I can make suggestions as to where you are to start."

Esmeralda breathed a sigh of relief, then took her first sip of tea. "Yes, thank you."

"I will contact the florist and order whatever arrangements you think will be suitable. Might I suggest a trip to the cathedral? You will be able to visualize what sorts of flowers would look best in that setting. I will also contact Madame Didier in regards to your wedding gown. I'm sure she will be honored to create the wedding ensemble of a future queen. I will send word that she is to report to you at once. I will also take you to my wife, Doris, the head cook, to consult her about the wedding reception ... which should be held here, of course."

Esmeralda's head began to spin as she soaked this all in, but she was grateful for the butler's help. "Jarvis, I have a feeling you and I will get along nicely together."

Another smile tugged at the corners of Jarvis' mouth. "I have no doubt in my mind that you are right."

FOOTMEN AND MAIDS scurried to remove themselves from the path of the Queen Mother as she glided down the hallway at a brisk pace. The only sound that could be heard was the click of her high-heeled slippers on the marble floors, and the rustle of her black skirts. Queen Alexandra could have been wielding a sword and shield, so quick were the servants to be out of her way. She was on the warpath, and they all knew not to cross her when she was in such a mood.

She marched toward her son's wing of the palace, moving gracefully past footmen toting trunks and various furnishings. Damien was moving into the king's chambers. She had already vacated the room adjoining the king's bedroom and now had her own wing of the house, which she found quite satisfactory.

This was not the issue that brought her before the new king. The news of his impending wedding to that insipid Gypsy girl had not been well received. She'd hoped that her son would be wise enough to know that his newly elevated status demanded he choose a more suitable bride.

Apparently, Damien needed some sense talked into him, and she was fully prepared to do battle with him on this. The two guards on either side of the door hesitated when she demanded entrance, but soon stepped aside when it became evident that she would not leave before gaining an audience with her son.

Damien was seated behind his desk, talking in hushed tones with a man in military dress, whom Alexandra recognized as a colonel in Cardenas' army. The two men stood and shook hands.

"Thank you for this opportunity, Your Highness," the colonel said as he turned to take his leave. "I know this decision could not have been easy for you, but I am honored to know that you trust me enough to reward me with this position."

"You will make a fine general," Damien replied. "I have no doubts about that. I shall assemble the High Council in a few weeks' time. General Stombol will soon arrive from Barony, and I'll expect a full report from the two of you. Use whatever information he can give you on the state of affairs in Barony and come up with a strategy. I will expect you to be prepared to share your plans with the council and myself—including potential costs and a list of needed supplies."

The newly appointed Colonel Adams bowed and turned to leave. He stopped to bow once more to her, and then was gone.

Alexandra stepped forward. "Damien, a word, if you please."

He sat back behind his desk, head lowered over a letter he was composing.

"Who let you in here?" he asked, never lifting his gaze from his work. "I asked not to be disturbed."

"I made it quite clear that I would not be turned away," she replied, approaching Damien's desk.

He glanced up at her, impatience edging his features. "State your business and leave. I have several other important meetings today and I don't have time for another one of your lectures."

"You will make the time," she insisted. "It has come to my attention that a wedding is being planned as we speak."

"Yes," he ground out, leaning forward to rest his elbows on the desk. "I assume you've come to congratulate me."

"I have come to talk you into coming to your senses! What on earth could you be thinking, choosing a peasant Gypsy dancer as your queen?"

"There is no law dictating my choice of bride, and since Father and Lionus both neglected to select one for me before their deaths, I have made the decision for myself. As well, the only people aware of Esmeralda's background are those who reside behind these walls—not that it makes a different to me one way or another. The court adores her ... the *people* will too. And, naturally, I love her. That is all that matters to me, and it's all that should matter to you."

"I won't allow it!" she shrieked.

The false mask of calm she had donned before entering was now slowly slipping away. Her cheeks flushed and her fists curled at her sides.

Damien stood, his fury a match for hers, his eyes blazing with green fire. "And how do you think to stop me? All I have to do is say the word, and you will be confined to your rooms for as long as I wish it. Or better yet, I could have you banished!"

"You wouldn't dare," she hissed, though she was not so sure. She had never shown Damien much affection and now her neglect of her youngest son might just come back to haunt her. It would be just retribution in his eyes to have her sent away.

"Are you certain?" he taunted. "Do you really want to test me and find out?"

Alexandra sighed, uncurling her fists and smoothing her skirts with her palms. She took on her smooth, cool demeanor once again.

"I warn you, you are making a terrible mistake."

"No," Damien said with a frown. "It is the only thing that makes this whole situation bearable. I had no desire to be in this position and yet here I am. I just appointed a general to take Serge's place leading our armed forces. I find myself responsible for the lives of everyone around me. When I think of a future with the woman I love, all of those things seem inconsequential by comparison."

"You are being unbelievably selfish," Alexandra said. "You haven't the slightest idea what being king really entails. Your father sacrificed much for the sake of duty and honor."

"Yes, and look what it gained him; a loveless marriage, and a vindictive bastard son. Do you honestly wish that kind of life for me? I am your only remaining child. I would think you'd want some form of happiness for me."

Alexandra sighed. It was clear that Damien was not going to listen to reason. All this drivel about love and happiness were blinding him to the truth. She decided to take her leave of him. Surely, within the few weeks that remained before the wedding, she could find another way to prevent the marriage from taking place.

"I hope you will at least think about what I've said," she remarked before leaving. "As king, you do not have the luxury of thinking only of yourself."

When Damien did not respond, Alexandra breezed through the doors of the library, which magically opened as she approached. The guards swung the doors shut behind her and she turned in the direction of her own chambers.

She encountered Jarvis as she neared her wing of the palace.

"Your Highness," he said with a stiff bow. "You have a caller."

"Who is it, Jarvis?" she snapped. "I do not wish to be disturbed at the moment."

"Lady Davina Russell was most insistent. She said that it was urgent, and she would be willing to wait all day if necessary."

Alexandra had never cared much for Damien's ex-mistress. The woman was vulgar and crass, but she would be more than grateful if Damien were to turn his attentions back to her instead of carrying on with a common Gypsy dancer. At least Lady Davina was of noble blood.

"Where is she?" she asked, allowing curiosity to overcome her desire not to be disturbed by callers.

"I placed her in the parlor overlooking the rose garden, Your Highness."

"Very well," she replied, waving Jarvis away. "See that we are not disturbed."

She entered the salon to find Lady Davina seated on a soft yellow chaise, holding a china cup in her gloved hands. She stood and curtsied prettily at the sight of Alexandra. Despite the girl's flaws, she was quite lovely. She possessed a confident air and an impeccable sense of style. With a little more polish, Davina could be transformed into a lady fit to be her son's queen.

"Your Highness. I am so pleased that you would take time out of your busy day to meet with me."

Alexandra took a seat on the other side of the coffee table, allowing Davina to serve her a cup of chocolate from the gilt tea service between them.

"I was assured that your reason for coming here was most urgent," she said, accepting the offered cup and taking a careful sip.

"Oh, yes," Davina replied. "It is most urgent, Your Highness, and I thought to come to you first since Damien has avoided me like the plague since ending our … association."

Tears welled up in her eyes, and she retrieved a white, lace-trimmed handkerchief to dab at her cheekbones with practiced vulnerability. Uncomfortable with the girl's simpering display of emotion, Alexandra set her cup in its saucer and reached across the table pat Davina's hand. The gesture felt awkward, completely foreign to a woman who had never tolerated weakness in herself or others.

"Pull yourself together, girl," she commanded between Davina's soft sobs. "Tell me what kind of trouble you're in, and I will tell you what I can do to help you."

"I am with child," Davina cried. "I am pregnant with Damien's child."

Alexandra's widened as she digested this. She knew that it had only been a few short months since Damien had last been with his ex-mistress. She also knew that the girl had spread her thighs for several other men since then. Nevertheless, the news was welcome. Even if the child wasn't Damien's, it would be just the leverage she needed to convince her son to marry Davina instead of Esmeralda.

"You mustn't worry anymore, everything will be alright," Alexandra declared. "Leave everything to me."

CHAPTER 22

Rothchester Hall had become a chaotic whirl of activity, and the wedding plans were now well underway. Esmeralda spent much of her time with Jarvis, following his guidance on nearly every aspect of the planning. The only thing she felt confident about was her wedding gown, which Madame Didier was designing with her typical style and flair. Each time the woman called on her for a fitting, the gown became more and more beautiful, more a work of art than a piece of clothing.

Esmeralda followed Jarvis' lead on everything, from the flowers to the wedding reception menu. Even Isabelle managed to shake off her somber mood to throw herself into helping plan the ceremony. Esmeralda sensed that her friend merely needed something to take her mind off her own troubles, and was glad to help offer a distraction.

The evening was growing late, but Esmeralda had just suffered through yet another fitting for her gown. Isabelle was being outfitted as well, having agreed to stand up as her maid of honor. The gray silk gown she was having created for the affair was still in keeping with the tradition of mourning colors, yet looked stunning upon her.

Once the fittings were complete, the two women retired to the dining room for a late supper. Once Jarvis served them, they ate in companionable silence, each lost in her own thoughts. Esmeralda wondered how her friend felt about her uncertain future. She would soon step into the role Isabelle had been born to fill and Esmeralda could not shake off feelings of guilt over it.

"Nonsense," Isabelle said when she voiced her concerns. "None of this is your fault. No one could have foreseen that things would happen this way. I must find my own place in this world now, whether it be here or in the country of my birth. You must find your happiness here with Damien. Believe me when I say I am truly happy for you."

"I've never been more nervous about anything in my entire life. I only hope that Damien does not regret making me his queen."

"There's nothing to it, I promise you. The men run the world and we are simply to bear their sons and congratulate them on their many accomplishments."

She giggled and Isabelle followed suit, her eyes sparkling as they hadn't in weeks. There were still tight lines of sadness around her mouth and eyes, but Esmeralda was grateful to see signs of her friend slowly rising back to the surface.

Damien found them a few minutes later, sipping coffee over dessert and chatting. He took a seat beside Esmeralda and helped himself to a bit of her custard.

Esmeralda slapped at his hand playfully.

"You horrid man," she admonished, though the sternness of her voice did not quite reach her face. "Do you think that just because you are soon to be my husband, you may now avail yourself to everything that is mine?"

"My love," Damien replied with a wicked smile. "That is exactly what my becoming your husband entails."

Isabelle stood. "Perhaps I should leave. The two of you have much to discuss."

Her impish grin told Esmeralda she knew exactly the type of business Damien would like to discuss just then. His gaze was fixed on the luscious cream topping on her dessert, and he looked very much like he wanted to lay her across the table and slather her with it.

Esmeralda pushed him away, her shoulders shaking with laughter. "Damien, behave, you're going to chase Isabelle away."

"Isabelle understands," he said, dropping a light kiss upon her shoulder.

That intimacy sent a jolt like electricity through her body. Long weeks had passed since they had last made love and Esmeralda found she was as desperate to have him as he seemed to be to have her.

"As I said, I'll leave the two of you alone now," Isabelle repeated, edging toward the double doors of the dining room.

Just as she reached for the knob, the doors swung open to admit Alexandra, who swept into the room, leading another woman in behind her.

Lady Davina, Damien's former mistress, looked as ravishing as ever in an emerald green carriage dress and matching redingote, a jaunty hat topping her auburn locks.

Esmeralda's stomach clenched at the sight of the other woman, wondering what she could be doing in the company of the queen.

"What is *she* doing here?" Damien spat, his expression and tone unmistakable in their disgust.

The courtesan gave them both a cat-like smile, but said nothing.

"Damien, there is an important matter we need to discuss," Alexandra said, motioning for Davina to be seated at the table across from them.

Esmeralda stood, uncertain why her palms were suddenly damp. She did not like this. Whatever was happening did not bode well.

"Perhaps I should leave, too," she said, moving toward the door where Isabelle hovered.

"You should stay," Alexandra said, clear command in her words. "This involves you as well, I suppose."

Esmeralda chose to remain near the door, unwilling to sit across the table from Davina, who had been shooting daggers at her with her eyes since the moment she entered the room. Isabelle clasped her hand in a show of support.

"I had hoped the two of you would be able to resolve this without my interference, Damien," said Alexandra. "But, Davina informs me that you have been avoiding her and have refused to see her on several occasions."

Damien shrugged. "That is because there is nothing more for me to say to her. I made myself quite clear before. What is this about?"

"Davina is carrying your child," she said, a self-satisfied smirk crossing her features at the look of sheer panic that overtook his expression.

His face had drained of all color and he stared blankly ahead, eyes widened. While she didn't want to believe it, Esmeralda knew that it was entirely possible.

Isabelle gasped, clapping a hand over her mouth to stifle the sound, while the other tightened around Esmeralda's.

Esmeralda remained silent, but felt as if she had been punched in the gut. She fell back against the paneled oak wall of the dining room and closed her eyes, wishing she could will herself to disappear. She did not want to be here for this, yet could not force herself to leave the room.

The silence persisted for a long moment, hanging like a thick, heavy fog in the air between them all.

"Are you certain?" Damien asked, his low voice the only sound in the otherwise quiet room.

"Of course," Davina replied, an edge of annoyance to her voice. "I was examined by my physician. I had hoped not to trouble you with this before your wedding, but Her Highness insisted you would do the right thing."

Damien stood, running a shaking hand through his hair. He lowered his head and examined the table silently for quite some time, his mouth pinched and his forehead creased with worry. Esmeralda clenched her skirts to still her shaking hands, her belly roiling as she waited with baited breath for what would come next.

Surely he must marry Davina now, and she would be cast aside. It would be the moral thing to do, the gentlemanly thing. However, knowing that did not stop the ache in her chest.

"This changes nothing," he murmured.

He turned his jade gaze upon Davina, their normally warm depths cold and hard. His voice raised when he spoke again, his tone sharp and brusque.

"Do you hear me? This changes nothing!"

"Damien, surely you do not mean to abandon your child," Alexandra admonished, clicking her tongue in disapproval. "Can you really be so selfish?"

"I have not said that I will not provide for the child," he retorted, keeping his steel-edged gaze upon Davina. "I want the word of a physician that you are truly pregnant."

"Of course," Davina replied, keeping her composure in the face of Damien's anger. "My physician can be here in a moment's notice to—"

His laugh was rough and harsh, cutting through the silence in the room like a knife.

"I want you examined by *my* physician. Do you think I would trust you enough to believe you without adequate proof? You forget, I know how vindictive you can be. You will return when I summon you to be examined. If the physician finds you to be pregnant as you say, I will settle whatever amount you request upon you and the child. I will not give you or the child my name, and you will speak of this to no one!"

"What am I to do?" Davina cried, her facade finally crumbling as tears sprang to her eyes. "Where am I to go? I'll be ruined!"

"Honestly, Damien," Alexandra admonished, placing an arm around Davina's shoulders. "Will you not think of this poor girl's welfare? She is quite right, you know. You've absolutely ruined her."

"I don't care where you go or what you do," Damien declared. "My decision will not change. I will not be forced into marriage by you or anyone else."

He grasped Esmeralda by the hand and led her from the dining room.

"When I return I want her gone," her threw over his shoulder before slamming the door behind them.

Esmeralda allowed him to lead her up the winding staircase

toward his new chambers in silence. She wanted to cry. She wanted to yell and scream at Fate for conspiring to keep her and Damien apart. She wanted to disappear. Instead, she followed him in docile silence until they were behind closed doors, every corner of her soul cold and numb.

He strode to the sideboard and poured himself a liberal splash of brandy. Then, he downed the first glass with one long gulp and poured himself another. Once he had drained the second glass, he turned back to Esmeralda, who had sunk silently into a chair near the door and sat staring in to the lit hearth without seeing.

"This changes nothing," he stated, coming down on his knees in front of her, grasping her hands in his. "We will still be together."

Esmeralda shook her head. A lone tear slipped down her cheek and splashed onto the back of her hand.

"Don't you see, Damien? This changes everything."

"No!" he bellowed, fairly shaking the walls of his chambers. "It can't. I won't let it."

"I know you, Damien. You are not the kind of man to abandon his child … even if you no longer care for the mother."

"I won't lose you," he protested, burying his face in her lap and clinging to her as if for dear life. "So much has happened to keep you from me already. I couldn't bear it if I lost you now."

"The selfish part of me wants you all for myself," she admitted, reaching out with one hand to stroke his hair. "But I know in my heart that I could never truly be happy with you, knowing what we did to poor Davina."

"There must be a way," he pleaded. "You must let me find another way."

Esmeralda pushed him away gently and stood. Breaking the contact hurt her to the core of her being, but she knew now what needed to be done. Damien wasn't thinking clearly, his emotional state overriding rationale. But, she could see very clearly how things must be now, even if she did not like it.

"There is no other way. Think of all that has happened because your father shunned his responsibility to Nicolai. Do you honestly want to have a hand in making this child hate or despise you?"

Damien shook his head, though his expression remained defiant. Esmeralda cupped his face in her hands and kissed his lips gently, longingly—maybe, she thought, for the last time. He clung to her, grasping her waist and pulled her close until she was starved for air. She threaded her fingers through his golden curls and drank her fill from him, memorizing the feel of his lips on hers to get her through the cold, lonely winter to come. She would never forget what it was to be held by him, kissed by him, loved by him.

She would never forget that for a short time, she had known what true love felt like. Esmeralda did not think she'd ever find it again, so needed this kiss to carry her through the rest of her life. It could never be enough, but it would have to do.

When they pulled apart, he cupped her face with one hand, his thumb stroking along her cheek.

"I won't give up hope yet," he insisted. "There is still the examination by a doctor to be seen to and … if it turns out that this is all a false claim, then we will proceed as we planned. I won't let myself believe this is over."

Esmeralda was determined not to cling to hope, but found herself doing it anyway. If Davina was lying about her pregnancy, then they still had a chance. However, reason told her that it wasn't likely.

"I love you," she whispered, pressing her lips to his one last time before turning to leave.

It took every ounce of her will not to look back.

Two days later, Damien sat in the corridor outside one of the many rooms in his wing of the house, waiting for Doctor Keane to finish examining Davina. The physician had asked him to leave the room for the sake of the lady's modesty, and though Damien had protested, he was eventually coerced into sitting in the hallway. He did not trust Davina alone for a moment, and had wanted to see her examined with his own eyes.

In the back of his mind, he realized he was being ridiculous. Doctor Keane had been a trusted physician to the royal family for years. He blamed his irrationality on the fact that he'd hardly slept in the past two days. He had lain awake both nights, praying that Davina was not really with child, hoping his relationship with Esmeralda was not too far beyond repair.

She did not blame him for this turn of events, he knew. This had happened before he'd even known her. Still, Damien blamed himself. He had been foolish to think he could outrun his past and make himself a better person with Esmeralda. Yet his previous deeds seemed to forever come back to slap him in the face. He had tried to change, but the consequences of his lifestyle were far-reaching and painful. How long would he pay for his transgressions? Would this be the end of it, or was there more to come?

Damien could not abandon the child, despite the things he'd said in the heat of the moment. If he did, he would forever have to live with the guilt of knowing his son or daughter would not have much of a future without him. He also could not be as callous as his own father had been, and pawn his ex-mistress and child off on some other man. His conscience would eat away at him, just as it had Adare.

Of course, he could always send Davina away and raise the babe himself, but knew he would forever regret that his child did not have a mother. He only hoped Davina would prove to be better than his own mother had been. Perhaps motherhood would soften her, change her. Anything was possible, as falling in love had gone a long way toward changing him.

If she were truly with child, he would have to marry her. The thought nearly made him sick, but there was no other option. If he'd gotten her pregnant, then he must face the consequences of that, no matter how much he didn't want to.

He stood as Doctor Keane appeared, adjusting his spectacles as he closed the door behind him.

All his hopes were finally dashed when the doctor spoke.

"She's most certainly with child. I estimate that she has been for two months or more."

Damien's heart sank as the noose of duty and responsibility settled itself firmly around his neck. Despair settled in the pit of his stomach. Just one more thing weighing him down, keeping him away from the things he'd wanted most.

"Thank you," he said to the doctor, dismissing the man from his mind as he disappeared down the corridor.

He stood outside the bedchamber for a few minutes, pulling himself together. He would go in and face his future, however unwelcome it might be. He might not be marrying for love, but his child would be cherished and well taken care of. His child would carry his name. It was the honorable thing to do, and he'd spent so much of his life living without any sense of honor or what was right. Now was the time to become the man his brother had always wanted him to be.

He entered the room to find Davina seated on the edge of the bed, her hands folded demurely in her lap. She watched him in silence as he crossed the room.

He folded his arms over his chest and looked down at her with contempt. Even the lust he'd once felt for her was absent, her opulent beauty nothing in the face of Esmeralda purity and goodness.

"We will be married as soon as possible," he declared.

Even saying the words aloud made him feel ill.

"I hope we can come to an understanding, Damien," she said, coming to her feet and reaching out to touch his chest.

He captured her wrist before she could touch him, derision turning his stomach at the thought of her laying her hands upon him.

"Do not make the mistake of thinking I care anything for you. This marriage will be for the sake of the child, and in name only. You are not the wife I want, nor are you the queen Cardenas deserves."

True to form, she grinned in the face of his anger, angling her body toward him and eying him as a lioness might her prey.

"Come Damien, surely you have not lost all the feelings you once had for me. I seem to remember you having one very strong sentiment."

"Lust," he spat. "And I find that it is no longer present when I look at you. This is not a love match, and were it not for the child you are carrying, I would have thrown you out the moment you walked back into my life. As my wife, I ask only for your loyalty to me as your king and your care of our child. You and I have hardly remained faithful to each other in the past, and I do not intend for us to start doing so now. So long as you are discreet in your affairs, I couldn't care less who you part your thighs for."

"I understand perfectly, darling," she said with a wide smile. "It will be as you say ... though I suspect that in time you will come to change her mind."

It wasn't likely, but he wouldn't waste his breath saying so. She would come to see he meant every word once they were wed.

"I will instruct Jarvis to send someone for your things. I suppose you can begin moving into your new chambers immediately."

With that, he released her wrist and turned to put her behind him.

DAVINA WATCHED HIM GO, then fell onto the bed with a whoop of delight once she heard his footsteps retreating down the corridor. She had not been so sure of her plan in the beginning. At first, she'd panicked when Damien had informed her that she was to be examined by his own physician. Surely, her lie would be discovered and Damien would throw her out the moment he discovered the truth.

Luckily for her, Doctor Keane had long been an admirer of hers. He wasn't the only man in Cardenas to covet her to no avail. He did not have the blunt to afford a courtesan of her caliber, and well he knew it. However, when his gaze had raked over her body with unmistakable admiration, she knew she could have the physician eating out of the palm of her hand with nothing more than a few sexual favors.

She had flirted and smiled suggestively, and had taken every opportunity to draw his eyes to her ample charms. When he asked her to disrobe for him so that he could examine her, she had done so slowly, tantalizing him as she removed each article of clothing.

Dropping her gown into a puddle around her feet, she had thrust her proud breasts forward as she dropped her corset, petticoats, and chemise to the floor. Then, she had offered herself to him, and he had leapt at the chance to discover the delights that awaited him between her thighs.

Doctor Keane was not unattractive, though he was a bit plain to look at and a little on the thin side. His dull blond hair did little to brighten his appearance, but when she removed his spectacles she found he possessed soft blue eyes—his best feature. Not without promise, and not a trial to open her legs for, she'd decided.

She'd had to clap her hand over his mouth to silence his moans and groans as he had lifted her and pressed her against the wall and drove wildly into her. Eventually, she had offered him a breast and he'd suckled hungrily, muffling his sounds of pleasure as he took her against the wall. She hadn't been at all unpleased with the doctor who was a bit clumsy, but not totally inefficient. She'd found more pleasure in the thought that they could be caught at any moment than anything else, reaching her peak seconds before he had.

Once they were finished, she'd secured a promise from the doctor that he would tell Damien anything she wanted. Of course, the man expected to bed her again, and Davina found she did not think the idea too repulsive. She rather liked the notion of taking the doctor as her lover for a little while, if for no other reason than to secure her secret until she could come up with a baby.

Orphanages were full of unwanted children, and of course Davina would find a boy. Her son would inherit everything that belonged to his father, including the throne. Davina's place at Rothchester Hall and under Damien's protection would then be secure.

CHAPTER 23

Tonight was the night. Damien didn't understand how he knew this. There seemed to be something in the air, some tangible thing that hummed with tension and promise. It resounded through him like the clash of a symbol, telling him that this would be the night he faced Nicolai for the last time. One of them would not walk away alive, and he was more determined than ever that it would not be him. He had to think of his family, of Esmeralda and even Serge, still comatose in his bed. Their lives and the well-being of his citizens depended upon him remaining on the throne, which meant Nicolai must die. His cousin would not rest until he'd achieved his aims otherwise.

He gazed out at the approaching sunset, stirred to attention by the howling winds and flurries of rapidly falling snow. A blizzard was upon them, another reason he felt confident Nicolai would come to him any moment now. He remembered his vision clearly: his cousin approaching as Damien stood on the palace steps, walking through darkness and whirling snow.

He sat before the fire in the green salon, slowly draining his second glass of brandy and staring thoughtfully into the fire.

Davina's things had been moved into the queen's suite beside his the evening before, and she was already making plans to redecorate. The project would cost him a great deal of money, but he did not care. So long as she stayed out of his way, she could do whatever the hell she wanted and he cared nothing for what it would cost him.

Guests had already begun arriving for the wedding ... the nuptials of King Damien and the mysterious Esmeralda, whom no one could quite figure out. Very few in his household knew about Esmeralda's background and for some reason his servants had not gossiped about her identity. Many members of the court still assumed she was some foreign princess come to be his bride, and adored her enough not to care whether or not it was the truth.

Of course, explanations to the contrary now had to be made. Damien left it up to his mother to make the announcement as to the change of bride, though the date and time of the ceremony were to remain the same. There would be much gossip and conjecture, but no one would dare to question him. One of the many perks of being king, he supposed.

Lost in thought, he did not at first hear the commotion just outside the doors of the salon. Damien turned and inclined his head in the direction of the noise, trying to hear over the pattering feet and mumbling voices in the main hall. Very faintly, he thought he could discern a voice being carried in on the winter storm. It sounded like a man, and as the sound became clearer, he realized it was his name being called.

"Damien! King Damien!"

The voice was unmistakable now, though it was hardly more than a whisper on the wind.

He strode toward to the doors just as Jarvis swung them open. The voice seemed to echo through the main hall from outside and he knew in that instant who it was.

"Damien!" the voice called, growing bolder and louder as if coming from the front courtyard.

Nicolai.

"My sword," he commanded, moving through the salon into the main hall.

Though it was freezing outside, he declined the greatcoat and gloves offered to him by a footman. Swords would be Nicolai's weapon of choice, and he needed to be as unencumbered as possible. He rolled his shirtsleeves to the elbow and accepted his blade from Jarvis.

Damien studied the ornate hilt of the weapon that had been wielded by generations of kings. He felt that perhaps some remnant of his father's spirit still lingered there, as well as his brother's. He could still hear Lionus' voice, commanding Damien to avenge him.

"I won't fail you, brother," he promised as he strapped the sword around his hips.

Jarvis grasped his shoulder, his face filled with concern, eyes emanating an unspoken fear. "Palace sentinels are prepared to take him into custody for you. He is mad to think he can just walk up the steps of the palace and murder our king."

Damien clasped Jarvis in a tight hug, clinging tight to a man who had been like another father to him for most of his life. The fear he felt in the older man's shivers was why he must do this. No one should live in terror because of a menace like Nicolai. Damien had to set them free, once and for all.

"No, Jarvis. The palace guards will stand by in the event that this is an ambush. But this is something I must do alone. Tell them to stand down as long as it is only Nicolai and I."

Jarvis relinquished his hold on him and nodded, his jaw set with the same determination that hardened Damien's features.

"Finish it, then."

Damien allowed a footman to open the massive door for him and then let ten palace guards followed him out into the night. The rest were ordered to stay in the main hall and await his command, while these ten stood vigil on at the top of the palace steps.

He paused at the bottom of the stairs, hand braced on the hilt of his sword. He could faintly make out the gleam of something silver coming toward him through the night. As the black-cloaked figure drew near, he saw the silver mask glowing in the moonlight over his cousin's face. The silver head of his cane glinted menacingly in his hand—the infamous figure of an eagle being constricted by a two-headed viper protruding from the top of it.

"All hail, King Damien!" mocked Nicolai's voice from behind the mask.

He came to a standstill at the center of the courtyard and bowed, the motion mocking.

"You were foolish to come alone, Nicolai. Even more so to think this plot of yours would accomplish anything more than your death."

Nicolai laughed through the twisted smile of the mask's mouth. "Who says I am alone? My men are ready and waiting, close enough to hear every word that is said. Once I have killed you, they will storm the palace. All who reject me as their king will be put to death."

Damien could hardly believe his ears. This man who had been so close to him had never sounded so angry or irrational. If he had gone insane, he'd done a good job of hiding it over the years.

"You've gone mad," he accused, taking the steps one at a time, down toward the center of the courtyard. "Do you honestly think you will ever be king? The people of Cardenas won't stand for it!"

"The people have no idea what is good for them. Once I am in power, I will make it known that all who oppose me will be put to death. Naturally, I will start with your mother and the most loyal members of your household. Perhaps I'll even have a bit of fun with your little Gypsy girl before I carve her to pieces."

Damien's hand tightened on the hilt of his sword, rage flaring in him in an instant. Taking a deep breath, he forced himself to calm. Nicolai was baiting him, playing upon his anger to make him irrational. It would put him at a great disadvantage in the fight.

"This is your last chance to stand down, Nicolai," he said, taking a few more steps into the courtyard.

The moon was full and high overhead against a cloudless sky, providing the perfect light for a late night fight. Snow still fell around them in sickeningly whimsical swirls, the powdery substance glowing in the starlight.

"Tell your men to surrender, and I will have mercy and allow you to live."

Nicolai's laughter was an ugly and harsh sound that caused Damien's blood to boil. He gripped his sword's hilt until he thought he would snap it in two.

"Surrender to you? Don't be ridiculous."

"Since you have refused my generous offer, I feel the need to tell you that you will lie dead at the end of this night," Damien declared. "I will not allow you entrance into this palace after your mindless slaughter of your family."

"*My* family? My family lied to me! Tricked me! My own father pawned me off on his spineless brother and turned his back on me!"

"Father loved you. He loved Aunt Margaret as well. He only did what his duty demanded of him. Perhaps he made the wrong choice, but he hardly deserved to die for it. And what of Lionus and Serge? Was being born their only crime against you?"

"Adare never looked back," Nicolai countered. "If he'd had any love for Mother, he would have seen how living without him had affected her. She spent the rest of her life sick with longing for a love she could no longer have. Even on her deathbed, when she told me that he was my father, she declared her love for him. As for Serge and Lionus … consider them collateral damage, just as you will be. Your deaths will rest on Adare's head, not mine."

"Take off your mask," Damien demanded, searching for Nicolai's eyes through the dark slits of the mask. "I want to look upon your face before I run you through."

Nicolai readily obliged, tossing the silver mask aside; it clattered against the cobblestones. A pair of green eyes met his and Damien wondered how he never noticed the resemblance. Even now in his anger, he had to admit that he and Nicolai had more similarities to each other than he had with his other brothers. The man was, quite frankly, the spitting image of Adare. How no one had ever puzzled out the truth was beyond him.

"I had hoped you would be smart enough to leave the country with your Gypsy dancer like you'd planned," Nicolai said once he was free of the mask. "I never thought I would have to wrest the crown from your grasp. Did you lie to me when you said you didn't want it?"

"No," Damien admitted. "Even now the crown weighs heavily on my head because of the way it has fallen to me. But I'll be damned if I allow it to fall to you after what you've done, you bastard!"

Nicolai smirked. "Bastard. Rather a fitting title for me, don't you think?"

Damien had grown tired of talking. The longer Nicolai stood before him, the greater his anger became. The time had come to end things. He unsheathed his weapon, holding it up in a silent challenge. Wordlessly, Nicolai grasped the head of his walking stick and pulled. A long, narrow sword was revealed from within the cane, which doubled as a sheath.

Nicolai tossed the scabbard aside and removed his cape, allowing it to fall to the ground. "This ends tonight."

Damien gripped his sword with both hands, poised for Nicolai's attack. They stood that way in silence for the span of a few seconds, eyes clashing. The wind whipped Damien's curls wildly about his head. In his mind, he saw Lionus dying a painful death as his lifeblood drained from his body. He saw Serge's battered and broken body lying upstairs. For them, he must emerge the victor this night.

Nicolai attacked first, as Damien had known he would. He charged at Damien with his sword raised, bringing it down to meet his with a loud clangor that rang out in the quiet of the courtyard. Damien timed his parries perfectly to Nicolai's thrusts, knowing his every move. They had sparred together many times, knew the other's strengths and weaknesses, and were equally matched.

He circled Nicolai, reaching out with the edge of his sword and finding his target. His blade sliced into Nicolai's sword arm. Damien watched in satisfaction as his blood dripped slowly to the cobblestones below, but did not celebrate for long. Nicolai was far too skilled to be bested by a simple cut on his arm, but Damien hoped that in a few moments he was going to have a hard time holding up his weapon.

Nicolai fought like a madman, growing angrier by the second. He aimed for Damien's neck and torso, while Damien concentrated solely on taking little slices out of his opponent's limbs. Before long, Nicolai's clothes were nearly in ribbons and blood trickled from several small cuts on his arms and legs. Damien had been deeply cut once on his thigh and the wound bled profusely, but he stood strong.

Nicolai grew sluggish, his movements becoming slower and sloppier with each passing second. Damien could have moved in for the kill at any moment, but was content to drag out his punishment for as long as he wished. He watched Nicolai squirm and writhe in pain before him even as he continued to fight for his life.

A carefully executed swipe caught Nicolai across the back and with a cry of agony, he fell to his knees.

Damien stood over his half-brother, watching as he fought for breath. White mist curled from his lips in the cold night air, and the blood he'd lost stained the snow beneath him. Though Nicolai seemed to know the moment of his death was upon him, his eyes were still filled with venom and hatred as he stared up at Damien.

He pressed the sharp edge of his blade to Nicolai's throat.

"For my father and brothers," he whispered before dealing his final blow.

With an expert flick of his wrist and a great deal of strength, he sent Nicolai's head rolling across the courtyard. The body remained in its position on its knees for a moment before it fell sideways onto the cold, hard ground.

Damien turned away, signaling the palace guards. They ran past him with their swords drawn, followed by those who had been waiting in the main hall. As he returned to the palace, he heard the clash and clang of sword and armor. He knew it would be only a matter of time before Nicolai's men were brought under their control and didn't even bother to look back to make sure things were well in hand. With their benefactor dead, the mercenaries had nothing else to fight for.

Damien ordered the captain of the guard to keep them alive for public execution, as a message to others who might think to plot against the royal family.

Jarvis stood just within the open front doors. He wordlessly accepted Damien's sword and handed it off to a footman to be cleaned. The butler followed him as he continued up the stairs and to his chambers. He turned to the other man and held out his palms, which were stained with his half-brother's blood. His face and neck were splattered with the crimson gore as well.

At last, the stoicism he'd held onto during the fight slipped away, and grief pierced him through the knife like the sharpest of blades.

"I killed him," he whispered, staring at his hands in disbelief. "I killed my brother."

He dropped to his knees on the carpet and Jarvis went down with him, pulling Damien into his arms. He sobbed against the butler's shoulder, the force of his sorrow and anger shaking him to the core. Jarvis held him until he was finished, seeming content to allow him to release everything he'd been forced to hold inside for the sake of presenting strength and dignity. Just now, he wasn't a king … he was a man—a broken one—who had lost nearly everyone he loved in one fell swoop. With no other eyes watching him, he could allow the feelings to claim him, to wash over him, and then wash away completely so that in the morning, he could become a king again.

Once he'd calmed, Jarvis helped him to his feet and rang for Hopkins.

"You have avenged your father and brothers," the butler assured him. "You did only what was necessary. Lionus wouldn't have done it any differently himself."

Damien nodded, though could find no words to express that he felt both grieved and vindicated at once. Though he was proficient with a sword and pistol, he had never before had to kill another living being. Cardenas had been in a state of peace his entire life and he had never even experienced war. Seeing the blood of another man—a man of his own family—on his hands had nearly been his undoing.

He squeezed his eyes shut and brought his breathing under control. The commotion had not alerted any of their guests, who were mercifully far enough from the main hall not to have heard. He felt a sense of peace and calm come over him as he realized it was really over. The threat to his family had been removed and now they could live without fear of an attack around every corner.

Once Hopkins arrived, Damien allowed the valet to strip him of his bloodied clothes and help him wash the blood from his hands and face. Then, he soaked in the tub for nearly an hour before the fire, sipping at the brandy provided by Hopkins.

He supposed his life could now take on some semblance of normality. Damien nearly laughed at himself for such a thought. How could anything ever be normal again, when his father and Lionus were dead? How could anything ever be the same when Serge lay abed in a state somewhere between death and life? To top it all off, when all was finally peaceful in his life, he had no one to share it with. Esmeralda was now lost to him forever.

DAMIEN COULD NOT SLEEP, even after he'd bathed and had another drink. Every time he closed his eyes, he saw Nicolai's head rolling over the cold stones of the courtyard and a gruesome spray of blood that stained his face and hands. Finally giving up on sleep, he went to his library to find a book. He settled on a volume of poetry he hoped would be soothing, and carried the leather-bound volume back to his chambers.

He had just settled into an armchair with a decanter of brandy at his side, when the connecting door between his room and one of his adjoining sitting rooms opened. A slender maid in black and white entered and stood in the shadow of the doorway in silence.

After a while she stepped forward into the light of his lamp, and Damien dropped the book absently to the floor and stood. He went to her and took her in his arms, crushing her against his chest. He breathed the scent of jasmine, and closed his eyes.

"Thank God you've come," he said, looking down to stare into wide amber eyes.

Esmeralda still did not speak, but then, she didn't have to. Damien knew from her expression that she had been informed of the night's events. She had come knowing how badly he would need her and how he might be feeling. Relieved, because it was all over. Angry, because he had lost his brothers in the process.

Tormented, because he'd had to kill someone he'd loved for all of his life.

"I've come to say goodbye," she whispered. "But I did not want anyone to know I was here, so I used the servant's entrance again. I know it is bad of me to be here when you're engaged to someone else, but I knew you would need comfort tonight."

"I'm glad you're here," he replied, not giving a damn if the entire castle knew she was with him.

Esmeralda opened her mouth to speak, but Damien swiftly covered it with his, causing an unmistakable surge of desire to unfurl in his middle, as it always did when she was near. He kissed her, long and deep, offering his tongue and accepting hers in return. Clinging tight to her, he wished he didn't have to let go, even knowing that at the end of this night he would have no other choice.

"Please don't say anything else," he pleaded, grasping her waist and sinking against her softness. "We do not need words to say goodbye."

Esmeralda nodded in silent agreement and raised her arms to wrap them around his neck. Where his first kiss had been soft and sweet, this one was anything but. His lips clamped over hers with an overwhelming force. Knowing this would be their last night together, Damien intended to make it count.

His lips and hands were everywhere all at once, touching her, moving along the familiar slopes and planes of her body for the last time. They undressed hurriedly, tearing at each other's garments in the desperation of their final joining. When they were undressed, they hurled themselves at each other and landed together on the lush rug before the fireplace, tangled in one another's arms. Damien rolled until he was over her and lifted himself onto his elbows to gaze down at her. She stared back at him brazenly as his eyes moved down over her bare skin, enhanced by firelight.

When he dipped his head to taste the dark peak of one breast, her fingers came up to tangle in his hair and she cried out in delight. He moved slowly, reveling in her taste, her smell, her softness. She roved her hands over his shoulders and chest, lifting her head to taste and tease his skin as he did hers. His seduction was slow and precise, a reminder of all that had been between them and a wish for what could never be.

After what seemed like an eternity, Esmeralda pleaded with him to take her. Tempted as he was to oblige her, Damien held out as long as he could, giving her all he could with his lips and his hands, showing her just how precious she was to him and committing the taste and feel to her to memory. She writhed and squirmed beneath him, shuddering at each touch of his lips. Esmeralda continued to plead and beg, and finally Damien could wait no longer.

Rising up to his knees, he pulled her onto his lap and wrapped her legs around his waist. He wanted to watch her, see the light of the fire play over her golden skin as he loved her. He went slow, thrusting up into her heated core and burying himself deep. He ran his hands through the wild mane tumbling down her back, pulling slightly to expose her neck to his hungry mouth. Kissing and nibbling the column of her throat, he loved her, reveling in the slow drag and slide of her tight sheath around him.

Her cries rose to echo from the high ceilings, but Damien didn't care who heard. He increased his pace, watching her face in pure enchantment as she neared the height of her pleasure. He reached down and gripped her hips in his hands, then moved within her even faster, allowing himself to reach that place with her. They climbed together and soared, clinging to one another as wave after wave of intense rapture washed over them.

Esmeralda collapsed against him, trembling, her head lolling against his shoulder, breath coming in ragged gasps. Damien fell back onto the rug with her, cradling her in his arms, and tried not to think about the fact that they were saying goodbye. He closed his eyes and pretended that everything was all right, that he and Esmeralda would awaken in the morning and go on as they had been for months.

As he felt the hot splash of her tears against his chest, he realized that he could not go on deluding himself. This was it for them. Instead of avoiding thinking of that, he would throw himself into their final night together.

He lifted her chin with his hand and gently wiped the tears from her cheeks. Then he stood and lifted her in his arms, his body already awakening again, his erection re-emerging as the urge to claim her once more overcame him. He carried her to the bed, where he laid her down and proceeded to show her once again just how sorely she would be missed.

Another hour later, he was able to find peace in sleep curled up beside her. When he closed his eyes, he did not dream of death or blood ... he saw only her face.

When he awakened in the morning, she was gone. Her glittering topaz ring sparkled on the pillow beside him.

CHAPTER 24

Today was his wedding day, and though Damien had tried his hardest not to dwell on that fact, he could think of little else. This should have been the happiest day of his life, but instead it was quite possibly the worst. He would be trapped forever in marriage to a woman he loathed.

He rose early and set out for a ride, knowing he would have little privacy in the hours before the ceremony. Already the servants were up and about, preparing Rothchester Hall for the reception to follow the ceremony. Damien made his way past servants carrying large floral arrangements, polished silver, and folded linen napkins, and turned in the direction of the stables.

Over the weeks that had passed, he'd tried fruitlessly to push Esmeralda from his mind. He knew it would be better for him to forget that she had ever been a part of his life, but such a feat proved impossible. Perhaps over time the heart could heal, but the mind could not be made to forget.

He found Desmond just outside the stables, grooming one of the horses that would be hitched to the carriage taking Davina to the church for the ceremony. Desmond stopped what he was doing and gave him a stiff bow. His face was blank and emotionless, though Damien detected a slight frown pulling at the corners of his mouth.

"Your Highness," he said before heading toward the open doors of the stable. "Can I saddle Persephone for you?"

"That would be fine, Desmond, but first I would have a word with you."

The boy stopped and turned to face Damien, his annoyance clear. "Of course."

Damien reached out and grasped the boy's shoulder in a gentle hold. Desmond flinched, but made no move to shrug him off. He had cast his gaze down to his scuffed boots and refused to meet his eye, but Damien pressed on.

"I am sorry for the way things have turned out," he said. "I am just as disappointed as you are that Esmeralda is not the woman I will wed today. My feelings for her have not changed in light of what's happened, and I doubt they ever will. But, sometimes … being a man means doing things you'd rather not do, choosing what's right over your own desires."

The boy nodded and sighed. "I know."

"I hope that you will remain here," Damien added. "You are the best groom I've ever had, and I appreciate all your hard work. I also hope that you and I can still be friends."

Desmond nodded again, but didn't speak. He turned to go back into the stable, leaving him standing there alone. He decided to give the boy time. He had not attacked Damien on sight and that was something, he supposed. Once everything blew over, Desmond would warm up to him again. At least, that was what he hoped would happen.

Once Persephone had been saddled, Damien swung up onto her back and took off at an exhilarating pace, breathing in the cold air of winter's morning. He pushed the mare hard and fast, thundering over the hard ground. Damien only wished he had the freedom to dig his heels into her sides and just keep riding, over the mountains and away from the world he had been born into. However, before long he had to turn back and face the inevitable.

ELISE MARION

Hopkins awaited in his dressing room, prepared to shave him. Damien endured the valet's fussing without a word, staring off into space as he was groomed. Jarvis entered just as Hopkins finished tying his cravat. He wore all black, save for his white shirt and linen, as he had decided that it was more than appropriate for him to wear mourning colors on his wedding day.

The butler stood watching him silently for several minutes, the disapproval on his face more than clear. Hopkins had been giving him similar looks all morning, but he'd ignored them up until now.

His patience snapped when Jarvis cleared his throat, giving Damien a knowing look.

"What the devil is it, Jarvis?"

"Your Highness, if I may be so bold—"

"You may not! There is nothing to discuss. I am marrying the mother of my child today, as it seems I hardly have a choice in the matter. It is over."

Jarvis inclined his head and bowed. "My apologies, Your Highness."

When Hopkins was finally finished, Damien went to the waiting carriage prepared to take him to the church. He did not know if Davina had gone before him or not and quite frankly did not care. He stared out through the window as he rode in silence with Hopkins and Jarvis, neither of whom said another word.

The rest of the morning swept by him in a blur. He faintly remembered standing at the front of the chapel, which had been filled to the rafters with guests. Even the courtyard outside had brimmed with Cardenas' citizens, all seeking to get a glimpse of their king and his new king queen. Damien had tuned out the priest's droning voice. He'd knelt for prayer when it was time and partook of the ceremonial communion. He'd repeated the vows mechanically, though he could not have told anyone later what he had promised.

The priest pronounced them man and wife and a stone weight seemed to settle itself within him. He lifted Davina's veil and barely brushed her lips with his. It was done. He was married.

A few hours later, he found himself seated beside his bride in the ballroom, where he downed glass after glass of champagne, effectively drinking himself into oblivion. Friends and well-wishers lifted their glasses in toast, one after the other. He was glad when the first course arrived and the toasting finally ceased. If one more person wished them a happy and prosperous marriage, he might go somewhere private and put a pistol in his mouth.

Of course, no one was so bold as to mention his previous betrothal to another woman. All of this seemed a distant memory to his guests, though there had been several rumors as to the reason for the sudden change of bride. Many speculated that Esmeralda had grown homesick and returned to whatever country she had come from, unable to go through with the marriage. Others thought that she had run off with another man to elope. Still, others were certain it was because the king's former mistress was with child. Of course, Damien said nothing to confirm or deny those rumors. Everyone would know soon enough, when the babe was born.

"Perhaps you shouldn't drink so much champagne," Davina hissed in his ear when he signaled a waiting servant to bring another bottle.

"Nonsense, my little wife," he said, accepting the open bottle and filling his flute. "This is a party. Come, join me in celebrating this joyous day!"

Alexandra shook her head in disapproval from her seat on Damien's other side.

"Shameful," she muttered before turning her attention back to the bowl of soup in front of her.

Damien barely touched his food. As course after course was brought before them, he ignored them all in favor of the bubbly champagne. At some point, he pushed his glass aside and took to swigging straight from the bottle, relinquishing it only long enough to lead Davina to the midst of the ballroom for their obligatory first dance as man and wife.

Despite his inebriated state, he managed to lead her gracefully through the waltz and dazzle their guests with his superior command of the dance. He then left Davina in the company of several young admirers and took his place once again at the table. Davina was partnered by an endless stream of men, and barely had time to notice that Damien was upon his third bottle.

Finally, it came time for the bride and groom to retire for their wedding night, and Damien was grateful to escape the stares and smiles of his so-called friends. He'd been on display the entire day and had grown quite weary of it.

He collapsed onto the edge of his bed and lay there for a few moments until the room stopped spinning. Perhaps it hadn't been a good idea to drink so much champagne, but he felt so deliciously numb and nonchalant. He hardly cared that a woman he detested was now next door to him readying herself for their wedding night.

He struggled into a sitting position and bent at the waist to remove his shoes. With slow, clumsy movements, he fumbled at his cravat until he had succeeded in removing it. Where the devil was Hopkins anyway? Probably off somewhere with Jarvis shaking his head in disapproval. Well, they could damn well hate their new queen all they liked; hell, he hated her too.

Just as soon as he had removed his shirt, the connecting room between his and Davina's suite opened and his bride entered. She was dressed in a wispy bit of white material that was nearly nonexistent against her fair skin. Her gleaming auburn waves had been brushed and fell loose around her shoulders.

She stopped and struck a provocative pose in the doorway.

"I hope I haven't kept you waiting too long, my husband," she purred, sashaying toward him. "I see you are nearly ready to receive your bride."

Damien studied her with a mocking grin, his disgust blatant. After a moment, he burst out laughing, doubled over and clutching his sides. When the laughter had subsided and he had composed himself, he rose from the bed, suddenly stone cold sober. She mistook his intentions as he walked toward her and smiled invitingly. Only when he drew near did she seem to notice the stubborn set of his jaw.

He grasped her by the shoulders, keeping her at arm's length before she had the chance to touch him. If she did, he didn't think he could be held responsible for his actions.

"You disgust me," he snarled. "Do you think you have anything to offer me that I haven't already had from you countless times before? Let me assure you, I'm not interested anymore."

"But ... but it's our wedding night," she stammered once he had shoved her away and turned back toward his bed.

He blew out the lamp near his bed and turned his back to her. "Good night, Davina."

Her rage-filled scream could be heard halfway down the corridor had anyone been near enough to hear. Immune to her tantrum, he curled up and closed his eyes, allowing the champagne to pull him under into oblivion.

ESMERALDA BURROWED her head beneath her pillow and tried to drown out the sound of her mother's voice from the other side of the door. In the time that had passed since she last saw Damien, she'd been feeling quite ill. She slept for hours during the day, and in the evenings had found herself too tired to give an adequate performance at The Golden Dancer. After one routine, she'd had to run through the dressing room and out into the alleyway where she became violently sick, spilling the contents of her stomach onto the street.

By now her mother and grandmother were worried sick wondering what was wrong with her. They attempted special teas and soups and tried to coax her into eating, but nothing helped. They assumed she was simply languishing from a broken heart. But her heart was the least of her worries.

She was pregnant.

So much had happened over the past several weeks that Esmeralda had not even realized she'd missed her monthly courses. By the time she'd noticed, it was too late.

Today was supposed to have been her wedding day, but now it was Damien and Davina's. The irony of her situation had not been lost on her. After she had finished crying over it, she'd laughed bitterly at how cruel a mistress Fate could be. How plausible was it, that mere weeks after Davina had appeared at Rothchester Hall claiming to be with child, she would discover her own pregnancy?

This revelation would have brought her endless joy a few weeks ago. Now, it filled her not with happiness, but despair. If Damien were to find out that she was pregnant, it would only confuse and upset him. He would be forced to choose between her and Davina, and though she knew in her heart that he would she would be his choice, she was not certain if his decision would be the right one. A child in the hands of that venomous woman would need the care of a man like Damien. Otherwise, they ran the risk of ending up with another Nicolai—something the Rothchester family did not need after all that had occurred.

Damien must never know, and Esmeralda would raise her child alone. The idea was not very encouraging, but what else could she do? The only thing Damien could offer her now was financial support, and that would make their time together seem cheap and tawdry. Esmeralda refused to tarnish their memories in such a way.

So much had gone wrong already, and she just wanted to find some peace in her life; she wanted the same for Damien. Surely, he had resigned himself to his marriage with Davina. Even now, on their wedding night, he could be making love to her.

Esmeralda tried not to think on that overlong, or else she'd become sick again. She thought instead of the last night they had spent together, loving each other desperately, neither of them knowing that his seed had already taken root within her womb.

Raina finally ceased knocking on the locked bedroom door and declared that she would leave Esmeralda's dinner tray outside the door. She was relieved when her mother's waning footsteps indicated her retreat. She needed time in which to think and devise a plan. When she was finally ready to tell her family, they would not be able to talk her out of whatever decisions she had made.

For now, she only wanted sleep. Her eyelids grew heavy, and though she had slept for hours already, she felt as if she had been awake for days without rest. Fighting the waves of nausea that swept over her when she even contemplated getting up to retrieve her dinner, she welcomed the open arms of sleep.

"But Tristan, I don't understand. I thought you loved me!"

Tristan crossed his arms over his chest, impatience putting him on edge. He did not have time for this nonsense. He had better things he could be doing, like comforting Esmeralda, who needed him. Instead, he stood in the dressing room of The Golden Dancer, where he had accidentally encountered Morgana while searching for her cousin.

The time had long passed for him to end their affair. The girl had been diverting enough when he'd needed something to take his mind off Esmeralda, but now that the woman he loved was suddenly available again, Morgana's usefulness had run its course. He had tried to let her down as gently as possible, and had been rewarded with an insipid bout of tears accompanied by an annoying amount of sniffling.

"I never said that I did," he pointed out, wishing that he had never gotten involved with her in the first place.

Morgana was young, barely nineteen, and taking her virginity had been a terrible blunder. She had obviously mistaken their affair as one that would inevitably lead to marriage, and now she saw all of her carefully laid plans falling down around her.

"Yes, but we made love," she whispered, as if this were explanation enough. "Did I do something wrong?"

She grasped his shirt and pulled him close, pressing her lips to his ear.

"Please Tristan," she sighed, pressing her soft, wriggling body against his. "Whatever I did, I won't ever do it again. I'll do whatever you want. I'll let you do whatever you want to me. Please…"

Tristan grasped her firmly by the shoulders and dislodged her from his clothing. Dark smudges of kohl streamed down her face and her cheeks were a mottled shade of red. Tristan grimaced at the sight and offered her one of his handkerchiefs.

"Keep it," he said, not wanting anything to do with her any longer … not even the bit of linen she ruined with her kohl and rogue.

Morgana swiped at her eyes and stuffed the handkerchief into the pocket of her skirt. "Please don't go. I'll do anything for you, I promise."

Tristan shook his head. "Morgana, it is time for you to grow up and understand the way things work between men and women. We had sex. That does not mean that I love you, or that you love me. You only think you love me because I was your first. Soon you will forget about me and some new man will catch your eye. You'll see."

Morgana's hands balled into fists at her sides and she flew at him, screaming her rage like a battle cry, pummeling him with her clenched hands.

It took a great deal of control for Tristan to fight her off without hurting her, for in her anger Morgana was surprisingly strong. Eventually, he managed to grab hold of her wrists and push her into a nearby chair. She struggled against him, but he tightened his hold on her wrists until she lowered her head in submission.

"That's better," he said, releasing her. "Morgana, this was a mistake. You are obviously too young to understand, but this is over. Someday, when you've married and birthed children, you may look back on all of this and laugh."

Tristan backed away toward the door, his eyes locked on Morgana as he watched the fight go out of her. She slumped her shoulders and remained in the chair he had placed her in, her gaze lowered to the floor. He regretted hurting her, but there was nothing for it now. Tristan hoped that in time, she would forget all about him.

As for him, he'd finally gotten the opening he needed to make Esmeralda his. He would not fail.

CHAPTER 25

"I am going to Europe."

Esmeralda's announcement left her gathered family stunned. Akira, Raina, and Desmond sat and stared at her in mute shock. After weeks shut away in her room, she'd become a whirlwind of activity, running in and out of the house as if on some mysterious mission. Of course, when asked what she was up to, she had promised an explanation later.

Her announcement must be even more shocking than her previous behavior.

"I'll be leaving on a ship at the end of the week," she continued when no one else spoke. "I've managed to sell some of my gowns and the black diamonds Damien gave me for quite a bit of money. I've already secured my passage."

Raina was the first to speak. "Why? Would we ever see you again?"

"Of course you will," she replied, sliding onto the sofa between her mother and grandmother. She put her arm around Raina's shoulders. "I'll come back to visit you often, I promise."

"You still haven't answered the question," Desmond said, standing and jamming his hands in his trouser pockets. "Why are you doing this?"

The time for the truth had come. She had rehearsed this moment over and over in her mind, but never supposed it would be this difficult to tell her family why she was going away.

"I am pregnant with Damien's child."

Various degrees of shock and dismay flitted across the faces of Raina and Desmond. Akira, however, barely even blinked, so Esmeralda had to assume her grandmother had known all along.

Of course, she had.

"No wonder you have been so ill," Raina murmured. "But Esmeralda, why are you leaving the country? Why have you not gone to him with this news?"

"No!" she practically shouted. "He must not know of this." She turned to Desmond, who encountered the king almost daily. "You must not tell him."

"Why not?" Desmond demanded, full of righteous indignation. "He should know. He would want to *do* something!"

"What can he do?" Esmeralda challenged. "He is already married to a woman bearing his child. He cannot offer me his name. The only protection he could give me would be as his mistress! Is that the sort of life you want for me?"

"Of course not," Raina said calmly, patting Esmeralda's hand. "We just think you're being a bit rash with this decision. Europe is a strange land and you would be all alone with a new baby. Surely you cannot mean to do this alone."

"I haven't spoken with her yet, but I intend to ask Tatiana to come with me. She always tells me how bored she is with things here, perhaps Europe will be an adventure for her. We will arrive in France first, and since I am so newly pregnant there will be time to decide if we will settle there and find a place to live. I have thought this through ... I have a plan."

Desmond shook his head. "No. This isn't right. Cardenas is our home. *Your* home. What about The Golden Dancer?"

She smiled at her little brother. "Soon, the time will come for you to take over. With Tristan and Morgana still here, you will do fine.

Morgana can train new dancers, and of course Dominic will be here, as well."

"It just seems as if you're running away," Raina said. "I know that this situation seems impossible, but if you decide to stay we will help you in any way we can. No one will tell anyone about the baby unless you wish it."

She cast a look at Desmond, who crossed his arms over his chest and glowered.

"I'm not running, I'm just starting over," Esmeralda replied.

Raina enveloped Esmeralda in her arms. "You are a grown woman. Whatever decisions you make, I will be supportive, even if I do not like it. It is time for you to make your own way in the world, and if this is what you want … then so be it."

She didn't dare tell her that this decision terrified her to no end, but it seemed like the only way. She could not bear for Damien to ever find out about the child, and going away where he could never see her again seemed like the best solution for both of them. For her, it would put an entire ocean between them so that she would not be able to run to him as she yearned to now.

Yes, she decided, this was the only way.

TATIANA AGREED to accompany Esmeralda to Europe, bringing her no end of relief. She'd known that she would hardly have to convince her cousin to come along on what she would undoubtedly think of as an adventure.

Hours after agreeing, Tatiana chattered excitedly as they walked arm in arm to The Golden Dancer. She'd been overflowing with excitement about the sorts of things they would experience. It had always been her wish to travel and escape her father, who had been a bit controlling since the death of Tatiana's mother.

Despite her lingering sadness, Esmeralda could not help but smile at her cousin's enthusiasm. She allowed herself to feel a small glimmer of hope. Perhaps she was making the right decision after all. A fresh start and a new life would help to put all the pain and sadness in the past.

Her cousin had not tried to talk her into going to Damien about the baby, and for that Esmeralda was grateful. Tatiana seemed to understand her need to start anew. She had decided to take on a new identity, one of a widow, so that she would not have to bear the stigma that would undoubtedly come with being an unwed mother. And, in truth, she felt very much like a widow at heart—as if she might never cease mourning the loss of the man she loved.

The plan was flawless, and she'd almost finished packing for the journey. All that remained was to meet with Tristan and Desmond, who would take over management of the tavern once she was gone.

Shivering against the cold, she was glad when they swung open the back door and rushed into the warm dressing room. Tristan was waiting for them in the back office. Desmond had not yet arrived.

Esmeralda could not meet his gaze, finding it difficult to look at him without thinking of the last words they'd exchanged. Somehow they had grown apart as friends and she deeply regretted the rift that her relationship with Damien had caused. Now that it was over, she hardly knew how to talk to him.

She could feel his eyes boring into her.

"Tatiana, would you give us a moment alone, please?" he murmured, never taking his eyes off her.

Her cousin gave them both quizzical looks, but seemed to know better than to question the tension thrumming between them. She slipped out of the office, and announced she would await Esmeralda in the taproom.

Tristan clasped his hands behind his back and paced behind the desk for a few moments once they were alone. Esmeralda knew he struggled with whatever it was he needed to say, but she could only stand there and wait for him to say it. Like everyone else, he would probably try to convince her not to leave.

"I know about the child," he began, saying each word slowly as if pondering each one before uttering it. "Your grandmother came to me this morning with the news. I think she hopes that I will try to stop you from leaving. But, you have been my friend since we were children, and I know that when you've set your mind to something you are going to do it."

"That's right," she said, sinking into the chair facing the desk.

She folded her hands together and waited for the inevitable.

He sat on the edge and crossed his arms over his chest, gazing down at her in that unsettling way of his, as if those black eyes could see straight through her.

"I know that I cannot say anything to stop you, but that does not mean I won't try," he said, coming off of the desk's edge.

He knelt before her and took her hand in his. Esmeralda suddenly understood what this private meeting had been all about, and felt her heart begin to hammer in her chest. She knew she should stop this, tell Tristan that she was flattered, but could not think of ruining his life by marrying him. She should tell him she was not ready, and her heart was still too injured for her to even think of moving on with someone else. But she could say none of those things, not when Tristan was gallantly down on one knee, the look in his eyes naked and vulnerable. She could only sit there and wait in numb silence.

"I know that you do not love me," he continued. "But I think in time, after your heart is no longer broken, you could learn to. I believe we could be happy together, Esmeralda. If you give me a chance, I could be a good husband to you."

"But the child..."

Surely, he was not thinking of the fact that she was carrying another man's baby.

"The babe is yours, and because it is yours, I will love it like it is my own. I will give it my name and no one has to know it is not ours together. Perhaps someday we will have children of our own as well. Please, Esmeralda, don't leave. Stay and marry me."

Her eyes stung with tears, her chest resounding with the phantom ache of a broken heart. Never had anyone given her such a selfless gift. She had known Tristan loved her, but she hadn't understood just what he would be willing to do for her.

Here he was, on his knees, saying all of these beautiful things and offering her the solution to all of her problems. If she said yes, it would mean security for herself and a father for her child. Didn't every child need a father?

If she said yes, she could keep The Golden Dancer and wouldn't have to leave her family. No one would have to know the child had been fathered by Damien.

Instead of becoming something she should refuse, his offer grew more tempting by the second. What else was there for her? Damien had married someone else and would soon be a father. There was no path that led her back to him. There was only a future for herself and her unborn babe—one that would take her across the world, or one that would see her safe with a new husband who would act as a father to her child.

"It hardly seems fair to you," she whispered, still examining his proposal from every angle in her mind. "I don't know if I could be a good wife to you, Tristan. You must know that my feelings for Damien are not gone. They may never completely die."

Tristan gave her that devilishly charming smile of his and shrugged. "I will be happy to spend the rest of my life changing that. Please, say yes."

Esmeralda sighed, her shoulders slumping as the fight went right out of her. She was suddenly more tired than she had ever been, not just physically but emotionally. She was weary of fighting and hurting, sick of wanting things that couldn't be hers and mourning what she'd lost. Perhaps it was time to take the easy way, and allow Tristan to care for her and her child. She would try her damnedest to return his love.

"All right," she said, hardly believing what she was doing. "Yes, Tristan. I'll marry you."

His smile widened and he pressed a gentle kiss upon her cheek before pulling her into his arms. She sank into the comfort of his embrace, grateful that she did not have to face the world alone anymore; thankful that someone would be there beside her, even if it was not the man she loved.

. . .

The date for the wedding was set for one week away. Raina and Akira thought it would be best for them to be married immediately in a small, private ceremony if they were to have any chance of passing off Damien's child as Tristan's.

It was hardly the ideal situation in which she once dreamed of planning her wedding, but it seemed her only option. Tatiana had been disappointed upon finding out that they wouldn't be leaving Cardenas, but had brightened upon being asked to stand with Esmeralda as her maid of honor.

No one seemed surprised by this development. Everyone she'd ever known since childhood had expected her to marry Tristan. No one even mentioned her short engagement to a certain prince, much to Esmeralda's relief.

On the morning of her wedding, she stood waiting for her mother to finish fastening the long row of buttons down the back of her ivory wedding dress. Tatiana had tried to talk her into wearing the gown that Madame Didier had created especially for her, but Esmeralda had refused. The gown lay at the bottom of a trunk in the attic, one of the few remnants she'd kept from her time with Damien. Esmeralda did not feel right about wearing it after all that had happened, though she hadn't had the heart to sell it.

She'd chosen the materials for this gown herself, an ivory satin with matching lace laid over the bodice. Raina had worked day and night to complete the gown. It was simple and modest, with long sleeves and a wide satin ribbon tied into a bow at her back. She wore the pearls her father had bought for her, as well as the white lace gloves. Her hair had been brushed and allowed to hang down her back, an ivory lace mantilla laid over the locks.

Both Raina and Akira had worn the mantilla on the occasions of their own weddings. Despite its age, it had been remarkably well preserved, and Esmeralda was proud to wear it.

Raina placed the bouquet in her hands and stood back to gauge the full effect with a smile.

"You look beautiful," she said, clasping her hands over her heart.

Esmeralda saw the glimmer of tears in her mother's eyes and prayed that they were born of happiness. She'd had enough of grief.

"Are you ready?" asked Akira, walking in a slow circle around Esmeralda, studying her with a smile and a nod of approval. "I think you are ready."

She supposed that she was as ready as she would ever be. She forced a smile, if only for the sake of her family and the groom who waited for her in the small church a few miles from home.

Esmeralda followed them down the stairs to the front door, where she pulled a cloak around her shoulders to ward off the cold. Desmond waited outside, perched on the driver's seat of the wagon that would take them to the chapel. He jumped down and helped Esmeralda into the vehicle, then turned and assisted Raina and Akira as well. She tried not to notice the grim expression that pulled at the corners of his mouth.

The ride to the church was surprisingly short, and before she knew it, she stood in the outer vestibule, waiting for Desmond to walk her down the aisle.

"Are you sure you want to go through with this?" he asked as he offered his arm. "You don't have to, you know."

Esmeralda's smile was genuine this time as she turned to kiss her brother on the cheek. When had he become taller than her? And when had he become so devilishly handsome? His charcoal gray coat and black trousers set off his dark hair and eyes to perfection. He'd gotten taller recently, and the shadow of a beard showed on his jaw even though he'd shaved this morning.

Esmeralda wondered how she had not noticed the moment he had actually become a man. Her heart swelled with pride and she felt the prick of tears behind her eyes. He was so much like their father, it was uncanny.

"What a fine man you have become, Desmond," she said as the doors to the chapel were swung open.

The small gathering of family and friends turned to watch Tatiana as she walked down the aisle, clutching her bouquet in front of her.

"I know that you are only thinking of my well-being," she whispered. "But I promise you that I'll be fine."

"Promise me that you'll be happy," he said, tightening his hold on her hand.

"I promise."

Damien did not know why he was here. It wasn't as if he could do anything to stop the wedding, but when he'd leapt into Persephone's saddle, he could think of nowhere else to go on this day. Desmond had told him about Esmeralda's impending nuptials days ago, and he had lain awake every night since, tortured by the news.

He'd awakened this morning and paced his chambers, trying to drive the image of Esmeralda as someone else's bride from his mind. He remembered clearly the vision that Akira had showed him and his heart plummeted even deeper into the depths of despair. He had been unable to see the groom in his vision, but knew now that it was not him.

After a few hours of trying fruitlessly to clear his mind, Damien had walked out to the stables to saddle a horse. He hadn't even realized what direction he had taken until he found himself in front of a small chapel. He saw the waiting wagon, decorated with ribbons and bells, prepared to whisk the bride and groom away after the ceremony, and knew that he was at the right place. He had managed to enter without drawing any attention to himself, and found a seat in the last pew, which was conveniently shrouded in shadow.

He had watched Tristan standing at the altar beside a priest and a man Damien assumed to be the best man. Tristan looked nervous, but also annoyingly handsome, damn him.

He knew that the man loved Esmeralda, so he did not have to worry over her happiness. Damien wished for it, in fact, even though his own life was decidedly miserable. He hoped that Esmeralda would come to love her husband, and that he would give her everything that Damien could not.

He did not know why he stayed, but he did. He remained to watch

Desmond lead his sister down the aisle. His heart swelled at the sight of her. Though he knew he shouldn't, he imagined that she was walking toward him instead of Tristan. He could not see her face, but he imagined that as he stood at the altar, she walked toward him, her face transformed by a smile, her amber eyes glowing in the candlelight.

He stayed to watch them exchange vows, and winced when they were pronounced husband and wife. It was torture, but he could not look away when Tristan leaned down to claim her lips in the kiss that sealed their bond as man and wife. Damien's fists clenched, and he had to fight down the urge to go stomping down the narrow aisle, declaring that no one touched what was his. He reminded himself that Esmeralda was not his anymore.

He remained in the back pew as the church emptied behind the newly wedded couple. He sat and listened to the sounds of friends and well-wishers, and knew they were tossing rice and cheering for the young couple as they went up into the decorated wagon.

He knew that they would now go to wherever the reception was being held, and they would dine and dance in front of all their guests, and that Tristan would spend most of the night holding Esmeralda close to him. Damien knew that at the end of the night, Tristan would take Esmeralda home and to his bed.

He knew that she was now lost to him forever.

ESMERALDA ATE and drank large quantities of spiced wine. She smiled and talked with anyone who approached. She danced with every man who asked, and with Tristan a few times as well.

She was stalling. She knew it, and she suspected Tristan did as well. Soon, their wedding celebration would be over. The food would run out, the guests would grow tired, and the time would come for husband and wife to retire together for their wedding night.

The party had lasted well into the evening, for which Esmeralda was grateful. She had not given much thought past the wedding, and was completely unprepared for what came after.

She noticed Morgana sitting alone in the kitchen. Most of the guests mingled in the spacious living room, as much of the furniture had been moved to make room for them, and some even stood in clusters outside smoking tobacco and sipping their wine. Music lilted through the air from outdoors, as well as the sounds of laughter.

The food had all been prepared earlier and now the kitchen was abandoned, the perfect place for a young girl to sit and brood. In fact, Morgana had been uncommonly cool toward her recently.

"Would you mind if I joined you?" Esmeralda asked, taking a seat beside her at the table.

Morgana looked up from her cup and frowned. She hesitated for a moment and then nodded before turning her attention back to her mug.

"I hope you're enjoying yourself," Esmeralda said after a few moments of strained silence.

"*You* certainly seem to be," Morgana replied, her tone brisk.

Esmeralda's eyebrows drew together in confusion. She and her cousins had been like sisters all their lives. Morgana was a bit younger than Esmeralda and Tatiana, but they had always been close.

"Is something wrong, Morgana?" she finally decided to ask. "You seem agitated. You know that you can tell me what's bothering you."

She laughed. It was a short, forced, ugly sound. Esmeralda could hear the malice dripping from her voice when her cousin swiveled toward her suddenly and grabbed her wrist.

"Why would something be wrong? I am here at this wonderful party, celebrating my cousin's marriage to the man I love!"

Esmeralda's chin dropped and her mouth hung open for a fraction of a second before she snapped it closed again. That Morgana was in love with Tristan was news to her. Esmeralda hadn't seen this, immersed as she had been in her own affairs. The rumors about town had swirled, and she'd caught wind of them all. However, their short-lived time together had been made out to be nothing more than a dalliance—one that had ended as abruptly as it had begun.

But, it was clear to her now. Morgana's wide brown eyes were filled with unshed tears and the misery that Esmeralda had caused.

She felt like the worst sort of person for having paid so little attention that she'd missed this one little detail.

"Morgana, I didn't know," she said, her voice a near whisper. "Why didn't you tell me?"

Her cousin's hand was still clamped around her wrist like an iron manacle and Esmeralda felt it tighten brutally. She winced, but was otherwise motionless. Fighting would only make this worse, and she didn't want to draw the attention of her guests.

"I wish you had told me before now," she said. "Surely you know I would not have married him if I had known you had such strong feelings for him."

"Would you have?" she retorted. "I wonder. You have ignored him for years and still he followed you around like a lovesick puppy. You never cared for his feelings!"

"That's not true," Esmeralda protested.

"It is true! You had your prince. You were supposed to marry him and leave Tristan alone. If you had, maybe he would have come to see how he really felt about me. Perhaps then, we would have had a chance. You have ruined everything."

Esmeralda shook her head, fighting to free herself from Morgana's grasp. People had started to notice them, since Morgana's voice had risen considerably since the start of their conversation.

"I didn't mean to hurt you," she whispered. "I'm sorry."

Morgana flung her arm away as if she had been burned and stood. "It is too late for that."

"Morgana!"

Two pairs of eyes swiveled toward the kitchen entrance, where Tristan stood. Arms folded over his chest, his dark eyes glistening with fury, he made quite a formidable sight.

"What do you think you are doing?"

Morgana's eyes met his and burned even brighter in their intense hatred.

"Nothing," she said, smoothing her hands over her skirt as she edged around him toward the sitting room. "I was simply wishing my cousin well. Congratulations. The two of you deserve each other."

Esmeralda sighed and buried her face in her hands. Everything had gone horribly wrong. She had not wanted to hurt anyone; she had only wanted a father for her child. Tristan was one of her best friends. Surely, she was not selfish in choosing him for her mate, even though she did not return his love. Was she?

Tristan's hand on her shoulder jerked her from her thoughts.

"I think it is time for us to leave," he said, gently lifting the wrist that Morgana had bruised with her rough handling.

He placed a lingering kiss on her tender skin. Esmeralda endured it, reminding herself that Tristan was her husband now and had every right to kiss her.

She nodded, coming to her tired feet. It was time to stop avoiding the inevitable.

"Yes," she replied, allowing him to loop her arm through his. "I am ready."

He retrieved her cloak and his coat, and then led her out to their waiting wagon. Their family and friends followed them into the night, seeing them off with cheers and waves before setting off for home themselves. Tristan drove at a brisk pace. He concentrated on driving, but Esmeralda could feel the tension mounting between them as if his eyes were on her.

He reached over and patted her hand in a reassuring gesture, but otherwise kept his own on the reins. When they reached Tristan's home—her home now too, she supposed—he jumped from the wagon and handed her down.

"Go inside," he said. "I'll just see to the horse and wagon, and join you shortly."

Esmeralda nodded, then went into the small cottage. Someone had come ahead of them and lit a fire. She glanced around the sitting room, which was simple and sparsely furnished. Esmeralda had brought several things from home to brighten the space, and would begin transforming it into a warm place to live first thing in the morning. As a bachelor, Tristan had never given much thought to such things, but his home had been clean and well-maintained, from the inside to the outer shelter where he kept his horse.

She busied herself with warming her hands before the fire and thinking over the small feminine touches she would add to the little house. If she were to live here, she would have to find some way to feel as if she belonged.

She was lost in thought when Tristan returned from outside. He stood next to her, holding his chilled hands out toward the fire. Staring into the crackling flames, he rubbed his hands together. After a few moments, he turned and took her into his arms. Esmeralda went willingly, knowing that she had no right to deny him anything after the sacrifices he had been ready to make for her.

She would yield to him on this night, and give him every right that was his as her husband. Esmeralda looked up at him as he gazed down at her, and realized that she was not afraid. She supposed she had Damien to thank for that. At the thought of him, she gave herself an inward shake. She would not think of him this night. He was in her past; Tristan was her future.

"It feels as if I have been waiting for this moment my entire life," he murmured, rubbing his hands slowly up and down her arms. "I know that you may be frightened..."

His worried expression only made her feel worse. He was concerned about her fear of men, and here she stood thinking of the man who had helped her to get over them.

Taking a deep breath, she looked into his eyes, determined to get through this, to commit to this new life she had chosen for herself.

"You don't have to worry. I am not afraid."

Tristan seemed relieved at this, and much of the tension left his tall, lithe frame.

"I will never forget this night," he said, inching closer until their bodies touched. "Hopefully, when I am finished, you will not forget either."

Esmeralda lifted her head for his kiss and closed her eyes. She concentrated on the lips that moved over hers and the arms that went around her, trying with all her might not to picture a tall, golden god of a man working at the buttons on the back of her gown. It was wrong to picture Damien's arrogant mouth moving over her throat as he removed her clothing and undergarments, but she couldn't help it.

She opened her eyes and watched Tristan, hoping that as he undressed her and led her to the bed, she would forget about the man that she wanted most but could not have.

Tristan worshiped her body with his hands and mouth, as skillfully and passionately as she knew he would. She clutched the sheets and suppressed the tears that came to her eyes as she found her release despite the conflict of her mind. Esmeralda felt like the lowest, dirtiest creature, a whore for experiencing pleasure at the hands of one man when her heart belonged to someone else. She felt like a traitor for thinking of her past lover when her husband was so fervently making love to her.

Tristan jerked and groaned before collapsing onto her, sated at last. Esmeralda was grateful that it was over, glad that the confused mingling of guilt and pleasure had ended. As Tristan rolled to his side and pulled her back against him, she finally allowed the tears to flow.

CHAPTER 26

In the months that followed Esmeralda and Tristan's wedding, their lives found a comfortable, serene sense of calm. They managed The Golden Dancer together, although Esmeralda no longer danced. She claimed that it could not be good for the babe she carried, although she knew in her heart that even if she had not been pregnant, she would not have danced. It no longer felt the same to her, the joy she'd once felt while performing a distant memory.

She spent most of her time in the small back office going over the ledgers and managing their modest income. She had hired a new dancer to replace her, and set Tatiana to teaching the girl. Her belly had begun to protrude a bit, and she'd started to feel the tiny flutters of the life inside her.

Tristan spent a lot of his time pressing his hands to her stomach, waiting to feel the kicks of the babe. Esmeralda felt tears spring to her eyes every time he referred to the child as 'theirs'. He was delighted by the impending birth, and one would never guess that he had not planted the child there himself.

He had insisted that she not spend all of her evenings at The Golden Dancer, declaring that she might as well get used to it, because when the babe was born she would not be able to anyway. Besides, she needed her rest. Esmeralda could not argue with his logic, and so spent many quiet evenings at home alone.

Her mother and grandmother often came to visit, but Esmeralda found that things were not the same as when they had lived together. At some point, the two women would have to depart, and she would spend the rest of the evening on her own, sewing clothes for the babe, or reading, or simply staring off into space. Loneliness often set in, and she was counting the months left until the child was born. She would then have enough to fill her days and nights, and prayed that it would ease the pangs of longing that never seemed to let up.

Of course, eventually, Tristan would come home and they would spend a quiet moments before the fire together. Then, it would be time for bed and the inevitable lovemaking that accompanied it. Esmeralda had found an odd sort of comfort in Tristan's arms. It was not so much a grand passion, nothing like she had experienced at the hands of a certain prince, but Esmeralda was grateful for it. She had worried that intimacy between them would be strained and awkward. Instead, it was easy and soothing if nothing else.

It was better that way, Esmeralda decided. Who needed grand passion? Those sorts of feelings only led to hurt, and she was glad she did not have to worry about Tristan hurting her. She had guarded her heart well, and though it would never belong to anyone else, it was safe from harm. It was the only way she would survive.

ROTHCHESTER HALL BUZZED WITH ACTIVITY. It often did now that Davina had been made its mistress. Flocked on all sides by her courtiers, she instructed the bustling servants with her shrill voice, sending them running off this way and that on various errands.

She was throwing a lavish dinner party for nearly one hundred members of the royal court, as she did at least twice a week, between the more intimate dinner parties and entertainments she hosted on other nights. There were also shopping excursions, sleigh rides through the winter snow, and trips to the theater—all with a flock of her admirers in tow.

Damien hardly had time to bother to attend her various events, burdened as he was with the impending war brewing in Barony. The citizens were growing restless, weary of being terrorized by the rebel army, who took refuge high in the bordering mountains. He had been working tirelessly with General Adams to gather and train soldiers and prepare to lend the war-torn land aide. It would be months before they could even think of marching toward Barony, but when the time came they would be prepared.

He had just returned from a meeting with the general, and was looking forward to a quiet, solitary evening, when Davina accosted him in the main hall. He could hear voices coming from the open doors of the green salon and sighed in agitation when he observed half the royal court milling about, sipping wine and chatting.

Davina, dressed to the nines despite her rapidly growing belly, wrinkled her nose at Damien's plain coat and breeches. "Would you mind making yourself more presentable? I have guests, you know."

"Perhaps it would be more logical to inform me when you do *not* have guests, since you have seen fit to open our dining room to every member of the royal court every night for the past six months."

She rolled her eyes. "Would you please just go upstairs and change? People are going to wonder why you are dressed like a commoner."

He pinched the bridge of his nose and felt the impending throb of a headache, as he usually did when forced to endure his wife's presence. "I have just come from a very long, tiring meeting with General Adams, and I have a staggering report on my desk to read on the state of affairs in Barony. I will trust you to convey my apologies for missing dinner."

Instead of going back into the bosom of her adoring court, she followed him when he turned on his heel and headed for his library. Her high-heeled slippers clicked annoyingly on the tiles as she struggled to keep up with his long strides.

"Damn you, Damien, slow down!"

When he finally stopped and turned, he found her slumped against the wall, breathing heavily and clutching her swollen belly. Damien felt the niggling pull of guilt upon his conscience. He did not care for his wife, but he did care for the child that grew within her.

He stopped and grasped her shoulders, finding it easier to abide touching her when it was the child inside her he thought of. "You should rest. You've been pushing yourself much too hard. The court will understand if you do not host so many parties for a while. You will wear yourself out."

Taking advantage of his nearness, she swayed closer to him and smiled suggestively. "Why don't you take me off to bed then?"

Damien pulled his hands away with a disgusted snort, and continued on his path. "I have business to attend to."

"Fine!" she spat, stomping her foot like a spoiled child. "Go! While you sit in your library and dream about your stupid university, I shall find some other willing man to warm my bed!"

Damien shrugged and continued down the hall without even a backwards glance. Once alone in his library, he sat behind his desk with a contented groan. He lit the cigar Jarvis had thought to leave lying on the desk for him in a crystal ashtray, and inhaled slowly.

It had taken some time, but he had finally grown accustomed to the flow of daily life that accompanied the crown.

He had never been more exhausted in his life, but when he collapsed into bed at night and thought of his father and brothers, he was quite proud of himself. Clenching the cigar between his teeth, he shuffled through the first stack of documents waiting on his desk. They were the plans for the university he hoped to begin building right away. He was putting quite a bit of money into the endeavor, but knew it was necessary to make the university worthy of his father and brother's memory. The Adare Rothchester School of Astronomy, and The Lionus Rothchester School of Botany would be completed within a year's time.

Damien was even mulling over plans for the Serge Rothchester School of the Sciences. His brother had held an interest in biology and chemistry, and Damien thought it fitting to name the place after him.

He signed and placed his seal upon the agreement that had been drawn up for the architect, and quickly signed a bank note for the full amount needed to erect and furnish the buildings. He had just chosen several acres of prime land just on the edge of the city, perfect for the installation of a sprawling campus.

His heart swelled with pride as he looked over the blueprints that had been drawn up by one of the most renowned architects in the city. His dream was almost a reality, and he couldn't be more pleased.

Actually, he knew he could be a lot more pleased, but tried not to dwell on it. But, as usual, he was unable to turn his thoughts away from hair dark as night and luminescent amber eyes.

Esmeralda had encouraged him, told him to make his dream a reality, and he had done it. He only wished she could be here to share in it with him. Damien shook his head to clear his thoughts and stood to pour himself a glass of brandy at the sideboard.

He was so busy these days he hardly had time to think of her. Of course, when he had a quiet moment to sit on his own and allow his thoughts to wander, he always wondered how different his life would be if she had become his wife as planned. She would be delighted that he was having plans drawn up for the university. She would tell him how proud she was, and give him one of her dazzling smiles. She would only throw parties for special occasions and would spend her time at more noble pursuits than flirting with the men at court or spending decadent amounts of his money.

Damien shrugged away his black mood and returned to his desk, pushing aside the university plans in favor of the generals' report on Barony.

The coming weeks held a plethora of things for him to attend to, and hopefully, when he busied himself with them his mind would be focused on something other than bronze-colored skin and the sweetest smile his eyes had ever beheld.

Anne Doyle was in a bind. She had served the queen for some time now, long before her ascension to the throne. Though she would not do anything to purposely incur the woman's wrath, she could not allow this deception to continue. King Damien had hired her when his wife had only been his mistress, and though he rarely spoke to her, he had been kind and courteous when he did. He'd showered the ungrateful woman with gifts beyond any of the things Anne could wish to own, and still it had not been enough.

When Queen Davina had taken her into her confidence, she had sworn Anne to secrecy and coerced her into helping pad her stomach each morning to lend her the appearance of pregnancy. She had also informed Anne that it would be her job to procure an infant boy from the orphanage whenever she was ready to "give birth".

Anne had gone along with it at first, afraid to anger her mistress and end up on the street without a job, but enough was enough. She had seen how miserable the king was with his new wife, and felt as if she were partially to blame. Everyone knew about the young lady the king had really wanted for his bride. Though the talk had died down, Anne had not forgotten.

She watched him sulk about the palace, his only joy found in the building of his university and the impending birth of his child. A child he thought was his. A child that she would bring from an orphanage and pass off as his.

It could not be allowed to stand.

She paced outside the king's library, reluctant to knock, but determined that the man would know the truth before the day was out. She knew he was in there, had been told so by the butler only a few minutes ago; or had it been an hour? She really should stop dawdling, but feared the wrath of the king when he learned of the deception she'd had a hand in.

Finally, she squared her shoulders resolutely and raised her hand to knock.

"Come," said the king's voice from the other side of the door.

Anne hesitated only a moment before placing her hand on the knob.

"Your Highness, I hate to disturb you," she said with a quick curtsy. "But I think there is something you should know."

. . .

DAMIEN WAS ANGRY. No, he was worse than angry, he was furious. No, he was something worse than furious, but at the moment he could not quite figure out the right word. He was barely aware of the flurry of motion he created while he stormed down the corridor, as servants flung themselves left and right to clear a path for him.

Davina had planned yet another dinner party, and he knew he would catch her in the middle of dressing.

Perfect.

He balled his hand into a fist and lifted it to pound on the door of her chambers. A wide-eyed maid—the one whose sole job it was to dress the queen's hair—swung open the door and then dropped into a curtsy. Damien breezed past her and came up behind Davina, who sat at the vanity table, applying a liberal amount of rouge to her cheeks.

She stared up at him in the mirror and frowned. "What are you doing here?"

"Leave us," he commanded the trembling maid.

When the frightened girl had closed the door behind her, he placed his hands on Davina's bare shoulders.

"Stand up, darling. I want to look at you."

Never one to miss an opportunity to place herself on display, she rose and turned to face him. His gaze dropped to what appeared to be her swollen belly and stayed there. By all appearances, his wife seemed to be pregnant. There was only one way to know for certain.

"Take off your clothes," he said, his eyes never faltering from her midsection.

He would have the truth, by God, and he would have it now. When Davina only stared at him in shock, he sighed and reached for her himself.

"I haven't got all day. Do as I said and take off your gown!"

Her lips turned upward into a smirk and she inched toward him.

"Finally," she said, her relief palpable. "You've come to your senses. I knew you couldn't stay away for too long. But, I know you wouldn't want to ruin all the work my maid had to do to get me into this gown. I have guests expecting me at any moment. But, I wouldn't be disinclined to lifting my skirts a bit."

Damien had long since run out of patience. Weary of Davina's games, he decided to take matters into his own hands. He grasped her by the wrist and swung her around before she had a chance to react. He grabbed her before she could pull away, and yanked her back against him. He caught a glimpse of her in the vanity mirror and was satisfied to see the sheer panic that crossed her face when she realized that he intended to undress her himself.

"No ... Damien, don't!"

She struggled against him, trying to twist in his grasp, but his unbreakable hold on her made it impossible. He worked at her buttons, exposing her back, inch by inch. When he moved his hands to remove the gown, Davina darted across the room.

"Please, Damien," she pleaded. "You're frightening me!"

Tears had sprung to her eyes and Damien could see that she was, in fact, frightened.

"Good," he rasped, leaping across the space that separated them.

They fell together onto a heap on the bed, and Davina swung her arms and legs in a final attempt to fight him off.

It took him longer than he had expected, and when he was finished her hair was tumbling down from its pins in a tangled mess, and his face sported a few scratches where she had used her nails against him, but when it was all over she stood before him, exposed. Over her chemise, she had fashioned some sort of cushion and tied it around her middle.

Damien had not known what to expect, but seeing the lengths she had gone through to deceive him snapped the last thread of control he clung to. He grasped a pair of scissors conveniently located on the vanity table, and snipped away at the cords tethering the false belly to Davina's middle.

She remained silent as he did this, resigned to whatever fate was to now befall her. When she was free from her bindings, standing there in only her chemise, petticoats, and sparkling jewels, he stepped back and eyed her with disgust.

He grasped her chin and forced her to look up at him.

"You were willing to deceive me in order to gain the crown. Did you really think I wouldn't discover the truth?"

"You weren't supposed to find out!" she wailed, her face and neck wet from her tears. "And I didn't know you were going to marry me at first. I only wanted to be back under your protection. When you offered marriage, how could I have refused?"

Damien's hand trembled at his side and he battled the urge to shake her, strike her, and curse her for ruining his life. But, he'd never harmed a woman in his life, and wouldn't start now no matter what she'd done to him.

"Doctor Keane. You convinced him to lie to me?"

She nodded and sniffled, dropping her head as if in shame.

"And my mother? Did she know about this too?"

"No," she whispered, her voice hoarse from screaming. "I believe she truly thought I was pregnant. She only wanted to stop you from marrying Esmeralda."

Deciding he'd heard more than enough, he took hold of her arm and began dragging her from the room.

"What are you doing?" she shrieked, pulling against him in a vain attempt to halt his progress. "I am not even dressed."

"Why should that matter, my dear? Most of the men you've invited tonight have seen you wearing far less."

"You think to shame me before the court?" she gasped, fighting him with renewed vigor. "Surely you cannot be so cruel!"

He halted, bringing her around to face him.

"You are the one who is cruel," he ground out, his jaw aching from how hard he clenched his teeth. "Do you have any idea what you've done?"

She did not answer, and he did not expect her to. Anything else she said would only anger him further and then he'd lose the last shred of dignity he'd managed to cling to.

"I want everyone to know that you are a fraud," he declared as they neared the dining room, where the invited members of the court had been seated for dinner. "I want them all to know why I will be petitioning the High Council for a divorce."

Davina opened her mouth as if to protest, but seemed to think better of it. Divorce was nothing compared to the many other things he could have done to her for her deception. She knew it was best not to speak, and Damien thought it was the most admirable thing she had ever done.

Two footmen hardly batted an eye when he approached the double doors of the dining room. They silently swung the doors open and stood aside to allow him entrance. Gasps and murmurs met them at the threshold, and Damien had to wait a few moments for the buzzing to die down before he could speak.

"Ladies and gentleman," he said, his voice surprisingly calm given the tumult of emotions raging war inside of him. "I present your hostess for the evening, the ever lovely Queen Davina. As you can see, she was not quite prepared when I chose to escort her before you this evening. I am sure you all have noticed that she has lost quite a bit of weight since yesterday."

He flung Davina away from him. She landed on her knees on the carpet and remained there, her head lowered. The murmuring continued to ripple through the assembled guests.

"I hereby denounce this woman for the vicious, lying, black-hearted bitch she is. I no longer claim her as my wife."

He turned away from his shocked guests to find Jarvis waiting for him in the doorway.

"Send for the captain of the guard and have her taken to the gaol until I decide what's to be done with her."

Jarvis simply nodded and summoned a nearby footman to lend assistance. Damien only stayed long enough to watch them haul Davina to her feet and drag her away. He refused to meet anyone's curious stare as he turned to walk away. They could all go to Hell, these lords and ladies who delighted in scandal and spectacle. He imagined he'd given quite a lot to talk about over tea tomorrow afternoon.

"Damien," a voice hissed from behind him once he'd reached the corridor.

He whirled to find his mother standing a few feet behind him, her mouth a grim line. She reached out to grasp his shoulder, a surprising gesture considering that she had not touched him in years.

"Surely you know I had no part in this."

Damien shrugged her hand away. "You may not have known about Davina's treachery, but you are just as responsible as she is for this. You were so desperate to stop me from marrying the woman I loved, you practically rammed Davina down my throat. I shall never forgive you for the part you've played in destroying my life."

Spinning on his heel, he set off down the hall at a mad pace, leaving Alexandra behind. He could have sworn he saw the glimmer of tears in her eyes, but wouldn't give her the satisfaction of caring. After all, she'd never shown him compassion when the shoe had been on the other foot.

Life was cruel, Damien decided hours later. He sat at Serge's bedside, nursing a bottle of brandy, still at a loss as to how to pull his shattered life back together.

"I suppose I could start with beheading the lying witch," he murmured to Serge's prostrate form.

His brother lay silent and motionless, as always.

Damien nodded. "Yes, you're right, of course. Executing her would make me seem a monster. Well then, what do you propose I do about it, since you know everything?"

He took another long swig of brandy and then smiled.

"Ah, yes. Transportation. I suppose shipping her off to some far removed place once I divorce her would be best. I certainly wouldn't want her near enough to cause any more trouble."

He watched Serge's face for any sign of life and sighed when there was none forthcoming. He visited his brother frequently, having never given up hope that he could awaken at any moment. Isabelle came often as well. She had even managed to persuade him that Serge could hear everything going on around him.

So Damien poured out his heart, telling his brother of the deception that had caused him to make the biggest mistake of his life. Now, it wasn't even possible for him to fix things. The woman he loved was married to someone else.

Damien drained the rest of the brandy and leaned back in his chair, closing his eyes. He wondered about the vision he had seen of the little girl running on the sloping lawns of palace. The girl's dark hair and wide, green eyes had seemed so real to him that he had dared to hope for the happiness she could bring to his life. Had it all been just hopeful thinking? Or had he ruined his chance for happiness by allowing Esmeralda to walk out of his life?

I should have tried harder. I should have sent Davina away and begged Esmeralda every day until she agreed to marry me.

He knew even as he experienced that thought, that it would not have been so. Esmeralda was too kind-hearted to aid a man in abandoning a child.

A child who did not even exist, much to his disappointment.

He turned back to Serge and shrugged. "Well, I suppose it's just you and me now," he said, raising his empty bottle in salute to his brother. "Just you and me."

CHAPTER 27

Tristan looked down at the face of his newborn child and smiled. He could never have imagined that something so small and fragile would capture his heart so completely. He had not known that he could ever feel for another person the way he felt for Esmeralda. Now he knew that it was possible.

They had named her Leila. She was a perfect little bundle of beauty, all dark hair and light brown skin like her mother. When she awoke from slumber and opened her eyes, they proved as green as new blades of spring grass. Tristan had thought that those eyes would haunt him, forever a reminder that he had not actually sired this child. But, he saw only Leila, whom he would raise and love and care for until he died. Perhaps someday he and Esmeralda would have more children, and Tristan would love them all just the same.

He glanced up at his wife, who stood over the fireplace stirring soup in a large kettle. He loved these moments, because he felt content to sit and watch her and hold his child, who fascinated him even in her sleep.

The labor had been long and hard, but Esmeralda had been strong. A few months later, she had completely regained her figure, with a bit of womanly softness that Tristan found added to her appeal.

She seemed happy enough with him, and he took pride in the fact that she and Leila were well cared for in addition to being well loved. Esmeralda had transformed his lonely house into a true home with her feminine touches, and for the first time since the death of his mother, he returned to this place each night to a warm fire and a pair of waiting arms.

If she did not love him back as much as he loved her, he did not care. All that mattered was that she was here, she was his, and would be forever. Love would come. Tristan was a patient man, and had loved her for too long to be put off by the memory of a former lover.

"Do you want me to take her now?" she asked, glancing at the tall grandfather clock in the corner. "It is almost time for you to leave. I thought you might want to have dinner first."

Tristan gave Leila over reluctantly, then plopped down at the table where Esmeralda sat a steaming bowl in front of him. Darkness had begun to fall outside, he noticed as he ate quickly. The Golden Dancer would open soon, and he needed to be there before it did. He wolfed down his dinner, then rose to take up his guitar case. He planted a swift kiss on Esmeralda's cheek, as was his nightly custom, and then he disappeared out into the night.

Turning in the direction of the tavern, he set off at a leisurely pace, enjoying the pleasant evening air. He whistled as he walked, swinging the guitar case at his side as he neared the back door of The Golden Dancer.

As he neared the tavern, he noticed the figure of a woman advancing on him from the corner of his eye.

"Morgana?"

She held out her arms to him, stumbling forward with tears in her eyes.

"Please," she cried, wrapping her arms around his neck.

His guitar case fell onto the ground as he reached up in an attempt to dislodge her.

"Please tell me what to do," she pleaded. "I don't understand why you do not want me anymore!"

"Morgana let go," he urged, trying to remain calm.

He'd hardly expected to encounter her, and in fact, hadn't seen much of her since the wedding. He supposed it had been too much to hope that time would be enough to help the girl move on.

He glanced up and down the empty street, grateful that no one was there to see him in this embarrassing position. He fought to untangle himself from her grasp, but to no avail. She proved strong in her grief.

"I'll do anything," she continued, seemingly oblivious to his attempts to free himself. "I'll even be your mistress ... no one has to know."

"Morgana!" he snapped, finally done with patience.

He grasped her shoulders and gave her a none-too-gentle push away from him. She landed on the ground a few feet away from him, her eyes wide as she clapped her hand over her open mouth. Tears streaked down her face, but Tristan was unmoved. He had grown weary of her childishness. It was time to end this once and for all.

"You do not love me. I do not love you. We have not been together in almost a year. It is time for you to move on."

Morgana shook her head, clapping her hands over her ears as if to block out his words. "No! Why are you saying this to me? I love you, Tristan. I have always loved you."

Tristan sighed. He was getting nowhere, and didn't know why he'd even attempted to reason with her.

"Leave me in peace," he said, turning his back on her to retrieve his guitar case. "I have a wife and I love her. Nothing you could ever do will change that."

Tristan did not look back, and so did not see Morgana rise to her feet. He did not see her unsheathe the curved dagger from the belt at her waist. He did not even hear her footsteps as she ran to catch up to him.

Her harsh, animalistic cry was the only warning that came before she plunged the knife deep between his shoulder blades. When he fell face-down onto the ground, she came over him and twisted the knife before pulling it free. Tristan's cries were heard by no one as she drove the knife into his back over and over again, until they were both drenched in his blood.

His vision blurred and he could barely see her, but could hear her sobs as she took him into her arms.

"I'm so sorry," she crooned, stroking his blood-soaked hair. "I'm sorry I had to do this, but if I can't have you for my own, then neither will she."

She lifted the dagger one last time, turning it toward herself. Then, she gazed down into his eyes and smiled.

"I love you," she whispered before plunging the dagger into her own heart.

She collapsed beside him, blood rapidly soaking the front of her blouse. She turned her head to look into his eyes, which were slowly closing. With her last ounce of strength, she reached out to take his hand.

And so it seemed, that even though she couldn't have him in life, Tristan was now hers ... in death.

ESMERALDA WAS NUMB. There really was no other way to describe it. As she stood over her husband's grave at the edge of the church burial ground, she found that she could no longer cry for him. Leila squirmed and wailed in her arms, and she absently handed the child into Raina's waiting arms.

When she had discovered her pregnancy almost one year earlier, she had thought then that she would die from the heartache. She never thought she could feel so utterly abandoned. As it turned out, she had been wrong.

Morgana had been buried the day before, but Esmeralda had refused to attend the service. She did not think she would have the strength to maintain her composure at two funerals, and felt she owed it to Tristan to attend his.

Feelings of guilt had been gnawing at her from the moment Desmond had burst into their home, carrying her husband's bloodied body.

This was all her fault. She should have left with Tatiana and the child she was carrying, and she should never have accepted Tristan's proposal.

Maybe if she had, they would both still be alive.

Ignoring the pitying stares and murmured condolences of those gathered around the grave site, she made her way back to the wagon that Desmond had driven them to the church in.

It was suddenly too much. She couldn't stand all these people feeling sorry for her, when she knew that this had all been her fault. She had hurt Morgana and caused Tristan's death.

Finally, the tears she had been unable to shed welled up and she did not try to hold them back. Her reasons for marrying Tristan had been selfish. She had wanted a father for her child, a companion so she would not have to go through the rest of her life alone. Now she would have neither, and her dear friend and husband had died, murdered at the hands of her own cousin.

Sobs wracked her body, and nearly threatened to force her to her knees. Esmeralda gripped the side of the wagon, giving herself over to the powerful force of her grief. She thought she might collapse, but found instead that she had been held up by a pair of strong arms. The feel of the embrace was familiar, and she nestled closer to the warm body those arms belonged to without thinking. She buried her face against a solid chest and breathed the scent of sandalwood shaving soap and tobacco.

The soothing hand that reached up to stroke her hair was one she had felt so many times before, and the voice that crooned and whispered comforting words was so achingly sweet that she ceased sobbing in an instant. When she had finally composed herself enough to look up, her eyes clashed with a pair of sympathetic green ones, and her heart was flooded with a heavy rush of relief.

ONCE AGAIN, Damien had no idea why he had come. When he found himself sitting outside the same church where he had watched Esmeralda marry Tristan, he had been unable to make himself leave.

His heart was broken for Esmeralda. Even though he had not really known Tristan, and from the limited experience he'd had with him found he did not much care for the man, he'd been one of Esmeralda's most trusted friends. For a time, the man had been her husband, and if the tiny bundle she held to her bosom was any indication, it seemed the man had been the father of her child as well.

Seeing her holding that tiny bundle did nothing more than remind him of the future he had let slip away. Thinking of her growing round with another man's babe filled him with a tangle emotion he could not unravel. Sadness, perhaps. Anguish. Despair. Envy. Some combination of those things.

He had not planned to step down from his carriage. Damien had stayed inside it during the funeral, watching from behind the curtains. When he had seen her run to the wagon and nearly collapse in her grief, he had been unable to stay away. Even an entire year apart had not dimmed the torch he carried for her.

Now he held her against him as she cried, ignoring the stares and whispers of the people nearby. He did not care what anyone thought of the King of Cardenas attending the funeral of a Gypsy dancer and holding the widow in his arms. He only knew that he had to be there for her. How could he not, after all they had suffered, both together and apart?

"Would you allow me to escort you home?" he asked when she had finally composed herself.

She gave him a slow nod, then turned to search the small crowd still lingering near Tristan's grave.

"I have to find my daughter," she said, avoiding his gaze.

He watched her walk over to where Raina stood holding the child. They exchanged a few words and then Esmeralda returned to him empty-handed.

"Mother will bring her along in the wagon," she explained, allowing Damien to hand her up into his carriage after she had given the driver directions to her home.

Once inside, she took the seat across from him and turned her head to stare out of the window. He was content for the moment to just sit and watch her. He realized that he had forgotten nothing, even after going without laying eyes upon her for so long. He traced the outline of her profile with his eyes, but knew that he did not have to. Even with his eyes closed, he could clearly see every feature that had been ingrained into his memory. He longed to reach across the space that separated them and pull her into his lap, hold her close, and kiss every inch of her face. However, it would be inappropriate given the situation, so he kept his impulses in check.

When they pulled to a stop before a small cottage similar to the one she'd occupied with her family before marriage, Damien linked her arm through his and walked her to the door.

"Perhaps you'd like to come in for tea," she offered.

"Yes," he blurted, before she even had a chance to finish asking. If she noticed his eagerness to remain in her company, she did not allow it to show.

He followed her into the house, taking in every detail of the home she had shared with another man. He felt like a stranger, an impostor, as he took the chair she offered him at the table. The evidence of her life without him, one in which he'd ceased to exist, hurt, even as he realized that his life had been just a devoid of her all this time.

"I am sorry for your loss," he said, and immediately regretted it.

I am sorry for your loss?

Nothing about that statement carried even one ounce of the pain he felt at seeing her so utterly abandoned. It said nothing of how wretched he felt to know the happiness he'd wanted for her had been destroyed, or how badly he wanted to be the one to make things right again.

"I know that Tristan meant a lot to you," he added, watching her put a kettle over the stove she had just lit.

"I did not love him," she stated.

Damien flinched, but was otherwise silent. He realized that her statement had not exactly been directed at him. She wasn't even looking at him, but stared at a point somewhere over his shoulder.

"I did not love him," she repeated. "But he loved me and he wanted me. I married him because I didn't want to be alone. Now he's dead."

Collapsing into a chair across the table from him, she sighed, head lowered.

"This is all my fault."

Damien reached across the table and took her hands in his. "Of course it isn't. How could you even think that?"

"I was selfish. I knew that he had a history with my cousin, and still I accepted his proposal. I took him away from her. She loved him in a way I never could have. She loved him so much, she could not bear the thought of being without him, so she took her own life."

"That is not love," he said, squeezing her hands tight between his. "Love is wanting what is best for the other person, even if it means not being with you."

A long silence stretched between them, as he comprehended how true his statement really was. Hadn't they both been forced to do what they'd thought was right at the expense of their happiness together?

"Besides," Damien added. "Your cousin did not just take her own life, she took his as well, thinking to rob you of your happiness."

"The way I robbed her of hers," Esmeralda interjected.

"You did not mean to take anything from anyone. I know you too well for that."

"I wasn't thinking clearly. I was too heartbroken."

He issued a dry snort as she rose to lift the steaming kettle from the stove.

"That would be because of me. So, in reality, this entire thing is *my* fault. I was trying to do the right thing, because I knew it was what you wanted me to do. Look what it has gained us."

He did not have to explain to her how things had turned out for him. By now the entire kingdom knew that the High Council had granted him his divorce, and Davina had been banished from Cardenas.

"Please," Esmeralda urged as she placed a steaming cup in front of him. "Let's not speak of the past. It is too painful."

Damien nodded his agreement and fell silent as she prepared their tea, presenting him with a steaming cup. He masked his surprise to find she still remembered the way he preferred it. Much the same way he remembered every single thing he'd ever learned about her.

They sat in silence and sipped their tea, and he could not help sneaking glances at her whenever he could. Even in grief her beauty made his heart ache, the changes apparent after carrying and birthing a child making her seem older, more womanly, alluring in a way he'd never imagined.

Raina entered moments later, carrying Esmeralda's child. He nodded his greeting as she walked silently through the sitting room and kitchen, into the open door he assumed was the bedroom. When she returned, she was without the babe.

"Leila is sleeping," Raina told Esmeralda. "I've laid her in the cradle."

Esmeralda nodded. "Thank you."

Raina nodded, then disappeared back into the room with the baby, giving him a friendly smile as she went.

"Leila," Damien said with a smile. "A lovely name."

Esmeralda returned his smile, causing his heart to accelerate maddeningly. "Tristan actually named her. He was such a good father."

They lapsed into silence once more. Damien did not know what to say. All he could think was that he would have been a good father, too.

"Perhaps I should go," he said when the silence became too much to bear. "I'm certain you want to rest after the day you've had."

She stood and led him to the front door where she smiled up at him again, the motion seeming less strained this time.

"Thank you for being here today," she said. "It was ... comforting."

"Nothing could have kept me away," he murmured, edging closer to her against his will.

It was madness to want to taste her lips on the day of her husband's funeral, but it was all he could think about. He settled, instead, on kissing her forehead, even as he fantasized about devouring her mouth and plunging his tongue in deep.

"Should you need anything, I am never too busy to assist you."

"Of course," she said, placing a hand upon his arm.

He jerked beneath her touch, which seared through the sleeve of his jacket like a branding iron. Damien could have sworn he still felt her hand there as he climbed up into the carriage. He could still detect the faint scent of jasmine that lingered on his coat as well.

ESMERALDA WATCHED Damien's carriage disappear down the road, her heart sinking lower with every second. One year apart had changed nothing. Her heart still raced at his nearness, her stomach still fluttered. She still loved him, even though she had spent so much time trying to force him into a tiny corner of her mind.

Now that she'd seen him again, the small space she'd compressed him into seemed to have burst forth, filling her with him to every corner of her soul. He was everywhere, even after he'd left her—his scent, his kiss upon her forehead, his voice. He'd looked so miserable, she'd wanted nothing more than to throw her arms around him and kiss his pain away.

And what sort of woman did that make her, to feel such things not an hour after her husband had just been buried?

Raina emerged from the bedroom when she heard the front door close. She stood across the room for a moment and studied Esmeralda with knowing eyes.

"That was kind of him to offer you an escort home," she said, still studying Esmeralda's face.

What Raina was looking for, she did not know. Surely, she was not so terrible at hiding the secrets of her heart, even after all this time.

"Yes," she agreed, moving about the table to clean up the empty cups and saucers. "It was lovely to see him again."

"Did you tell him?"

The question froze the blood in her veins. She'd been expecting it, but was in no way prepared to answer it.

"No," she said, hoping that Raina would not expect her to elaborate.

"He should know," Raina pressed, moving about the small sitting room, picking things up here and there.

"You did not think so when Tristan was my husband."

Raina sighed and straightened, holding Tristan's guitar case in one hand and a pair of his boots in the other. "Everything is different now. He was married to someone else, someone we thought was also expecting a child. You did not want to burden him. If the expression on his face today was any indication, he would be nothing but pleased if you were to tell him now."

"And I suppose he will bend down on one knee and ask me to be his wife like he did before," Esmeralda snapped, slamming the tea kettle into the basin.

She was sick to death of people trying to advise her on how to live her life. She was still reeling from the loss of two people she had dearly loved and was in no mood for a lecture.

"No one would be surprised if I were to say yes. After all, who would refuse a king? I suppose you would all stand around with handkerchiefs pressed to your teary eyes as he swept me onto his horse and rode off with me into the sunset. I once thought that love worked that way, but I learned otherwise. The hard way."

Raina shook her head and heaved a weary sigh. "I am not telling you that you should marry him tomorrow. I am not saying that you should marry him at all. I am only saying that he has a right to know about the child, and now that Tristan is gone you must think of Leila's future. You must think of your own future."

Esmeralda grudgingly admitted that her mother was right. Even though the fantasy of Damien riding off with her into the sunset still lingered on the edges of her mind, she knew it would not be that easy. Life had taught her that painful lesson.

"My husband has barely been buried an hour," she whispered. "I need time."

"I understand," her mother conceded as she turned to leave. "Just don't take so much time that you miss out on something wonderful."

"I still love him," she admitted, swiping away a tear with frustration.

Esmeralda did not want to cry anymore. She had spent an entire year avoiding heartbreak and sadness, and although she had not been deliriously happy, she had been safe and comfortable.

"How do I stop loving him?"

Raina leaned against the door and shrugged. "It's possible. But only if you truly want it to be."

CHAPTER 28

*D*amien could not stay away. He knew that he should, but only four weeks after Tristan's funeral had passed before he found himself standing on Esmeralda's doorstep again. He understood he had to give her time and space to grieve, but he could not deny himself the sight of her any longer.

She seemed surprised to see him, but he could tell that she was also pleased. She accepted the yellow roses he offered her with a smile, and ushered him into the sitting room.

"I hope you don't mind," he said, watching her fill a pitcher with water for the bouquet. "I was thinking about you, and wanted to see for myself how you and Leila are getting on."

She took a seat on the sofa beside him, nearly unmanning him with her nearness. He wanted nothing more than to crush her against him and smother her with kisses. He had not touched a woman since his last night with her, had not wanted to until the moment he'd been close enough to reach out and touch her. He folded his hands in his lap instead and watched her lips when she spoke.

"We are doing well," she said, indicating the small cradle where Leila lay sleeping a few feet away from where they sat. "Desmond comes whenever I need him to fix things or to bring me firewood. He has been a great help to us."

Damien nodded and smiled, thinking of the young man. He still kept his post as a groom at Rothchester Hall, and had warmed to him again over time. Though, they never spoke of Esmeralda.

"I am glad to hear it."

He turned to study the sleeping infant in the cradle. Swirls of inky black hair covered her little head, and dark lashes lay like crescent moons on her plump cheeks while she slept. Her skin was the same shade as Esmeralda's, and she had her mother's nose as well.

"She's beautiful," he murmured, rising to take a closer look at the sleeping child. "Just like you."

"She does take a bit after her father," she said, coming to standing behind him.

Leila began to squirm in her sleep, and within moments she was crying, a little mewling sound that warmed Damien's heart. With her eyes squeezed closed and her tiny fists balled up, she kicked her tiny feet as she wailed.

"May I?" he asked, turning to Esmeralda for permission.

He'd never had the chance to hold the child he'd thought would be his, and he suddenly had an urge to hold this one.

She hesitated for a moment, and Damien clearly read apprehension on her face.

"Don't worry," he assured her. "I've held a baby before."

He had meant to put her at ease, yet she seemed even more anxious with each passing second.

Leila continued to cry and after a few seconds, Esmeralda nodded her assent.

He bent over the cradle and slid his hands beneath the babe, one at her head and one at her bottom, then lifted her against his chest.

"Shh, hush now," he crooned to the tiny thing, swaying gently from side to side as he held her.

She fussed for a few seconds before nestling against his chest. Then, she found her thumb and began to suck with a loud smacking sound. He could not have described the emotion that welled up within him as he stood there watching her suckle at that thumb. Damien felt as if this child had always belonged in his arms. It was the same feeling he experienced when holding the mother in his embrace.

He looked up to see Esmeralda with her hands clapped over her mouth, her eyes filled with tears.

"What's wrong?" he asked, his brow wrinkled in concern.

"Nothing," she sobbed. "It's just that holding her comes so naturally to you."

Damien studied her for a moment in bemusement, wondering why the sight of him holding her child should bring tears to her eyes. Then, he glanced down just as Leila opened her eyes. He felt as if the wind had been knocked from him as he stared down into them, captivated by what he found.

Leila's eyes were the color of emeralds, jade, or new blades of spring grass. They were his father's eyes. His eyes.

His head jerked up and he found Esmeralda's gaze. The look upon her face confirmed his suspicion.

"Tristan's eyes were brown," she whispered.

Damien could hardly believe what he was hearing and seeing. The child from this vision, this child, was real. She was real and she was *his*.

"Why didn't you come to me?" he asked, though he was sure he already understood.

He could not even be angry with her for not telling him. All that he had been through in the past year faded into nothingness, as he held his firstborn child for the first time.

"I'm sorry," she said with another sob, swiping at her eyes with the back of her hand. "I didn't know until after you had already married Davina. By then, you had been through so much, I did not want to burden you."

"This child could never be a burden."

"Yes, but I know how difficult it was for you to make the decision that you did. I thought it was better that you never knew. I had planned to leave Cardenas and start over ... that way I could be sure you would never find out. But then, Tristan discovered that I was pregnant and offered me marriage. He did not care that Leila was not his by blood. He loved her because she was mine."

"I owe him a great deal," Damien said, unable to tear his eyes away from the child he held in his hands. "For taking care of the two most precious things to me, I will never forget him."

Esmeralda edged toward him tentatively, as if afraid he would reject her. He smiled, reaching for her and pulling her against his side. She buried her face in his shoulder, her body trembling as she wept against his coat. He held Leila with one hand, while rubbing Esmeralda's back with the other, nuzzling the top of her head.

"It's all right, love," he whispered. "It's all over now ... I'm here, and everything will be all right. I'm not angry with you. I could never be angry with you for doing what you thought was right. It was an impossible situation."

After a while, she calmed, seeming to accept his words as truth. He meant every one of them, and found that instead of anger he felt only relief and joy. The future he had seen hadn't been destroyed ... it stood right here in his arms.

They stood in silence for a long while, gazing down at the life they had created together out of love. Leila quickly drifted off to sleep again, her thumb falling free of her open mouth.

Damien laid her gently in the cradle and then turned to Esmeralda. Their eyes locked and they stood there wordlessly, their gazes communicating things that could not be said with words.

In an instant, he was across the space between them and sweeping her into his arms. She did not resist him when he leaned down to kiss her. She responded with unrestrained ardor, opening her mouth to accept his invading tongue, wrapping her arms around his neck. Her taste was achingly familiar, but it had been so long since he had experienced it that Damien could not get enough. Her knees weakened, but his arms tightened around her waist to keep her from falling.

"I've missed you," he murmured against her mouth.

"I've missed you, too," she whispered, her voice husky with desire as he began backing her toward the open door of the bedroom.

All logical thought had fled the moment he tasted her, and now he could not stop, would not stop until he had her naked and spread beneath him.

"I need you," he murmured, kissing her cheek, her jaw, her ear. "Now."

"Yes," she said breathlessly. "Yes, Damien."

He tore at her dress. She tore at his shirt. Articles of clothing flew in every direction until they tumbled onto the bed together, naked flesh pressed to naked flesh. Damien looked down at her body, noting the changes carrying Leila had made in her—fuller breasts, a softness in her middle, a widening of her hips.

Beautiful, lush, and his.

Then, his hands were everywhere, traveling over the hills and valleys of a body that had haunted his dreams since the last time he'd gazed upon it. He tasted every inch of bare skin he could reach, and then she was over him, head bent as she returned his kisses with heated ones of her own.

He wasn't certain if minutes went by, or hours, but when they'd both been reduced to a panting, writhing mass of tangled limbs, he flipped her onto her back and sought out the wet opening of her passage.

Esmeralda's voice rung out in a joyous, passionate cry when he entered her for the first time in what had felt like forever, mingled with his hoarse groan at the feel of her.

He took her slowly, fighting against the climax that nipped at his heels. It had been too long and he was dying to sink into her and lose himself, but held it in check, longing to savor the silky grasp of her sheath around him and her thighs gripping his. He gritted his teeth and rocked against her, angling his body so he also stimulated the sensitive nub buried within her mons, determined to make her shatter right along with him.

She clung to him, kissing his neck and shoulder, whispering her love for him in his ear and reaffirming all they'd ever had, what they shared now, and all they would have now that they'd been reunited.

It wasn't until she screamed his name at the force of her climax that Damien buried his face against her shoulder and let go. His thrusts became frenzied and uncontrolled, pounding out a frantic rhythm against her as he soared over the edge and beyond.

When it was over, he knew she understood just how much he had missed her, how he had longed for her.

As they lay tangled together in the bedclothes, he held her close. He whispered in her ear, mindless love words that he'd been dreaming of saying to her night after night for a year. She clung to him, burying her face against his neck, and he reveled in the familiarity of her skin against his.

"How soon do you think we can be married?"

She stiffened in his arms, and the question hung between them unanswered. Esmeralda struggled into a sitting position and reached for her shift. She pulled it on over her head and began searching for the rest of her garments, which were scattered around the room.

"Esmeralda?"

She turned her back to him and pulled on the rest of her clothes.

"Surely you know that I will not live the rest of my life without you and Leila," he continued as he left the bed to find his clothes.

She faced him again once she was completely dressed.

"You have to give me time," she pleaded. "My husband has only been dead a month. I cannot even think of marrying again until more time has passed. It wouldn't be right."

Damien came forward and cupped her face in his hands. His fingertips were gentle as he lifted her face toward his. He kissed her. Once. Lightly.

"We have waited long enough," he said. "Tristan is dead, but that doesn't mean we have to be. It is time for us to live again. Together, as a family, as it should have been from the beginning."

Esmeralda squeezed her eyes shut, almost as if looking at him would make it too difficult to be rational.

"So much has happened to keep us apart that I just don't know if I'm brave enough to risk heartache again. I love you ... you know that. But, so much as happened, and I ... I'm afraid, Damien."

"I know that nothing has turned out the way we planned. We have both been through a lot apart, but we have also been through so much together. And, I know that together we are stronger. Whatever happens, at least we'll have each other. We'll have Leila."

"I need more time," she whispered. "It's too soon after Tristan and … so much has gone wrong, that we should at least do this one thing right."

"We have spent enough time apart. I don't think I can wait any longer."

"Please, don't make me decide now. If you truly love me, you won't deny me that. I'm not saying no. I'm saying yes … in time."

Damien heaved a weary sigh, but nodded his agreement. He didn't like it, nor did he want to spend another moment away from her or his daughter. However, he had to accept that while he'd spent the entire year pining after her, she'd spent that same amount of time married to someone else. She might not have loved Tristan, but she'd cared for him and would mourn him. That she was telling him yes at all renewed his earlier hope for the future.

Esmeralda would be his, permanently. He'd wait another hundred years if that was what it took.

"At least you did not say no," he said with a grin. "I will give you all the time you want, but I will not give you space. I shall be here, every hour of every day until you give me an answer."

When Esmeralda groaned in frustration, Damien merely chuckled.

"You didn't think I would make it that easy, did you?"

HE DID NOT MAKE it easy. Less than one month later, he stood in the garden at Rothchester Hall, watching as Desmond led her toward him through tall white pillars wrapped in garlands of spring flowers.

He'd been a constant presence since the day he'd discovered Leila was his daughter—spending as much time with them as his schedule allowed. He spent afternoons holding and lavishing love on his daughter, and his nights in Esmeralda's bed, reminding her how things between them had been, how they would be once they were wed.

Day by day, her resistance began to slip away and he felt her walls begin to fall down. The hardened woman who had suffered through loss and pain had faded away, and the vibrant, optimistic woman he'd fallen in love with had re-emerged. He'd asked her each morning he had awakened at her side to marry him, waiting with baited breath to receive the answer he most wanted to hear.

At last, she had agreed, even as she had worried how it would look for them to marry so soon after his divorce and Tristan's death.

But, none of that mattered to him, and in time others would forget the scandals surrounding their union. All that mattered was their love, and the rest of their lives stretching out before them.

They had decided on a private ceremony in the garden with only their families and closest friends. His first wedding had been grand and lavish, yet hollow and without meaning.

As Esmeralda walked toward him in Madame Didier's opulent creation of white silk and lace, a wreath of flowers set on top of her unbound hair, Damien's heart leaped for joy in his chest. As she came near and smiled at him, he knew that this time would be different.

This time, when he knelt before the priest for prayer, he silently added his own plea that God would keep them together for eternity. This time, when he said his vows, they meant more to him than any words ever had in his life, and he meant every single one. This time, when he slid the ring onto his bride's finger, he did so with the knowledge that it would never be from her hand, and he found joy in that revelation. This time, when he kissed his bride, he could not stop kissing her.

So they kissed, and they kissed, and they kissed … until the priest cleared his throat noisily.

Then they kissed some more.

When, at last, Damien relinquished his bride from his arms, he found her smiling up at him with so much happiness in her eyes. He reached up to cup her face and smiled back.

"Didn't I tell you, love?" he murmured so only she could hear. "Everything will be all right."

Wrapping her arms around his waist, she pressed against him, heedless to their applauding guests.

"It already is," she murmured, before coming up on tiptoe to kiss him again.

Princess Isabelle Rothchester smiled from her seat in the garden, applauding just as boisterously as the other guests. The sun beamed down on them, and the fragrant flowers surrounding them created a small cocoon where only happy endings occurred and fairy tales came true. It was a fitting end for her brother-in-law and her friend, who had been through so much before coming back together. She'd been delighted to learn of their reconciliation, and had thrown herself into helping plan their intimate ceremony. It had turned out to be the most beautiful wedding she'd ever witnessed.

A tear came to her eye as she thought of Lionus, and how close they had been to their own happy ending. She wiped it away and forced a smile for the benefit of those sitting around her. Today was about happiness. It was about her closest friend and her dear brother-in-law finding each other again and coming together in love. There could be no place here for her tears or grief. She would save them for when she could be alone, as she always did.

Akira, who had sat beside her during the wedding, took her hand and gave it a squeeze.

"It's so beautiful, isn't it?" she asked, her smile wide.

Isabelle could not be sure why, but for some reason she always felt as though Akira could see right into her soul. Just now, it seemed the old Gypsy woman searched for something inside of her. For the life of her, Isabelle couldn't figure out what.

"Yes," she agreed. "I am so glad that they have found their happiness."

"Not to worry," Akira said with a reassuring pat on her shoulder. "Yours is closer than you think."

Isabelle turned back to the newly married couple and sighed. No. Hers had been dropped into her lap and then snatched away before she'd ever gotten the chance to truly enjoy it.

"I'm not so sure about that," she murmured, a touch of sadness still lingering in her voice.

The old Gypsy woman only chuckled, her eyes twinkling with mystery and mirth.

"Oh, but I am."

EPILOGUE

Sunlight streamed through the window, and why that should bother him when his eyes were closed, he was not certain. The drapes had obviously been thrown open and the sun had decided to stream directly into his eyes as he lay in bed *trying* to sleep.

He tried to turn his head away, but to no avail. For some reason, his neck would not obey the commands of his mind. A part of him wanted to drift back into darkness and oblivion, but another part fought against that urge. It was almost as if the light was reaching out to him, calling him, beckoning him to wakefulness.

His body ached. He could not recall what he had done the night before, but his head was pounding something awful, and his mouth was so dry he could barely swallow.

What the hell had happened to him?

Then in a flash, he remembered. The dark night on the side of the road, his brother run through by a sword, the fear in his sister-in-law's eyes as she'd taken the reins in her hands, the evil glint in his half-brother's eyes as he had ordered him lashed to the back of a carriage.

He remembered.

His eyes flew open and a sharp gasp emitted from deep within his chest—as if he had emerged from a long time underwater.

An answering gasp from a corner of the room alerted him to someone else's presence. He searched the room, panic settling in as he realized he couldn't move, his limbs jerking as if detached from the rest of him. His gaze fell upon the woman seated in the chair at his bedside, and he widened his eyes, parting his parched lips and trying to communicate.

She rose slowly from her chair in the corner, looking as if she'd seen a ghost, as if she could hardly believe her eyes. The book she had been reading clattered to the floor, forgotten. For a moment, she did not move or even speak. She continued staring at him with an open mouth, not moving as if she were afraid she would frighten him off if she so much as breathed.

He stared back at her, awed as he had always been by her beauty. Her wide blue eyes were filled with tears as she walked slowly to his bedside. Then, her arm was behind his head, and she lifted him, shuffling cushions beneath him until his upper body sat erect. His muscles screamed in protest, the pain almost sending him back under. He fought to remain conscious, focusing upon her face.

She was moving faster now, rushing to the bedside table and returning with a cup filled with water. One hand holding his chin, she lifted the cup to his lips and tilted it, flooding his mouth with cool water.

He drank greedily, savoring every last drop, his throat so dry that each swallow pained him. When he had finished, she set the cup aside, still staring at him as if she could hardly believe her eyes.

How he had longed for her to gaze at him this way. For so long he had loved her, watched her from afar, yearning for what could never be between them.

His heart pounded in his chest when she hurled herself against him, wrapping her arms tight around his neck, practically lying on top of him as she embraced him.

"Serge," she sobbed, her tears wetting him through the nightdress he wore. "My God ... Serge."

"Isabelle," he croaked, his voice rough and heavy, sounding so unlike himself.

He could only lie there and revel in the feel of her against him, both painful and exquisite all at once. He closed his eyes and inhaled. She smelled heavenly and felt like his every dream come true.

Those thoughts were wrong ... dangerous. She was his brother's wife, and it was wrong of him to love her.

Still, he couldn't seem to tell her she should let him go, to ask her how long he'd been ill, and where the rest of his family was.

He could only let his head loll against the top of hers and drink in her scent.

He did not know why she was crying and holding him as if she had not seen him in years. He only knew that he did not want her to let go.

THE AWAKENED PRINCE

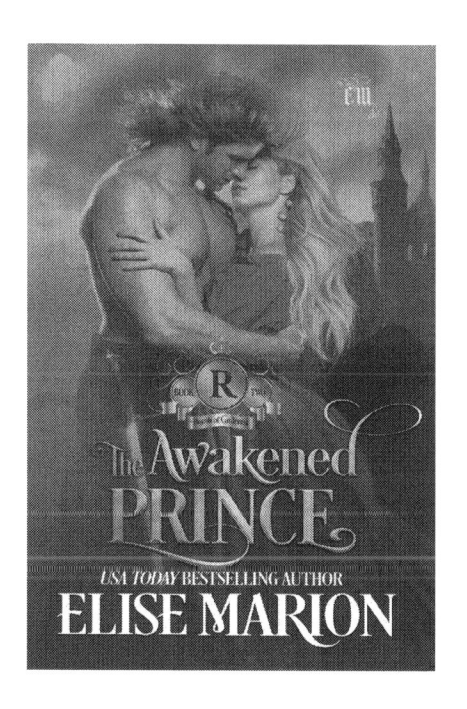

When a devious plot against the royal family results in her husband's death, Princess Isabelle Rothchester is left with a broken heart and an uncertain future. Only one year after his brutal murder, she has no choice but to choose a new husband and return to her own kingdom, taking her place as queen and repairing the war-torn land.

After a deadly scheme against his family leaves Prince Serge hovering on the edge of death, he awakens from a coma to find that his elder brother has died and his youngest brother has taken the throne in his stead. When it is suggested that Princess Isabelle take him as her husband, Serge begins to hope that all his secret dreams will now come true. He has secretly loved Isabelle his entire life, and the fact that she was promised to his brother has brought him no end of pain. Now, he has the chance to claim her for his own, hopefully earning her heart in the process.

Despite the unexpected spark of desire between them, Isabelle resists the new path her heart is taking as she clings to her first husband's memory. Can she let go of her past and learn to love Serge in return, or is she destined to a life tied to one man as she mourns the other? And in the midst of it all, the rebellion washing over Barony comes to a boiling point. Together, they must fight to save their kingdom … and in the process, each will unlock the hidden potential they never imagined they possessed, learning that they truly are stronger together.

ROYALS OF CARDENAS READING ORDER

The Rogue Prince
The Awakened Prince
The Lady Warriors of Barony
Wild Gypsy Rose
The Gypsy Lord

The Courtesan (Bonus novella, can be read in any order)

ABOUT THE AUTHOR

I first picked up a pen with with dreams of writing at the age of 12. Sitting at a little desk in front of my bedroom window, I wrote (by hand with pencil and paper) my first novel. It wasn't very good, but I'd never been more proud of anything in my life. I've been writing ever since, and have found a love of romantic stories both sweet and sensual.

When I'm not wrangling my three rambunctious kids, or spending time with my retired Army husband, I'm stretching the imagination with stories of people from all walks of life (and worlds) falling in love.

I love coffee, chocolate, music (listening and singing), shoes, jewelry, and food! I am always in the kitchen whipping up something new or

ABOUT THE AUTHOR

watching the pros do it on TV. You can often find my characters eating or cooking something delish and sucking down mass quantities of coffee.

Made in United States
Orlando, FL
16 November 2023